THE SWEETWATER PEACE

Jeffrey R. Sanderson

THE SWEETWATER PEACE

TATE PUBLISHING
AND ENTERPRISES, LLC

The Sweetwater Peace
Copyright © 2014 by Jeffrey R. Sanderson. All rights reserved.

No part of this publication may be reproduced, stored in a retrieval system or transmitted in any way by any means, electronic, mechanical, photocopy, recording or otherwise without the prior permission of the author except as provided by USA copyright law.

This is a work of fiction. It is a novel. The places described or mentioned are real, but the characters and their exploits are fictional. This story holds many truths, but it does not reflect the life of any one person, real or imagined. Any resemblance to any real person or persons, living or dead, is purely coincidental. The story is the original work of the author.

The opinions expressed by the author are not necessarily those of Tate Publishing, LLC.

Published by Tate Publishing & Enterprises, LLC
127 E. Trade Center Terrace | Mustang, Oklahoma 73064 USA
1.888.361.9473 | www.tatepublishing.com

Tate Publishing is committed to excellence in the publishing industry. The company reflects the philosophy established by the founders, based on Psalm 68:11,
"The Lord gave the word and great was the company of those who published it."

Book design copyright © 2014 by Tate Publishing, LLC. All rights reserved.
Cover design by Rtor Maghuyop
Interior design by Jimmy Sevilleno

Published in the United States of America
ISBN: 978-1-63268-844-6
Fiction / War & Military
14.10.23

This work is dedicated to Staff Sergeant Jens Schelbert, United States Army who was KIA in Iraq in 2005. All the Panthers know how much it hurt me.

To Lech,

Kennst Ignoto

vir

Giorgio A. Tsoukalos

13 Jan 2012

ACKNOWLEDGMENT

I GRATEFULLY ACKNOWLEDGE the following people:

Teresa who keeps me sane, encouraged, and loved. I don't deserve it.

Jake who keeps me young even when I want to be old.

Judy and Perry who make family a real word.

Frances who was the ultimate earthly encourager.

Granny Ila who taught us all character and perseverance in the Lord.

Andrew and Lillie who taught us faith by their daily example.

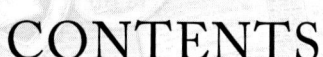

CONTENTS

Hard Times 11
Swimming in Darkness. 18
Fresh Air 24
Serge 30
Things Fall Apart 42
Ambush 61
Border Crossing 70
State Officials 79
Down on Sweetwater 85
Lorraine 97
Crisis 106
National Crisis 116
To the Far Ends of the Earth 122
Breaking into a Foreign Country 143
Back in the Zone 157
The Bloodiest Day 172
Momentum Shift 192
Men from Chechnya 198
Firefight 204

Good Followed by Bad 219
Helen, Georgia 231
The Last Mission 238
Building Roads 244
The Stinking Place 265
One Last Target 281
Heartbreak 287
Clay County Jail 310
Lawyers 317
The Good Judge 328
The Peace 339

HARD TIMES

The Command Sergeant Major entered the room first and said, "Gentlemen, the Commander."

We stood. He walked directly to his seat and said, "At ease. Take your seats." The lights dimmed in the amphitheater briefing room and a red sign over the door illuminated the words *Top Secret*.

The Operations Officer cleared his throat and began. "This briefing is classified Top Secret Exit Marker." A map appeared on the screen. "Our mission is to infiltrate a four-man team into Belgrade, Serbia, to conduct strategic targeting. The timeline begins with isolation at the conclusion of this briefing, followed by movement and ingress reconnaissance. We anticipate the team in place and operational in Belgrade in twelve days."

He aimed his laser pointer toward the map and showed a series of photographs of the ingress location. "We anticipate a ground force invasion of the country within the next fifteen days. Once the invasion begins, our team links with friendly forces and conducts missions as required. I will be followed by Intel."

The Intelligence Officer stepped forward. "Per our previous updates, air power continues to weaken Serbian static defensive positions. They are making maximum use of cover and concealment to avoid detection and damage. The majority of their forces are away from the larger urban areas. The Serbian Army is successful in its efforts at movement control with numerous complex defensive positions and checkpoints along all major and minor avenues of approach."

He pointed at a series of aerial photographs and maps detailing the enemy positions, and then transitioned to maps and photographs of Belgrade. "The town of Belgrade itself is at the intersection of the rivers with two prominent mountains which dominate the surrounding terrain. I will be followed by Operations."

The operations officer walked to the podium. "The concept of the operation is based upon the enemy requirement for fuel. The regime requires fuel, and we will infiltrate our team in the back of a fuel truck. Once inside the city, the team will link with other governmental agencies that will provide both sanctuary and the strategic targets. This is a targeting mission, so the only major equipment will be the device, communications, and pistols. The cover, as we previously discussed, will be Spanish pipefitters. I will be followed by Science and Technology."

Dr. Mullins took the stage. "This has been a challenging project. I refer to it as our Trojan horse. Mixing fuel and oxygen is dangerous business as most of you now know." Laughter broke out across the room. A week earlier, a fuel truck exploded, requiring the services of the entire Fort Bragg fire department.

"Suffice it to say, this only works with specific fuels coupled with a specific type of fuel truck. The team will harness itself using advance suction technology and basically remain submerged inside the tanker for the duration of the journey." He looked directly at the CIA liaison officer and said, "Of course we are counting on other governmental agencies to ensure we receive the correct fuel and the correct truck before we begin the mission. I will be followed by Operations."

The Operations Officer looked at the Commander and said, "Sir, your intent?."

The Commander stood and looked at the team. "You all know I don't like this mission." He stared at the CIA Liaison officer and continued, "The CIA was gutted as a result of the peace dividend. I don't know where their agents are located, but we have the mission. It's common knowledge I fought this all the way to the Vice Chairman level." He paused. "And lost."

"We are armed combatants, not a surrogate for clandestine operations." He looked at me and continued. "My intent is to get you into country and linked up with the CIA asset. Once on the ground, you take your target missions from them. Operations briefed a follow on ground invasion, but as of now, we don't have a decision. If for whatever reason you fail, we send in C2." He pointed toward the back of the small theater where the reserve team was sitting. "So my intent is to get you in and then assist you in any way possible." He turned and sat down.

The operations officer nodded. "Standard mission protocol in effect. C2 will undergo isolation and rehearsal with the primary. Pending your questions, this concludes the briefing."

The lights came on, and the Commander and Sergeant Major stood. The Commander shook my hand and said, "Good luck and God speed, J.B." They walked the line shaking hands with the team.

I knew the Balkans. I lived in safe houses throughout the region from its largest and most historic cities to improved outhouses on the side of a mountain. Somalia was bad, but this place was worse. Somali clan leaders bartered for power and threatened violence, but here it was just violence. Evidence of war crimes abounded. We tended to go after the ring leaders, thinking it will cure the problem, but in the Balkans atrocities and mutilation were the norm. The theory was simple. Kill the Indian Chief and the braves will run away. In this region, it's not that simple. Military leaders forgot that war is a test of wills, and politicians wanted it off the nightly news. Serbian leaders were the bullies on the block, but there was plenty of evil to go around.

In Hollywood, it was easy. Movie stars spoke multiple languages, memorized all aspects of the local culture, charmed their way through bad situations, and always won. In reality, everything in war was simple, but the simplest things were difficult.

The bombing campaign would continue, and we expected a ground offensive to follow. We were correct about the bombing. The buzzword was precision targeting. It meant we hit the target with minimal damage to its surroundings. We went after specific high-value targets designed to sap the enemy's will to win. Precision targeting required a guy on the ground to view the target, laser designate the target if required, and send a report of the damage.

We rehearsed each aspect of the mission. We would climb into the fuel compartment and harness ourselves for stability until the truck reached its destination. We would exit the truck and conduct linkup operations and execute our missions. Our asset would provide transportation and sanctuary. Once we were mission complete, we planned to link up with invading forces. We went into isolation.

Isolation was tough. Designed to eliminate all distractions, it allowed total focus on the upcoming mission. You underwent two unpleasant tasks during isolation. First, you sat with an Army lawyer who covered all aspects of your life from financial planning to your last will and testament. Second, you wrote a letter to your wife. It was sealed, dated, signed, countersigned by the lawyer and placed in your locker. It was not new to me, but I hated it.

> Lorraine,
>
> You know the drill; if you are reading this, I am dead. I love you. You bring joy into my life. You made it fun. Words can't do justice. You are the best person I know. Thanks for the wonderful times. I adore you.

The kids will be fine. You are their lifeline, and I regret being a lousy dad. When they ask about me, please tell them the good things. You are good with money but pay off the mortgage. The Army will see that the kids go to college free as long as it's in-state.

Please take me to Clay County and bury me there or at least have a ceremony there. It is home. Ten years from now, they will give you a briefing on how I died. Don't be mad We talked about this; don't ever believe I am missing in action. You have my permission to remarry when you reach the age of seventy…Just kidding. You'll know when.

Love,

JB
Major JB Smith

We conducted reconnaissance on the fuel farm for more than a week. We determined the fuel routes throughout the region, we used satellites to determine which trucks went on which route, and we knew the arrival and departure times. The right fuel was delivered in a series of blue Mercedes trucks and we carefully selected the exact make and model of the trucks. We anticipated a five-hour swim in the fuel. We didn't know what we didn't know.

Jessie was second in charge. He was a large black man from Georgia who spoke fluent Spanish. He could do anything with nothing, had been with this unit for more than nine years, and swore every operation would be his last. Rabbit and Zeus rounded out our four Soldier excursion.

Rabbit was short and thin. He might have weighed one-fifty with all his combat gear. He was as quick as his nickname implied and he was the best pistol marksman I ever saw. Rabbit spoke French and some Spanish, but he was a very quiet man. He was comfortable with silence. Zeus was the junior member, and this was his second mission. He was as handsome as handsome gets. He was confident in his skills and impressed us during both his previous mission and during training. He underwent Serbian language training by immersion, but we pulled him for this mission.

We climbed from our observation perch just after dark. Jessie cut the fence with Rabbit covering from the high ground. Zeus and I were the first ones through the fence. The others followed. We found the right truck, put on our extended swimming gear, and climbed up and through the small hatch into the fuel compartment. Our first task was to suspend our gear in the rear of the compartment using advanced suction technology. We went to our prearranged corners and began building our swings. Zeus and I were in the back, and Jessie and Rabbit were forward. It wasn't so bad. It was like working in a very dark and slick cave. Our flashlights worked. The only fuel was on the bottom. Just after midnight, we heard the engine start and began moving. That's when the trouble started. Our advanced technology suction devices weren't so advanced. Zeus's suction gave way. He fell hard and slid forward along the bottom. It was comical until the truck stopped sending him to the far forward portion of the compartment where Jessie grabbed him. We heard the footsteps on the roof. We cut our lights. The worker opened the main entry hatch and inserted the nozzle.

The fuel flowed into the tank. In the blackness, you saw nothing, even with your eyes wide open. I felt the fuel rising against my wetsuit. I rechecked my oxygen tank and prayed for a solid seal on my mask. Just as the fuel level reached my shoulders, my suction gave way, and I collapsed to the bottom of the compartment. I panicked. I could not see my hands; I could not tell which way was top or bottom. My heart was going to explode. I grabbed anything that might give me a grasp on reality. I felt the equipment bag. It was still in place. I grabbed the securing rope and pulled myself upward. The securing line was not built to hold my weight, and it gave way. I attempted to stand on top of the equipment bag in an effort to get my head closer to the roof. I reached a stable place. The truck began moving. My back slammed hard against the rear of the truck. I felt bubbles through my suit. My heart rate soared. The only thing that caused bubbles was oxygen. I felt my legs and lower back. The bubbles were intense. I had shattered my secondary oxygen tank. I began the math problem in my head as to when my oxygen would run out. The good news was that it didn't explode; the bad news was that I was going to die inside a Serbian fuel truck.

SWIMMING IN DARKNESS

The Hiawassee River is beautiful cutting its way through the mountains. The water was crystal clear, and we were fishing for rainbow trout. Dad was farther downstream, and Mr. Samuels was behind me. Nothing hit a dry fly like a rainbow trout. The bow kept his nose against the current so he could get the easy food that drifts downstream. The trout grabbed a floating fly and charged toward the bottom. My feet flew out from underneath me and I felt the cold bottom of the river. I was submerged and couldn't get up. I had fallen with my head upstream, and my waders were filling up fast. I felt the cold water going to my legs. I couldn't move. I was paralyzed with fear. I opened my eyes. The water was clear, but I couldn't breathe. I opened my eyes and saw the murky figures above me. Mr. Samuels grabbed me and touched my legs and back. I saw the light; it was intense.

In the fuel tank, something grabbed me and shined a light in my mask. I remembered where I was. But he was leaving me. Where was he going? I grabbed after him, but I couldn't reach him. I felt a sensation. Something was moving my feet from the bag. I kicked hard but hit nothing. I saw the light again, moving closer. Two lights, I saw two lights. The other light shone in my mask. I blinked, but felt frozen, paralyzed with fear. The lights were communicating, but I couldn't understand what they were saying. They dove into the compartment. I felt them moving my legs and moving the bag. They were grabbing at my face and pulling at my head. My mask cover was removed, and the smell was awful. It was a stench—a wicked, evil smell. I wanted to vomit. With the flashlight, I saw Rabbit. Jessie was on my other side holding me up.

"I opened the valve," he yelled.

The fuel was draining fast and was neck level. Eventually, the driver would realize he was losing fuel. We picked a fuel trailer with an internal cleaning and draining system, and we picked the right trailer. As the fuel drained, the compartment became more and more wavy. My head was clearing. Rabbit motioned for me to grab the makeshift line he had rigged. It was dark, but we felt the tank draining. The truck was still moving. Each lane change was an event inside the compartment, and we swayed from one wall to the other. Rabbit and I hugged each other and held on to the line. I was standing on the equipment bag, and Rabbit's feet were on my thigh. The fuel was draining fast and was just above my chest. The stench was awful. It overwhelmed my senses, and I gagged. Rabbit vomited on my head. Jessie returned. He closed one valve. It would still continue to drain but not as fast.

"Where is Zeus," I asked. Jessie shook his head. "What does that mean?"

He screamed, "I don't know!"

"Get out of the compartment," I yelled. "Open the hatch."

Rabbit was already moving.

I had a history of doing tough, physical things. Nothing compared to Rabbit, Jessie and I pulling ourselves along Rabbit's makeshift lifeline and attempting to open the main cylinder. There was no grip. It was like playing chicken in the water, but we were all swimming. The fuel continued to drain. Jessie found something on the bottom and lifted me up. I thrust Rabbit and he grabbed something on the roof of the compartment. We had to find the hatch.

"What if the driver locked it from the outside," I yelled. Rabbit screamed something, and Jessie pushed me upward. Rabbit was spinning in midair. He screamed again, but I couldn't understand what he was saying. I saw a light inside the compartment. The light faded away, and I felt another thrust from below. Rabbit was back on my shoulders and I saw light.

In an amazing display of upper body strength, Rabbit pulled himself through the opening. The truck changed lanes. We fell. We were back in the fuel. I grabbed for Rabbit's lifeline. Someone was climbing over me going up through the hatch. It was Zeus. I worked my way toward the light. I saw Jessie; his face was bleeding. Another rope was dangling from the hatch. I grabbed it and was pulled from hell. Clean air, headlights from oncoming traffic. I held on to the bars.

"Jessie!" I shouted. "We must get Jessie." He tugged and we pulled him from the compartment.

We held on to the rails on the flat part of the truck. Although it was in early May, it was freezing, and I shivered. We turned and faced inward, so we could hear each other. We had immediate problems. We were freezing and exposed on top of the truck. The fuel vale remained open. We would soon pass a checkpoint where we would be seen. We had pistols strapped against our skin, but that was no match for the firepower at a local checkpoint. Our equipment bag was inside the compartment and one of us would have to retrieve it. The time was 0247 local. We hadn't been inside the compartment long.

Success in combat was defined by finding or choosing options. The combatant who retained options won. The best Soldiers created options. Most soldiers preserved options, and bad Soldiers forfeited them. On the roof of a fuel truck, we needed options. If we went back into the compartment, we would be there another two hours minimum. I wasn't certain we would survive. Mentally, the compartment did me in, and it appeared the others were of a similar view. Infiltrating in the back of a fuel truck was a bad plan, but there was no time to dwell on that now. We could take the truck, but we didn't have the language skills to clear the checkpoints. We could take the truck and ditch it and attempt to infiltrate by foot or by stealing a vehicle. It seemed reasonable, but we still had the problem of checkpoints. Rabbit turned around and began crawling forward toward the cab of the truck. I grabbed his foot. I was not ready to take the truck. He mouthed the word "recon" to me. I nodded.

We needed the equipment bag. I noticed Jessie's face. He had a deep gash from the bridge of his nose across his forehead. He constantly wiped blood away from his face. There was no way Jessie could go back inside the compartment, and the bag would be a two-man lift. Zeus and I decided to go back inside to get it and Jessie would have to pull us out. We used Rabbit's line as a guide.

Zeus went first and I heard the splash of the fuel. It took all the courage I had to descend back into the compartment. I grabbed the line. It was warmer inside the tank. I breathed without gagging and the fuel level was at our waste. It was still slick, but manageable. We worked our way toward the back of the compartment. We found the equipment bag tangled in suction ropes. We freed it and began moving forward. The driver downshifted; Zeus slipped and fell. I let go of the equipment bag and held on to Rabbit's original rope. The driver downshifted again. Stopping, the driver was stopping. I heard a thud and a splash. Jessie was back inside the fuel compartment. He went under but came up quickly; his face was a mix of blood and fuel. It was a checkpoint; we must get to the back of the compartment. We sloshed backward. The main cylinder remained open with Rabbit's rope attached. We could hear talking but no gunfire. If they spotted Rabbit, he would engage and expect us to join. We unzipped our wet suits and grabbed our pistols. We heard voices, but no yelling or excitement from the outside. If they noticed the open hatch, Rabbit had to engage or we were dead men.

We heard more talking outside. I had my pistol. I took it off safe and aimed at the hatch. The truck began moving forward and I secured my weapon. I heard yelling. The driver hit the brakes hard and we slid forward. I listened for gunshots. We heard yelling outside the rear of the truck. They discovered the draining fuel. Seconds passed. Minutes passed. We heard what sounded like a wrench on the outside drain valves. I checked my watch. It was 0311 local and we must be getting closer to the city. We would encounter more and more checkpoints. We heard voices from the outside and someone climbing the ladder from the back of the truck. The driver would see the rope we tied to the hatch. We heard his footsteps clanking across the top of the truck. Our pistols followed his movement. We heard him say something, and then the hatch closed. Again, we were in total darkness. He didn't see the rope? The driver turned and reversed his route, and we heard him climb down the ladder and speak to someone. The voices were muffled. We remained frozen with pistols aimed at the hatch. We heard the driver start the engine and begin going through gears to get the truck to speed. Finally, we placed our pistols underneath the suits. All three of us were huddled and braced in one corner. We were standing on the equipment bag. We were speechless.

Minutes passed. The truck driver again began downshifting to stop. The truck stopped. I checked my watch, and it was 0339 local. We heard muffled voices on the outside of the compartment. The truck began moving, and we passed another checkpoint. The driver brought the truck to speed. The fuel sloshed around us and we knew we were on a winding road. I had memorized the map, and I thought, because of the motion, we were running parallel to the river.

We were in a daze. It was easy to kick ourselves for the stupidity of attempting this infiltration method. This was miserable. We were trained professionals and familiar with hardship. One thing was certain: our exit from this mission would not include a fuel truck. We heard a banging noise above us. All of us reached for our pistols. The hatch opened. It was Rabbit. He partially closed the hatch behind him and slid his way toward us.

"I hid under a blanket behind the diver's luggage rack," he said. "The checkpoints are too dangerous. We are beside the river. This is the best way."

It was 0417 local. We must be getting close.

The truck slowed and made frequent stops. We were entering the city. Soon, the truck began making a series of tight turns. We were close. We heard muffled voices. We felt the truck backing and stopping. It was 0512 local. All was quiet outside. We had roughly two hours before daylight. We had to change clothes, get our bearings, and begin the march. Our link-up time was 0730 to 0745 local. If we missed this window, the next was tonight. Our link-up point was a secluded scenic overlook roughly seven kilometers away but almost straight uphill. The linkup vehicle was a white Toyota pickup truck with an extended cab and a light-blue towel on the passenger side dashboard.

FRESH AIR

We moved the equipment bag. Without the engine noise, it was much louder inside the compartment. Rabbit went first. I felt a great sense of joy as he opened the hatch, and we saw light. He moved to establish security. Jessie went next and positioned to pull the bag to him. Zeus and I lifted and pressed the bag to him. I went out next, followed by Zeus. Jessie roped the bag off the side of the truck to Rabbit. We were in a fenced truck farm. To our left, I saw twenty fuel trucks, but I also saw a small makeshift tower. To our right was twenty meters of open space and another six or seven trucks. We were roughly on eye level with a makeshift tower, and we needed to get off the top of the truck. We slid off between the trucks and away from the tower. Rabbit and Jessie had security. Zeus and I worked the bag. We unzipped the bag and pulled individual clothing packages and peeled off our suits. I stank from the fuel and sweat.

We were in transition. Combat leaders micromanaged transitions. During transitions, you were vulnerable. We rehearsed this action. I had two minutes to relieve Jessie, so he could change. I conducted my personal equipment check. We didn't carry a global positioning system device because it could be traced. We couldn't afford to forfeit our location to anyone. There were several private companies around the world that specialized in selling specific GPS locations, and in this case, we didn't want the Chinese selling the Serbians all GPS device locations within their country. This was a targeting mission. We carried only pistols and our equipment was designed to ensure accurate targeting. Besides, rifles were much easier to spot. I gathered my equipment and placed it into my worn out, old, civilian backpack. Our plan was to move roughly halfway to the link-up point and then ditch the wet suits.

Jessie was at the front of the truck behind the driver's side wheel and facing outward. I tapped him on the shoulder and he moved back to the equipment bag. Just as I placed my knee on the ground, I heard a whistle blow. Not good. It was a series of long blasts from a referee's whistle followed by shouting. I saw a fat man running toward us carrying a rifle or shotgun. He was heading directly for us. I saw a smaller, thin man blowing the whistle running behind him. Both would be within my range in a second. I raised my pistol, took off safe and squeezed the trigger. Nothing. It failed to fire. I pulled the slide to the rear and aimed. Again, nothing, My pistol was useless.

I grabbed my knife and crouched behind the wheel. As the large man passed, I kicked him in the side of his leg. He fell hard. I plunged the knife into his heart and quickly removed it. The thin man rounded the corner. I flipped the knife into throwing position and let it fly. It struck him on the left side of his throat. Both Rabbit and I were on him in a second, removing the knife and thrusting it into his chest while pulling him to the ground. We removed the knife and Rabbit went back to the equipment bag to finish changing.

We were taught to slit the throat and cut the windpipe, preventing the enemy's ability to make sounds. I couldn't do it. I pulled the fat man underneath the truck and did my best to hide him from view behind the wheel. He was white headed with wild white eyebrows. He was carrying an old shotgun. I pulled five shells from his pockets. I pulled the thin man underneath the far truck wheel. He was a smoker, and I could smell the smoke from his clothes. He was carrying an old revolver.

The men were not soldiers. They were security guards and thought somebody was stealing fuel. I had killed in Panama, in Iraq during the first Gulf War, in Somalia, Columbia, and on three different occasions in the Balkans. It didn't get easier. I hated myself. I always remembered things about them. Here, I would remember the wild white eyebrows of the fat man and the smell of smoke from the thin man. My right hand trembled, but I rubbed it hard and it subsided.

Jessie came forward and whispered, "Zeus is cutting the fence."

I disassembled my pistol and rubbed it hard with my cleaning cloth. It smelled of fuel. I had the pistol from the thin dead man and I cleaned it. Jessie had a large green bandage over the gash on his forehead, but his black toboggan covered most of it. It was 0533 local. We had infiltrated from the south, and we had to get moving toward the mountain. The city was flat and sat at the intersection of two rivers. It had two mountains that overlooked the city and we had to reach the smaller one.

On missions like these, we didn't have squad intercom sets. We used hand and arm signals or miniflashlight signals to communicate. We saw Rabbit signaling behind us and we broke for the fence. Zeus cut the fence on the opposite side of the fuel farm. When they discovered the dead guards and found the cut fence, they would initially follow the trail downhill toward the city. My best guess was that we had an hour before someone discovered the bodies, maybe two.

We worked our way through and away from the fence. We dashed through the urban area and started uphill. It was steep. We moved in an extended diamond formation with roughly thirty meters between men. Rabbit was on point. A control freak, he refused to be anywhere else except in the lead. Zeus was on the right flank, Jessie on the left, and I was the swing man in the rear. It was a thick forest, but we all knew we had to make the link-up times. If we failed, we would live in the woods for twelve hours. By that time, the police would be swarming the area, attempting to solve the murder and catch the fuel thieves. No wonder the Air Force had problems targeting the enemy in this stuff. I thought about home.

We made good time and I continually looked behind me. As we climbed higher, I had two clear views of the fuel farm and saw no movement or activity. We took a break. Rabbit found a good spot to bury the wetsuits. We dug quickly and resumed the march. We should have no problems making 0730. The terrain grew steeper as we climbed higher and we were in twilight. The scenic overlook was on a cliff. We had veered hard to the right to avoid the cliff. According to the plan, we were to enter and observe the parking area from above the overlook. We stopped. Rabbit moved forward alone to conduct reconnaissance of our objective rally point where we would gather prior to link-up. We needed to observe the parking lot without being detected. During planning, satellite photos showed two promising spots, but far more vegetated than we anticipated.

We were dressed to look like migrate workers. If it came to it, our collective cover was Spanish pipefitters who entered the country illegally and were looking for work. We hoped it never came to that. Our Spanish language skills were solid and we had taken a crash course in pipefitting. There were enough Spanish journeymen workers in the country to make it plausible. Business, industry, and the military always needed pipefitters, even during a war.

It was cool enough in early May for us to wear jackets and it helped us conceal equipment. We carried worn-out backpacks. When we divided out the equipment bag, we split the load. Jessie carried our targeting equipment. Zeus carried our communications equipment. I carried additional pistol magazines and my mission notebook, which was a slightly modified *Popular Mechanics* magazine. We all memorized and repeatedly tested ourselves on the word and letter sequence along with the specific page numbers. If we got into trouble, the mission notebook provided the data for potential safe houses in the area as well as the signals associated with each site. I carried sixty-five thousand US dollars in small bills, twenty thousand in local currency, as well as five solid gold pieces. I didn't know the value of the gold pieces, but I knew they could make a poor man rich. Rabbit carried our small first aid bag and additional clothing. It was 0652 local.

Rabbit called us forward. We moved carefully to a spot above the scenic overlook. Several cars and two large trucks were below. Truck drivers would stop here for the night and they were getting up and preparing to move. More importantly, we had a great view of most of the city and the fuel farm. Zeus took far side security and Rabbit moved to determine how we would get off the spot and into the parking lot. Jessie began initial equipment checks and I maintained observation of the parking lot.

"All set for targeting and can laser designate," Jessie said.

He replaced Zeus who began his equipment checks. He grabbed my foot. I turned. He had a pale look. He pointed at our communications equipment. We carried this equipment in three small suitcases, each about the size of a high school textbook, and two of the three cases were damaged. When we placed the components together, we had a digital encryption device. During my rampage in the fuel compartment, or when all of us were standing on the equipment bag, we crushed two portions of the equipment. This was bad. It was very bad. Our last report was at 2300 prior to entering the truck. We were required to report every twelve hours. We had until 1100 local to send a message telling the higher-ups we were in compliance with the plan. Having been on the other end of this experience, if we failed to report by 1100, it would be noted. By 1300 local, it would be serious.

By 1500 local, my entire chain of command would know, and by 1700, general officers would be involved. They would barbeque me in molasses when I returned, but they didn't spend the night in the back of a fuel truck. We would adapt. We would fix it or check the CIA's communication capabilities. We had our targeting equipment so we would accomplish our mission.

It was 0717 local and twilight was fading. I saw movement below and heard police sirens. They found the bodies in the fuel farm. I was focused on watching the city. Suddenly, I heard a tremendous explosion on the far northeastern horizon along the river. The enemy fired some sort of surface-to-air missile and we saw it trekking into the sky. I didn't see a secondary explosion and I doubted they could hit our aircraft, but it reminded us we were in a war zone. We saw a white extended cab Toyota pickup truck coming down the road and slowing to make the turn. The truck entered the parking area, but the driver parked the nose of the truck outward. We needed to get a clear view of the light-blue towel. I glanced at Zeus and Rabbit, both shook their heads, telling me they did not confirm the presence of the blue towel. I was concerned about the fuel farm and the missile made me nervous. We needed to get out of here and into a safe house. I signaled Rabbit to begin working his way into the parking lot. The missile made the truckers nervous. They were packing, throwing away their breakfast and moving out. We were in another transition. We must avoid looking like four guys walking out of the woods.

SERGE

Rabbit made his way to the parking lot, trying to get a visual on the light-blue towel. I noticed more activity at the fuel farm. I saw groups of people forming and walking the fence line. It wouldn't be long before they found the cut fence. The driver of the Toyota got out and stood beside the truck. He was smoking. Rabbit was at the opposite side of the overlook, but moving toward him. I looked back toward the fuel farm. I heard dogs barking. Then I saw them being unloaded. This place had smart cops, and they weren't wasting time. We needed a blue towel, and we needed it fast. Otherwise, we would have to steal a vehicle and begin reading the *Popular Mechanics* magazine. Rabbit closed in on the man and took a cigarette from him. I saw Rabbit nod.

I told Zeus, "Get Jessie."

The explosion and missile strike stirred the parking lot. The people sleeping in their cars were moving around. They placed their bedding on the hood and were walking toward the bathroom. I scooted down the hill. As I walked across the parking lot, I placed the revolver I took from the man at the fuel farm inside a bag on the hood of one of the cars and kept walking. Rabbit got in the back of the truck. Jessie got in the rear passenger side, and I got behind the driver. Zeus sat up front. In most places in the world, it would not matter, but the Serbs were known for their racists views, and we didn't need any undue attention. We didn't speak. The driver pulled away from the scenic overlook and headed up the mountain and away from the city. We drove down the far side of the mountain through a series of interconnected towns. We were heading east and then north toward the city. I pointed at the river, and the driver nodded and said, "Sava."

We were in a working-class neighborhood with small houses and small yards. The good news was many appear to be fenced. We could not park on the street; we must pull into a driveway, better yet a garage. Places like this have curious neighbors.

The driver turned into a small house and pulled toward a building in the back. We were blocked from the neighbors by a large overgrown fence on one side and the house itself on the other. This house was slightly offset from the one across the street. We exited quickly and entered the house. Rabbit began a room-to-room search. Jessie moved from window to window, observing in case things went wrong. Zeus moved to the kitchen table and began working on our communications devices. It was 0808. The curtains were closed, and the furniture was old and musty.

Our CIA asset, now our contact, was an older balding man with a large belly. He was a chain-smoker.

"Good observation of the surrounding neighborhood from the second story," said Rabbit.

Jessie transitioned into hunting for listening or camera devices and was looking through the small bookcase, under the tables, and was checking all the outlets. Listening and camera devices were getting smaller, but they required some power source, so checking all electric outlets was the quickest way to ensure we were not being monitored.

Our contact lit another cigarette and said, "You are paranoid." We continued. If this mission went bad, it wouldn't be because we were ill-disciplined.

Our checks were complete. We reassembled in the small living room. Zeus stared at the communications gear and said, "I can't repair it."

We had a problem. Rabbit took first watch from the second-floor bedroom, Zeus went down for sleep, and Jessie took his shot at the communications gear. The contact's name was Serge. Most of our contacts were contracted foreign nationals, but I didn't ask and he didn't tell. The less we knew of each other, the better. He spoke English with a slight Slavic or Russian-like accent. He was well paid as most of these folks retire in their forties to island nations. He had communications with his superiors but only via dead drop. He made wooden models of historic churches and other older buildings and sold them in the open market. The tourists' market had fallen off since the war, so he sold cheap pottery. He took me through his outdoor workshop where he built the models and made the pottery. He began loading pottery into the back of his truck. He also loaded a beautiful small country church made of wood into the backseat. It reminded me of home. He told me he must get to work and he must follow the routine. He was due a dead drop. The neighborhood would be quiet until the children got out of school. He told me to rest. Somehow, I didn't think that's going to happen.

We were most vulnerable when he left. If he was corrupt, the enemy would descend upon us. If that occurred, we would not fight back. Our best option was to work the Spanish worker cover for as long as possible. We had no viable escape and killing even a few of the enemy here would just lead to more brutality upon us later. We would retain a local watch and work a disciplined sleep plan until we received orders. In most cases, we got orders quickly, but on occasion, we ended up waiting. The waiting was unbearable. Eventually, NATO and US Forces would invade and we would link up and assist in targeting. I would feel much better if we had communications with headquarters. They were above the fray, could think clearly, had lots of toys, and could direct us around or through bad situations. I took full responsibility for the communications equipment. I panicked. Maybe the others had something to do with it, but I was the leader and was responsible for whatever we accomplished or failed to accomplish.

Jessie yelled for Zeus. They worked on the gear, and he said, "We won't be able to receive, but at least, we can report." We sent the report. We got a green light, meaning it went somewhere. We rotated watch and each of us got a few hours of sleep. Serge was right about the neighborhood. When the kids come home, it exploded with several soccer games up and down the street. Finally, Serge returned. He didn't have much to unload, so he had sold some pottery. He came inside with canned food and a baked chicken. We immediately opened the canned food. We were afraid of eating local meat. We couldn't afford to lose a team member to sickness. The chicken smelled good. If we were here for another couple of days, we would eat it.

Serge told us that he had his drop. We should expect our mission list tomorrow. He followed routine and went to church that night. We continued to rotate on six-hour shifts and eat canned food. During the night, we heard two or three distant explosions but nothing close. The next morning, Serge loaded pottery and left for work. We spent the day studying Serge's city maps. They were old maps, but we needed to develop a thorough understanding of the terrain. Each of us placed the targeting device into operation to ensure we were ready. We had only one device. In the past, we had carried several plus additional communications gear, but we had significantly downsized our profile for this specific mission due to concerns about our infiltration.

It was Friday afternoon. We ate canned food, rested, and executed mission prep all day. Serge returned. He showed me the target list. It was only one target. One target was unusual. Tomorrow night. We moved quickly to the maps. It was a fenced compound. Jessie used a piece of string to determine the distance we required using the targeting device. We thought we could pull this off from the scenic overlook. We would have to move off the scenic overlook down the mountain about a kilometer to ensure we had the right distance. I recalled the spot where I looked back at the fuel farm. I had clear observation. Although our targeting device had a sophisticated and powerful sighting system, we wanted to execute a drive-by to ensure we were all seeing the same target. We needed to conduct ground reconnaissance tonight to ensure success tomorrow.

Zeus and I conducted the recon of the target. Serge drove. We couldn't afford to draw any attention to ourselves, so smaller was better. Our plan was to conduct the reconnaissance of the target first, go to the overlook, park, and work our way down the mountain to the spot. If we could see the target and both of us reassure ourselves that we had a good visual of the correct building complex, our portion of the recon was complete. Once we returned, Jessie and Rabbit conducted a similar recon designed to find a safe observation spot where they could make the estimated damage report.

It was twilight as we departed the safe house. The soccer games were ending. Serge knew all the local roads and we worked the side streets. The enemy didn't have enough combat power in terms of troops for total control so they generally placed movement control checkpoints only on the main roads. Additionally, they were concentrating more on movement control outside the city and we had already infiltrated past those checkpoints. We worked our way across town, leaving the small working-class neighborhood and headed into the working-class business district. We didn't stray anywhere near the wealthy side of town or in the vicinity of the wealthy businesses district. Just like America, rich people protect themselves. If you didn't look like you belonged, then you were in trouble. We didn't look like we belonged. I saw a series of blue lights to our front and I feared it was a checkpoint. It was not. A military convoy was moving through a major intersection from north to south and the police were directing traffic.

The roads were wider and prettier now, so we were getting closer. We had an old tourist map that we were using to navigate. If we were stopped, we would simply throw it into the floor; however, Serge knew where we were going from our map reconnaissance. We saw the building. It was an impressive facility with an enormous brick fence surrounding and it covered an entire city block. It was designed to show power. I noticed the signs but could not read them. Zeus noticed some type of flag, but in the darkness, we could not determine its significance. We circled the block and determined all the major landmarks. This area was the exact target location, and it would be much easier than we thought to pick it out from the side of the mountain. We were confident it was the exact target. We drove a wider circle around the target area to ensure our accuracy. There were more prominent landmarks. I wondered why they wanted it designated as it was the most prominent building within a six-block radius. It appeared they could easily see this area with satellite imagery, target and destroy it, but we continued with our mission. Wherever we aimed our laser was where the laser-guided bombs would land.

We began driving toward the mountain. Zeus and I continually looked back to see the prominent landmarks. I could see the fuel farm where this all began and we started up the mountain. We parked at the scenic overlook. It was far more crowded than before. We heard the sound of music. It was a young crowd, and we could smell dope. This place was the Friday night party spot. We parked in the corner. I told Serge to back the truck into the spot. Serge got out and lit another cigarette, walked around to the rear of the truck, and sat on the tailgate. This crowd was not going to notice us. Zeus and I headed into the woods. I had point, and he had the device. We moved down the mountain, making good time. As we approached the small clearing, I heard giggling. A couple was making out. I found a good-sized rock and threw it off to the side. They either didn't hear it or didn't care. Zeus threw a stick. They heard it but were finished. They walked hand in hand back up the trail, passing right beside us. If they were here tomorrow night, we could have trouble. Zeus set up. We used a folding tripod to ensure stability. If someone came near, we would point it toward the sky and appear to be stargazing. If we were asked anything, we would rely on Zeus and his immersion language training. He had little confidence in his language skills, and I had even less. We began aiming. Zeus easily found the target, and I confirmed it. We were well within range with a clear view. We broke it down in reverse order and began moving back up the mountain. Serge was still on the tailgate smoking when we came out of the woods. We loaded up and began the circular drive back to the safe house.

We pulled into the driveway. Zeus and I got out and Jessie and Rabbit got in. Zeus and I discussed how we would handle the parking lot if it was crowded tomorrow. We also discussed the make-out spot. We had a very small time window and we needed to ensure we were set to execute the mission. If our favorite couple was there tomorrow night, we would need to scare them away to execute our mission. We didn't want to harm them, but if it came to that, we would be prepared. We ate more canned food and continued to study the older maps. This must be a major target. We were going to great lengths to ensure its destruction. It was also our only target, which was unusual. We sent our report telling headquarters we were in variance with the plan; we had our target and would be in position to execute tomorrow night. We got the green light, so we sent the message. I anxiously awaited the return of the rest of the team.

The Toyota pulled in the driveway. It was 2347 local. Serge, Jessie, and Rabbit returned. They found a good spot to observe. We began mission planning. We would depart together. We navigate the side streets and drop Jessie and Rabbit at an intersection where they would move to an overpass and could safely observe the shot and target destruction. Serge would take us up the mountain to the overlook, drop us off, and we would move to the clearing and set up. Serge knew our engagement window, so he would pick up Jessie and Rabbit minutes after the target was destroyed. He would drive back to the overlook where Zeus and I would jump in the truck, and we would return to the safe house and await our next mission. We had a plan.

It was Saturday, and the neighborhood soccer games began early. Although this was a nation at war, it was modern war. In modern war, people go on with their lives. The people of this city have not felt the war. At night, they heard the distant thunder of explosions, but that was about it. The strategy thus far had been to use airpower against their army, which was away from the city.

We rechecked all equipment. We rehearsed all aspects of the mission, which included a vehicle breakdown, a compromise of the vehicle, and a compromise of the targeting or observation site. We also established rally points. If we thought it a potential for failure, then we rehearsed it as well as all of our follow on actions. Serge watched the soccer match on television. We sent another report and got a green light. We tried to sleep in the afternoon. Serge left to go shopping. He returned but didn't unload the cases of cigarette he purchased.

Darkness came and we continued to prepare. We all went into separate rooms to think about the mission. Each of us had a major role, and each of us depended on the others for survival. We could not fail. It was 2212 local. We will departed at planned to depart at 2300 local and execute the mission from 2345 until 0015 local. Basically, we would laze the target for thirty minutes.

A police car came screaming down the narrow street with lights and sirens blaring. He stopped in front of our safe house. We were up and moving. Seconds later, an old model fire engine came down the street. I heard Jessie yell, "Fire!" and I thought our safe house was on fire, but then he pointed. The house opposite us was on fire. Kids and families came running from all directions and stood in the front yard and driveway of the safe house. More police arrived as well as another old fire truck.

"Go now before they block the driveway," I said. "Move slowly, we don't want the neighbors to think we are arsonist." We would be spotted on our exit, so we waved at the crowd as we slowly backed the truck out of the driveway. We got several odd looks, but soon, Serge had the truck moving down the street away from the fire.

"We will be early," Jessie said. "My drill sergeant told me on Day One in the Army, you can be early, but you cannot be late."

Serge abruptly pulled the truck into a crowded gas station, got out, and began fueling the truck. I was astonished. We were at risk. The gas station was adjacent to a crowded late-night restaurant. We avoided looking. If anybody spoke to us, all we could speak was Spanish or English, and both would bring suspicion.

"Avoid eye contact," I said.

Serge went out earlier and should have filled his fuel tank. He went inside and purchased more cigarettes and tossed them into the back. We were angry, and I said, "You put us in jeopardy."

Before I could finish my sentence, Jessie interrupted and said, "Being stupid can get a man killed."

He shrugged and said, "I needed petro." He was either brave or stupid, but his being stupid now would get us all killed.

Jessie grabbed his shoulder and said, "This mission is hard, but if you continue to be stupid, it will get harder." He shrugged his shoulders again, changed gears, and continued to drive.

We arrived at the drop off intersection and pulled to the side. It was 2302 local. We were somewhat early, but this was the best option. We would be exposed a little longer, but the streets were generally empty in this part of town. We needed to watch for the police as we were prime candidates for profiling. We were good on time. Jessie and Rabbit dismounted and began walking toward the overpass. Serge drove us up the mountain and pulled into the scenic overlook. It was even more crowded than last night. More music and more dope smell. This was the party spot for the crowd that couldn't afford to go into the clubs. We pulled into the far corner.

"Good luck," Serge said in his thick Slavic accent. His tone and mannerisms struck me as odd, but we had a mission. People were everywhere, and I worried about our observation spot being occupied by energetic young lovers. It was 2321 local when we dashed into the woods. We followed the same path as our recon. They were there; we heard the giggling and soft talking. Zeus and I followed our plan. He moved below them, and I moved above them. Zeus had filled an empty food can with small rocks, cut holes in the can, and taped the top. He threw the can high in the air, and it sounded like a bear tearing through the woods as it bounced limb to limb off the trees. He then growled. His deep voice sounded like something snarling in the woods. The couple ran up the hill. We moved into the observation spot and set up our equipment. We leveled the tripod, mounted the device, and we clearly identified the target. By 2335 local, we were set.

We heard them coming down the hill. They were loud. There must have been ten or twelve. I pointed the targeting device skyward and began stargazing. Zeus engaged them and I prayed he could speak the language. He stopped them. Basically, we had ten to twelve drunken teenagers carrying sticks and ball bats all looking for a bear. Zeus started laughing and then began speaking to me in some language that I couldn't understand, but I also started laughing. He laughed harder; I laughed harder. We initially got stunned looks from the stoned teenagers; then, they began laughing themselves, saying something I didn't understand, and slowly working their way back up the mountain to the overlook. We continued to fake laugh until they were gone.

It was 2341 local, and we reacquired the target and conducted a final systems check. We both verified the target and placed the crosshairs at the base of the building. We began lasing. We were painting the target. Any laser-guided bomb released from an aircraft magically moved to the spot we illuminated. The neat thing was nobody could see it. We made mission.

"What did you say to the teenagers," I asked Zeus. He shrugged.

"I don't know. They were looking for an animal of some sort, and all I knew to do was laugh." He was agile and adaptive.

At 2359, the building exploded. I never saw it coming. The noise was deafening. The shock wave so intense, I felt it tug my jacket and we were roughly eleven kilometers away. I was no stranger to big explosions, but this was the biggest and most intense I had seen. I was concerned about Jessie and Rabbit. We dropped them roughly three kilometers away from the target to observe. I didn't know what munitions we hit the target with, but I knew we hit it hard. We checked the sights; it was completely destroyed. There was nothing but a large hole in the ground. We both verified the target was destroyed. The smoke cloud was easily three or four hundred feet in the air. We didn't need to separate the team, but we didn't know the delivery munitions we were going to use. If they used bombs, we would have had to target verify, but none of us knew. This must have been a Tomahawk missile of some sort and our nation wanted this building completely and utterly destroyed. It must have been some type of bunker busting or ground penetrating missile. It was a building with several underground facilities; they were all gone now. There was nothing remaining in the entire block but a huge hole in the ground. It was at least fifty or sixty feet deep. The amazing thing was the precision. We could see the hole that used to be a building because of the fire in the hole and the lights and power grid on the surrounding blocks, which never faltered.

We took the targeting device down, collapsed the tripod, and moved back up the hill. Serge should have picked up Rabbit and Jessie and would be on his way back here by now. Once we got to the overlook, we should be able to see his truck coming. We needed to get out of there and back to the safe house. We made it to the overlook. The explosion stopped the party, and most of the young crowd had either left or were in the process of leaving. We stayed in the woods, looking for the Toyota pickup truck. I sent Zeus back to our original perch where he would have a better view of the road. I knew Jessie and Rabbit were outside of the safety danger zone, but I also knew that, given the intensity of the explosion, they were probably deaf and dazed. It was 0011 local. I was doing the math in my head. Serge should have been back by now with Jessie and Rabbit. I was getting anxious. I waited another five minutes and then moved to Zeus.

He stared at me and said, "Serge has failed us."

THINGS FALL APART

WE MOVED UPHILL to the first designated contingency rally point. If Jessie and Rabbit were not in trouble, they would join us, but it was a long, uphill hike. Under our contingency plan, we were to stay here not later than 0200 local waiting for them. If they failed to show by then, we moved to the alternate and attempted another link-up. If Serge was corrupt, he knew portions of our plan. By now, he had notified local and Army authorities and we would soon have company searching for us. If that was the case, we would fight it out. We were on good ground with lots of pistol ammo. Serge would tell them our cover story so they would execute us. We might as well go down fighting. If he had simply vanished, then we would regroup and begin working our way out of this place. I thought about how he didn't unload the canned food and cigarettes and how he suddenly stopped for fuel. Best case for us was him just driving away. He was signaling us that he was running away, and I missed it. We all missed it. I have never, ever trusted the CIA or their hired assets. I was angry and venting. They were a poorly run, gutless, and an overall sorry, and ill-disciplined outfit. They rewarded failure. It was their ethos. Regardless of what happened to us, Serge would report back that he destroyed the target and his mission was complete. I needed to calm down. Maybe something else happened. We continued to watch the city.

It was 0200. Nobody had come near us, and we saw only a few cars on the road. We watched the police and fire response around the building. They continued pouring water into a big hole in the ground. Jessie and Rabbit had yet to show, so we moved to the next rally point. Serge ran away with our transport or they had been captured. We didn't know. If they had been captured, they could resist the torture for a while, but would eventually begin talking. We had trained and rehearsed for this contingency. The next rally point was on the other side of the mountain, facing away from the city. It was six kilometers away and would require us to cross the top of the mountain. We started uphill.

As we moved toward the top, I heard dogs barking. The noise was coming from our left flank, not from our rear, so I didn't think we were being chased, but we established ambush just to ensure we were safe. Here, we would execute a near ambush, meaning we would fire at point-blank range. It would work if the enemy didn't have night vision. Night vision was getting more and more common among military and police units so it was a concern. By killing at point-blank, we increased our lethality and enabled ourselves to steal their rifles and ammunition once the mission was complete. I cringed. From the top of the mountain, we saw multiple explosions in the far southern horizon. Our Air Force was bombing somebody tonight. I couldn't gauge the distance, but it appeared twenty to thirty miles distant.

We had pistols. We were good with them, but the game had changed and if we were to survive, we needed long rifles and a basic load of ammunition. Zeus and I found good spots along the mountaintop path. Once we were set, we no longer heard the dogs. We remained set for roughly five minutes and then resumed the march, this time going downhill. It was 0247 local.

I was keeping the pace count in my head. It allowed me to gauge how far we had traveled. I don't know why, but I was very good at navigating through the woods in the dark. We were roughly two kilometers away. Serge knew the first rally point above the overlook, but only the team knew this one. It was the top of a cliff that overlooked an intersection. At the base of the cliff to the right, was a small store on the uphill side of the road. From there, we could observe and plan while being somewhat safe. The enemy would have a hard time spotting or shooting us. We needed time to think. We needed time to study the modified *Popular Mechanics* magazine and determine the other potential safe houses in the area. We needed to steal a vehicle. I heard the explosion; it was another significant airstrike to the south. Somebody or something was getting hit hard tonight. The biggest problem we faced now was to avoid walking off the cliff. We thought it was substantial at about sixty feet. We moved slowly. It was easier to be quiet going uphill. Regardless of how much effort we placed into being quiet, I feared we sounded like an elephant herd coming down the mountain.

Zeus closed in fast on me and whispered, "I heard something."

We set ambush positions facing uphill. It was a partly cloudy night and, once we were stationary, we could see much farther than I anticipated. We spread out with each of us covering a designated sector of fire. We had each other's back. I heard movement. I was uncertain if it was an animal. We heard it, and then we didn't. We needed to get set on the cliff so I prepared to move and then we heard more movement. We remained in position. It must have been an animal, probably a raccoon or something. I started to move again. Just as I stood and turned, I heard a thud as if somebody had fallen. This was weird, so I was back in ambush again. Then I saw him.

"Contact, right flank," I whispered to Zeus. The target veered toward us. I saw further movement behind him. If this was a patrol, we were screwed because they are not going to bunch up and let us take them in a near ambush.

I was praying that I knew who was coming. Rabbit was in the lead, being quiet and deliberate, with Jessie lumbering through the woods behind him. My heart was soaring. I stood up quickly. Rabbit raised his pistol and then lowered it. I hugged him and Jessie. We all took a knee on the side of the mountain. They were winded.

Rabbit stared at me and said, "We just destroyed the Chinese Embassy."

"What?" I exclaimed. "That can't be true. Embassies are sovereign soil. Destroying a country's embassy, a country we are not at war with, is an act of war! How do you know?"

"You know we arrived early and I sent Rabbit to check out the surrounding area. He saw the sign," Jessie said.

I stared at Rabbit.

He cleared his throat, gasped for air, and said, "I saw a sign, on the corner, in English, with an arrow pointing toward the Chinese Embassy. I ran down the street about two hundred meters. I saw another sign fixed to the brick fence, which said Chinese Embassy in several languages. I saw it in English, French, and Spanish. I ran back to J, and we went behind the embankment so I could tell him. That's when it hit." He shook his head. "It's gone. The whole thing…nothing left. It must have been a Tomahawk."

"It was the target they gave us," Zeus interrupted.

I nodded and said, "Serge?"

Jessie shook his head. "Nowhere to be found, but I will find him one day."

"Are we all okay," I asked. They all nodded. Jessie gazed at me, took several deep breaths.

"We were off the road when it hit," he said. "We were expecting bombs, not a missile. We ran to the link-up point, expecting to see Serge, waited only a minute, then began the move up and over the mountain. Lots of police and fire trucks moving along the roads so it was slow. We should have either stayed with the truck or stolen it from Serge."

My mind was spinning. Jessie looked around and said, "We in it now, baby. We in it."

Were we setup by this guy? What should we do next? How do we get out of here? Were we now war criminals? I tried to focus.

"Move to the next rally point," I said.

Rabbit took point, and we moved in the extended diamond. I was still reeling about the fact we destroyed an embassy. Infiltration was critical. We only received one target, and our asset was flaky at best. We didn't have communications, but we followed our standard protocol. We destroyed the target we were provided. Was this some national plot to blame us? What would we have done different? A mission is a mission, embassy or no embassy. We got the targets and we executed. We did what was asked and we did it well. How high did this thing go? I thought only the president could order the destruction of an embassy. This was a deliberate and well-planned mission. The embassy had a significant understructure, and it was all destroyed. Maybe the Chinese were providing intelligence to the Serbs on our movements and activities, and we needed to spank them. It was a hard spanking.

Rabbit had us in the slight clearing at the top of the cliff. We conducted a short recon of the area and marked our exit routes in case we needed to leave in a hurry. We did this because none of us want to fall off the cliff. We stopped and looked south at another airstrike. This one was somewhat closer. We had excellent observation and could see more than a kilometer in every direction except behind us. We could see the store. We needed to steal a vehicle, but before we executed, we had to know where we are going. We went into a rest and guard cycle. Zeus and I took the first watch and Rabbit and Jessie went to sleep immediately. We needed daylight to plan and to work our way through the magazine, determining the next safe house. Maybe we would see Serge again, and I would keep Jessie from killing him, or maybe not.

It was a lazy Sunday morning without much movement and I thought of my childhood home in Clay County. The sun was up and we had all gotten some sleep. Sleep, even a nap, was critical. Without it, we became paranoid and stopped thinking clearly. We were not prepared to sleep in the open, but the weather was not bad, and it was not unusual for us. I examined Jessie's head. It was infected. It was a significant gash that would normally require ten to twelve stitches. I was sure the fuel didn't help it. We were out of bandages and ointment. He was the toughest man I knew, but if we were forced to live off the land for more than a couple of days, the infection would spread. It would eventually take him out of action. This changed the state of play. Our protocol was to find another safe house, but without two-way communications and any internal asset, it was foolish. I was thinking more and more about either going north to Budapest, Hungary, or east to Bucharest, Romania. In both cases, we must figure out how to cross the Danube River, and either way, we would end up at the American Embassy. West and South were not good options because those areas had become Air Force bombing ranges. Macedonia was our stretch option as we had friends there, but it didn't seem worth the risk because it was both south and would require multiple border crossings. Border crossings were dangerous. If we were going to invade using ground forces, we would have executed by now. We had massed both the air and ground combat power. However, going anywhere to the south might put us between defending and invading ground forces.

Rabbit was convinced east was the best route. We studied the magazine. We had three viable safe houses, but all three were well to our north, requiring us to move back through or around the city. We didn't have an asset to work with, and they weren't expecting us, which could be a dangerous undertaking. It was over a four-hundred-kilometer trip without transportation.

From where we sat, we were roughly two hundred kilometers to a border crossing area followed by more than three hundred more kilometers to Bucharest. We also needed to cross the Danube, which made this border crossing even more difficult. Overall, we needed to move a long way before we were safe. We needed fresh bandages as well as any type of over-the-counter ointment to fight the infection. The one hole card we had yet to play was money. We discussed bribing our way to some sort of an advantage. Our problem remained language. We were fighting a cultural war and we were unarmed because we couldn't speak the language. I kicked myself hourly over the fact we couldn't talk to these people. If we could speak the language, bribing them would be much easier. We would go east, but that required transport. We were all skilled car thieves, but that was a last resort.

We trained for this situation, but I couldn't remember a team being isolated this long without communications. When we executed similar missions in the past, we always went from safe house to safe house whether it was here in the Balkans, Central Africa, Columbia, or Somalia. Each safe house had a code from the modified *Popular Mechanics* magazine. We would report from here as we thought we had enough battery power to send one more report. We would send the number for a safe house located to the east. Higher would know we were heading east. We developed a plan. Zeus and I would move along the mountain for roughly a mile and then return up the road to the store. Our plan was to casually enter the store and attempt to buy supplies. We would continue the Spanish worker ruse. It was the only one we had. Skilled workers walking away from a war zone and looking for work. It was plausible. Once we exited the store, we would move up the road, climb the mountain, and circle back to the cliff.

We went uphill and then worked our way across the mountainside. We were roughly a mile down the road from the store when we emerged and began walking back. I scanned the cliff, knowing my teammates were watching us, but I saw no signs of life. The country side was beautiful. On the other side of the mountain was a city with over a million people, but on this side, it was farms and rural area with a few scattered houses. We didn't see traffic in either direction. We casually entered the store and provided a friendly wave to the clerk. He nodded politely. This was a local country store with wooden floors that creaked as we walked. No need to worry about cameras here. The shelves were sparse, but he did have large Band-Aids, some medications, and lots of canned food. We continued to talk in Spanish. I forced myself to relax and play the part. As we walked to the counter, I added four candy bars to our purchase. He rang the cash register, and I paid him in Euros. He frowned when he saw the money but took it anyway. He asked me some type of question. I smiled at the man, quickly replied in Spanish, and called for Zeus. Zeus came forward and I motioned that the man had a question for me, so he would need to interpret. Zeus carefully worked his words and unintentionally butchered his sentences. The man understood. I pointed to the sink in the corner and then made a gesture as if that is what we do, and he appeared to comprehend. Zeus attempted to thank him in his language, and he smiled and waved. We walked out the door, stopped at the bench, placed the items in our worn-out backpacks, and began walking up the road. We saw a truck coming. It parked and we looked back and watched the driver going inside. We continued walking past the fork in the road and were getting close to a point where we could get into the woods. We heard the honking first. It was the truck that stopped at the store. The man pulled beside us, and we waved. He was speaking fast, and I looked at Zeus to translate.

    Zeus tried hard to understand. The man obviously wanted us to go with him. Zeus broke into a smile. He spoke to me in Spanish saying, "He thinks we are plumbers looking for work, and he has work."

    I nodded and said, "We cannot say no, or we blow our cover."

    Zeus got in the front, and I jumped in the back. He turned the truck around, and we started back down the hill toward the store. I scanned the cliff as we passed and signaled for them to stay put. We drove past the store roughly a mile and then turned down a long and winding dirt road. The ground had been tilled on the right side and the left was pasture. We followed this route for another mile and pulled into an old farmhouse. The man had a pasture full of horses on one side, an old barn with an ancient tractor, with the remaining sides all plowed. He was looking to plant lots of something. We could have been anywhere in the Midwest.

We were isolated, even by Yugoslavian or Serbian standards. An older woman came out and greeted the man. Two barking, but friendly, dogs surrounded the truck. The driver and Zeus got out of the truck and I cautiously jumped out and petted the dogs. The woman went back into the house as Zeus and the man attempted to communicate. The woman returned with some sort of flavored drink in a glass. Zeus continued to point toward me and I thought he was deferring to me as his boss. We drank the flavored drinks and the man and his wife talked.

In Spanish, I said, "If we barter for anything, it must be a four-man job because I am concerned about Jessie."

Zeus looked at me with confusion and said, "I don't know anything about farming."

"We need this place. It is isolated," I said. "We get Jessie and Rabbit here and we will do whatever work he needs."

He began to engage the man in a broken monologue of words. He tried hard. The man could see he was trying. He sent his wife inside. She returned with pencil and paper. He drew a picture. He had a well. He wanted us to attach lines to his well pump that would pipe the water first to the horses, then to the center of his field. He wanted an irrigation system. He wanted us to build it.

I drew on the paper and looked at my watch as if I was determining a date. I told him I needed two other men and I could supply them. He didn't understand. I counted slowly in Spanish from one pointing at myself, then two pointing at Zeus, then three and four. He was concerned about paying for four laborers. I pretended to do math in my head and scribbled some numbers. I should have known the currency exchange. All foreign workers would, but I didn't. He gave me a very puzzled look. I nodded my head and talked to Zeus in Spanish asking him to determine if he had the pipe and tools on hand. Zeus translated what he could and the man got up and insisted we follow. We walked to the back side of the barn and he showed us a massive amount of white PVC pipe. We all nodded and smiled. He wrote a figure on the paper and handed it to me. It was twelve hundred in local currency. I pointed to the barn and made a sleeping motion. He nodded yes. He smiled and we shook hands. We were in the contracting business. I told Zeus to explain to him that he wanted to borrow his truck and get our mates. He didn't like the idea. I finally told Zeus to tell him that I would stay and get to work today. This seemed to pacify him somewhat and he handed Zeus the keys. The farmer and I walked the farm. He showed me the water well and we drew diagrams and nodded at one another. He showed me a series of small pumps, we drew more diagrams, and we walked. We ended up back at the barn where we counted PVC pipe.

I heard the truck. Zeus grabbed the team, and they understood the game. Both Jessie and Rabbit walked directly to the man, shook his hand, and overly thanked him. While he was somewhat shocked to see Jessie, he seemed pleased. I was relieved to have the team together. Rabbit looked at me.

"Our last message to higher didn't get out. We got the red light," he said. This was bad.

The wife came out with more flavored drinks. She immediately noticed Jessie's worn-out bandage. They asked about it and Zeus told them he cut it on our last job, but that he was a valuable and skilled worker. The woman went into her home and retrieved some sort of smelly salve. She presented it to us and we applied it to Jessie's forehead. Jessie was nervous but played the part well.

In Spanish, I said, "We are going to work for this man and emplace an irrigation system." They looked at me as if I was beyond crazy. I continued, "If the ground invasion begins, we are placed to pick up and join. If it doesn't, then we plan our escape to the east. Act like workers. They are looking for labor, and we will provide labor. For the next few days, this is our new safe house."

As afternoon approached, we went to the barn, ate canned food and then went to work. I walked the ground, and I told the team the scope of the project and how I saw this working. We also talked about what would happen next and, if it came to it, how we would get across the border to the east. We were in a good spot with a solid cover. We walked back to the barn. Rabbit cranked the tractor. He dug a narrow series of trenches out into the fields. Jessie attempted to carry large sections of pipe when the farmer showed up, laughed, and motioned him to put it down. He returned ten minutes later with a horse hitched to a cart. We loaded the pipe and began putting it together. By nightfall, we had connected the pipe to the far fields. We returned to the barn.

The farmer came and took us inside his house. It was very small and the furniture looked homemade. They had electricity from a generator and the wires ran throughout the house. They used oil lamps for light, and used a generator to pull water from his well. He appeared a smart and industrious man. His wife cooked us a meal. It was mostly fried vegetables, and they insisted we eat it all, so we did. As we ate supper that night, we heard the distant explosion of another airstrike. The explosion reminded me we were in a war zone. The farmer told us that soon, the British Army would come and they would need food and he would be prepared to provide them fresh vegetables. The farmer reminded us wars always produce a profit for somebody.

Zeus carried the conversation with the family and understood most of the main points. The farmer always lived on the farm. It was a collective communist farm at one point; however, communism didn't stick in the former Yugoslavia. There economic system was far more socialist than communist. He sold most of his crops to the government and the remainder on the open market. His best crop was soybeans, but he also grew corn and potatoes. When communism fell, he continued to farm because it was all he knew and people needed to eat. He made more money than ever before because they took their crops directly to the suburban market. Apparently, this was how he bought the new generators. During the early part of the civil war, the Army occupied his southernmost fields. They built a large camp, stayed for three years, and tore it down. He was somewhat adamant that nothing ever grew on that ground anyway, and he didn't need to farm there. When the Army left, they told him not to farm the southernmost portion for twenty years due to chemicals. We were intrigued by the mention of the Army and chemicals, but we simply nodded and agreed. In exchange for not farming the southernmost fields, the Army gave him the PVC pipe to irrigate his fields. When the Army came, many of his neighbors moved away, but he stayed. When his neighbors left, they gave him their workhorses, so he kept them but had plenty of pasture. The couple had a daughter who lived in Belgrade with their two small grandchildren, but they rarely went into the city. The conversation then turned to grandchildren. We thanked them for their hospitality and went to the barn. Because we were who we were, we took turns keeping watch so the other three could sleep.

It rained during the night, and we could hear it on the tin roof. Around midnight, we heard the high-pitched scream of jets overhead, but nothing more. If they hit a target, it was out of our earshot. We were up early the next morning working. We completed the pasture project. Attaching the water well pipes to the main pump was a half-day job, but Rabbit and I were persistent, and it finally worked. We had to get water to the horses. We began attaching pipes all over the farm starting with the distant points and moving closer to the well. Some of the smaller pumps worked while others needed repair. The farmer and his wife left in the truck to buy fuel for the generators.

Rabbit and I rode the tractor to the southernmost part of the farm. We could see where the Army built their outpost but not much remained. They built on high-level ground. We would call it a Forward Operating Base. Probably a Battalion-sized operation, but I didn't understand why it would be here. We were roughly thirty kilometers from the city, and a camp here did not make operational sense. It wasn't on any major avenues of approach. It had only one bad road for both entry and exit. Rabbit and I dismounted and began exploring. They were a disciplined force. If the farmer didn't tell us, we would never know a camp existed. We spotted a wood and metal structure in the woods. It might have been a gang latrine. If we repaired it, it would make an excellent water trough for the horses. We brought the tractor and chained it so we could pull it back to the pasture. Rabbit drove, and I was on the back of the tractor. The structure was heavier than we thought. We pulled the structure and began plowing the ground.

Rabbit leaned forward and yelled, "Oh God!" He pointed. It was bones. We were plowing bones. They were coming up everywhere. I grabbed his shoulder.

"Over there," I said, pointing to the side. He moved the tractor down a small gully, and we saw more and more. We were plowing through a mass, but very shallow, graveyard. We saw skulls and faces, large and small, buried with clothes. Rabbit stopped the tractor. We were staring at the face of a small child holding onto another small child. The older child was a girl, roughly six, and the younger one was three or four. Both were wearing winter clothes and their bodies were only partially decomposed. I saw only half of her face. We found another genocide spot. We were tough men. We gagged. I vomited.

We dragged the device back to where we found it and dumped it. I was certain if the farmer wanted it, he would have gotten it by now. He may have seen the same things we saw today. The official term was ethnic cleansing, but it was state-sponsored mass murder. I didn't know how many they killed or how long this camp of horror was in operation, but now it made sense. If you were going to commit mass murder, you needed a very isolated place relatively close to the city. The PVC pipes were a bribe. I didn't know if the farmer was part of this or if he was one of the millions who turned a blind eye. I did know that he didn't want or need the southernmost part of his farm, and I understood his reasons. We returned to the barn and carefully plotted the site on our tourist map. We didn't have a GPS device so we made a good guess.

Jessie and Zeus completed the pipes to the northernmost part of the farm. We hooked up the system and turned it on. The smaller pumps worked and water sprayed over plowed ground. The farmer and his wife returned. They were ecstatic. By doing this job for him, we had increased his total wealth ten-fold, at least until his well ran dry. To him, I thought, the PVC pipe bribe was worth keeping his mouth shut. His wife cooked fried vegetables for us. Jessie's gash was healing. It was approaching twilight. We held a team meeting and I reviewed the situation.

"If the ground invasion was coming, it would have happened by now. We are isolated, and our last message didn't get through to our higher headquarters," I said. "They don't know if we are dead or alive. The longer we wait here, or anywhere in this country, our risk increases. Our asset is long gone and we have destroyed the Chinese Embassy. We need to get out and head east." My mind continued to spin over the idea that we were sent to fail.

"We will mentally record everything to date and everything to come," I continued. "We can't write statements for fear of compromise, but we will remember everything."

We walked with the farmer out to his horses. They were workhorses, not pleasure horses. They were huge animals. They were mostly Belgians, with each being well over seventeen hands tall. Zeus asked the farmer if he was willing to sell them to us for our future travels. He agreed and took it from our wages. We told him we were traveling to a job in northeast Serbia, near Vrsac, and we had to get there by midweek. We also told him we were confident we could sell the horses for a profit when we got to our next job. They were strong and obedient animals, bred for pulling a large metal plow. He didn't have saddles to fit them, but he had blankets that he gave us for our trip. He had a collection of bits, bridles and ropes that we pieced together to control them. He also gave us grain bags. These horses generally won't gallop or run, but it beat walking. We were going to ride our way to the border.

We would leave tonight. We would move in darkness and rest during the day. Rabbit was our navigator. If we moved generally east and followed our tourist map, we would be close. Once we crossed the border, we would steal a car and drive to the embassy. The farmer told us we could have any of the horses we wanted. I was not a good judge of horses and wished I had paid more attention when I was a kid. We always had several work horses, but we didn't ride them. Dad said it would spoil them. The rest of the team knew less than I did about horses, which left me making the best guess. The farmer attempted to help us, but it was not in his best interest to give away his good horses. We picked four very strong horses that stood still long enough for us to mount them. This would be interesting.

Stealing a car was the fastest option, but we wouldn't steal from the farmer. We didn't know enough about him or his contacts. If he survived while all his neighbors died or fled, then he either knew something or somebody, or he was of the right ethnic tribe. Either way, it was not worth the risk. Our Spanish worker ruse worked thus far and the horses would get us farther east. We would ride through lots of open land and several mature forests. The horses should not have a problem. Many of the roads in this part of the world had dirt trails that ran beside the main roads. We attempted to use as many as we could. People had traveled these roads for centuries, so us crossing on horseback was not uncommon. The main highway was at least twenty kilometers to the north and anyone trying to get to the east in a hurry would use it instead of our roads. Our roads were commuter roads and in poor repair.

We conducted our last preexecution checks. It was 2112 local. We waved farewell to the farmer and began riding back toward the road and the store. We then turned due east. The horses were broad animals, and it hurt to ride them regardless of how many blankets we put on their backs. Rabbit took point. I was amazed at how high I was on the horse's back and how much I could see. We continued to spread out as if in a formation, but the horses wouldn't cooperate. They followed the horse in front of them, and the closer, the better. It remained overcast, but we were riding mostly in the open. I thought about old Western cowboy movies and us crossing the Great Plains. As we entered into a wooded area, Rabbit stopped. His horse continually ran into trees. I took the point. We came to our first road crossing. It was a good road with multiple lanes. The road was running north and south. I dismounted and worked my way to see both directions. Seeing nothing, I moved back to the horse and remounted. Just as I nudged the workhorse forward, we heard another airstrike. The noise made the horse nervous and he became skittish and irritable. I coaxed him across the road and back into the woods on the other side. We were making very good time, but I didn't have a pace count, so we estimated and kept moving. After midnight, we stopped at a small stream and took a short break. We were all sore. We could see the lights of a town to the north. Our best estimate was we had traveled roughly fifteen to twenty kilometers to the southeast.

We attempted to remount the horses. They were more irritable than ever. Maybe they were tired. After several attempts, I managed to get on his back. Jessie manhandled his horse and mounted. Rabbit climbed a tree and jumped on the back of his mount. Zeus kept trying, but the horse wanted no part of this exercise. Rabbit's horse began moving in circles and my horse did the same. Zeus finally mounted and we attempted to get moving again, but all the nudges to their hindquarters were in vain. They weren't moving. It was 0143 local. We had another four hours of good travel time remaining. We tried the gentle approach and fed the horses and relived the same drama of attempting to mount them. We weren't on good ground. We needed to move at least a kilometer downstream if we were going to stop for the night. After an hour of pulling, tugging, biting, and absolute frustration, we arrived on suitable ground. We were on a slight rise with good observation in all directions. The horses were in a small clearing and were grazing. I didn't feel comfortable. I sent Rabbit and Zeus on foot to conduct an area reconnaissance to determine future options. We might be able to steal a car. Maybe the horses would cooperate in the morning. They returned and told me that a north and south paved road was roughly two hundred meters to our east and they continued their reconnaissance mission.

Leadership had many components. There was the component of leading by example and never asking people to do something you were unable or unwilling to do. There was the component of having physical and intellectual skills and being able to demonstrate those skills to the people you lead. There was the component of judgment: being able to quickly discern the good, bad, and acceptable risk in any operation and deciding the best option. Another component was building trust. We earned trust over time. Good leaders built trust and said what they meant and meant what they said. All these components were important, but it was always the final component that separated the good from the great. In my world, the most important leadership component was having good ideas. Right now, I was in desperate need of a really good idea.

Rabbit and Zeus returned.

"Enemy forces. Probably platoon-sized outfit but maybe larger," Rabbit said. "We saw two large trucks and a couple of scout cars. They are probably infantry. The town itself is more like a village."

We could not engage as we didn't have the people or firepower to conduct any offensive operation. Our best option was to move south downstream and away from the enemy.

Rabbit said, "We drifted to the north." We quickly discussed options. Heading south would eventually get us in a better long-term position. Our tourist map showed three roads that traveled east and west to our southeast, but we had yet to see any of them. We all knew it was about getting to the east, but we also knew that crossing a river border was much more difficult than a land crossing. This was the agrarian part of the country and, even with the bombing, it was much safer here than heading in any other cardinal direction.

I talked to my horse before I mounted him. "I expect you to cooperate. This is a tough mission, and you need to do your part."

"Boss, the horse doesn't speak English," Jessie laughed.

We all mounted our horses except Zeus. His horse wouldn't cooperate. We boxed his horse in with the other horses and he mounted. We moved, but his horse didn't budge. I gave the order to keep moving, banking on the fact that Zeus's horse was a herd animal and wouldn't like the idea of being left alone. We moved down the stream. I was on point only because my horse had the best night vision. I strained to see if Zeus was moving. It worked. The horse was more afraid of being alone and he closed in with the others. We followed the stream for several kilometers. We were heading almost due south. It was now 0511. We needed to find good ground and wait for dawn. We were in open ground with several large hardwoods. I stopped the patrol. Jessie conducted reconnaissance to the east, and I moved to the south. We needed to get a sense on how exposed we were from the surrounding areas. I traveled roughly two kilometers to the south. I found another stream but no east/west road. It had some elevation with hardwoods and was surrounded by pasture lands. It had good observation in all directions, but it was dark, so I couldn't see the whole picture. I thought this was better ground than our last spot. I rode back for the others and brought them forward. Twilight broke, and we established for the day. It was overcast, and looked like rain. We pushed the horses to graze and began our sleep and guard cycle.

As daylight came, we were in a good position; however, there was a north/south road to our east. It was roughly three hundred meters away, and we had good observation of it from our position. The horses meandered around, grazed, and drank from the small stream. Jessie and Rabbit slept first, while Zeus and I kept watch. We switched over before noon. I stank and I was working on a good beard. We probably looked more like goat herders than Spanish workers. I was down for three hours when it began raining. It started as a drizzle and then it poured. We were under the hardwoods and horse blankets, but all of us got a good soaking. It was 1435 local. Moving in daylight was a risk, but it beat sitting in the rain. We hadn't seen anyone or anything all day. We moved out in daylight going southeast. We were very close to the east/west road, which ran parallel to the border. The horses were cooperative and we moved quickly. In daylight, Rabbit took the point and we slowed the main body as best we could to give him maneuver room.

We made good time. The horses traveled much faster in daylight. It was a steady drizzle, and it was getting foggy. We stopped along the stream to let the horse's water. We dismounted. It was not yet dark and Rabbit was confident we were close to the road. I sent him forward in reconnaissance. I also sent Zeus to the east.

"I think we traveled too far south, and I can't find any terrain features." Jessie said. I saw them first and Jessie and I both hit the ground. We had bigger problems than being lost.

AMBUSH

A CAR MOVED along the road to our east. It was moving from north to south. Our horses were in the open and could be seen. They had blankets all over their backs and would draw attention.

"Jessie," I said, "get in the woods." I heard engine noises. A truck followed the car. They looked at the horses. They were Serbian Army. It was a four-wheel drive command or scout vehicle. The truck was full of Soldiers. They moved at a good rate of speed, and while they spotted the horses, they didn't slow down. A third command car followed. It slowed down and stopped. The driver attempted to find a decent path over to me. I waved a friendly wave, hoping to discourage them from coming over, but it didn't deter them. I had my pistol in the small of my back and, if it failed me, I was a dead man. I concentrated on the truck full of Soldiers, but it continued down the road and out of sight. If they saw Rabbit, their natural curiosity would compel them to explore. I was not confident the Soldiers in the truck ever saw the final command car slow and detour off the road.

Jessie was hidden in the trees to my right. I moved to the left toward the horses. It was a European style Range Rover command car with the steering wheel and driver on the right. It was a hard top vehicle so we had to make our first shots count. If I didn't engage the curious passenger, then I would mask Jessie's potential shot should we get in trouble. I couldn't speak the language, so I predicted trouble. All were wearing combat helmets and the windows were rolled down. An officer of some rank sat in the front passenger seat. He had two guards with Kalashnikov rifles in the back seat. One of them was a NCO of some sort. I could see his chevrons. They were a disciplined outfit. This was a first-round kill situation. We wouldn't get second shots. I continued to move to the left toward the horses, hoping to ensure we could get more than one of us shooting.

There were only three rules in tactical combat. Throughout history, winners followed the rules, and losers died. The first rule was to see the enemy before he saw you. In large scale warfare, we used everything from satellites to ground cavalry scouts to accomplish this purpose. If you could see the enemy first, you could shape the coming action. If you didn't, you became shaped by the enemy. We were on good ground and saw the enemy first. They hadn't seen Jessie. The second rule was to make contact with the least amount of combat power possible. The winner always retained options, and the best way to retain options was to make contact with the enemy with minimal combat power. In this case, it was me. Finally, all tactical battles and engagements were won or lost by fire distribution and control. Know the target you were going after, hit and kill it, and don't waste ammunition.

I moved farther left in order to give Jessie a clean view of the targets. I could not mask his fire. I grabbed the reins of one of the horses. It was raining harder. They pulled the vehicle to within ten meters and yelled at me. I could make the shot, but closer would raise both my probability of hit and first-round kill. The man in the back passenger seat aimed the Kalashnikov directly at me. I held the horse reins and began pulling the horse forward and then let go and slightly lowered my head to show deference to a higher authority. My eyes were fixed on the man in the back aiming his rifle at me. He was the immediate threat. I walked slowly toward the vehicle. I clearly saw the muzzle. I talked in sign language as if I was deaf. I heard them say something and the senior officer looked me dead in the eye. I heard a bolt go forward from the Kalashnikov rifleman sitting behind the driver. I heard the shot. The Sergeant in the back looked in horror at the man sitting next to him. Jessie fired again and hit the driver. The officer yelled and held his hand out as if it would stop a bullet. I fired two rounds in the man and quickly transitioned to the other passenger. The forty-caliber flat-nosed bullets penetrated, and they showed no movement. Jessie sprinted forward. I pulled the senior officer from the vehicle. I could not leave him in the open. Anything coming back up the road would see the tire tracks going into the pasture. He helped lift the dead senior officer and we threw him on the back of the horse. We grabbed the driver. He was much heavier and it was a chore to lift him. We used ropes and tied him onto the horse's back. It was messy because there was always blood. I hated killing. Why did they come over here? Jessie jumped into the vehicle and began driving it off into the woods. I grabbed the horses and ran behind him. I saw Zeus coming from the east. His horse was at a slow gallop, which was about as fast as a workhorse ran. I motioned him to join Jessie. The horses seemed to understand the danger and were cooperative.

Jessie drove deep into the woods. He and Zeus unloaded the dead men from the back of the vehicle onto the horse's back. I pulled the blankets from Jessie's horse and cleaned up the blood in the seats. It was dark and raining harder. I was concerned about Rabbit. We tied the horses together with a rope. Jessie drove and I was on the passenger side. Zeus held the horses and we slowly moved deeper into the woods. We moved roughly two kilometers. The rain was steady. The fog was quickly engulfing us. We had driven as deep into the woods as possible. The trees were thick and we couldn't go farther. The tire tracks were deep in the soft ground. Stevie Wonder could track us to this spot. We were in bad ground. We turned around and headed back out of the woods to a small clearing. We made a circle, and if someone was following us, they would follow the original tracks. The clearing would give us some observation and fields of fire. The cleared area was roughly fifty meters long and maybe thirty meters wide. Jessie and Zeus carried the dead men's Kalashnikovs. I grabbed the driver's short stock Kalashnikov. The Soldiers we killed were carrying full loads of ammunition with multiple magazines. Jessie moved to a slight rise on the left, and Zeus, into the woods on the right. I was in the center using the truck engine as cover. We pushed the horses deeper into the woods, but they were content to carry the dead bodies and graze. The rain continued.

I moved forward into the clearing. I carried an eight-foot long limb from one of the trees. I got as far forward as possible and placed the limb on the ground. This designated the spot where we wanted to kill the main body. Jessie began to adjust immediately. I moved back to Zeus. He was new and didn't understand the significance of the tree limb.

"The tree limb is a target reference point, and all of us must be able to place effective fire into that general area. If they dismount, we will be forced to fight twenty or so individual Soldiers, so priority is the truck," I said. "This is as far as they can get a truck into the woods. They will eventually see the Range Rover and stop. I will initiate. Kill quickly."

The problem with all dismounted ambushes was protecting the flanks of the ambush. If the enemy was smart, they would dismount early and enter into the area moving in a series of squads. If they did that, we were in trouble. It was raining, and they were following tracks. Like most Soldiers, I suspected they were tired and hopefully ill-disciplined enough to stay mounted.

I moved back to the Range Rover. Jessie whistled. Rabbit ran toward me.

"My horse is night blind and useless," Rabbit said. "I left him about three clicks back. I found the road to the south. It's an intersection between the north/south road and the east/west road. It's got Soldiers all around it, but they mounted up and started this way. They probably left a squad at the intersection. They are moving with four Soldiers in the Range Rover and two squads of roughly eight men each in the truck plus a driver and assistant. They are following the tire tracks with white lights, we will be able to see them coming. I maintained contact as long as I could, but they are close." He took a deep breath. "Range Rover first, and then the truck."

I pointed to the limb in the clearing and said, "Target Reference Point." He nodded and glanced at his pistol. I nodded. He moved off to the left to find a good spot.

We heard the whine of the truck engine, and soon, we saw the white light of the lead Range Rover. Someone was in front walking and guiding the vehicle, and they were dead on the tracks. He was using a large flashlight and walked right past the tree limb. He was yelling back toward the truck. He realized he could not get the truck any farther into the woods. The truck began making a large slow turn. As he made the turn, his headlights shone right at our captured Range Rover. The flashlight man yelled something and walked toward me. His Range Rover was following. They were getting closer. His rifle was across his chest with a sling, and as he walked closer, he reached for his rifle. All of the windows on our captured Range Rover were down, and I was crouched behind the right rear wheel and observed him through the open windows. I pulled my pistol as this would be much closer than I anticipated. He noticed the open windows, and I could see curiosity come over his face.

As he peered forward and looked into the vehicle, I fired. I hit him right between the eyes, and blood splattered everywhere.

Jessie began firing, Zeus began firing, and I heard Rabbit's pistol. I grabbed the short stock Kalashnikov, began firing, and rushed toward the enemy Range Rover. They were confused. I rushed forward and killed the driver and two guys in the back. I heard yelling and screaming from the truck and could see tracers flying toward the vehicle from both the left and right. Jessie appeared to have the best effect into the back of the truck from his position. No return fire. I emptied my magazine on the truck. Someone was attempting to get out of the passenger side of the truck. I pulled my pistol and fired. I changed magazines and saw Rabbit running toward the truck. He found a Kalashnikov. Jessie and Zeus moved forward to secure the area.

"Kill their radios!" Jessie screamed. I checked the fuel gauges for both Range Rovers. They were about equal. I pulled bodies out of the enemy Range Rover. Zeus helped me. Blood was everywhere. The Kalashnikov fired a heavy bullet and it damaged at close range. Jessie and Rabbit ran to me.

I took a long breath and said, "Take both vehicles. Rabbit and Jessie, in the lead, and Zeus and I will follow. Clear the area, stop prior to the intersection so we can figure out how we deal with the squad at the intersection, and follow the same tracks on the way out."

It was raining harder as we left the area. As we drove past the truck, blood and water were pouring out the back. We made a clean exit from the engagement area. The trail was difficult to see and the Range Rovers were sliding all over the trails. We attempted to go without white headlights, but that was impossible. We turned on the headlights and eventually made it back to the original small road where we first encountered the enemy. It was 2149 local. It continued to rain hard.

We parked on the road, and Zeus and I joined the others in the back of their blood-soaked Range Rover. I shook the rain off my head.

"My guess is they have standard four-point security. They will have two guards facing outward along all four points of the intersection. They probably have one machine gun, but best guess, it's pointed either east or west but not along our entry road." I took a deep breath. "The most important thing is to begin our engagement from inside the perimeter. We need to kill quickly. Use the Range Rovers to drive directly to the guards and begin the engagement, and then keep driving. The rain coupled with them thinking we are their leaders should allow us to get close. If we fail to penetrate the perimeter, we risk facing the machine gun. Even if it is a light machine gun, we all die. Again, kill quickly, drive, and find targets. Jessie and Rabbit, circle to the right, and Zeus and I circle to the left. Break inside the perimeter and shoot out. Once we're done, hustle to drag the bodies into the woods. Kill them all, we cannot have anyone chasing us to the Danube. One vehicle follows the other. Everybody got it?"

They all nodded in unison.

I always asked, and they expected me to ask, so I said, "Questions, comments, opposing viewpoints?" All shook their heads.

"Check your weapons and don't miss," Jessie said. "We're in it, baby."

We ran back to our Range Rover. The heavy rain continued. The fog was thick in places. The rain and fog gave us an advantage. We moved down the road. Jessie was driving the lead vehicle. He hit his brakes signaling he made visual contact. He stopped. I saw three armed Soldiers approach on both sides of the vehicle. All were wearing helmets and ponchos. Two were on the passenger side. Because the steering wheel was on the right side of the vehicle, I engaged with my pistol and hit the farthermost target. Rabbit hit his target, and Jessie engaged, and his target dropped. Immediately, their vehicle pulled to the right, and we broke left. We ran over the bodies and felt the vehicle bump up and down. Zeus accelerated. We hit them quickly, and the rain somewhat muffled the sound. They were confused. Zeus drove the Range Rover between the two groups of guards. Zeus fired before I did. I engaged. We were roughly ten meters away, and I engaged the Soldier on the left side of the road. I hit him, and he fell. I continued firing. It was not a clean kill. Zeus continued to fire and drove the vehicle, but I didn't understand why he was still firing. We should have been turning right inside the perimeter at this point to kill the final group. We were taking fire from Zeus's side of the vehicle. I felt a sharp pain on the underside of my right leg. I was hit. We continued forward and I saw two more Soldiers off to my left. The one on the right was struggling to get his weapon out from under his poncho, but the one on the left was up and ready to fire. His bullet hit the top of the windshield. The glass didn't shatter, but I saw the holes. The shooter on the left was my primary target. We were less than five meters apart. This was close. He was aiming lower. I fired. I hit his rifle. My bullet tore through the front stock just underneath the barrel. He was stunned, flinched, but raises his rifle to fire again. He was aiming right at me. The whole scene was in slow motion. I squeezed the trigger on my pistol. My bolt was locked to the rear. I was out of ammunition. I glanced to see the other Soldier raise his weapon. This was not good. I saw a flash from my far left and both enemy Soldiers turned just in time to be run over by Jessie's Range Rover.

Jessie and Rabbit jumped from the vehicle, shooting those they just ran over. Zeus turned the vehicle to the right and Jessie stopped us. The enemy only had two points: one where we entered their perimeter and the other facing east. Better yet, they didn't have a light machine gun. We guessed wrong on the enemy disposition, but we penetrated the perimeter and came in behind the majority of the squad.

"Eight dead. Three as we entered the intersection, and five where we are now," Rabbit said.

We got out and dragged the bodies into the woods. The road was full of blood. It was pouring rain and the water was washing it away. Both Range Rovers were full of bullet holes. Zeus caught a ricocheted bullet that grazed the back of his left arm.

I had a gash on the underside of my right thigh. It ripped my jeans, bloody, but only superficial. Rabbit threw us bandages. It was 2239 local.

We examined the Range Rovers. Both had first-aid kits as well as canned rations. Ours had taken the most damage, but both were drivable. I looked around and motioned for us to huddle.

"We take both vehicles," I said. I stared at the blood in the road and watched the water wash it away. I shook my head hard.

"Okay," I said. "Right now, we have a time advantage, and we must move to turn that into a time and distance advantage. If we are lucky, the enemy may think they have rouges in their formation. Most of our killing was with Kalashnikovs, and it will take some smart folks to figure out the differences between those killed with a forty-caliber pistol and a Kalashnikov. We need to ditch the other Range Rover down the road, but we have to get out of here first. Conduct one last sweep of the area and go."

My right hand trembled. I began rubbing it hard. Rabbit checked to the right, and Zeus to the left. Jessie pulled me close to his face.

"You okay," he asked, grabbing my hand.

I jerked it away and said, "We need to get moving"

BORDER CROSSING

We had options. We were on the road east toward the National Forrest area. It was good ground, and we could hide. We looked rough, and we needed to stop and think our way ahead. We could cross in the vicinity of the famous Iron Gates Dams, or we could move farther south and steal a boat. Both Romania and Bulgaria were on the highest of border alerts to avoid large numbers of refugees crossing their border. It would be easier to cross farther south as the ground was more supportive, but would increase our risk.

Steam was coming from our engine. At first, it was hard to distinguish from the waves of fog, but we knew the smell. They had hit our radiator, and the engine was overheating. Zeus flashed his lights, and Jessie and Rabbit turned off into a small side road in a densely wooded area. The ground was much hillier with lots of tall beautiful trees. They towered over us and mitigated the rain. We drove deeper into the woods and ditched the Range Rover in a thicket. We took the first-aid kit and the rations and turned the vehicle on its side and worked to cover it with some camouflage. It would be a while before they found it. I felt the pain from my flesh wound every time I moved, but I knew Zeus was in worse shape.

It was 0012 local, and we were now all in one vehicle and back on the main road. We avoided the major river towns, and suddenly, we were on the side of the Danube. It was a gorge, and it was deep. The rain and fog made it harder to see. It was going to be a challenge. We needed to plan our way across the river. Our tourist map was not helpful in terms of reconnaissance. We saw more and more road signs. We were getting close to a riverside town. It was dangerous driving in a gray military-style Range Rover with bullet holes. We turned around and worked our way back in the direction we came. Thus far, we haven't seen any traffic, but that could change. We drove roughly ten kilometers back and found a small trail. We got out and ground-guided the vehicle as deep into the woods as we could. Zeus and Rabbit went back to the road and camouflaged our entrance. We were on a hillside, and it was thick with vegetation. It was not good ground. We had little observation and no real escape route, but we were exhausted. We were going to get as safe as we could and then rest.

I took first watch. The rain let up, but the fog was heavy. We had three options. The first was to scale down the cliff, swim the river, and climb the opposite cliff into Romania. While it seemed simple, it was the most complex in execution. We didn't have any ropes; we didn't know the angles of the cliffs or the water temperature. Moreover, it would be difficult to conduct reconnaissance of anything but the far cliff, and that presented a risk. Our second option was to wait another night and then drive the Range Rover past the town in an attempt to find a better crossing site to the south and either steal or bribe our way across the river. Finally, we could simply ditch the vehicle here and begin walking the ridge line in a very long movement to contact and see what opportunities developed. It was 0330 local, and I was convinced I heard voices. I could be dreaming while standing up. I woke Jessie as he had the next watch.

I whispered to him, "I think I heard voices toward the top of the hill."

He looked and said, "Get some sleep." I crawled into the backseat.

I felt the sunshine in my eyes. It was 1043 local. The fog was lifting. We were, at most, two hundred meters into the woods. I still had pain, but it's not as bad as it was last night. We could see a small portion of the road. As I looked around, I was amazed we got the vehicle this deep. We had a good view of the side of the mountain and better observation than I thought. It was spring, and the ground was not overgrown. Jessie was awake and had sent Rabbit on an area reconnaissance over the mountain. Zeus and I changed our bandages. Jessie and I discussed options.

Jessie shook his head and said, "I don't like the idea of swimming and then climbing the far cliffs, but I can strip the Range Rover to get us some flotation devices. Water will be super cold. It's a risk. Maybe we try a homemade raft."

Rabbit returned and said, "I saw the town. No visible boats. Small town but I didn't see any military. It has a couple of houses and stores. I don't think it helps. I saw multiple trails, but I don't know their purpose."

The vehicle got us here, but now it's a distracter. Jessie said, "The Rover is no good, We need to strip it, and we may need stuff later."

I nodded and we began stripping it. We pulled off multiple cables and belts and began putting them into our backpacks. Jessie attempted to jack up the vehicle and harvest the rubber from the tires, but the vehicle was on too steep an angle. We turned the vehicle over to strip the tires and to mask its outline and then applied camouflage. We ate a decent meal of Serbian Army rations, and I briefed our plan.

I began. "We can't swim the river. It's not worth the risk. The current is too swift, the water is too cold, and we don't have the climbing gear we need. We will move south on foot until we find something. We take the Kalashnikovs, the first-aid kits, and the canned food. We parallel the river. When we get away from the gorge portion of the river and farther south, we will see more and more patrols. It's not in Romania's best interest to allow a mass exodus of Serbs fleeing into their country. They will be alert and dangerous. As we move farther south, we will steal a boat or flotation device. If we have enemy contact on this side of the river, we fight. However, once we cross the Danube on the Romanian side, then we surrender and insist they take us to the US Embassy. As usual, we will move at night and rest during the day. Do we have any questions, comments, opposing viewpoints, or better ideas?" I looked at them; they looked tired and worn but didn't say a word. I continued, "You know the drill, and check your weapons."

We began moving. We took up the extended diamond with Rabbit on point, Zeus on the left, Jessie on the right, and I was in the rear. The ground was hilly, and it was a beautiful forest. We had good observation and decent light. We moved up the mountain and past the town. We crossed several well-worn trails. The town was probably a tourist town, and these were the associated hiking trails. We avoided them as best we could and continued south making decent progress.

Rabbit stopped. I moved forward to his position. Although we were deep in the forest, there were several garden plots to our front that had been hacked out of the wilderness.

I whispered to Rabbit, "During communism, this is where they kept their gardens."

Rabbit was not interested in a history lesson, and he pointed to my front.

I said, "Is it a trip flare?"

He nodded and moved back to brief the others.

Why would a trip flare be in the middle of the forest? Rabbit returned and I sent him to the flanks looking for other devices. We continued to observe a series of small garden plots carved out of the wilderness. Rabbit returned. Each of the major trails as well as most of the open ground leading into this area were rigged with trip flares. We needed to be cautious.

Rabbit moved us to the left to avoid the trip flares. We heard and then saw movement. They were carrying flashlights. We scrambled for cover and quietly moved to gain observation over the series of small garden plots. We saw them coming. It was roughly fifteen to twenty people moving along three different trails. They were not concerned about noise. We heard them talking. They were followed by a couple of strong young men pushing several wheelbarrows. They immediately broke into groups with about four or five moving to each square and began hoeing, fertilizing, and planting. There were several older and a few young women in each group. They were working by flashlights. If we moved, we would be seen, but all of us found good hiding spots. They were planting now, expecting a harvest in late summer. I saw Rabbit and Zeus to my left, and I think Jessie is on my right. We are generally on line, and we can fight from here.

An older man meandered toward us. He was smoking. He was less than a body's length away from me. He flipped his cigarette butt in my direction then looked down, unzips, and pees. Once complete, he went back into the field. I slowly check my watch; it was 1243 local. Finally, they all moved to the far side of the field and take a break. We started our movement, crawling backward into the woods and then moving laterally around the fields. We slowly moved undetected away from the midnight farmers.

We continued to move southeast and, at times, saw the road. On at least one occasion, we saw the river itself. The far side cliffs were impressive. I was confident we made the right choice in moving on foot to the southeast looking for different opportunities. It was hilly ground with multiple hidden coves. We stopped in one gully and refilled our water bottles. Rabbit was on point, and we crossed over another series of heavily wooded hills. It was 0337 local. We were moving too far away from the river. We were paralleling the road, and it was moving away from the river to the southwest. We conducted a short halt and huddled. We needed to cross the road and work our way south along the banks of the river. We continued to move, and Rabbit has us overlooking the road. He found a good area to cross between the curves. We moved from our perch one at a time, and the bank was much steeper than it appeared. I hit a slick spot on the bank and slid down. I felt a sharp pain in my thigh. I ripped the bandage free, but I hobbled across and climbed the opposite bank. This side of the road had more gullies, and we moved up and downhill for a couple of kilometers. We needed to begin thinking of a place to stop for the day, and I needed a new bandage on my thigh before it rubbed raw. We crested another hill.

Rabbit stopped. He had contact. I crawled forward. We saw light reflecting from the trees and heard a small motor running. Whoever it was and whatever they were doing, they wanted privacy. They had a generator of some sort. Rabbit crawled to the top of the hill. We were attempting to get above them where we could look down into the gully. It was very steep and slow going. He moved above them and I followed and crawled next to him. They established themselves in a gully with high ground on all three sides to muffle the noise. I could see the river through the trees. Rabbit stared at me.

I whispered to him, "They are moonshiners." We were in the middle of the Serbian National Forest, and the place was crowded.

We saw two of them and possibly a third on the side of the bank sleeping, but he was just out of our sight. The generator was running a small light as well as a small motor, which cooked the brew. One looked older, was giving the orders, and was clearly in charge. The copper tubing was in a long coil running from the boiler to the spout. They built sawhorses to hold it. They were pumping fresh water from the river. They were draining the brew into a series of large jugs. You can't make it if you can't get it to market, so they had to have some transportation system to move their product. Jessie and Zeus crawled to us.

I whispered, "Eventually they will move the product. Rabbit conduct the recon."

Rabbit nodded and worked his way back down the hill. We continued to observe. It was 0547 local, and the fog was beginning to engulf us. They began moving the large jugs down a trail toward the river.

Rabbit returned and grabbed our feet. We turned downhill to face him. He says, "I didn't see a boat. They are moving jugs to the river. They must have one coming. We need to move now."

I nodded and said, "Zeus and Jessie, move left, and I will follow Rabbit to our right. When the boat arrives, we take it and move across the river. Remember, they are smugglers so they know the routes. In this fog, we will need a pilot, or we wait until it burns off. Go, be quick."

The moonshiners were covering their equipment with an army-style camouflage net. They placed the boiler into a hole in the bank and covered it with a brown tarp. They killed their generator, and it was dark and quiet. Rabbit and I moved closer to the shore behind a large muddy bank. The older man continued to bark orders. The others continued to move jugs to the river. We were close enough to smell their cigarette smoke. We saw daybreak approaching in the trees above, but we were engulfed in the fog.

We heard commotion and the smugglers readied themselves. The boat was bigger than I anticipated. It was a large green boat powered by some type of trolling motor. The pilot easily placed the nose directly into the small covered inlet. A rope flew toward the shore, and the older man grabbed it and pulled it around the backside of a tree. An older, ancient-looking bearded man is on the boat. They began loading.

We moved forward. Zeus and I had the short stock Kalashnikovs. They were shocked we were behind them but they were submissive. The younger men raised their hands. Rabbit pointed his weapon directly at the ancient-looking boat pilot to ensure he didn't move. Zeus spoke to them and pointed toward the far shore. The older man was defiant and snorted in disgust. He spoke in a loud and uncompromising voice. Zeus didn't answer back, and the older man raised his voice as if asking a question. He turned and dismissed us with a wave of his hand and reached down to begin loading the boat. Jessie grunted and pointed his pistol directly at one of the jugs. Again, the older man shook his head, waved his hand, and began loading the boat.

Jessie fired. The sound from the bullet piercing the jug shocked them. They froze. I threw the Kalashnikov over my back, ran forward and tackled the man. Jessie ran to me. We tied his hands together with a fan belt we stripped from the Range Rover. Zeus moved the boys back toward the bank. The older bearded man stepped forward and began to speak. We had another language barrier. We didn't understand. He turned and spit, as if disgusted and then began speaking in French. Rabbit answered.

We kept our weapons ready as Rabbit and the man talked.

Rabbit said, "The man on the ground is his son. The boys are his grandsons. He will give us a safe ride to the Romanian side of the river but wants us to take his brew and his family. Same story, they are a poor family. It's not safe here during the day, and he only moves his boat during the morning fog."

We had heard sad stories like this before. He spoke to his son in Serbian, and they spoke around us. We couldn't understand. In a show of faith, I untied the man on the ground. He stood, saluted, and shook my hand.

The ancient one began talking, and Rabbit translated, saying, "The old guy fought the Germans and later the Russians. His son served in the Army."

I nodded. We boarded the boat.

The boat was long with a semiflat bottom. The ancient man, and Rabbit went to the rear. I sat with my back to Rabbit facing forward. They loaded the jugs in front of me. Jessie and the older man sat side by side in the middle, facing me with the jugs.

The boys and Zeus sat in the front facing forward. I don't know what the whiskey weighed, but we are very low in the water. It was 0612 local. The boys pushed the boat back, and the ancient man cranked the trolling motor. You could barely hear it. Within seconds, we were engulfed in the fog. The bank disappeared. A minute passes, and I could no longer see Jessie or the older man sitting less than two feet in front of me.

Rabbit talked softly to the ancient man. I placed my hand in the water. It was freezing. I was a good swimmer, but I could not swim this river. The river wasn't a hundred meters wide, but I had no clue which direction we were traveling. I know we were moving, but I could not tell which way. I saw the outline of something to my left. It was a mud bank. We crossed the river and were moving along the far shore. He turned the boat sharply to the left, and we entered into a small tributary. I was amazed, but cautious. The man had skill to navigate in this fog. The boys jumped to the shore and pulled the boat. We remain seated until Zeus was out and could cover us. The older man and Jessie shook hands. I hoped we were on the safe side of the river. We moved into the woods and formed a small perimeter. We watched the smugglers push the boat back into the water and disappear into the fog.

Rabbit talked all during the crossing to the ancient man. He said, "I believe him. There is a small junkyard roughly a kilometer to our southeast. The man who owns it always has something to drive."

STATE OFFICIALS

I said, "Remember, we are no longer in a fighting stance." I handed Zeus my Kalashnikov, and he took both mine and his, separated the magazine from the weapon, and tossed them into the river. I hoped we were in Romania. I pulled the money out of my backpack. Our mission would be to buy transport to Bucharest. Rabbit moved out. Less than fifty meters later, we were walking on a trail.

The trail turned into an unimproved road. The fog was less dense on the ground. It was 0709 local when we spotted the junkyard. It was larger than I expected with all makes and models of car bodies. We moved toward a small building. Nobody was around. We ate and waited. After an hour, we went into our standard sleep and watch cycle, and I took the first shift. The fog burned off. It was a beautiful morning. I saw the outline of the high ground to our west. The land on this side was less hilly and looked more like a flood plain with multiple dunes.

I saw an older model Mercedes box truck coming over the small hill. The man pulled directly in front of the building. Zeus stepped forward to speak, and he walked past him and directly to me.

He spoke English and said, "Sorry I am late. I have arranged transport for you to Bucharest."

I was shocked. He walked past me, opened his small shop, and began moving around inside the building. I was stunned. I turned to Jessie and said, "What just happened?"

He shook his head and said, "How did he know we spoke English?"

Before we could move into the building, a small red car came barreling down the road. A younger man was driving. He spun the car around and handed me the keys. In English, he said, "Drive seven kilometers east, then turn on a two-lane road due south. From there, about seven kilometers to the main east highway."

I nodded. The original man returned with four cups of coffee. I asked, "How did you know we would come here?"

He smiled and pointed toward Jessie. He says, "Please don't shoot the whisky jugs. They are expensive to replace."

I handed him a wad of money. He gladly accepted and said, "Leave the vehicle on Tudor Street with the keys under the driver's seat."

I shook his hand and moved to the passenger side. We loaded up and began driving.

As we pulled onto the highway, I fell asleep. I woke as we entered Bucharest. We spent forty minutes lost and wandering the streets of an ancient city. We finally found Tudor Street. We placed the keys under the seat and walked away. It was 1145 local, and the embassy workers were exiting the building going to lunch. We walked into the building and looked for the Chief of Mission. I anticipated seeing a security desk, but we couldn't find one. We scanned the boards looking for room numbers. We found the room number for security, walked up the stairs, and entered. An older man was sitting behind a cluttered desk and listening to the radio. I gathered our military identification cards and handed them to him.

He looked at us in amazement, jumped up and began closing doors behind us and making phone calls. Per our protocol, I said, "I need access to a secure telephone and dozens of sworn statement forms."

He ushered us into a small conference room and showed me his security badge. I told the team we are not going anywhere for a while, and Jessie and Rabbit knew the deal.

I gave specific orders to the team. "Mark the top of the page Top Secret/Sensitive Compartmentalized Information and begin writing down in chronological order everything that has occurred to this team since receipt of the mission."

The security manager took me to the communications room, and I asked for privacy. I dialed the number from memory.

After a series of switches and access codes, I was talking to our Operations enter. They transferred the call to the commander's home. Within seconds, I was talking to my Commander.

I said, "Sir, it's JB, and I have my team at the embassy in Bucharest, Romania. We are tired and bruised but okay. We completed the mission, but the asset ditched us, and we had to escape and evade our way out. It's been a tough couple of days."

He said, "Thank God you are safe. I need you to stop worrying me! Listen carefully. Do not follow normal end of mission protocols. Do not take statements, and do not discuss anything relating to the mission with anyone at the embassy." He was more blunt and direct than usual. He continued, "This mission is high profile. It involves lots of politicos, and you did exactly what you were told. We have been fighting it out with the Agency for the past week over this mission. So keep quiet and I will arrange transport and get you home." There was a short pause, and then he said, "JB, it's good to hear your voice."

The line went dead.

I asked the security officer for as many English newspapers as he could gather. I said, "Keep writing, but our orders are to keep silent when it comes to the embassy. The boss didn't say anything other than keep quiet."

The security officer returned with a stack of newspapers and handed them to Jessie. Jessie closed the door and said, "You need to see this. The Chinese Embassy was destroyed. Three people were killed. The US denied involvement. The US accepts responsibility for the bombing, the US calls the strike a mistake, and finally, the US says that the strike was made at the wrong coordinates."

I pulled out my sworn statement form and began writing.

The security officer knocked on the door and announced the Ambassador. We all stood. He was a tall gray-haired man with glasses. I stood at the position of attention and was completely motionless.

He was very direct and asked, "Who is in charge?"

I nodded.

He stood directly in front of me and said, "I want to know your involvement with the Chinese Embassy." He moved closer and repeated his question. I stared past him. He was visibly agitated and said, "Well then, I guess I will need to call the president."

I said nothing.

He looked first at the team and then back to me and said, "We have an international crisis on our hands. Embassies are sovereign soil. Do any of you know the implications?" The team remained silent, and he continued, "This could result in another war." He shook his head in frustration and said to me, "Come to my office. We have some things to discuss."

I followed him. We moved up the back stairway and entered into a huge office. It was the most luxurious room I had ever seen.

He said, "You look like you could use a stiff drink."

I nodded and said, "I would love a Pepsi."

He grunted and poured himself a drink. He motioned for me to sit down, and I sank into a chair. I stank and am probably an awful sight with a scraggly beard and shaggy hair. He began with an intellectual treatise on how we need the Chinese in our war against the Serbs. All I could think about was the pain in my thigh. The phone rang, and he initially ignored it and then jumped out of his seat to answer it. All I heard was "Yes, Madam Secretary" and "No, Madam Secretary."

He hung up the phone, pointed at me and asked, "Do you know who that was?"

I answered, "It was Madam Secretary."

He stared at me in disgust and began a lecture on how diplomacy is the art of the cultured and the military is the art of the ignorant.

The same phone rang again. He jumped up and answered. He stood silently and said, "Yes, Mr. President, and I fully understand, Mr. President." He hung up the phone and asked, "What are your current orders?"

I said, "Not to talk to anybody about anything."

He said, "You can leave, and my staff will provide whatever assistance you require."

I returned downstairs. The team was writing. I asked the security officer for baths and any clean civilian clothes. We bathed and got haircuts. I felt like a new man. We ate a great meal. I wrote down the details. I took the remainder of the team's summaries, read and reviewed them, and placed them in my backpack. Later that night, I made copies of the documents and placed the original in a small box and with a Clay County, North Carolina, address. I placed the documents into the mail box and went to sleep. We were up early the next morning and, around noon, were driven to a local airport.

We arrived at Fort Bragg some fourteen hours later. I went directly into the Commander's office. He was waiting. He said, "JB, I have good and bad news. The good news is you are promoted and going to school. The bad news is you are out of here, and we will miss you."

He handed me a coin and bid me farewell. I walked to my locker and ripped my letter to Lorraine into small pieces. My guys and many others were waiting. Word traveled fast. We shook hands and this mission was over.

I drove home. The kids were at school. I opened the door, and Lorraine was in the kitchen. We hugged. She smiled and said, "How was your trip?"

DOWN ON SWEETWATER

Sweetwater is seven miles south of Hayesville, North Carolina. We farmed nine acres of bottom land between the house and the Hiawassee River. Behind the house, we had a barn and twenty acres of mountain. My dad worked for the county as an electrician, and my mom was a teacher's assistant. Members of my family lived in this cove since the Cherokee were sent west. Our roots were deep.

Clay County is rural. It sits deep in the southern Appalachian Mountains. When describing its location, you start by saying roughly ninety miles west of Asheville and let the hillbilly jokes begin.

Most folks worked a normal job and tended a large garden as a supplement. We had three or four beef cattle, a hog every other year, and an acre garden beside the house. We grew corn and soybeans in the big field because they were easiest to sell.

My dad was drafted right after high school. He was on leave one summer and spotted a pretty young girl at her mailbox. Every afternoon for the rest of the week, he drove by at the same time. Finally, on Friday afternoon, the girl stepped in front of his truck and stopped him. She walked to his window and said, "Mr. JD Smith, how long are you going to drive by here without stopping and talking to me?"

My mother was a very straightforward lady.

A bunch of wealthy men parked on our road to go fishing on the Hiawassee River. They drove nice cars, had the most expensive fishing rods my dad had ever seen, and smoked cigars. They fished all day and didn't catch a thing. When they returned to their cars, one of the men gave me a five-dollar bill. He thought I was poor. If you looked at our life through his eyes, you might see the same thing. Looking back, I was raised in paradise.

One summer, when I was about eight years old, the Green Berets held a major training exercise in Clay County. They set up a base camp near the river. We went down to greet them and Mom brought them fresh-baked biscuits. They treated us well, and each day, when school was out, my little sister Lynn, and I took biscuits to them. My sister claims they are the reason I joined the Army.

My parents' goal for us was college. We were pushed. No one from our family ever attended anything other than the local community college. My sister and I were reminded daily. We were going to attend a real college. They didn't care what we studied or our career goals, only that we went to college. Our life centered on the three routine events of school, church, and our small farm.

From my earliest memories, there was always Mr. Andrew Samuels. He and his wife lived on the farm next to us. To say he was famous doesn't give him his just due. When describing where we lived to someone local, we said we lived behind Mr. Samuels's. He knew more about my family than I did. He was a farmer who sold seed, ran a small mill, and bartered for what he needed. He was also a man of great faith. He wore an old brown hat, suspenders to hold up his pants, and always tucked his pants legs into his boots.

Mrs. Lillie Samuels was a sweet woman, and she and my mother were close friends. She was a school teacher and taught almost everyone in the community to read and write. Sometimes, the best teachers don't need college degrees. One morning, when I was seven years old, Mom couldn't get her on the phone and sent me over to their house to see about her. I found her lying in the chicken coop, and her body was cold. I shook her as hard as I could, but she wouldn't move. I ran back to our house yelling for Dad. He was near the river on his tractor. He saw me and knew something was wrong.

"Mrs. Lillie is in her chicken coop, and she's cold and won't move."

He nodded and said, "Tell your momma and call an ambulance." I ran to the house and told Mom. She called the ambulance and began praying. I ran back over to the Samuels, and Dad moved her out of the chicken coop. Mr. Samuels's truck came up the road. Dad ran to him. Mr. Samuels went over to his wife, kneeled down, touched her, and began praying out loud. I looked over at Dad. I had never seen him cry, and I was scared. Mr. Samuels prayed and prayed and thanked God for his wife and their life together. We could hear the ambulance siren from across the river as it crossed the bridge and turned up the driveway.

Suddenly, Mrs. Lillie opened her eyes, and color returned to her face. She coughed hard, looked directly at me, and said, "JB, run fetch me a glass of buttermilk." Mr. Samuels and Dad kept praying, and I ran like the wind into the house after buttermilk. When I returned, they were all standing in the yard, talking to the ambulance crew.

From the time I was twelve until I got my driver's license, I worked for Mr. Samuels. He sold every type of seed and ground corn for everybody in the community. I helped with everything but mostly with the seeds. On most days, it was just me, him, a black lab named Scratch, and an old mule named Moses. We started and ended each day with him praying. If we were working on something that made me nervous, like grinding sugar cane into molasses or robbing his bees, he would preach. He would go about his work and preach as if he was standing in front of a congregation and preaching the gospel.

"Mr. Samuels," I said, "who are you preaching to?"

He smiled and said, "Mostly to myself, but if you have a mind, you are welcome to listen."

It was a bit odd as Mr. Samuels never preached a single sermon to anyone other than himself during his whole life. When I would go home at night, Dad's first question to me was if Mr. Samuels preached. If I replied that he did, I was expected to recount the highlights of his sermon.

He seemed to know everyone in the county. Almost every day, someone would come by and ask Mr. Samuels for advice. Sometimes, it was advice on building something; sometimes, it was advice on growing something. Most of the time, they asked him to pray.

I said, "Mr. Samuels, why do you listen to all these people and then pray with them?"

He nodded, smiled, and said, "My only reason for living is telling people about the Gospel of Jesus Christ and help as many as I can along the way."

Mr. Samuels taught me to shoot, but more importantly, he taught me ballistics. One of his prized possessions was an M1903A3 Springfield Rifle. He was lethal with the rifle at any range. We shot the rifle several times a week, and it was always the highlight of my time with him. He taught me calculus and geometry by tracing the trajectory of the bullet during each phase of its flight working my way from close to far targets. He taught me science by keeping his spent shell casings and teaching me how to reload ammunition.

When I was thirteen, Mr. Samuels got a nasty gash across his face when the mill got bound. A spring flew loose and cut his face. He couldn't see out of his right eye. He went to the doctor and wore an eye patch for several months. While his eye was healing, I was his driver. He taught me to drive his old Chevrolet truck with the gearshift on the steering wheel. We were never stopped by the police, and when we did pass them, they just smiled and waved.

As his driver, my whole world opened up. We drove all over the county visiting people. We drove across the mountain to Franklin and once through Murphy all the way to Andrews. We always took food. Mostly potatoes, but on a couple of occasions, we emptied the can house and loaded it before departing. I stayed in the truck most of the time, but occasionally, he would ask me inside.

We drove to Standing Indian late one afternoon. The house wasn't much more than a pieced-together shed. It was miles away from anything or anybody. We weren't on a road but more of a worn path. It had an outdoor toilet. When we entered the house, there was an old woman and a young boy. We visited lots of folks, and many of them were poor, but for the first time in my life, I saw real poverty. The house only had one old couch that smelled, and I sat on one end. The young boy was sick. He kept going to the one window in the house, sticking his head out and throwing up. Mr. Samuels called the boy to him and began telling him about Jesus. He talked for over an hour about how Jesus was the Son of God and how whoever believed in him could have everlasting life. He began praying over him. The boy accepted Jesus as his Savior and the old woman cried and cried.

As we went back to the truck, I said, "Mr. Samuels, I could give the boy my Bible."

He adjusted his eye patch and said, "It do no good. They can't read."

One of Mr. Samuel's best friends was Mr. Fred Willet. He drove an old Ford truck, which didn't have a muffler, and you could hear him coming a mile away. Clay County only had about seven black families, and Mr. Willet was the head of one of them.

Mr. Willet visited us two or three times a week. Some folks didn't like Mr. Samuels because of his friendship with Mr. Willet.

Once, when we were sorting seeds, I asked Mr. Samuels, "Why some people didn't like you because you are friends with Mr. Willet?"

He smiled and said, "When we get with the Lord, we won't be fussing over the color of skin."

Joel Johnson was the only other kid my age that lived close. Joel was a great athlete and could run faster and throw harder than anyone. His dad was the biggest and strongest man I had ever seen. He worked at the Fires Creek sawmill. He had a baby sister, but she was much younger than Lynn. Joel and I were best friends. We explored every aspect of the Hiawassee River and all of the mountain ridges around Sweetwater.

I asked Mr. Samuels if I could have Saturday off so Joel and I could go fishing at Carroll Lake. He agreed, and early that morning, I gathered my gear, waved to Mr. Samuels as I walked across the bridge, and went to get Joel. As I approached the house, I knew something was wrong. Mr. Johnson's car was running with the headlights on, and two doors were open. As I walked on the porch, the screen door was busted in half. I knocked on the doorframe and yelled for Joel. Mrs. Johnson came running toward me holding the baby. Her eyes were swollen shut, her lip was splintered and bleeding, and she was pulling her leg behind her like her ankle was broken. The baby was crying.

She cried out, "Joel! Joel!" And she squinted at me to determine if I was Joel. I could not speak, and she recognized me. She straightened up immediately as if to defuse the horror of what I was seeing. Joel came running up the porch behind me.

He grabbed his mom and yelled at me, "Go home!" The entire right side of his face was purple and bruised. I was astonished and stood there, staring at them, trying to determine what was happening. Joel yelled again, "Go home!"

I turned and jumped off the porch and began running. I ran straight for the woods as it was the shortest route back to the bridge.

I had to find Dad. I fell. I tripped over something. I hit the ground hard and rolled. I looked back, and there was Mr. Johnson. He was on his knees.

He looked at me and growled, "Boy!"

I jumped and ran across the bridge and down the road. I saw Mr. Samuels walking Moses toward the river. I yelled and ran toward him. Between breaths, I said, "Mrs. Johnson is in bad shape. Joel and his dad must have been in a fight, and Mr. Johnson is in the woods growling at me."

Mr. Samuels said, "Get your dad."

I ran to the house and told Dad. We jumped in the truck and drove over the bridge. Dad slid the truck into the front yard, and we saw Mr. Samuels standing on the porch. Mrs. Johnson and the baby came out first. Mrs. Johnson was carrying a suitcase. Joel followed. Mr. Samuels looked at Dad and said, "Take the family to my house. I will deal with this."

I could tell Dad was uneasy, but Mr. Samuels just pointed toward the truck. Dad nodded.

We took them over to Mr. Samuels's house. Mrs. Samuels laid the baby down and began working on Mrs. Johnson.

Joel said, "Dad's bad to drink. All that war stuff from Vietnam and all. He came home last night and began beating on us. I hit him to keep him off Momma."

Mrs. Johnson interrupted and said, "Please don't call the law."

Dad said, "We will see."

Mom came over and cared for the baby. Mrs. Johnson and Joel went into the bedroom. Hours passed. I could tell Dad was getting restless, and I was worried about Mr. Samuels. Dad called me aside and said, "Stay put. I'm going to check on Mr. Samuels."

I jumped up and said, "I want to go!"

One of the few times in my life, Dad yelled at me. He said, "Stay put! Mr. Samuels can handle himself. Watch after Joel!" Dad returned a short time later. He seemed calm and relaxed. He apologized for being harsh and told me not to worry, all is well. Finally, around five o'clock, Mr. Samuels and Mr. Johnson came walking up the road. Mr. Johnson's eyes were swollen, and he was squinting. Joel started toward him, and I grabbed after him. Then he slowed and approached his father with caution.

His father said, "It's okay, Joel. I'm sobered up, but I need some help."

Mrs. Johnson and Mom stood at the door. Mr. Johnson lowered his head in shame. We stood silently for a few seconds. He raised his head, looked at Dad, and said, "I'm in need of a ride to the VA Hospital on the far side of Ashville."

Dad nodded and they were gone. A short time later, Mrs. Johnson's brother arrived. They loaded the car and left.

Dad returned after midnight. Mr. Johnson was admitted to the VA hospital. I rode home from church the next day with Mr. and Mrs. Samuels. I boldly asked Mr. Samuels, "Mr. Johnson is a great big man. What happened?"

Mr. Samuels seemed reluctant to talk, glanced at Ms. Lillie, and said, "I prayed for God's intervention, I prayed for the courage to talk, and I prayed for the courage to listen and forgive. I reckon you saw. The Lord answered." We rode in silence the rest of the way home.

July 24, 1973, was my sister's eighth birthday, and we had a party for her at the house. Mom invited all her friends. Dad dressed up in a clown suit. By two o'clock, when the party ended, a fierce thunderstorm hit. Jenny Parker was Lynn's best friend and was the last to leave. Her dad was one of the three doctors we had in the county.

Jenny's mom and dad drove up but didn't come all the way to the house because our driveway was so ruddy and muddy. We stood on the porch and watched Jenny run toward the car. Lynn realized Jenny forgot her purse and darted out after her.

Jenny reached the car with Lynn running after her and yelling, "Wait! wait!" She was wearing her new birthday dress.

Mom yelled, "Don't be going out in the rain in your new dress!"

The lightning bolt hit Lynn, and she fell into the mud. The flash was intense. Mom screamed. Dad ran down the driveway toward her, and I followed. She was face-first in the mud. Dad grabbed her and ran back on the porch. Dr. Parker ran up the driveway. Dad put Lynn's lifeless body on the porch, and Dr. Parker immediately began beating her chest and breathing into her mouth. All I could smell was burning flesh, and all I could hear was Mom screaming. I leapt off the porch and ran to Mr. Samuels's house and began beating down their side door. Mrs. Lillie opened the door.

"Lynn," I managed to say between breaths, "has been hit by a lightning bolt, and she's dying."

Mr. Samuels grabbed his hat and marched past us. Mrs. Lillie said, "I'll call for an ambulance."

He walked as fast as I had ever seen him. Dr. Parker was exhausted from beating her chest and breathing into her mouth. Ms. Parker, Jenny, and Mom were huddled in the corner of the porch, crying.

Dr. Parker's eyes were filled with tears. He looked up and said, "I'm sorry, JD. There's nothing more I can do."

Dad collapsed backward and screamed, "Oh God!"

Mr. Samuels went to his knees, placed his hands on Lynn's forehead, and began praying. I looked up and asked God for help. Just then, Lynn coughed. She opened her eyes and began blinking.

Mr. Samuels grabbed her, saying, "Sit up now, child."

Dad went to his knees. Mom ran to Lynn and began squeezing her as hard as she could. Dr. Parker looked as if he had seen a ghost. Mr. Samuels turned to me and said, "JB, run get sissy a glass of buttermilk."

The ambulance arrived and took her to Gainesville, Georgia. Dr. Parker and Mom went with her in the ambulance. Dad and

I followed in his truck. Dad couldn't stop crying and praying the whole way. They treated her for her burns on her head and neck, and she stayed in the hospital for over a week.

One Saturday morning, while sorting seeds, I asked him how he could talk to God. The conversation started over nuclear war. In school, we talked constantly about the Russian threat and the potential for nuclear war with the Russians. I told him I had been praying that it wouldn't happen.

He asked a simple question, "If I died right now, was I sure I would go to heaven?"

I told him I wasn't sure, and he told me that God wasn't obligated to listen to my prayer. It hurt my feelings, for we went to church every time the doors were open, and I listened and paid attention both in Sunday school and to the preacher.

I told him, "God was listening to me!"

He smiled, realizing I was angry, and said, "In order to gain all God's blessing, you must be born again. You see, son, the only prayer an unsaved person can pray is the prayer of salvation. Once you are saved and are reborn in God's spirit, then you are his child and can talk to him, the creator of all, about anything you want, whenever or wherever you want." He looked away, thought for a moment, and then said, "If you commit to the Lord, the Lord will commit to you."

I thought for a while and then asked when he started talking to the Lord. He didn't hesitate and said, "July 15, 1918, on the banks of the Marne River in France. I was in a war, and I was scared. I had several close calls, and I was downright certain I was going to die. I told a buddy of mine, and he sent for the Chaplain. The Chaplain walked me through the Bible and told me basically the same things I am telling you now. I accepted the Lord as my risen Savior that day, and I am sure glad I did."

"So," I said, "what happens after that?"

He smiled and said, "It's pretty simple. I reckon that's why most folks don't get it. You pray and you obey." He became quiet and lost in reflection; then, he turned to me and said, "Prayer is the greatest thing God gave his children. Most folks just don't use it. The key is to ensure you are one of his children. Now, don't get me wrong, son, living for the Lord is no piece of cake. It takes work and dedication. A man fights the devil, the world, and himself throughout his life. Once you're saved, the old devil can't get you, but the world will give you a fit. Most of all, you got to conquer your own flesh, and that be the hardest part."

I began thinking about all we discussed.

We remained close to the Samuelses, but once I got my license, I went to work for Mr. Charles Johnson. He owed a small dairy farm and sold milk to Biltmore farms. I was a fast learner, and he paid me two dollars an hour. I was at the dairy every morning at five fifteen and worked until seven thirty when I left for school. When I wasn't playing ball, he let me milk in the evenings and doubled my income. My grades were good, but I had a miserable SAT score.

I chose Appalachian State University in Boone, North Carolina. I chose them because they chose me. I wanted to go to North Georgia College. It was a military school, but it was out of state, and we couldn't afford it. My parents saved enough to pay for my tuition, but I had to earn the remainder. Dad bought Mr. Willet's old Ford truck, rebuilt the motor, and put a muffler on it for my transportation. The speedometer didn't work, nor did the odometer, so we had no idea of how many miles were on the old truck.

He said, "Without a speedometer, you will slow down." He was right.

The day before I left for college, Mom told me that Mr. Samuels wanted to see me. Mrs. Lillie made an apple stack cake for me and wrapped it up for the ride. Mr. Samuels had a small gift for me. It was wrapped as if it were a Christmas present. When I opened it, it was a small box of stick matches. He encouraged me to slide open the box, and I did. Inside was one small brown mustard seed.

He smiled and said, "I told you this a dozen times or more, but it's all about faith." He pulled out his ink pen and wrote Hebrews 11:6 on the outside of the box. As I walked out the door, he said, "With faith, JB, you can move mountains."

LORRAINE

College life was not what I expected. The professors didn't really care if you came to class, cheating and drugs were rampant, and I didn't fit anywhere. I had to make the most of it as my folks were counting on me. Not fitting in didn't matter much, as most of the time, I was working. The college had a program called work-study. Under the program, the student was the labor force and conducted a wide variety of jobs across the campus. I landed a job with Larry and Bill. They were the fix-it specialist in the Department of Public Works. Larry was the boss, and Bill was his understudy. I learned to fix everything from toilets to the university boiler system. Bill was a Vietnam Veteran and got cancer from Agent Orange. When he got sick, Larry couldn't keep up with the work orders, so I was given my own truck and work schedule. There were limits on how much money a student could make under the program, and I reached my limit. I told Larry I needed to work and asked if he could help me find another job.

On the side, Larry cut grass. One of his clients was the University Chancellor. During one of his grass-cutting sessions, he talked to the Chancellor about me. My work-study went into the unlimited category, and I continued to fix all that was broken across the campus. I would fix a toilet in the history building and then dash down the hall to attend class. It was a very good deal, and I parked my campus DPW truck wherever I wanted.

My grades were good. I enjoyed the history classes but loved the ROTC classes. College was not hard. If you did what they asked and did it with some quality, you made good grades. By my junior year, I had friends. I dated occasionally, but not often. Shortly after Thanksgiving, while sitting in history class, my radio went off. Larry was in a mess in the girl's dormitory. An air-conditioning coil on the roof of the dorm froze, thawed, and flooded the top floor of the dorm. I left class and made my way to the dorm. The water went everywhere, but one room was devastated. I began cleaning it as fast as I could and moving furniture into the hall. The two girls who occupied the room were called out of class and came running down the hall. One was a large brunette, and the other a smaller blond girl. The brunette became hysterical and began cussing me for all I was worth. I said nothing and continued to move furniture. I picked up a desk and was moving it into the hall when the brunette stopped in front of me said, "You!" in anger and slapped me. I dropped the desk and walked down the hallway to another room.

The small blond girl followed me down the hall. I was in fear of getting slapped again.

She said, "I'm so sorry for Sarah. This is too much for her to handle right now. Our room is flooded. Will you please keep helping us?" She was calm and carried herself with such poise. Her eyes were blue. A mysterious blue and I couldn't help but stare at her. I said nothing; all I could do was gaze at her.

Finally, using her hands and making pointing gestures, she said very loudly, "Will you please help us? We really need"—she paused and pointed—"your help."

It dawned on me. She thought I was slow! I nodded and followed her back to her room. I worked for an hour, drying off what could be salvaged. I didn't speak a word, but I took every opportunity to stare at her. She was beautiful. I went to the furniture storeroom and picked out the nicest furnishings I could find and took them back to the room. The room was empty, and I began setting up. As I finished my work, they returned with several other girls and two big jocks.

The brunette came in first and then walked back into the hallway and said, "The retarded boy is still working." They began mimicking sign language to one another. They all laughed.

I saw her again about a week later coming out of the Music-English Building. She was with a jock. She saw me sitting in my truck and waved an exaggerated wave. I just nodded. She was an amazing girl who thought I was retarded.

During the Christmas exodus, the campus was flooded with people, but mostly parents coming to pick up their students. It was a good time for me. I finished my exams and could work nonstop up until Christmas and then go home for a week.

Larry sent me to fix a door in one of the buildings adjacent to where many of the parents were staying. It had been very cold for several days, and the wind chill in Boone was below zero most of the week. As I finished the door, I noticed a couple looking under the hood of their car. They were obviously parents, and we were under the strictest orders to be exceptionally nice to parents. I walked over, introduced myself, and offered assistance. The wife was upset with her husband, and he was frustrated with his vehicle. He placed the transmission in reverse, but the vehicle wouldn't move.

He said, "My transmission is busted. Do you know anything about them?"

I shook my head and said, "I think your brakes are frozen." I grabbed a plumbing pipe wrench and climbed through the slush underneath the car. It was freezing. Larry would beat me up if he got a complaint on me from parents. I took the wrench and began pounding on the rear brake drums. I yelled, "Now try it!"

He did, and the vehicle moved a few feet. The man was overjoyed. As I came from underneath the car, I looked up, and there she was staring down at me. She was wearing a long white coat and white earmuffs.

For whatever reason, I had self-confidence that day. I jumped up and said, "Please don't fall. I'm not good at catching angels." It was a lame line, but she thought I was retarded. She turned red with embarrassment. Her father came over and shook my hand. I loaded her luggage in the trunk and escorted her to the back seat. As she got into the car, she said, "I'm so sorry."

I smiled and mimicked sign language saying good-bye. She laughed. She was clearly out of my league, but it was fun to flirt with a girl that pretty.

We had a wonderful Christmas. Lynn was accepted on a full scholarship to the University of Georgia, Dad finally received a promotion from the county, and Mom seemed especially content. I went to see Mr. and Mrs. Samuels, and they looked much older, grayer, and, for the first time I could remember, feeble. There was talk of putting them in a nursing home, but Dad cut enough wood for them to last out the winter. Mr. Samuels asked me lots of questions about college, and what I was going to do when I graduated.

He said, "The Lord has a purpose for all of us, and a man is blessed if he sees his purpose during his life here on this earth."

When I told him about the Army, he just smiled. He went into his back room and gave me one of his most prized possessions, a M1903A3 Springfield Rifle. He had fought World War I with it and said he knew I would take great care of his rifle. As I left their home that day, he began thanking me for being such a good boy and listening to him all through the years. I didn't know what to say, so I hugged them and left.

I returned to school just after the turn of the New Year so I could work full days until classes began. By midmonth, the other students returned. One afternoon, I was tackling the boiler. Larry taught me how to repair it, and it was dirty work. Larry called me on the radio and told me to return to the DPW shop. I was covered in grease. I walked into the shop, and Larry said, "You have a visitor," and there she sat.

Larry wandered down the hall, and she looked at me and said, "You were wonderful to us when the room flooded, and you made my folks happy with the car." She hesitated, and I felt my heart beating out of my chest. She looked away and then back at me and said, "I want to buy you dinner at Pizza Hut."

I was dumbfounded but remained calm enough to say, "Yes, yes to everything."

She smiled and said, "You might want to clean up before we meet again."

I nodded, and she walked away. I ran out the door after her and said, "What's your name?"

She smiled and said, "Lorraine, Mr. JB Smith, my name is Lorraine."

As far as first dates go, it went as well as could be expected. I bought three long-stemmed red roses, was polite, smiled, and listened. Her father was a minister, and she was from Asheboro, North Carolina. I didn't talk much, but as the evening progressed, I continued to stare at her. When it was over, she kissed me good night, thanked me for a wonderful evening, and left me on cloud nine.

I returned to the room with a note on the door telling me to call home for an emergency. I made a collect call to the house. Mom answered. She said, "JB, son, I have terrible news." She was crying, and I could feel her pain. She took a deep breath and said, "Andrew and Lillie were killed in a car wreck. They were struck by a drunk driver and died. Lillie got sick, she'd been sick a week, and I should have driven her, but Andrew said he would. He took her to the emergency room over in Murphy. She was treated and released, and they were hit on the way home."

My heart sank. She continued to cry and said, "The gathering of the faithful and receiving of friends will be later this week, and we will bury them over the weekend. They want you and Dad to be pallbearers. You need to bring your good suit home. I will buy you a new shirt and tie."

The gathering of the faithful took place at the home. Once the funeral home had completed their work with the bodies, they brought them both home, set up both caskets in their small living room, and people began arriving. It seemed all of Clay County came to that small house that night to pay respects. When it was over and the family had gone home, Dad and I locked the doors of the house for their final night together. Early the next morning, we prepared for the funeral. They were buried at Sweetwater Baptist Church on the side of a steep hill. Dad and I were the lead on both caskets, and my muscles were aching by the time we reached the graveside. It was a cold day, and the wind was strong. Lots of people come to the house, but not that many come to the graveside service. In this case, most of Clay County was there and marched up the hill with us to see them in their final resting place. Five old mountain preachers were as brief as God would allow, and then it was over. This wonderful old man who taught me about hope, faith, love, and all aspects of life was gone. It didn't hit me hard until I was driving back to school. I began to think about his lessons and how much each one of them meant to me. It was a long trip back to Boone.

Life returned to normal back at school with one great exception. Lorraine. We saw each other at every opportunity. One night, walking Lorraine back to her room from dinner, I told her that I loved her. The words just shot out of my mouth. She told me that she loved me, and I floated all the way home.

As the summer approached, we decided it was time to officially meet her parents in Asheboro. One Saturday morning, we drove to Asheboro. Her mother liked me, but her father was much more skeptical, even though I fixed his car. Her mother,

Marge, was a nice lady who moved with a sense of grace and was comfortable wherever she was in the world. I admired her for that. Her father, Walter, was an odd man. Our first real conversation took place with just me and him in his home office. He began slowly by seeking my political views. I had few so that part of the test was easy. He seemed to sense that I could be persuaded and appeared encouraged. Next, he went to religion. He was a Presbyterian minister, and I impressed him with my biblical knowledge. Mr. Samuels taught me well.

The next morning, we went to church. It struck me that I had only attended two churches in my whole life: Sweetwater and the Campus Baptist Church. Walter preached. His sermon, if you can call it that, was boring. Most seemed happy when he concluded, not necessarily by the sermon, but by the fact that it was over. It didn't matter. I was sitting next to Lorraine.

Three weeks later, we loaded up in Mr. Willet's old Ford and drove west to Clay County. Mom and Lynn were ecstatic. They grabbed Lorraine and talked her ears off. Mom seemed content, but I sensed something was wrong with her.

I asked Dad, and he said, "She's been feeling poorly and been to the doctor over in Murphy."

Mom, Dad, and Lynn all loved Lorraine. It was a great trip. When we arrived back at campus, I called to tell them we had arrived safely and to thank them for making Lorraine feel so welcome.

Lynn answered, "Mom is coughing up blood."

I followed her condition over the next several days. Dad and Lynn took her to see several different doctors. Finally, they went to Duke Medical Center, and she was diagnosed with cystic fibrosis. The months passed, and Mom's condition deteriorated. Mom was insistent Lynn go to Georgia in the fall. Dad and I promised that Lynn would go to college. Dad hired Mr. Willet's youngest daughter, Alidade, to stay with Mom while he worked. It was a very tense time.

By October, the end was near. Lynn stayed by her side all summer and drove from Athens every weekend. Lorraine came home with me for fall break and was a great help. Dr. Parker came every afternoon and gave Mom pain medicine. We had lots of company from the Church, and they all brought food. Thursday night, Mom died. Lynn cried all night. Dad went on a long walk along the river, and Lorraine and I sat in silence on the porch.

Lorraine's parents came for the funeral. They stayed in a motel in Murphy. We placed Mom's casket in the living room. Hundreds of folks came that night. Most came after work and were dressed in their work clothes. Lynn couldn't handle it and broke down crying several times. When it was over, Lorraine and I drove them back to their hotel in Murphy. Walter droned on and on about the unique people he had seen that night. I remained quiet.

As he was getting out of the car, Walter said, "I am glad to be away from all those hillbillies." It hurt.

We buried Mom. The sky was Carolina blue, and the mountains were at the height of the color season. Dad insisted that he and I be pallbearers. In her last days, Mom told Dad the details of her funeral. As we approached the graveside, Mom's friends sang "Swing Wide the Gates." The preacher preached a very short sermon, and the choir sang hymns. We cried.

We went back to the house, and people came and brought food. As folks departed, Dad took another long walk along the river. Lynn and Lorraine cried, and I walked over to Mr. Samuels's house. It was boarded up. I recalled the lessons he taught as well as the miracles I witnessed. I thought of finding Mrs. Samuels in the chicken coop, of Lynn getting struck by lightning, and the whole hosts of other things I saw him do for people. I missed him.

I went back to the house and started a fire. Dad returned and slumped into his chair. Lynn and Lorraine sat quietly on the couch.

I turned to Dad and said, "I sure do miss Mr. Samuels."

Dad sat up, rubbed his eyes, and said, "He and I talked about it, and her purpose was fulfilled." He stood, stretched, and walked quietly to his bedroom.

Lynn stared hard at me and said, "He's so tired, he can't think straight."

I wasn't convinced. He seemed fine to me. I told Lorraine about Mr. Samuels and the lightning strike, about how Lynn came back to life.

Lynn spoke up and said, "It was Dr. Parker, not Mr. Samuels and buttermilk, who saved me."

I could not believe what I was hearing. Lorraine noticed my anger and suggested we go for a walk. As we walked along the river, I told her the things I witnessed growing up on Sweetwater.

She listened patiently but skeptically and finally said, "Sweetwater, what a peaceful place."

CRISIS

Lorraine handled doctor visits, school visits, and all the other major parenting tasks associated with raising two children, but she refused to go the dentist. The oldest was John, but we call him John-boy. The family princess was Jessica, and we call her Jess. For whatever strange reason, I agreed to oversee dental care. Almost all dental visits result in some sort of pain, and even the dullest among us know what is coming and will do anything to avoid. They woke with an attitude, and simply arriving at the dentist office on time was a victory. Our kids play off one another. If one had minor pain, the other had a major pain. I was sitting in the corner on a small chair surrounded by toys, watching *Barney* the purple dinosaur when the cell phone rang. I didn't carry the secure pager anymore, and some days didn't really feel like the Soldier I had once been. My job was to resource training. I was a Lieutenant Colonel who commanded a cubicle.

It was Lorraine. Uncle Ray called her twice looking for me. I hung up with her. It rang again. It was Uncle Ray. He sounded desperate and said, "JB, he's in the hospital in Murphy. His heart is bad, real bad. I don't know what's going to happen, but I just know it's bad. I called Lynn. I think you best come."

I hung up and dialed Lynn. She said, "I am packing and leaving now. I called the hospital. He is critical."

I made my way to my office. Colonel Bishop was in his office. I told him my situation and asked for emergency leave. He agreed and found the paperwork. It had to be signed by our General. He told me to wait, and he would get it signed. He was gone for a long time. I thought the General was in a meeting. I wandered down the hall to the command group section. I heard the General's voice.

"Training is my top priority. Smith is working on our Quarterly Training Briefing, and it's a critical mission."

I moved closer down the hall.

Colonel Bishop said, "Sir, the guy's father is in bad shape. Please sign the form. We will get it done."

The General raised his voice and said, "I don't think you realize the importance of these briefings."

I stood quietly beside the door.

Colonel Bishop cleared his throat and said, "Sir, I deal in bottom lines so the bottom line here is we will get it done. Also, I'm well past retirement eligible, so if you don't sign, you can find another flunky Colonel to lead this staff. It's your call."

He put it all on the line for me. Then silence. Finally, the General said, "Colonel Bishop, you are great because of your passion. Give it to me."

I moved down the hall. When the Colonel returned, I thanked him for being a great boss. He smiled and said something I had not heard in a very long time. He said, "I will pray for your dad."

It was a six-hour drive. Uncle Ray sounded worried, and I was scared. I made good time. As I stepped off the elevator, I saw Uncle Ray stretched across two chairs in the small waiting room. A young black kid was sitting across from him, and I stepped cautiously over his outstretched feet. Uncle Ray woke and jumped to meet me. I could see fear in his eyes.

Before I could speak, he said, "Is he still alive?" I felt pain. I knew it was serious, but the possibility of Dad dying hadn't crossed my mind.

I said, "I just got here. Where is he?"

Uncle Ray looked exhausted and said, "It's his heart. It's just not working," and then he pointed at the double doors down the hall. As I was moving down the hall, he yelled, "JB, only two in the room at a time." I kept moving. I buzzed the door to the small Intensive Care Ward and it opened. A heavyset nurse was sitting behind the counter, and she pointed toward the door on the right.

The room was dark except for a small light over the bed. Dad was hooked to everything. Monitors were silently flashing, and I tried to make sense of all I was seeing. I reached down and touched his hand. He turned his head toward me and gripped my hand. I leaned in toward him and said, "Dad, I'm here. I'm here."

He gripped my hand. He was wearing an oxygen mask. I glanced around the room and saw movement. It was Lynn. She was sleeping on a small couch in the corner and was up with her arms open. We hugged. She whispered, "It's bad." I noticed movement in the room.

Lynn stepped back and turned on the small light. I looked across Dad's bed, and there sat a pretty graying black lady. She was holding Dad's hand and talking softly to him. I knew her, but I couldn't find her name. My first thought was that she was a nurse and Dad was getting great care. She leaned in and lovingly kissed him on his forehead and told him she loved him. She crossed the room and hugged me tightly.

She spoke softly and said, "He's been anxiously waiting for you. I am so glad you are here." She turned to Lynn and said, "I will leave you for a minute and take a break, but I will be right back." I knew her voice.

Dad squeezed my hand. I bent over him. He attempted to take off the oxygen mask with his free hand. I stopped him, but he was persistent.

"Dad," I said, "it's going to be all right. You're getting the best care."

He shook his head as if to disagree. His voice was raspy, and it took great energy for him to speak. He stared at me, and I wondered how much pain medication they were giving him. He whispered, "Son, I'm going home."

I shook my head and said, "No, you're going to make it through this."

He gripped my hand, harder this time, and turned his head. I replaced the oxygen mask, and he took several deep breaths and then removed it. He seemed calmer now, and he smiled at me, and then, he whispered, "Remember Mr. Samuels?"

I said, "Yes, Dad, of course I remember him."

He moved closer to me and said, "I have talked with him, and it's going to be fine."

I couldn't make sense of what he was saying. It must be the drugs. Lynn leaned in and said, "Daddy, we all remember Mr. and Mrs. Samuels."

Once more, he shook his head, smiled, and said, "Going to be fine." He looked at us and said in a whisper, "You must take care of Alidade and Israel. I love them" He grabbed for the oxygen mask. We helped place it over his mouth. He turned his head and drifted to sleep.

Lynn held back tears. This was bad. Lynn lowered her head as if to pray and suddenly looked up and said, "I've got to call Roger, and you need to call Lorraine." She grabbed her cell phone. As she was walking out, she looked at me with tears running down her face and said, "JB, we got to be tough."

I stood there, holding Dad's hand. He was a great father, a great man. I was tired. The drive had been hard, and each time I closed my eyes, I felt a slight burning sensation. The tears weren't helping. I grabbed one of the small straight chairs in the room and sat down next to Dad. I lowered my head and began to pray. I hadn't prayed in a long time. I tried to pray, but I had forgotten how. I heard movement behind me and turned to see who was coming in the door. It was the young black kid from the waiting room. What is he doing here? He walked slowly around me to the other side. He took Dad's hand and gently rubbed his forehead. I stared at him and thought, from the side, he looked like Uncle Ray. I was confused. Who is this?

The pretty black lady walked gently into the room and stood beside the young boy. She touched Dad's head. Dad turned slightly. The woman leaned into him saying, "We are all here, JD. We are all here." He smiled through the mask. I felt a hand on my shoulder. It was Uncle Ray. I looked up at him. He was wiping the tears from his eyes. Uncle Ray was tough. I didn't recall every seeing him cry. I looked at him, and he nodded.

Finally, he said, "You want coffee?"

The black lady said, "The doctor won't be here until six or six-thirty, so get some breakfast."

I nodded. Uncle Ray and I walked out of the room.

We walked through the doors. I turned and said, "You have a fine family, but I didn't know you had a son."

He gasped and stared at me. He shook his head and said, "He didn't tell you. He promised, but he didn't." I was confused. The last several minutes were the most confusing of my life. I knew bad places; I saw and did bad things. I took pride in my ability to read any situation quickly, but my senses were failing me. Uncle Ray pulled me into the corner of the waiting room and told me to sit down. He lowered his head searching for words. He spoke slowly.

"The woman in the room is Alidade. She was Fred Willet's youngest daughter. Your dad hired her to watch after your mom when she first got the coughing cancer. Your mom knew she was dying long before they ever told you and Lynn. Alidade loved your mom and took great care of her when she had some really bad times. Your mom made JD promise he would remarry. Three years after your mom passed, JD and Alidade were married, back in eighty-two. A year later, Israel was born. The woman is JD's wife, and the boy is your brother. There, now you know, and it's over and done, and he promised me he would talk to you about all this. Son, I didn't know that you didn't know."

My brain was racing. What had he just told me? It just didn't make sense. Uncle Ray got up and said, "I will find coffee." I was alone in the room and staring at a painted picture of a boat tied to a grassy dock. Dad wanted me to come home. The last time we talked, he wanted to tell me something, and I missed it. I never really gave him the opportunity. Every time he visited, it was always about me and my family and kids. He visited us several times. Why? I remembered watching a Holiday bowl game one year, and he was trying to tell me something. That was years ago. Had I been gone that long? I lowered my head and cried. My mind was racing. I was crying more for me than for him.

Lynn sat beside me, patting my back. I kept crying. Dad was such a great man, and I took him and his life for granted. Lynn put her head on my shoulder and cried with me. Lorraine, I must call and tell Lorraine. Lynn, I need to tell her.

"Lynn," I said, "I have something very important to tell you." She looked up in fear. "Dad was married to the woman in his room, and the young kid is our brother." She shook her head as if not comprehending what I was saying. "It's true," I said. "Uncle Ray just told me."

She just stared at me, shook her head, and said, "I know that." Then it hit her. Her eyes widened, and she said softly, "Dad never told you, did he?"

I shook my head. "No," I said. We sat in silence.

Finally, I said, "How long have you known?"

She smiled, reliving the memory. "Dad drove to see me just before Roger and I got married. He told me. When Alidade got pregnant, they were concerned about her age. Israel was born early in the children's hospital. Dad and Alidade stayed with me in Atlanta until he was ready to travel." Then, she raised her head as if she was having a revelation. "You were off fighting in some war. Dad was worried sick about you and about little Israel. He would get up every morning and watch the war news, turn off the TV, get on his knees and pray, and then turn it back on and watch more war news. He prayed so loud my neighbors complained. I think he prayed you through that war."

Uncle Ray returned with coffee. He stood over us, ran his hand through his thick gray hair, and began to speak. "When Dad died, it was just me and JD. He was fifteen, and I was thirteen. What was left of our raising was done by Mr. and Mrs. Samuels. He was always there for me. When he went in the Army, he sent me money. When I got into trouble with the law, he paid my bail, and when I was sober and working steady, he was proud of me. When I got bad sick, he prayed me through it." His voice cracked. He choked, wiped away tears from his face, and said, "I reckon I can't stand to be without him."

Israel entered the room and said, "The doctor is here and wants to talk to the family."

The doctor was a short older man in his late sixties. He finished examining Dad and asked that we all step into the adjacent room. We gathered, standing in a tight semicircle. He looked the part with a white hospital coat and the stethoscope around his neck. He had seen his share of death. He looked directly at Alidade and began speaking. "Your husband has congestive heart failure. Frankly, I don't know what is keeping him alive. His heart is very weak and growing weaker by the minute. I am very sorry, and I detest having to tell you this, but he is expectant." Alidade, Lynn, and Uncle Ray began crying. He continued, "I cannot offer any prediction as to when he will pass, but I would think soon. If I, or the staff, can be of any assistance to you, please don't hesitate to ask." He turned and walked out the door.

I walked into Dad's room. I sat in the straight chair and held his hand. I squeezed his hand to tell him I was with him. I felt no response, so I squeezed again. He squeezed back, but his grip was leaving him. They all entered the room holding each other. I needed to call Lorraine, but I was afraid to leave. Alidade walked to the other side of the bed, bent over, and kissed his forehead. She lowered her head and prayed. I felt Dad's hand as if his muscle twitched. Lynn lowered her head on the foot of the bed and began crying. I squeezed Dad's hand, bowed my head, and tried to pray. I couldn't find words. For several minutes, the only sound was each of us crying. Dad squeezed my hand hard, and then the machine alarms began their wide-ranging torrent. Alidade was unfazed. She prayed aloud over the sounds of the machines. The heavyset nurse and the doctor quickly walked into the room and silenced the alarms. Dad was dead.

Death is final. It sounds lame, but it's the reality of life. I felt pain all over my body. He was such a great man. No matter what becomes of me, I will never be as genuinely good. It's my fault. After Mom died, I made him come to me. I was living my life, and I expected him to meet me on my terms. The incredible thing is that he did, over and over again. I was selfish and ashamed.

Alidade was a comforter. Lynn cried and Alidade comforts. Uncle Ray pulled up a chair in the corner and stared at Dad. He looks much older now than he did just a few minutes ago. I stared at Israel. He is my father's son. I can see it in his eyes, his face, and his mannerisms. He moves like Dad, talks like Dad, and has the same inner strength as Dad. I am ashamed. I'm ashamed of missing all this and not knowing her and Israel. I can't place anger or blame on Dad. He tried to tell me, but I was all consumed with my life, not his. He loved me anyway.

I stared at Dad. I was stunned by what happened. I am guilty. I wonder if I am as distant from my children as I was from my father. I focused on the past.

The door opened, and Uncle Ray greeted the visitor. He was the preacher from Sweetwater Baptist. He hugged Alidade. Israel ran to him for comfort, and they embraced. He pats me softly on the shoulder and moved to comfort Lynn. He was a very big man. I heard the talking around me but am in a trance, trying to determine the opportunities I missed. I am a master of excuses.

Finally, the preacher came to me. I didn't want to be bothered. I needed to work a resolution in my head as to how I missed all this. He sat quietly with me. Lynn was crying harder and they all helped her from the room. We sat in silence. I keep coming back to my selfishness and shame. Finally, the preacher said, "JB, it's been a long time."

I looked at him. He looked familiar, and I wondered if we were related. He said, "It's okay if you want to cry." I stared at Dad. He cleared his throat and said, "You know, if it wasn't for your dad, Mr. Samuels, and you, I wouldn't be here today." I turned and stared at him. It was Joel Johnson.

A hospital orderly came into the room and began moving equipment. Joel sat beside me and didn't speak. He was a comfort to me. The orderly returned with the heavyset nurse, and she asks that we leave the room, so they can prepare the body for movement. Joel asks their patience, and they leave. Finally, he said, "We need to go and find the others."

I stood and moved to the far side of the bed. "Dad," I said, "I am so sorry."

The family was in the waiting room. Lynn asked if I called Lorraine. I was embarrassed. I have not. Am I so selfish that I can't call my own wife? Lynn told me to go to the end of the hallway to get reception. I called Lorraine. She answered, and I said, "Dad is dead." I began rambling about my new family and how horrible I felt that I didn't know. I confessed to her my selfishness and guilt that we weren't close. Nobody comforts me like Lorraine. She is loving and steady. She told me that she will pack and get the kids out of school. They should be on the road before noon and she will call her parents.

I walked back into the waiting room. Alidade took my hand, and we walked down the hallway. She was a graceful woman. We sat in two small chairs.

She said, "I loved him. He wants to be buried at Sweetwater next to your mother. I think we ought to receive friends at the house if it's all right with you?"

I nodded.

She continued, "Israel and I will be buried on the other side. We have already purchased the plots."

I nodded. She knew him well.

We conducted the gathering of the faithful at our house. Lots of people came. It was overwhelming. We buried him the next day. John-boy and I were lead on the casket. He was stronger than I thought. Joel preached, people sang, and I felt ashamed.

Lorraine and I walked along the river, and I told her how I felt. She hugged me. Finally, it was time to go back to Fort Bragg. I got the family up early. We locked up and drove through the fog alongside the Hiawassee. I glanced toward the shed and swore I saw Mr. Samuels standing there. My mind was playing tricks on me.

NATIONAL CRISIS

I WAS FORTUNATE. Over the past year, I slept with my wife every night. I drove my kids to school and watched ball games and plays. I missed Dad. I called Alidade once a week to see how she was doing. I regret not taking my kids to Clay County to see Dad. It haunted me.

By 0930 on September 11, 2001, it all changed. We knew it was Bin Laden. A year or so ago, the president ordered a missile attack on one of his training camps in Afghanistan. We didn't have anyone on the ground. The new way was to shoot from afar, fly over, and guess the damage. The strike made people feel good, but other than that, it didn't accomplish a thing.

We worked through the night on September 11. By midmorning on the twelfth, I was eating a candy bar in my cubicle. I finished a never-ending cycle of meetings and was compiling my notes. The Army knew it was going to war. Money and resources were already flowing.

Colonel Bishop walked in and said, "Pack your stuff. You have orders." He handed me the orders and continued, "You are now working for the Intelligence Support Activity assigned to Fort

Belvoir, Virginia, with duty here at Bragg. They put in a byname for you, and it's approved. Hand over your work to Major Lewis. Good luck." He shook my hand and walked back down the hall to his office.

I drove to the building. A large photograph hangs in the entry foyer showing wrecked aircraft and helicopters. It is the failed Iranian hostage rescue mission. The words underneath say, "Don't confuse your enthusiasm with your capabilities." It is prophetic. I gained my credentials and began trying to find my new unit. I rounded the corner and saw the boss. He looked tired, was much grayer than I remembered, and needed a haircut. He smiled and said, "Welcome. We are at war. Your desk is over there."

It was a happening place with more brass arriving hourly. I didn't know the Army and Air Force had that many Colonels. The navy sent every SEAL they could find. I was openly introduced as the guy who blew up the Chinese Embassy.

The military communicated with Video teleconferencing or VTC. You see and talk to each other over large television screens. With all things military, there are pre-VTCs to set agendas for upcoming VTCs and pre-brief VTCs prior to the actual decision-making VTCs. For several days, it seemed we lived in the secure VTC suite existing on black coffee and whatever stale product remained in the vending machines. If you went home at all, it was to sleep, shower, shave and get back.

The big guys VTCs were interesting. The Three Stars shut up, the Four Stars actually thought before they spoke, and the Secretary of Defense and the CIA Director held everyone's attention. After three full days of back-to-back VTCs, the only conclusion drawn was this was going to be a tough mission. I hated the CIA. Observing them on the VTCs reinforced my opinion. The Air Force and Navy continually pitched the idea of a massive air war, the Army didn't have any ideas, and the Joint Special Forces community clung to their roots by arguing the only solution involved working with the local forces. During those VTCs, a nuclear bomb could have exploded, and it would kill everything except a good idea. We didn't have any.

The Secretary of Defense wasn't one for listening. He ordered everybody to build plans. The Four Stars didn't ask any specific questions such as what we were planning for, how long, or the strategic end. They simply echoed the orders to plan. We began planning. Central Command, the Joint Staff in Washington, all of us at Fort Bragg, and a dozen other semi-intelligent government agencies began doing the same thing. One Saturday night, I sat in the very back of the VTC room and listened to eleven different plans, each with a different twist and all focused on killing the mastermind.

A brave Air Force Colonel from the Joint Staff finally said, "Gentlemen, we tried the killing of the Indian Chief theory before in Somalia when we chased the ring leader and lost lots of good men. Dead Rangers were dragged through the streets on television. We need a comprehensive strategy." The previously dead VTC roared to life. I didn't know how many were on the VTC, but it suddenly seemed as if the whole world was watching, and they all had a comment. It was getting interesting.

The boss poked me and motioned me outside. I followed him to the courtyard. He wasn't a smoker, but these were unique times, and he needed the temporary relief of a cigarette. He was an old school guy. He didn't have much humor, he spoke softly and directly, but he was widely considered the best thinker in the building. He was blunt.

He lit his cigarette and said, "Go home." It was odd, and before I could respond, he said, "Get some rest. You are going to deploy. I will call you when we get the details sorted out. You will be my lead for whatever happens next."

I was angry over the terrorist attacks, and I wanted revenge, but I thought I would continue to ride a desk. I figured my days of grand adventures were behind me. He crushed out his cigarette, and said, "It might be another week, maybe two, before we get our act together, so rest up." He turned and walked away. I went home.

Lorraine was surprised to see me. I told her I was going to be off for a few days. She immediately went into hyperchatter. She knew. She wouldn't ask, but she had been through this drill before. There was only one reason I was home in the middle of a national crisis. We hugged a lot. We held hands, we cried for the people in those towers and in the aircraft, and for the first time in a long time, we prayed.

It had been years since I talked to God. Mr. Samuels and Dad drilled me since birth that prayer was the answer to all things, but as I got older, I felt it was under control, and I didn't need God. I survived numerous close calls, firefights, and dangers of all sorts, but this was a national tragedy, and the entire nation was in mourning. I wished I could pray like them, but instead, I just sat quietly and mumbled. I missed Dad.

The call finally came. In times like this, you instantly realize what a sorry father and husband you really are. My kids grew faster than I could control and had a life of their own. School, sports, plays, dance, activities of all kinds. They weren't raised on the banks of the Hiawassee River. They never worked until they hurt, never knew the value of firewood on a cold night, never understood the rural life, and they never listened for hours to old men talk about the gospel. They lived in a small subdivision where we would occasionally see the deer at night. They were good kids. They gave us no trouble, and they were exactly the same as every other kid in the neighborhood, but that was the wrong standard. They had little self-reliance and were so sheltered, they often corrected one another over the most minor of safety issues. I realized the wisdom of my raising. I could correct these things, but first, I had another deployment.

Leaving is always hard. I was glad the report time was early. Lorraine was clingy. It was unusual for her. We checked the kids and checked them again. I assured her it would be fine. This time, there was hesitancy in her voice. She was kind but candid in telling me, "You aren't ten-foot tall and bulletproof. You are slower and older, and you need to be careful. I need you." For the first time since I had known her, I could see worry in her face. I reassured her and walked to my truck.

Everything, minus weapons, I needed was packed inside a sixty-five-pound large framed rucksack. Socks, underwear, cold weather clothing, ultralight sleeping gear, and an emergency pocket with everything from fire starters to fishing gear. Survivalist had nothing on me. I drove to the special lot, shouldered my rucksack, and handed my keys to the civilian guard. He bid me good luck and told me he would ensure it got cranked weekly to keep the battery charged. Although I had no real idea where I was going, I suspected it would be cold, and furthermore, I had no idea how long. I thought to myself, as I trudged along, that all my papers were still in order so if something did happen, Lorraine could sell the truck. Stories abound about this particular Fort Bragg parking lot as it has several vehicles that have been there for years, but this is a place where it is best not to ask questions.

It was just over a mile from the parking lot to the headquarters. After Somalia, many of the guys called it the Mogadishu Mile. I had walked it many times before, but this time, the rucksack seemed heavier. I dumped my rucksack and went looking for the boss. He wasn't in his office, but instead, he was sitting in a lawn chair, smoking a cigarette in the outside courtyard. I had been off for almost two weeks. After the attack, the news program experts speculated on every possible war plan. After a while, I had become numb to the talk and watched *The Andy Griffith Show*. I was clueless to the situation.

He looked worn out. Somebody had brought in some nice lawn furniture with the canopy umbrella and a nice black iron round table. The boss set up a temporary office outside where he could smoke and think. He was glad to see me and actually smiled. He shook my hand quickly and said, "You ever been to Uzbekistan?"

I shook my head and said, "No, sir, I have not."

He smiled and said, "The plan is a hybrid. The diplomats are working to gain use of an old Soviet airbase in Uzbekistan. From there, we would infiltrate into Afghanistan, work with several of the tribal leaders we presume are friendly, use massive amounts of air power to bomb the place, and recapture the country. If we killed Bin Laden, then good, but if not, recapturing the country is the objective." He crushed out his cigarette and continued, "You are on the first plane. Negotiate with the Soviets and or Uzbek's on the ground and set up initial operations for our follow-on forces. We will fill the place fast and begin infiltration. I will get there as soon as I can with the staff."

I nodded. It sounded simple enough.

He hesitated and said, "During the first phase, you will be under the operational control of the CIA." He smiled, making me think he was kidding. He looked at me and said, "JB, place nice with the fraternity boys."

TO THE FAR ENDS OF THE EARTH

THE BRIEFING STARTED at 0900. The CIA was clearly in charge with a guy named Chad giving the briefing. Twelve people would execute the advance reconnaissance mission. Our destination was an old Soviet Airbase known as K2 in southern Uzbekistan. It official name was Karshi-Khanabad Airbase, and it sat just east of the town of Karshi. The diplomats discussed our use of the airbase with their counterparts in both the Russian Federation and directly with the Uzbeks, but nothing was certain until we landed. If we didn't receive full cooperation from our hosts, we were to take whatever actions necessary to gain control of the airbase and barricade ourselves until help arrived. Help, in this case, was a SEAL Team on alert available to us from our ships in the Persian Gulf. I tried to do the flight math in my head to determine how long we would need to barricade ourselves within the tower, but the best I could figure was ten hours. That is a long time to barricade. Chad was convinced we would be warmly received. I got the feeling we bribed access to the airbase.

Officially, our mission was to coordinate the arrival of follow on forces. Approximately twelve hours after we landed a series of transport aircraft, carrying a wide variety of military equipped four-wheel drive trucks common to the region, a complete communications suite, a large medical contingent, rations, ammunition, and a water purification unit would leave Germany en route to our new home. Once we had the infrastructure on the ground, we would begin infiltrating all sorts of Special Forces teams across the border where they would link up with local tribal leaders and encourage them to fight a war to run the Taliban out of Afghanistan. We would rely heavily on the ability of our Soldiers on the ground to play laser tag with targets and fly bombs to their ultimate destruction.

Key to the overall operation were two prominent tribal leaders. We often used the words "tribal leader." It was not an accurate description. They were drug lords. Aside from the cultural differences, they were just like the drug lords in Bogota, Columbia, who exported cocaine. Dealing with these guys would be interesting. They preferred solo power and worked alone as opposed to combining their strengths in a cartel. They grew and exported opium around the world, and they owned more black markets than the Russian mafia. They were rich, powerful, had everything they ever wanted. Those conducting the negotiations needed to convince them it would be in their best interest to remove the Taliban from power.

The Taliban and Al Qaeda were separate and distinct organizations. Each had its own pecking order. Both organizations knew a major attack was planned on the United States on September 11 down to the key leader level. Their plan was simple. They would continue to project power aboard using terrorism as their weapon. They collaborated to assassinate the one leader who stood in their way. On the ninth of September, they killed Ahmed Shah Massoud. He was the Lion of Panjshir. He had leadership ability, the respect of the people, and the financial backing to thwart their operations, so they killed him. This left the two remaining tribal leaders in the north vying for power and influence.

Negotiations are interesting. The person with the power in any negotiation is the one with the ability to say no and kill the deal. That was why I never won an argument with Lorraine. All negotiations must be in the best self-interest of the person with whom you are dealing. It all boiled down to Mr. Samuels using carrots and sticks to train his old mule. If the mule did what he wanted, he rewarded with a carrot. If the mule failed, he used a stick to punish. The negotiators would use a carrot to incentivize or a stick to threaten. The worst-case scenario was losing the deal. We could threaten punishment but certainly didn't want to follow through. Losing the deal meant we would be forced to punish. When you hit that level, most folks called it war. What we didn't need was a subwar within the war we were attempting to start. We could not go into Afghanistan without the support of somebody. Worst case was us fighting the Taliban, Al Qaeda, and the drug lords.

Two men were critical to our success. The more powerful of the two was Mr. Kalid. He had ties to everything, and the theory was that unless he assisted us in this mission, the US Navy would shut down his drug export shipping lanes. We had a stick, but we didn't have a carrot. The less powerful was Mr. Obar. The initial intelligence estimate was that he would be easier to convince because his area of influence was located more to the north plus he had numerous public run-ins with the Taliban. Both were reportedly "good" Muslims who claimed to have their faith as the centerpiece of their life. I knew many Christians who professed to have Christ as the centerpiece of their life and didn't, so I wasn't convinced. Both were mujahedeen and fought the Russians. Both were fierce. The mujahedeen were world famous "Holy Warriors," but I didn't give much credence to the idea of beating the Russians. While the Russian professional troops were as good as any in the world, their conscripts were worse. A disciplined group of bad guys is called a gang but an undisciplined group is called a mob. The Afghans had beaten a mob. Kalid and Obar gained power and influence after the Russians withdrew and kept massive amounts of drug money flowing into the economy, which increased their power and kept the Taliban at bay.

Once we established, the CIA would infiltrate into Afghanistan and begin the negotiations while the military built strength on K2. The CIA would conduct a battle hand-off by conducting the introductions and linking up our teams with tribal leaders. Although everyone in the briefing had faith in our ability to execute an intensive air operation, we all knew this would require troops on the ground. If we were going to hold the ground and do something positive, it would take much more than teams of Special Operators. It would take an Army. The people who owned the Armies in the region were Mr. K and Mr. O, so in order for this to be successful, we needed to rent their personal armies.

Twelve of us were going to make this happen. Six would-be CIA and six would-be military. The CIA gang was young. Chad was the oldest, and he might have been in his midthirties. The others were in their mid- to late twenties. Karl was either Chad's deputy on this mission or was actively bucking for the position. He worried me. He was young, brash, and appeared to have far more Rambo than common sense. He was the reason the military went to great lengths to determine who was fit and unfit for these missions. The military can teach anybody to shoot, but it's not about shooting. It's about knowing when and, more importantly, when not to shoot that counts.

The CIA recruited heavily from Ivy League schools. They sought bright young folks who were physically fit and highly motivated. Being book smart and fit are important, but the military went to great lengths to find the intangibles of common sense, resilience, and a resolute calmness in any situation. The CIA and the military didn't see it the same way. I couldn't blame young folks for going to the CIA as they certainly paid more, but it was never about the paycheck. Maybe I was stirring up bad old memories. Maybe I was prejudging the guy and the Agency, but I had good instincts, and they were telling me to keep a close eye on this cowboy. Maybe I was jealous. Maybe I was angry over the Belgrade incident, or maybe I was scared. The remainder of the CIA team included Kwan and Curtis who I suspected were their language guys, and Rolf and Ray who I suspected were their ex-military muscle guys.

The military team was a collection of Fort Bragg's best. I wondered why the boss wanted me. I was a used up old Soldier with a long history and limited potential. Maybe I was expendable. I was pleased to see an old master sergeant known only as Hustler. He was a master logistician, master negotiator, and was legendary for making things happen. He was joined by his apprentice who was known only as Midget. Midget was a former team operator who had more missions under his belt than anyone else on the plane. He was half blind and walked with a severe limp. I doubt he would have made it in the conventional Army. If you saw him in polite society, a short little balding man, you would feel sorry for him. When he could no longer serve on operational teams, he pulled strings and became Hustler's apprentice. Also on the mission were Brian and Corchado. They were both well-known for their ability to make communications happen with anything from anywhere. I worked with them in the past, and I knew firsthand how good they were. Finally, there was Travis. I don't know how old he was, but my best guess was fifty at a minimum. If it could fly, Travis had flown it. He was old school to his core with a sharp tongue and a quick wit. He came into the Army post-Vietnam and learned to fly from the Vietnam helicopter pilots. Rumors had it that he was one of the junior pilots during the disaster in Iran in 1979 with Charlie Beckwith, but I never asked him. At first, I wondered why he was on board, but then I figured if you had to run an aircraft control tower, Travis was your man.

When the briefing ended, we went to the Arms Room and drew our weapons. I drew an M4 rifle, a .40 caliber pistol, and a .44 Magnum revolver. While the Arms Room was full of new, interesting, and experimental stuff, I went with what I was most comfortable. The M4 was a great weapon, and although I had done my share of sniping at a distance with heavier weapons, almost all engagements are well within the M4s capabilities. I carried the .40 caliber because I am very good with it, I know the ballistics, and the ammunition is light. I drew ten magazines and loaded them on the spot. I carried the revolver on previous missions, and it was my lucky charm. I didn't draw it on the mission to Belgrade, and it costs me. I never used it in combat, but I had always come home, so it must be lucky. I grew up watching *Dirty Harry* movies with Clint Eastwood blowing up cars with a single bullet. It wasn't nearly that powerful, but every time I pulled the trigger, I thought about feeling lucky. As I grew older and became more and more proficient with weapons, I began to seek reliability. When really bad things happen, the most important thing is the ability to shoot back. It's hard to jam a revolver. I watched as Karl drew a M240 machine gun as well as the ammunition. This was going to be an interesting.

The boss met me as I exited the Arms Room. He pulled me aside, and we walked to the corner of the building where he could smoke. He said, "I am concerned about the CIA team."

I looked at him, nodded, and said, "You're telling me."

He smiled and said, "I'm suspicious. They seem more interested in getting into theater than getting follow on forces into K2. It's their job, to gather human strategic intelligence, but as long as I have been doing this, they have been far more wrong than right. I worry about these guys. They negotiate and leave us holding the bag with no options."

I understood. The boss was always talking about options. Warfare is all about options. He turned his head, exhaled the cigarette smoke, and said, "I'm concerned—no, I'm actually worried these dudes will forfeit our options. They will enter into treaties leaving us with only a few ways to accomplish our mission. It wouldn't be the first time. They get in and make the deal and then fade back into the shadows leaving us holding the bag." He looked at me and said, "You keep an eye on them. We can't afford free radicals on the battlefield."

I understood. The CIA doesn't answer questions. They don't answer to the press or even to historians. They operate within a different sphere and under different rules. When things go wrong, they just fade away and leave the military to clean up. The distrust between the military and the agency started long before I ever donned a uniform. For my generation, much of it stemmed from the failed Iranian hostage rescue attempt in 1979. While there was plenty of blame to go around, the military version always had the CIA as the culprit. They loved the role of middle man where they could make strategic negotiations and then turn over the dirty work of fighting the war to the military and fade into the shadows. Plus, there were still many Vietnam Veterans around at the senior levels of the Army, and they wanted as much control over the military portion as they could get. The CIA made promises we had no way of keeping, and when things went bad, they were nowhere to be found. They were desperate to make the strategic deal. Once the deal was struck and we were on the ground, our hands are tied with no real way out other than to play by the existing rules.

He shrugged, lit another cigarette, and said, "The worst-case scenario for us is they make a solo deal with the drug lords. They tell them whatever they want to hear. Once the shooting starts, they are gone leaving us with two choices. Either we honor the strategic deal they made, or fight the people we hired to fight the war for us. It's a bad situation." He thought for a moment and then said, "This is going to be a long war, and we will bear the brunt. We have a vested interest in getting a good start. We can't afford to fight Bin Laden, the Taliban, and the drug lords." He smiled and said, "At least it's not boring."

I had marching orders.

We loaded vans. I suspected we would go to the green ramp at Pope Air Force Base and was surprised when we headed toward the vast Fort Bragg training area and then to the Special Forces area known as Camp McCall. The vans bounced along dusty roads, and then we turned to an old airstrip on the backside of the camp. We began to unload our gear when an unmarked Gulfstream jet landed and taxied to our location. It was sleek and looked more accustomed to moving business executives around the nation than moving us into a combat zone. I expected something far more military and far less comfortable. It had twelve seats for twelve passengers with two pilots driving. It dawned on me that the reason twelve were chosen for the mission was because that was the size of the best plane available. The pilots were exacting in their instructions. We cleared all weapons, and they loaded our equipment into the aircraft. This proved far more painstaking than I anticipated as it seemed to take forever for them to move our rucksacks, communications gear, and weapons around in the small cargo area, and in the area behind the last row of seats. Finally, they were satisfied, and we boarded. Chad and Karl moved to the front seats followed by the remainder of the CIA men. We filed into the back of the plane. The only instructions were to sit down and buckle up. We were off.

We were airborne for an hour or so when we began to take breaks, stretch, and walk around the cabin. We started talking. Hustler and Midget slept while Kwan said, "I didn't think learning languages would be dangerous."

I nodded and asked for the languages.

He said, "I speak seven languages fluently and read and write in another three, but am weaker in reading than in writing."

I nodded and asked, "Do you speak Pashtun?" He looked at me and shook his head.

Travis interjected and asked, "Why can't Spanish linguist talk to Puerto Ricans?" It was a great question, and Kwan was articulate in his response, giving us a dissertation on dialect.

I finally interjected and said, "What languages of value do you speak?"

He nodded and said, "Uzbek, Tajik, and all varieties of Turkish Russian spoken in the region."

Ray, sensing my discomfort at this news, turned and said, "I speak Pashtun, as well as Tajik and Russian."

I smiled. At least somebody was thinking ahead.

After several hours, we moved around enough to generally know the folks on the plane. We began a descent ending in a bumpy landing in Reykjavik, Iceland. The plane taxied to a far corner of the airfield where we deplaned for roughly an hour to refuel. This gave me an additional opportunity to speak to more members of the CIA team.

I started with Rolf. He was the muscle man. He was a weapons expert, and we had a great conversation about ballistics and sniping in general. He was an American citizen but was raised in Germany and served a tour in the German Army. I didn't ask how he got into this line of work, but it appeared this wasn't his first major mission. He wasn't as young as I initially thought and was pulled from a mission elsewhere to be on the plane.

Karl joined our conversation. He was knowledgeable with weapons but not in Rolf's league. He spoke with an accent. He was from Boston and with a degree in International Relations from Harvard. He was slightly older than I guessed at thirty-one. He was in excellent shape. The more we talked ballistics, the more out of his league the conversation became for him, but he did appear interested and eager to learn. Still, he retained an overly aggressive tone to all his words and actions. I probed him to determine his experience, but he was evasive. The more we talked, the more it became apparent that he and Rolf didn't know each other.

Finally, I said, "Have you guys worked together before?"

Rolf said, "No, Chad just assembled this team. I think we all have worked with Chad but not with each other." Chad moved toward us and gently moved Karl away from the conversation. They went into the corner and talked. He returned and then he and Rolf walked toward the corner and talked. I attempted to restart my conversation with Rolf, but he was aloof. It's lunch time in high school. Chad doesn't want his folks mixing.

Once the plane was fueled, we boarded and buckled. At cruising altitude, folks began moving around. On long plane trips, you can get a sense of the people around you by what they are reading. Curtis was reading some sort of textbook on engineering. It was odd. Normally, folks who have done this line of work, only pack what they need. I certainly didn't need the extra weight of a textbook in my rucksack, but it did enable me to start a conversation with him. He was the other muscle man for their team and a weapons expert. It didn't take long to see how bright and articulate he was. He was a mechanical engineer by training and an MIT graduate. He was young and very smart. I notice Chad turning to make eye contact with him, and the conversation ended.

Looking out from the aircraft, I stared into darkness. It was like watching a vast nothingness. It reminded me of the fuel truck. Occasionally, the pilots would turn from their cabin and speak to Chad, but overall, the cabin was dark and quiet. I watched as Chad and the pilot underwent an extensive conversation. Once complete, Chad moved toward the back of the aircraft, pulled a small chair from the side of the fuselage, and began plugging things into the wall. He had done this before. He dropped a panel and plugged in a set of headphones with a voice mike. He attached his cell phone and dialed a series of numbers. I could not hear the conversation. I watched Chad nod his head and make a couple of points. When he was complete and started to put away his gear, I asked if we are still in a go status for the mission. He nodded. I attempted to engage him in conversation, but he returned to his seat. I watched as he woke Karl, and they had a conversation. He had things to say, but not to me.

We began to descend and land. I didn't know where, but it was a well-lit and modern airfield. The pilots taxied us to a small hangar and cut the engines. Two men in coveralls boarded the aircraft. We listened to the conversation regarding some sort of special sensor. Finally, Chad said, "Yes, put in the sensor."

I don't know aircraft, but if having a special sensor increased my chances of survival, I was in favor of emplacing the special sensor. We unloaded the aircraft and sat in a pilots lounge inside the hanger. The pilots moved to a small room in the back which had two half-beds.

I have trouble sleeping on airplanes. I am always afraid something will happen, and I won't be able to react. Not that I had any skills to influence the outcome, but at least, I wanted to see it happening rather than sleeping through it. I wandered around the lounge until I began to feel drowsy. I didn't know the local time, but back on the East Coast, Soldiers would soon start rising for their morning physical training routine. The lounge had several large, oversized leather seats, and I had just settled into one and was dozing off when Brian woke me.

He motioned me to follow him, and we walked out the side door into a dark hallway. He handed me a phone. It was the boss. He said, "You're in for a warm welcome. The diplomats did their job. That's the good news. The bad news is the CIA team will ditch you at K2 and head south. We can't let that happen. We've played this stupid game before, and they will leave us holding the bag. Give Hustler the airfield mission, but you stay with them. Do whatever it takes to make mission. You got it?"

I thought for a few seconds and began to speak, but he said, "Good luck." The line went dead. I handed the phone back to Brian and thought about the best way to accomplish my mission.

They would separate from us. My guys would immediately begin working on logistics, communications, and tower/airfield operations while they quietly slipped south into Afghanistan. If that happens, I will have failed. I thought about my options. I could approach Chad directly and simply ask to go with him and his team. It wouldn't work because he will be forced to admit that his team had a separate agenda. I could force my way into his team by seeing how they divide themselves when we land and then bully my way into a vehicle where Chad doesn't see me. Nothing appeared feasible.

Young officers learn quickly in the Army or they become Burger King Managers. One of the first lessons an officer learns is to work closely with noncommissioned officers. Lieutenants are presented with a problem. The problem is simple. The flag is stuck at the top of the flagpole. The Lieutenant is directed to build multiple courses of action to solve the problem. Some begin to work options where they requisition a cherry picker or a fire truck; some get bogged down in the fact that it is our national colors and must be treated within a certain protocol. Others simply cut the lanyard and catch the flag. After much debate and discussion, the instructor tells the Lieutenants that there is only one solution. Tell your Sergeant it's his mission to get it down. Basically, put a noncommissioned officer between you and every problem, and your chances for success increase substantially.

I walked back into the lounge. The lights were low. I poured coffee in a Styrofoam cup and began to think. Brian returned to his side of the big leather couch and which caused Hustler to stir. I caught his attention and pointed at the bathroom. I drank down the coffee and walked into the bathroom. The door made a squeaking sound as I pushed it open. I leaned against the sink, and in a few minutes, Hustler opened the door. I turned on the faucet and acted as if I was washing my hands. He used the bathroom and then pulled alongside me washing his hands.

I spoke in a whisper saying, "My mission is to go with the CIA wherever they go when we land. Yours is to handle the flow of all follow on forces. The boss says we will not have a problem when we land."

He nodded in understanding. I turned off my faucet and began to dry my hands with the rolling hand towel machine. I cleared my throat slightly and then whispered, "I need help in ensuring I go on the CIA mission." He nodded, wiped his hands, and we both opened the door as we walked back toward the coffee machine. We poured coffee and stood there silently, staring at each other.

He drank down the coffee and poured himself another cup. He walked to the window, looked out at the lights on the far side of the airfield, surveyed the passengers sleeping, and walked back to me. He put down his cup, pulled his notepad from his pocket, and wrote down, "Engineer?" I didn't get it. He then pointed at Curtis and then pointed at his stomach. Again, I was slow.

He leaned into me and whispered, "Who do you want to get sick, the engineer guy?"

I thought about his question. Rolf and Curtis were the muscle for the CIA team. Where they were going, they would need all the muscle they could find. If one of their muscle men went down, they would need to replace him, and I would be on the mission. I nodded. The flagpole problem was going to be solved.

One of the men in coveralls returned and woke the pilots. On his way back, Ray asked the salient question, "How much longer?"

He replied, "Another fifteen minutes."

This caused the crowd to rise, stretch, and head for the bathroom. I asked Hustler if he knew where we were. He smiled and pointed at a small sign above the room where the pilots were sleeping, which said, "Pilots' Lounge, Istanbul, Turkey." I felt stupid. One of the pilots came out of the bathroom and poured himself a cup of coffee. Hustler asked him the time to K2. He replied roughly three hours but maybe less with some decent wind.

Midget slept most of the way. He was short enough that he could almost lie down in one of the reclined seats in the aircraft. He walked out of the bathroom and to the window. He fished his pockets and came out with a small bottle of eyedrops. I never knew the extent of his injuries but heard he spent over a year in and out of hospitals recovering from his wounds. He held up his head and began to squirt the drops into his eyes. Hustler moved beside him and quietly took the bottle causing Midget to give him an odd look. Hustler walked back toward the coffee machine and began pouring cups of coffee. The line in the bathroom ended, and they were walking out toward the coffee machine.

In his best Noncom voice, Hustler said, "The party is just starting. Everybody get coffee and get your brains moving." He began handing coffee cups to those walking out of the bathroom. He handed Curtis a cup and said, "This will put hair on your chest." Curtis smiled and began to sip not only the coffee but also half a bottle of eyedrops.

We loaded the aircraft. The pilots went through their preflight and started the engines. The Gulfstream roared, and soon, we were at our cruising altitude. Curtis was the first to stand. Hustler looked at me, nodded his head slightly, and winked. Curtis headed for the onboard latrine. Shortly, he returned to his seat and began dozing off. I looked at Hustler. He raised an eyebrow. Thirty minutes passed, and Curtis continued to sleep. An hour passed and nothing. I was beginning to formulate a plan B as this plan obviously failed. I would need to confront Chad and tell him of my command's vested interest in working with the tribal leaders. My mind was working overtime as I rehearsed my speech and words. Curtis sat straight upright. He turned and almost ran down the corridor of the aircraft and opened the latrine door. All heads turned to see what was happening. He dropped to his knees and began vomiting. We watched but turned our heads away to allow him some dignity. Hustler and Midget jumped up and offered assistance. I looked forward and saw the worry on Chad's face. His plans were unraveling.

Hustler and Midget were great medics. Once Curtis emptied himself, they escorted him back to his seat. Midget went to the rear of the plane and returned with an IV bag. They quickly inserted the needle and began pushing fluids into him. They hung the bag above his head, and Chad came back to look. Midget magically produced a thermometer and took his temperature. He walked to the back of the aircraft to get better light, turned and announced, "One oh two."

Brian and Corchado cleaned up the bathroom. Vomit has a unique smell, and it seemed to linger. Cleaning the bathroom made it look better, but the smell remained. Chad touched his forehead and said, "He feels hot."

The pilot turned and told Chad we were beginning to make our initial decent into K2. Curtis jumped up again and pushed past Chad back to the bathroom. More dry heaves. Midget stood above him holding the IV line. Curtis turned and dropped his pants. He exploded. He sat on the toilet, and we heard the splash. Midget attempted to close the door, then made a face, and we turned and looked forward. Chad sat down across from me.

He tried not to look anywhere near Curtis. The smell of vomit was mixed with stench. Finally, Curtis came from the bathroom and sat down with Midget following. His face was flushed and red. Hustler said, "We may need to put on masks just in case he is contagious." Midget shuffled through his medic bag and found a small white mask and slowly placed it over Curtis's nose and mouth.

Chad leaned forward and began talking to me. He said, "Once we land, my team will meet transportation and begin moving toward the border. We have a contact on the Afghan border. We will begin working our infiltration." I listen carefully and nodded. He lowered and then raised his head and said, "Curtis won't make the mission."

I interrupted him and said, "No worry, our guys are trained medics, and we will take care of him."

He shook his head and said, "Not my point." I feigned surprise. He said, "We need your skills." He stared at me for a few seconds and then said, "I know we blew the mission in Belgrade.

We only had one operative in the county, and we paid the asset when we gave him the coordinates. He left, and you were in a bad spot, so I know you're angry. We thought you and your team were dead. Somehow, you survived. The nation needs you, and I need you." I began to formulate questions, but he said, "You're ISA and we need you. I will inform my higher that you are added to the team."

I shook my head and said, "I have strict orders to get follow-on-forces into this airfield. My mission is time sensitive."

He stood and said, "Be prepared when we land because you're going with us."

I said, "I am an old Soldier who follows orders." Hustler looked at me. I nodded at him. Once again, he made a miracle happen.

As we lost altitude, we could make out shapes. It looked like we were landing on the surface of the moon. The aircraft landed, and we followed a small truck with flashing lights. It was dark, but dawn wasn't far away. We stopped and saw the ground crew moving around the aircraft. The pilots cut the engines, and Chad motioned for Ray and Kwan to move toward the door. The pilot walked down the corridor and opened the door. Chad moved behind the language specialist as they stepped down. I stood and gathered myself. Karl rushed past me and followed Chad. I heard voices but couldn't make out the language.

Midget and Hustler helped Curtis to his feet. He removed the mask. He was regaining his strength and was adamant the IV be removed. This was a concern. A man in a tie with a white lab coat entered the aircraft and moved toward Curtis. He placed his hand upon Chad's head and, in broken English, asked him to sit back down. Curtis complied and Hustler began giving the man his medical diagnosis and continually asking if Curtis was contagious. This prompted Kwan to return and act as an interpreter. They talked and the man in the white coat listened and nodded. Kwan told us he is the base doctor, and he would have an ambulance move Curtis to their infirmary. If his injuries required more advanced care, they would move him to a better facility. The doctor said he didn't know the extent of the illness until he ran test. We heard the sirens moving across the airfield. Two Soldiers attempted to enter with a stretcher, but Kwan and the doctor managed Curtis out of the aircraft and into the ambulance. Midget followed and handed over the IV bag. As the ambulance pulled away, he nodded at me.

Chad and Karl departed into the main building with the arrival entourage. The pilots began the slow process of unloading the aircraft. Hustler said, "That guy was really tough. It usually works faster, especially with half a bottle. We should have waited longer before we started the IV. I guess it flushed him pretty quick. If you're going somewhere, you need to get moving."

Two Nissan Pathfinders pulled in front of us. Chad and Karl emerged. Chad asked, "Who will be responsible for the follow-on-forces mission and who is your tower guy?"

I pointed toward Hustler and Travis. He motioned and they followed him into the building. Brian gave me the super cell phone, and I placed it in my cargo pocket. Corchado found a cart and began moving communications equipment into the building. Rolf and I stood guard. Hustler, Travis, and Chad returned.

Hustler said, "No worries. Most of them speak English."

Chad pulled the team together and said, "Lieutenant Colonel Smith will join us on the mission in Curtis's place. Now load up."

Ray, Chad, and Rolf loaded the point vehicle while I joined Kwan and Karl in the second. Karl drove and Kwan moved to the back, leaving me with the shotgun seat. I locked and loaded my rifle, causing Kwan to do the same.

Karl said, "No danger here, buddy. I will let you know when we need to get serious." I nodded but didn't change my weapon status. We followed the point vehicle off the airbase and began moving on one lane roads almost due south then southeast. The sun came up, and it was a cool and clear morning. The sky was beautiful, but the landscape was barren. The Uzbeks were cotton farmers and gold miners, but I didn't see any viable agriculture, and the mountains look rugged in all directions.

I asked Karl, "How are we navigating. Do you have a map?"

He snorted and then offered a half smile and said, "You don't really need to know. We just follow the point vehicle." I started to speak but held my tongue. Our nation's been attacked, and we were on the verge of a major war and invasion of a foreign country, and I didn't know where we were going. It didn't require a degree in strategy to figure out this old Soviet airbase would be a good place to launch an invasion. The best way to stop an invasion was to start early and interdict initial arriving forces. Either way, I thought, it wouldn't take long for the Taliban or Al Qaeda to know something was happening here in Uzbekistan.

The road widened as we entered the M39 Highway heading south. We pulled into a roadside stop. Everything in this part of the world moves by truck, and trucks need fuel. It was crowded and it was also prayer time. We could hear the speakers calling for prayer. Truck drivers were assembling their prayer mats and facing toward their holy cities. I thought it wise to stay in the vehicles as it showed respect and doesn't draw attention, but we didn't do that. As if oblivious to all around us, we got out and began fueling.

Gently, I approach Chad and said, "We should hold off until prayer is complete. We are out of place here."

He looked at me as if I stunned him, thought for a second, and then agreed. We all moved back into the vehicles. Karl was furious and almost jerked the door handle off as he sat down. I looked at him and said, "When in Rome, we ought to be good Roman citizens."

Kwan wanted to diffuse the situation as Karl and I stared at each other. He talked about being raised as a Muslim. I just sat there and waited until the prayers were complete. We finished our fueling, and Ray paid the attendant. I approached Chad and asked for a map. He said, "I only have one map, but I have the

GPS, which is guiding us toward the link-up location. We are about three hours out from our destination."

We drove another hour on a narrow two-lane road winding its way across a mountain range with commanding views of the surrounding valleys. The lead vehicle pulled over to the side of the road on a small turnout. We all dismounted and relieved ourselves. The road was not overly busy, but we followed several trucks through the narrow mountain passes. We were well into the afternoon and it remained cool at this altitude. Chad produced the map and laid it out on the hood of our vehicle.

We gathered and he said, "We will link up with a contact near the border town of Termiz. We believe the contact can assist us in getting across the Amu Darya, which is the river separating Uzbekistan and Afghanistan. The two countries are linked by the Uzbekistan-Afghanistan Friendship Bridge built by the Soviets in the early 1980s to get Russian Soldiers into the country. The Taliban shut it down in 1997. We need help in getting into the country. If we can't cross here, we will need to move seventy-five miles to the west and attempt another crossing. We must be able to cross with these vehicles and our equipment. We wouldn't be much good on the other side on foot."

I replaced Karl as the driver in our vehicle. He went to the backseat and immediately went to sleep. After another hour, the road widened and we entered the outskirts of Termiz. It was a good-sized city with a population of over one hundred and forty thousand. It was getting late, and we were all tired. Kwan was drifting off to sleep and kept hitting his head against the window. We turned east off the main highway. Our objective was to avoid the town and link up with the contact on the northeastern outskirts of the city near a reservoir. We saw the lake off to our right flank. There were several open picnic areas around the lake. The lead vehicle pulled into an open area, and we followed. The lake was on our right flank, A large hill was on our left. We waited. Karl and Kwan were asleep.

I dismounted and walked forward to the point vehicle. I woke Chad, and he, said "We are waiting for the contact to arrive." All in his vehicle were asleep. I was the only one up and moving. I moved back to our vehicle and opened the trunk. I pulled guard. The road was quiet. I needed a bathroom break, so I grabbed my rucksack and looked for paper. I attached my rifle across my chest and strolled into the woods. Just as I was walking back up the trail, I saw headlights coming down the road. It was a small truck. I assumed it was our contact, but as soon as it saw the reflections of our vehicles, it began speeding up, which didn't make sense. It stopped at about one hundred feet away.

The flash was extensive. I knew it instantly. A rocket-propelled grenade produced a distinct signature. It looked like a small nuclear weapon exploded with a tremendous flash, and it illuminated the truck. I saw two rifles standing in the back of the truck, one dismounted on the left side and one firing from the passenger side behind an open door. They were firing at my vehicle, which was the trail Pathfinder, but they haven't seen me. The RPG penetrated the center of the engine block on my vehicle. The sound of metal on metal as the grenade entered the engine compartment was ear–splitting. They were firing small arms, and I heard the ricochet of bullets from the metal. I raised my weapon and fired first at the dismount on the left side. He fell. I emptied the magazine, firing at those standing in the back of the vehicle. All fire from the truck stopped, but it quickly made a wide left hand turn, exposing the passenger's flank. I hadn't executed a change-magazine drill in almost two years, so I initially fumbled my way and lost my grip on the magazine. I told myself I had to be faster. I slapped the magazine into the rifle and aimed directly at the passenger. The door was open, so I had success. The truck continued to turn, and I instinctively raised my weapon and moved toward the vehicle. I had a clear view of the truck bed and fired at the gate and at the rear window. I was within sixty feet. I concentrated on the driver emptying another magazine. I ejected the magazine and grabbed another, quicker this time, as my hands and fingers regained lost muscle memory. The truck rolled to a stop. I moved forward and double tapped two dead in the truck bed. I moved to the passenger side and double tapped the passenger and the driver.

BREAKING INTO A FOREIGN COUNTRY

I HEARD THE fire, then saw the rounds impacting into the back window and looked to see the muzzle flashes. Two weapons were firing from the vicinity of our vehicles. It's too late. We were surprised and too ill-disciplined to protect ourselves.

I shouted, "Cease-fire! Cease-fire! Check wounded, check wounded!"

Rolf rushed forward, and we searched the dead. We found nothing of value. I told Rolf, "They probably aren't alone. Get forward and establish somewhere to protect us."

I ran to the vehicle. A fire was burning underneath the hood. They filled the Pathfinder with bullet holes. Chad and Ray were working to determine the damage. Kwan was dead, and it looked like Karl had been hit in the side and was in bad shape. The RPG struck just above the engine block. It brought a hailstorm of deadly shrapnel into the front seats, exiting out the roof above the rear seats. We moved Karl out of the vehicle to the ground. He was bleeding. Ray and Chad looked at me. I began feeling his side. I couldn't find anything. It had been years, but I knew I must find entry and exit holes and patch them. I moved to his arm. He was in and out of consciousness, and when he was awake, he rolled to his side and tried to vomit. Ray grabbed the medic bag, and we found morphine. It was in the small vials, but I couldn't remember the dosage limits. We gave him one stick, and it appeared to ease the pain. I finally found the wounds all in his arm. His arm was cut to pieces. I didn't know if it's from small arms fire or shrapnel. I couldn't tell the difference between an entry and exit wound, so I bandaged his entire arm. It was bad. He had lost a lot of blood. I screamed at Chad, "Put the fire out and get the equipment out of the vehicle. Throw it into the back of the other Pathfinder!"

Karl was knocked out with the morphine. He was out of pain and still breathing. We must get him out of here, or he would die. We had no internal communications gear, so it was hard to gain control of the situation. Chad finally extinguished the engine fire.

I told Ray, "Find Rolf and get him back here."

We needed to get moving. I checked on Karl and noticed Chad wandered off into the woods, talking on his cell phone. It infuriated me, but I didn't have time to explode on him.

I saw Rolf and Ray running back. We rearranged the gear and then lifted Karl and placed him in the back of the pathfinder. His breathing was strong and steady; however, I noticed the bandages were soaked, so he was still losing blood.

I told the others, "We must get him back to the doctor at K2 and soon, or he will be KIA."

Chad joined us and said, "We have our orders, and we will continue the mission! We will leave them here and keep moving south. I am working another contact now."

I exploded and said, "That is stupid! We won't do that. We've got to get him to medical help."

He was dumbstruck. He buffed up and yelled, "This is my mission, and I am in charge!"

I was angry and I yelled at him, "How is your *mission* going so far? You morons are too ill-disciplined to secure yourselves, and we are lucky we are not all dead and your mission along with us!" I shook my head and then yelled again, "This is not a sightseeing tour! These people want to kill us. They know we are here and what we are trying to do." I walked away and turned back and screamed, "I don't do amateur hour!" I pointed at Chad, lowered my voice, and said, "I have a vested interest in staying alive, despite your best efforts."

Rolf and Ray nodded, and Chad stared at them. I walked toward the enemy truck. I needed a solution, and I could hear Chad, still angry, telling the others something about orders directly from Langley.

I turned and said, "We steal a vehicle heading north. Rolf drives it back to K2 with Karl and with Kwan's body. We continue mission. Once Rolf drops Karl and gets a vehicle, he and the other guy will return to link up with us."

Chad looked at me as if I was crazy. Rolf nodded his head in agreement. Ray said quietly, "Curtis is the other agent's name, but how do we steal a vehicle here?"

It was a good question. I moved to the enemy truck. It was full of holes, and the back windshield was mostly gone. I pulled the bodies from the cabin, sat down, pushed in the clutch, and turned the key. It cranked, and it had almost a full tank of gas.

I moved it alongside the Pathfinder. "Rolf," I said, "here is your transport to K2." I pulled the dead enemy from the back and wiped up as much blood as we could. The others joined me, and we carefully loaded Kwan's body into the bed. He was young, had a good sense of humor, spoke so many languages, and was another casualty of the 911 terrorist attacks. I doubted he would ever be recognized for his service to the nation. It was sad. I stripped his gear and found a lightweight sleeping bag. I rebandaged Karl's arm and threw the bloody bandages off to the side. If he lived, he would lose his arm. We placed him in the sleeping bag and laid him in the bed of the truck. Rolf grabbed his gear and drove off in the night, heading north.

I looked at the others and said, "I don't know how they found us. Maybe it was the truck stop, maybe they followed us, and maybe someone from K2 knew our general route. Maybe one of our vehicles is bugged." I then said, "What did we expect? We are Westerners, looking Western, landing at K2 in daylight, driving south to coordinate the invasion of a foreign country, and they knew we were coming." Why we were so lax, I will never know.

We gathered our gear and loaded the vehicle. I cranked it but felt a sudden hesitation. I killed the engine. They stared at me, and I said, "Check for bugs." If we were bugged, we would invite another attack. Chad's eyes opened wide. We gathered our flashlights and began an extensive search of the Pathfinder. We found nothing. We then went back to the destroyed vehicle. Ray crawled underneath, and I searched the inside. We found nothing.

Just as we were starting to move, one of Chad's multiple cell phones rang. He answered. It was the contact. Chad activated the speaker, and we could hear his voice in broken English. He would be arriving soon, and we should stay put and wait on his arrival. It didn't make sense. Chad asked for a new meeting location, telling the contact we already passed the previous link-up point. This caused obvious consternation on the other end of the phone, and Chad motioned for me to move out. The contact set us up for failure and played the agency into the ambush. Chad hung up, called Langley, and asked for a trace on the phone. Getting across the border was proving difficult.

We discussed going east to the M41 highway and then south but decided to get off this route and work to blend into the population. It should be easier with just one vehicle. We headed west and merged onto the M39 and drove into the heart of Termiz. The initial shock was wearing off, and we were thinking. Ray spoke fluent Russian, and Chad could speak some Russian. I would be the mute within the group. We drove to the river and began a search, slowly circling a working-class neighborhood until I spotted our target.

It was a garage and a junkyard. It had roughly fifty old cars and trucks alongside a cinder block building, with a vacant lot on one side and the river on the other. It would work for tonight. We parked the Pathfinder in the middle of the junk cars for safety, and Chad began talking on his cell phone to establish another contact. This time, we took turns sleeping. As with most CIA operations, Chad and Ray were carrying millions of dollars. When the garage opened in the morning, we would either trade or buy ourselves another automobile. Before I went to sleep, I wandered off and called the boss. I briefly told him about the day's activities. He told me the CIA Liaison officer briefed him and that he had not heard any reports on Rolf or Karl. He told me to continue the mission and to keep him informed. I returned to the vehicle, stretched out in the back seat, and went to sleep.

Chad's phone buzzed all night. He was up at least six times. His higher headquarters eventually agreed with our assessment that the contact was burned. We had one dead and one wounded to prove our theory. The sad thing was that in an era when America was the one and only super power, this was our only viable contact in the region.

I took the final guard shift. I was up and moving when Chad's phone buzzed again. He was groggy. He placed the phone on the hood, activated the speaker, and went to relieve himself. The voice on the other end began briefing before Chad was ready, but apparently, he was used to this routine. It was some sort of battle update briefing, and I assumed it was at the CIA headquarters. The briefer acknowledged our plight and discussed their coordination with the British government. Within hours, they supplied a viable contact. The British contact would meet us at our current location, get us across the river, and facilitate the link up with the weaker of the tribal leaders. From there, we would have to work a relationship with the other leader. It was a start, and I was impressed that somebody was thinking about how to solve this problem, even if it was the British.

We were to stay put. The British contact knew exactly where we were located. As the sun broke over the horizon, Ray and Chad took out shaving kits. I thought they were just kidding when both began to put shaving cream on their faces. I nodded my head and spoke up, "How many men have you seen so far who are clean-shaven?" I paused, looked around, and then continued, "I know its cliché, but when in Rome, we best act like the Romans."

We ate breakfast and listened to the prayer calls along the river. It was a pretty city. Around midmorning, a blue Nissan pickup truck pulled into the station. We could see his bad attitude as he got out of the truck and slammed the door. The man didn't like the idea of people at his worksite or around his stuff. I couldn't tell if it was because he wasn't a morning person or because he thought we were thieves. Ray greeted the man in Russian. The man threw up his hands as if to acknowledge our presence, but it wasn't a warm reception. Ray told him we broke down and needed transport and that we were willing to trade or buy. He walked past us, found his keys, and opened the main door and then the garage doors. He wasn't in a talkative mood and Ray pressed him slightly. The man waved and disappeared into the back room.

Chad and I stood outside looking through the garage doors when an older Ford station wagon pulled directly toward the garage door opening. A ruddy-faced, white-haired older man threw up his hand and waved as he pulled forward. He was a large cumbersome man, and it took a few seconds for him to get out of the vehicle. I heard the unmistakable sound of a bolt moving forward. We turned, and the garage owner was staring us down with an old Soviet era rifle.

He began yelling in a language I couldn't understand, but it was clear he meant to kill us. The gray-haired fat man ambled toward the hood of his car, threw up a beefy hand as to stop the incident, and said, "He thinks you are Russians, and he hates Russians." He began speaking to the owner in another language, but the owner was not backing down. Ray began speaking to him in yet a different language, and I assumed it was Pashtun. Any sudden move and this guy pulls the trigger, leaving one of us dead. The fat man talked to him in low and measured tones. He appeared unafraid, as if this was second nature to him. He continued talking to the owner, and after a few minutes, he lowered his weapon and stormed back into the backroom.

The fat man turned to us and chastised us for being stupid. He said, "Only a fool would speak Russian in this town." He spoke with a thick English accent, and said, "Speak only English, Uzbek, Tajik, or Turkmen in this area. They hate Russians." He looked at us and then said, "Surely you can't be as stupid as the Russians. Load your gear into my wagon. We are leaving."

Chad stared at the man and said, "You are to assist us in crossing the Uzbekistan-Afghanistan Friendship Bridge and then link us up with the Afghan Tribal Leaders." It was half statement and half question. The fat man again held up a beefy hand, shook his head, and said, "You are arrogant and stupid. The bridge has been closed for years. It is mined with at least a company of Infantry defending it. Maybe your computers and satellites didn't tell you?" He sat in the seat with a thud and then said, "Whoever sent you here thinking you could bribe your way across here is an idiot."

I stepped forward, grabbed my rucksack, swung open the back hatch, and threw it into the rear of the Ford. I grabbed my rifle, opened the passenger door, and sat down, just as I was told. Chad and Ray, looked at each other in disbelief, loaded their gear, and took the seats in the back.

He cranked the engine, shook each of our hands and said, "Call me Scottie, just like the guy in Star Trek. We are in for a long ride, so get some rest." We pulled out of the garage and headed due north back onto the M39 highway.

I said, "Where are we going?"

He looked at me and said, "Home for now, then to Turkmenistan." I sunk into the seat and went to sleep.

I awoke in time to see the road signs announcing the next major city as Qarshi. He noticed I was awake and nodded at me. He had a full head of long and wavy gray hair, and was easily a three-hundred pounder, probably in his early to midsixties.

I reached for a chew of tobacco.

He said, "You are from the American south?" I nodded and he asked, "Where?"

I said, "Clay County, North Carolina."

Without missing a beat, he said, "Have you ever had any luck fishing on Lake Chatuge?"

I was shocked. I was world away talking about fishing in Clay County. I stammered and said, "I don't know of anybody who has been lucky on that lake, but I know some folks who have killed up at Fontana."

He nodded in agreement and said, "I have been there and had some good days. I think the best is Nantahala, but it's hard to get to."

"Well," I said, "I prefer trout and fly fishing."

He nodded and said, "Have you ever fished the Tuckasagee?"

I looked at him. "Mister," I said, "how is it you know the mountains?"

He smiled and said, "My first wife was from Sylva. We met in college at North Carolina State. We spent every vacation, wandering the mountains." He paused in deep thought and said, "She was killed in an automobile accident, and I was adrift for a couple of years. Then, I joined the Diplomatic Service as an Agricultural Specialist." He looked at me and said, "You are not CIA. If you were, we would not be talking." I glanced toward the backseat and noticed Chad listening to every word.

He ran his hand through his hair and said, "My first posting was to the Uzbek Soviet Socialist Republic. I met a wonderful woman and married her. You will meet her. Her father was Sharif Rashidov."

He looked at me and then glanced into his rearview mirror to see if the name registered with either of us. It didn't. He continued, "Rashidov was the unquestioned leader of the Uzbek's and a crony of Brezhnev. My specialty is agriculture, and I grew cotton and poppies. You know what we make from the poppy, don't you?"

I nodded.

He said, "The cotton production kept the Supreme Soviet off our back giving us autonomy, and you must know the opium trade is profitable." He shifted lanes and then continued, "When the Soviets invaded Afghanistan in '79, I had a front-row seat. My first contact with your agency was in early 1981 when they paid me to give away opium and heroin to Soviet Soldiers. That was profitable and good for all."

He was in a talking mood. I glanced to see Chad hanging on every word. He moved his frame in the driver's seat and said, "In '82, the old man died, and it was sad."

I interrupted and said, "Old man?"

He replied and said, "Rashidov. It caused a great deal of uncertainty within the family and within the government, but we did well until Gorbachev's anti-corruption campaigns forced us back to England in '87. By that time, even the Soviets knew they lost Afghanistan and were trying to minimize their losses and keep control of their empire. We moved back in '91 when Uzbekistan declared its independence. The Soviets were bled out in Afghanistan and couldn't do anything about it, so they conceded."

He glanced again into his rear view mirror and said, "Now, my family farms just over three thousand hectares with mostly wheat."

I wasn't certain if he was a spy, a politician, or a major drug dealer. However, he seemed to know what he is doing, and that was good enough.

"Agriculture," he told me, "is all about fertilizer and water. Keep the soil strong and wet, and something will grow."

I thought to myself, *I've heard similar thoughts from Mr. Samuels, except Mr. Samuels would have added that God gives the increase.*

We turned off the highway and began heading southwest. Soon, we turned off the paved road onto the dirt, and we could see nothing but wheat on both sides of the valley. Large combines were working the fields. If it wasn't for the mountains, it would look much like the American Midwest. We entered pavement again and turned into a driveway, and a mansion loomed before us. It was a Southern-style plantation with large pillars and a veranda.

He said, "You will stay here tonight as our guest. I am too tired to drive, and I need to make calls." Several men came out and offered to assist us with our luggage, but I politely waved them off. He said, "We will come get you for dinner, and then we will talk."

The men escorted us into the mansion. A graceful older lady and two younger women greeted us. We exchanged pleasantries and were shown to our rooms. My room was immaculate and looked like something out of *Southern Living* magazine. I got to see many things, but never with Lorraine. She would love this place and this room. I took a bath and changed clothes, but I didn't shave. I dressed in carpenter jeans and a dark-gray sweatshirt.

We gathered in the dining room. It was a feast. Mutton and a wide variety of noodles were spread out across a magnificent table. The young ladies were his daughters. The men were his son-in-laws. It was a large extended family and they put on a show for us. Ray relaxed long before Chad and was conversing in all the languages he knew. Chad was the most social I seen but remained aloof. Apparently, they don't have many visitors, so we were a big deal. In broken English, and with help from Scottie, I had a discussion with the ladies about my family. I don't carry pictures but do my best to describe my family. Chad doesn't like the conversation and, during a short break said, "We are a nation at war and watch your tongue."

I just smiled and walked away.

The evening ended and Scottie and I moved to the veranda. A pit fire was burning, allowing warmth against a cool night. These people were wealthy. Chad and eventually Ray joined us. The view was wonderful and the night sky was clear. We began with small talk, and then Scottie started his strategic lecture.

He said, "Americans are stuck on using hard power. If you can get it close to a military solution, you take it. Your military learned the hard lessons in Vietnam, but your political leaders don't get it and don't understand power. Power is at its zenith when left unstated, unused, and dormant. You Americans always think power makes you powerful and the answer to all problems." He stood and warmed his hands but continued preaching. "Nobody can live like that. If you have a disagreement with your neighbor, you don't attack his home. If you are foolish enough to attack his home, you find that his children and later his grandchildren will hate you. It's easy to start a war, but once it gets going, it's impossible to stop."

"You," he said, pointing at me, "should have learned that lesson in Bosnia and later in Kosovo." I wondered what he knew about me.

He had our attention and continued, "The Afghans feed on it. Its blood hatred and it's taught from one generation to the next. That's why they invited you here. They need it, to keep radical Islam alive. The Internet is killing them, and they know it. The only way their lifestyle survives is a bloody war with the West. War keeps them in power. They love war, and they love radical Islam. Alexander the Great married a Pashtun princess to get out of the place, so I hope you brought wedding rings." He laughed at his own joke and then continued, "If peace comes, they will make war against each other for a while, and that's bad for business but good for you."

He waved his hand and said, "The Chinese are masters." I winced at the mention of the Chinese. "In ten years, they will be the major influence on the planet, and they won't ever fire a shot in anger. Americans keep twenty trained diplomats in their embassies around the world, while the Chinese keep thousands. They influence everything, and they keep their ears to the ground. They have no interest in a shooting war, but they seek power, and they know real power is soft power not military might. They will soon own all the natural resources of Africa and South America, while the United States will bleed in Afghanistan. They realize power is diplomacy, economic interest and open markets, and the wise use of information. They don't yet own the Internet, but in ten years, they will, and just like the Russians, if you control information, you control people."

His arguments made sense, so I said, "I am only a Soldier stuck in this situation, but I think you underestimate our capabilities. We learned the lessons of Vietnam."

He smiled, laughed, and then continued his lecture. He said, "America knew 911 was coming, yet you did nothing about it. You may start this war with surrogates, but eventually, you will send Regiments, Brigades, and Divisions, and when that day comes, you will have played directly into their hands. All Al Qaeda attacks are designed specifically to draw you here, and magically"—he snapped his finger—"you are here."

I interrupted and said, "What do you mean about the 911 attacks?"

Chad turned his head quickly, and Ray looked on with renewed interest.

He said, "As early as June 2001, you knew you would get hit. By July 2001, you knew it would be a major terrorist action. By August 2001, your government knew it would be somewhere in the greater New York City area, yet your government did nothing. You have no one to blame but yourselves." I raised my eyebrows. This was the first I had heard of any such forewarning intelligence. I looked at Chad. He looked away. Judging by Chad's reaction, at least, some parts of this story were true. This was turning out to be an interesting discussion, but it was all history, and we had a mission to work, so I pointed the conversation toward in Laden, the Taliban and Al Qaeda.

He smiled at the mention of Bin Laden. "Tomorrow," he said, "you will meet some very powerful men and when you mention Bin Laden's name, they will laugh. He is a lightweight. He is an amateur who is not well considered by the old guard. He was a late comer to the mujahedeen and never really proved himself. He is looked upon here as the spoiled rich kid who has never worked for anything in his life." His voiced deepened as if to emphasize his point, and he said, "These people are tribal and brutal. The West is not ready for the brutality." He turned back toward the fire and said "You have a choice. The choice is Islamic fundamentalist who requires a war to retain power or those in the drug trade." He tugged at his belt, then said, "The fundamentalist need you. They must have an open war with you in order to indoctrinate their young. They are generally opposed to drug trade. Those in the drug trade, while claiming great allegiance to Islam"—and I noted the sarcasm in his voice—"need unencumbered production and shipping routes. The Taliban has some success against the drug lords over time, appealing to Islamic values, but it has been overemphasized and far less accurate than reported. The drug lords would fight the Taliban for a while, but once you begin to interfere with the drug business, they will quickly find common ground." He pointed at Chad and said, "And that, gentlemen, is what you must avoid." He then said, "Al Qaeda will move to Pakistan and work to destabilize that government, providing the West with a much greater problem than planes flying into buildings."

I asked, "So how would you solve the problem?"

Using my line, he said, "I am only a poor farmer trying to inch out a living." He thought for a few moments and said, "The only strategy that works is to punish and leave. Form an alliance with the drug lords against the Taliban and Al Qaeda. Gain control of the cities, if you must, transition power quickly, within months, back to the Afghans, and get out of the country. Leave only small cells, but never, ever, bring Regiments, Brigades, and Divisions." He turned slightly as if talking directly to Chad and said, "Find the common ground now with the Pakistanis. They are infiltrated, but many want closer ties with you. Work with them to mitigate Al Qaeda within their borders. Do whatever it takes to make Pakistan a staunch ally. Eventually, the Taliban will lose strength because it has nobody to fight. It may fight itself and fractionalize, but that is the Afghan way. Civil wars happen. America always over reacts. Let them sort it out. Eventually, the strongest will survive." He pointed a fat finger toward us and said "Either way, it's not, nor will it ever be, worth your blood and treasure to fight a long war here."

Chad was processing every word. He turned to warm his back against the fire, raised his eyebrows and said, "Most importantly, don't screw with the opium trade. It is the Afghan economy. The last time the CIA was here, it encouraged the mujahedeen to grow opium to finance their war with the Russians, so if you're looking to see how the drug finance operations work, I suggest you start with your own files. If the West has a drug problem, then decrease the demand, but don't mess with the suppliers. Those in the drug trade will be your staunchest allies with two preconditions. First, you don't mess with their business, and second, allow them to fight the war in the traditional Afghan way with brutality. If you come here and start an antidrug campaign, they will turn quickly. The Taliban are not the best and brightest in this society, but the drug lords are. They are capitalist, and they are smart."

He nodded, as if he had given us all the wisdom we required. Maybe he did. At this point, all I wanted to do was think and get ready for tomorrow.

BACK IN THE ZONE

We awoke early the next morning. It was a beautiful fall day. Scottie and his family greeted us warmly. We thanked them for being gracious host. As we exited the mansion, I noticed three well-kept Chevrolet Suburbans. Scottie gathered us around the hood of the lead vehicle.

He said, "I need eighty-eight thousand US dollars to bribe our way through Turkmenistan and into Afghanistan. You will ride in the middle vehicle. My boys will provide security in the front and rear vehicles. Once we get there and I introduce you to Mr. O, you keep the middle vehicle." His asking for the bribe money up front didn't seem to startle Chad or Ray. Chad nodded at Ray who went to his gear, came back, and counted out the money on the hood. Scottie divided up some of the money to his crew. Soon we were driving.

These were comfortable vehicles with plenty of room, and they were not uncommon in this part of the world. We continued to travel north, and occasionally, Scottie would take out his phone and call someone as he finalized the deal. We crossed the border at Charjew. It was smooth, and I watched closely as one of the boys handed cash to the officer in charge. Turkmenistan is a desert county, reminding me of the high California desert. The Soviets built canals for irrigation. They were massive projects and needed repair. We were on a southwesterly track and soon entered the town of Mary. Legend had it that Mary, the mother of Jesus, was buried here. It was an oasis town, and we stopped for an extended lunch break. Scottie liked me, but he was cool toward Ray and downright cold toward Chad.

As we traveled, Scottie reemphasizes all his points from the previous night. He told us, "The Russians attacked using two main avenues of approach. One from where you previously tried to cross at Termiz, attacking south to Kabul and then to Kandahar. The second avenue was farther to our west from Kushka to Herat, then to Farah, and linking up with the other forces at Kandahar. They gained control over the major cities but never really expanded their control into the countryside. Their logistics were so poor that reports of Russian Soldiers starving to death were accurate. They did install an air bridge into Kabul, but it became an excellent target. As a result, all the Soviets ever really controlled were a few major towns and, about half the time, the routes between the major cities." His attention to detail was remarkable, and he often referred to Soviet Motorized Infantry Regiments by their numerical designations and then referred to those who replaced them over time.

I said, "You have a remarkable memory."

He replied, "When it's your job to know other people's business, then you best know it well, or you either starve or die. As you can see, I didn't starve." He may have been a spy, a drug dealer, or whatever, but he was helpful.

We crossed the border and the river about one hundred kilometers east of the town of Gushgy. Once again, the bribery operation went smoothly. We were in Afghanistan. We turned east toward the town of Meymaneh. It was high desert with rings of mountains in every direction. As the sun went down, we saw the outskirts of the town. I noticed three other vehicles joined our convoy. One was in the lead, and the remaining two were trailing our last vehicle. We made contact.

We moved through the town and began to climb in the darkness. It was becoming difficult to see anything beyond the headlights. We rounded a sharp curve, and the lead vehicle stopped and then moved away to park. Several men with rifles were directing traffic. They moved us to a very specific spot. A group of bearded men wearing the traditional Afghan headdress were waiting for us. Scottie pulled himself out of the vehicle, while the rest of our crew lingered behind him. He spoke to them in a language I didn't understand, and they were full of hugs and smiles. It appeared to be a reunion of sorts as all were genuinely happy to see him. Chad followed directly behind him, then Ray, and I pulled up the rear. Scottie turned and reached past Chad and Ray and grabbed me by the arm. He introduced me to Mr. Obar. He was an older man with a big smile and bad teeth. He hugged me. He was a stout man who sent me shaking hands and hugging several others within the impromptu receiving line. I was followed by Chad and then Ray. We were ushered into the home. It was a brick home with a commanding view of the valley and town below. A table filled with hot steaming dishes was placed in front of us. Mr. Obar made a short speech and insisted we sample the food. I grabbed my plate and moved to a corner where I had a better view of the crowd and my surroundings. There are nine of us including Scottie's men and seven of Mr. Obar's folks. I saw several men outside with rifles slung over their backs. They were guards, but I was uncertain as to the threat. You didn't need to speak the language to realize that Scottie was the most popular man in the room. He knew each of the hosts by name and seemed to have some sort of a joke or story on each one of them. They, ate and laughed, listened to his stories, and then laughed some more.

We continued eating for several hours. At times, it appeared the conversation got serious, but Scottie remained the life of the party. It took him a full hour to say his good-byes. He worked the room like a pro.

Finally, he grabbed me, and we walked out to his vehicle. He said, "Good luck with your mission and your invasion. When you leave your mountains again, come here and visit. You are always welcome."

I said, "I appreciated the gesture, but I was just an old Soldier along for the ride."

He smiled and held up two fingers. "Remember two things, lad. Don't screw with the opium trade and let them fight the war their way." He moved into the back seat and stretched out. We shook hands, and he said, "Start moving. It's a long ride back to Uzbekistan." The room was much quieter when I returned. Chad and Ray attempted to corner Mr. Obar, but he wasn't talking strategy tonight. We would start fresh in the morning.

The three of us were shown into a large room on the backside of the house. The only view from the window was the side of a mountain.

Chad said, "Now that Scottie is gone, we will make progress." Within minutes, I was asleep.

I heard the buzz, but I couldn't determine its source or location. It continued to buzz, and suddenly, Chad bolted upright and began rummaging through his pockets. It hit me. It was my cell, not his. I jumped and grabbed for my pants and found the cell phone. I answered. Chad was standing nearly on top of me. It was the boss, but I could hear numerous other voices in the background.

He said, "I'm putting you on speaker. Give me an update?" and we both spoke nearly at the same time.

He was quicker than I on placing me on the speaker, and I said, "I really need to pee."

This was met with some laughter on the other end. I handed the phone to Chad and walked into the toilet and relieved myself. I walked back, took the phone from Chad, and said, "We made link-up with Mr. Obar, and tomorrow, we begin discussing options."

A gruff voice that I didn't recognize interrupted and said, "What is your view of the situation?"

My response was quick. I said, "I just told you my view of the situation." A silence fell over the phone, and all of the background noise was gone.

The boss said in a quiet tone, "I think maybe introductions are in order. You're on the phone with the Secretary of Defense."

Chad's eyebrows rose in arches. I shook my head and said, "I don't normally pee in front of the Secretary of Defense, so my apologies." I heard laughing in the background.

The Secretary of Defense said, "Very good, who is this guy?"

The boss interrupted and said, "Sir, I will brief you." I heard a series of whispers that I couldn't make out over the phone lasting for more than a minute.

The Secretary's voice then said, "Since you are from Carolina, I will call you Sandlapper." Hillbilly would have been more appropriate, but it wasn't the time to correct the Secretary of Defense.

"Sandlapper," he began, "tell us what you think of the situation thus far." I was put on the spot and the only reasonable military response I could give came from our conversations with Scottie.

I said, "We were greeted warmly by Mr. Obar. Our first impression is if we want his assistance, then we don't interfere with his business operations." I listened and then said, "He is the less powerful of the two, and we are counting on him to arrange a meeting with Mr. K." I listened and then continued, "I don't have a clue as to how K2 is going."

I heard talking in the background but could not make it out. This went on for several minutes. I anxiously held the phone. Finally, the boss came back on the line and said, "Call me back once you talk to Mr. Obar. Work fast."

And the line went dead. I had known him for years. He was as calm as they come. He understood tough missions, and he knew we were doing all we could, so his last comment caught me by surprise.

Chad and I couldn't go back to sleep. We moved cautiously through the home and found a seat on the small outside deck. We startled several guards, but once they realized we were not attempting to exit, they calmed down. We sat silently for a while; then, he began to speak.

He said, "Africa is my specialty. I was successful so they rewarded me with missions in China, then Bosnia and Kosovo." He looked at me and said, "I have a family in Virginia, but I never see them." I nodded, wondering what prompted the conversation. He continued, "I have been run ragged since the attack, and I don't know if it's worth it. It used to be an adventure, but now it's all stress."

I nodded, and we sat in silence. Finally, I said, "Look, the faster we get this mission complete, the faster we can get home." He agreed and we sat in silence waiting for the rest of the household to wake.

We ate breakfast and dawdled the morning away. We didn't see Mr. Obar until midmorning. We were escorted to a small room with a table. There were the three of us and three of his men, with two standing guard on the inside of the door. Ray was a proficient interpreter who often assisted his man with several English phrases. As with most meetings in this part of the world, we started with tea and pleasantries. I continued to hear the boss's words telling me to work fast. Finally, around noon, I began to speak.

I said, "We have been attacked, and this is personal. We are anxious to gain new alliances to help us with our mission." Mr. Obar rarely spoke; he just listened intently and smiled. I had been willing to talk and listen to Scottie, and he enhanced my reputation with Mr. Obar. As a result, when I spoke, all listened. He thought I was the man in charge. Chad was okay with the situation as long as it produced results. Chad's phone began to buzz, and he gracefully exited the room. They brought a wonderful lunch, and we continued to socialize without much business. Chad returned, and we continued with the small talk.

Finally, after lunch, Mr. Obar spoke directly to me. Ray didn't miss a word in the translation. He said, "I understand your situation and your mission. I am willing to help, but if we are going to fight and die together, then we must know one another." I took it as a sign he was willing to help, but it would be slowgoing. We took a long break and wandered back out into the open portion of the house. I noticed several beautiful race horses' photos hung in the hallway. Somebody here was a horse person. Mr. Obar noticed me looking at the photos and grabbed his interpreter. He began telling me the story behind each horse. Most were stallions, and he was a breeder.

I listened and said, "I would love to see them." He smiled and nodded. I was immediately escorted out the door and into the back seat of a large Ford Dual Tire Farm truck. Mr. Obar joined me on the other side, and the interpreter jumped in the passenger seat. The driver sped off with a vehicle in front and one in the back. My rifle and pistol remained in my room, but I kept the Magnum revolver on my hip. The speed loaders were in my vest, so I only had six rounds. If this was a capture scenario, I would at least get off a few rounds.

As the truck moved down the mountain, Mr. Obar continued to talk horses, and the interpreter continued to turn toward me, and I would smile. I was out of intelligent questions. We arrived at an immaculate stable, which easily housed twenty horses. I was in Central Asia, but it looked like Lexington, Kentucky, with a series of white fences in all directions. He jumped from the truck, and we walked down the line, discussing each horse through the interpreter. The stalls were the largest I had seen and immaculate, almost as if they were mucked hourly vice daily. Finally, he began to smile as if showing me his most prized possession, and we were in front of Galaxy. Galaxy was his prize stallion. He was a big horse and easily stood well over sixteen hands. He opened the stall door and invited me in. I slowly approached the stallion and began stroking his neck. I began bragging on him, and then with some confidence, I reached down and squeezed his front leg, forcing him to raise his hoof. Mr. Obar was in full smile at this point and was yelling. Soon, one of the stable hands produced a hoof pick, and I cleaned the horse's feet. This thrilled him. The good news was he was happy; the bad news was I was out of horse knowledge.

We stayed around the barn for another hour or so, walking and talking. Before long, the sun would set. I noticed he waved off his security, and they were no longer following. We entered into a large feed room. A servant brought tea, and we sat in small wooden straight-backed chairs. The interpreter began to pull up a chair, but Mr. Obar waved him out of the room, and we were alone. I drank my tea, not knowing what to expect. He removed his turban and rubbed his hair. He was balding with gray on the sides.

Then, in English, he asked, "What do you propose?" I smiled; he smiled.

I said, "We want to overthrow the Taliban, kill Bin Laden, and destroy Al Qaeda as an organization." He nodded. I continued, "We are massing forces now and will use all available military means to see these objectives met. Our strength is in air power, and ideally, we use that power in cooperation with local forces to destroy the enemy." He nodded. I continued, "We have sophisticated equipment enabling us to kill the enemy with precision, and we will use massive air strikes to weaken the enemy prior to executing direct fire assaults."

He nodded again and then asked, "And what of the Afghan?"

I said, "The Afghan is our ground force. We will embed our forces with the Afghan units bringing communications and access to air power." I then stated, "These things allow victory over the Taliban."

He nodded again and said, "When do you propose to begin?"
I answered, "As soon as possible."

I was impressed by his language skills and his sentence structure. He was a well-educated man. He leaned forward and said, "Al Qaeda will continue to attack you as long as they exist, but it is possible to run the majority out of the country. They live with the Pakistani pigs now so that is where they will run." This time, I nodded and he said, "The Taliban are crazed zealots who have committed atrocities against the Afghan people. They preach in the name of Islam, but they defile everything they touch."

I nodded and said, " Bin Laden?"

He leaned back in his chair and said, "You have made him what he is, but he is nothing more than an errand boy. He is a weak man. In the West, you might call him a sissy boy, and he is rich and arrogant, but he is not one of us." I nodded. He continued, "I can raise an Army, but I have many enemies in my own region that will fight against me. Armies costs money, so I assume you are willing to pay?"

I nodded. I didn't understand his statement about his enemies, but I had his help. I wasn't a diplomat, and I wasn't a negotiator. I had a 2.6 in history from Appalachian State and learned to barter with people at the local flea market, but I was making deals. He stood and walked to a corner of the feed room. He reached and pulled out a large sliding map of Afghanistan. It was an old acetate overlay, which showed the Soviet Troop Concentrations as of 1989. He motioned me forward, and for the next several hours, we discussed in detail how the Soviets failed and what a successful operation entailed.

By the time we returned to the house. Chad was in a low hover. I recounted my afternoon and conversation. He was mesmerized. Mr. Obar told us that we would talk more after the evening meal.

I said, "He speaks English better than I do."

Chad said, "You don't have a Master's Degree from Oxford." When we met again, he spoke English and entertained us with how stupid the Russians were. Some of his stories were a bit off-color, but he was an excellent talker. Even Chad was laughing. After we finished, we moved back to the original room. He began by telling us that he and Mr. Kalid had a long history and some of it was unpleasant.

We discussed how to recruit an Army, how to provide for it logistically, and how to control it by embedding US Soldiers. We discussed the wise use of air power and how it would allow ground forces full freedom of maneuver. We discussed major objectives, targets, and built an initial timeline. Chad continued to raise the Kalid issue, and each time, Mr. O avoided the question. We continued to discuss and draw plans on an old teacher's chalkboard. After each drawing, Chad photographed and stored it on his phone. Around midnight, we took a break and Chad went outside to make his nightly report. When he returned, he told me to push for a union between Kalid and Obar.

We reconvened, drank more tea, held more discussions, and talked further. We pushed for an alliance between Kalid and Mr. Obar. He did not concede but began talking to us about other leaders in the northern portion of the country that would be profitable in an alliance. It was clear he was providing options. He told us the men were strong warriors and would accomplish the most difficult missions. He strongly encouraged us to research them, knowing he had piqued Chad's interest. We listened, took names, wrote on the chalkboard, photographed the chalkboard, and talked more. Finally, after much pressure, Mr. Obar conceded he would arrange a meeting with Mr. Kalid. We broke for the night, and I walked to the road to call.

I dialed the number and heard a dull roar in the background. It wasn't the boss. Being polite, I asked for the boss and was told to render my report. I hesitated and was told to hold. The next voice I heard was the gruff voice of the Secretary.

He said, "Please be quiet, I need to hear this report. Sandlapper tell us what you know."

I reported our conversations and concluded that he would arrange a meeting with Mr. Kalid. I also said, "There is tension between Mr. Obar and Mr. Kalid and that Mr. Obar provided us a list of his recommended allies." Finally, I said, "The CIA took photos of our planning session notes and sent them to their headquarters."

I heard a groan. The Secretary gave an order to go off-speaker. He was blunt. "Sandlapper, you send all reports to us. Get the photos and get them to us as soon as possible. This is a military mission, not an intelligence mission. You report to me, not to the agency. I want everything the CIA collected, do you understand?"

I was standing at attention, as if I was being admonished by a senior officer. I answered with a firm "Yes, sir." The line went dead. Apparently, cooperation was not the order of the day in Washington.

Chad was sleeping when I returned. I asked him to step outside with me. He gave me a puzzled look but complied. I told him what I needed. He shook his head and said, "When we say we're all in this together, it really means me, you, and Ray." He went back to his bunk, grabbed his phone, asked for mine, and within minutes, sent everything he had photographed. He turned to me and said, "From my first day in training at the agency, it was drilled into me that the CIA has two lifetime enemies, the Russians and the US Military." We went to sleep.

I slept as long as I could and wandered around the house. We did not see Mr. Obar until the afternoon. He took all of us to the feed room where we continued the discussions from the previous night. He was called away several times to talk, and we could see him pacing with a cell phone on the other end of the barn. Chad's phone buzzed and he went to the opposite side of the barn.

Chad returned and said, "We have vetted the names Mr. Obar gave us, and all are second-tier guys. They are mujahedeen with warrior backgrounds, and they all hate the Taliban. They are not all in the drug business. It will take months to determine if they have ties to Al Qaeda."

Mr. Obar returned and said, "I have arranged a meeting with Mr. Kalid. I have business to attend, but you stay here and plan. We will bring you food."

I called Scottie. He said, "You made a good impression on my family and must come back and visit."

I went to the point and read the list of names as best I could pronounce them to him. I said, "We need your assessment on this." He laughed and said, "You are beginning to see the world through Afghan eyes. Remember, lad, the enemy of my enemy is my friend." He knew two of the men, told me they were great warriors and several of them tie directly to Ahmad Massoud.

We were escorted back to the house, again with no sign of Mr. Obar. Our only instructions were to be ready to travel. Chad and I called in our reports but, this time, without much fanfare. It occurred to me it was the weekend in the States, and people had lives to lead, even in the middle of a war. I wondered if the entire furor had died down, and if the television stations were still showing planes flying into the buildings. Americans would be patriotic, but I wondered for how long.

We were up early and ready to travel. One of his men told us we were going to Kala to meet Mr. Kalid. Kala was a long drive, and we would skirt south of Mazar-e-Sharif. It was a Taliban stronghold. In some ways, the Taliban were akin to the Russians. They had firm control of the cities, but their influence and power decreased the farther you went into the country. I was thinking about Clay County, which is about as far from Raleigh as you can get. We were closer to six other state capitols than our own, so the state-level politicians didn't come often. People who live away from cities are different. They are self-reliant and independent.

We passed several checkpoints. The Taliban was expecting a repeat of their Russian experience with an attack from the north. They were everywhere. Our convoy consisted of five vehicles. Mr. Obar wanted to show strength. He was well-known in these parts, so we easily navigated the checkpoints. All three of us had scraggly beards, so we were beginning to blend in with the population. We were passing through the high desert. It reminded me of the trip from Las Vegas to Barstow, California, except here there were no casinos.

We veered sharply to the east as we approached Kala and climbed a steep mountain. It took a while for the vehicles to climb the steep road. The next to last vehicle got stuck, and it required a chain to pull the small truck up the steep mountainside. The summit was a sizeable plateau with several good-sized tents and warming fires. He has put on a show. It's no wonder it took him most of the day yesterday to coordinate. We entered into this place via the back side using a very steep road. Chad pointed and said, "There is a much wider and better road on this side of the mountain. I wonder why we didn't come up from this side. It's a great view."

Several smaller convoys arrived. They came up the mountain using the same steep road. Mr. Obar began the introductions. He invited several of the second tier men we discussed earlier. To a man, they apologized for the attacks undertaken by the rouge group Al Qaeda and insisted an attack of that nature is not the honorable Afghan way. They apologized for knowing Al Qaeda. They all said that they were ready to fight the Taliban.

Mr. Obar introduced us to Mr. Kamil and Mr. Mannel. Both were in their midforties, were ambitious, with significant political and social ties. Both fought the Russians as young men. Mr. Kamil was a man who liked to posture. Using Ray as an interpreter, he immediately began telling us of his military exploits. In the end, he spits as if to spit on the Russians.

The crowd continued to grow. By late afternoon, over two hundred people gathered on the mountain plateau. It had a commanding views in all directions, and we could see Kala in the distance. We were mingling as if this were a social gathering. Many of the men exchanged hugs and were visibly excited. Mr. Obar's troops began calling for our attention. We gathered looking down the gentle slope. They wanted us to come closer. They wanted a formal receiving line for Mr. Kalid. We were ushered toward the front. We saw the convoy of vehicles working its way up the gentle slope. It had a small truck in the lead followed by three Chevrolet Suburbans with another small truck in the rear. As they worked their way closer, Mr. Obar turned and faced toward the arriving convoy. It was less than a half mile away.

The sound was deafening. I winced from the explosion. The sand slapped hard against my face burning my eyes, and several of the Afghans standing next to me dropped to the ground. My hand instantly grabbed for my pistol, but there were no targets. The ball of fire raced toward the afternoon sun. I focused on the convoy. Nothing remained but twisted hulks of burning steel. My first thought was a missile strike. I heard the wailing all around me. Mr. Obar quickly turned to the crowd and ordered his men to go forward and help survivors. They raced down the hill. He then turned and yelled at the crowd, "The Taliban killed Brother Kalid, and we must take a mujahedeen's revenge against the Taliban." All those around me screamed in unison. I looked at Chad. This was very suspicious. Anything resembling a Northern Alliance must revolve solely around Mr. Obar. He killed the competition.

Mr. Obar is a bright and industrious man. His men publically confirmed Mr. Kalid and his men are dead. He gathered us in the large tent and spoke calmly to the crowd. Ray listened and scribbled notes where I could read them.

Obar said, "War with the Taliban is now. Go home and bring Afghan men to fight. America helped us defeat the Russians. The attack on America was cowardly and not the Afghan way. The Taliban ruined our country. We will observe three days of mourning for the great Kalid. Two days later, we will assemble in the northern caves." He walked to his convoy. We followed. I pulled out our driver and took his seat. We needed to talk and report.

I called the boss and reported the assassination. He said, "Tier one infiltrating now. Two Special Forces companies with communications gear, along with Air Force Special Operations teams, infiltrate tomorrow. We need the Termiz Bridge. It allows easier access to the country."

Mr. Obar was masterful. Radio stations as far away as Pakistan were already reporting Kalid's assassination by the Taliban. Tier One conducting special reconnaissance meant that special people were seeking strategic targets. I wasn't sure if that meant Bin Laden or Taliban leaders or just plain reconnaissance. More Americans on the ground made me feel better, but I was mindful of Scottie's words. Feeling better didn't win wars. The Special Forces companies as well as the Air Special Operations teams would link up with Mr. Obar's forces. The Afghans would provide the Infantry, and our teams would provide communications and air support. We needed to seize the bridge. To accomplish that mission, we needed Mr. Obar.

Chad said, "Ray and I are to work the capture of the bridge with you." I nodded. He looked at me and said, "We will work the capture of Mazar-e-Sharif. Once we get those objectives, we drop from this mission."

I was shocked. I assumed we were in this until the end, but that was not the case.

THE BLOODIEST DAY

The next several days were busy. We greeted the Special Forces companies, established communications, and did our best to keep those in America informed. We worked a plan to seize the Termiz Bridge. The Uzbek's were cooperative, but it was tense in Turkmenistan.

We linked the teams with Afghan forces. Each was self-sufficient and brought the critical capabilities of communications and air power. Even with these, we needed an Army. We required Mr. Obar's. For the majority of our Soldiers, this was their first war.

Mr. Obar was busy marshaling his forces and he and Chad continued to engage daily over money. Most of the time, their conversations were friendly, but as the size of his ground forces grew, these negotiations became worrisome. We were paying him to build a large Army, and he was producing. Each day, I would walk to his feed room, which served as his Tactical Operations center, and see the numbers increasing. We were initially concerned about weapons and ammunition. We worried how we would equip our newly bought Army, but we soon realized

Afghanistan was awash with every type of Soviet weapon manufactured as well as numerous ammunition caches.

Chad paid Mr. Obar in the millions, Obar paid his lieutenants in the thousands, the lieutenants paid their underlings in the hundreds, and the poor private at the bottom got paid a dollar per day. I had no idea of how much money was involved, but it was an everyday occurrence. Two additional very young-looking CIA agents showed up daily with more money. Mr. Obar saw it as an opportunity. From my perspective, I wanted retribution against Bin Laden, but I also didn't want to make the same mistakes the Soviets made by coming here for an extended campout. I thought often about Scottie's advice. The war is winnable, but don't send your Regiments, Brigades, and Divisions. It might costs us a fortune, but better to have them fight for their country than us fight for their country.

Our first action would be the bridge at Termiz. I spent one day in reconnaissance of the bridge. I sought out Mr. Obar, who was becoming increasingly harder to talk to due to the dramatic rise in his stature, to discuss the bridge. Mr. Obar spoke better English than I did, but he was insistent that his two new generals, Kamil and Mannel, attend the briefing, so I used Ray as the interpreter. I briefed a simple operation with a force attacking from west to east and flanking the Taliban position guarding the bridge. The Taliban were expecting us to use the bridge so they reinforced it with members of the Afghan national Army. We did not require more than a company of his Infantry.

He listened politely and said, "It is unnecessary to capture the bridge." I was puzzled but insistent that we gain control of the bridge. It was our lifeline from K2, and without it, things would be difficult. Mr. Obar smiled and said, "The Taliban will abandon the position." Sensing my frustration, Mr. Obar walked me over to his board and said, "An attack on the bridge is viable, but a better target is the capture of Mazar-e-Sharif."

I was thinking small, and he was thinking big. All along, he envisioned to capture the most populous city of the north and use it as a base of operations. It had political and social significance. The Taliban massacred thousands here in 1998. He continued, "Once those on the bridge know we are attacking the city itself, they will turn and run away as we are behind them."

It was viable. Mr. Obar was not one to write detailed operation orders; he simply told Kamil that he would attack from west to east, and he told Mannel that he would attack north to south. He asked when each General would be ready, and both replied the day after tomorrow. It worked for me, and I agreed to work the link-up operations and promised air support.

I dialed the number and waited for a response. I didn't know who would answer, but they needed to know that we were going after big targets, and this war was getting underway. The boss answered. I was relieved. He sounded exhausted. I told him our plan, and he listened quietly. I could hear him thinking from a world away.

He said, "Seize the bridge tomorrow, see if Obar will assist, and then work the town the next day. Use our guys, if required, but gain control of it. They will be ready to cross."

I was confused. I said, "Sir, I like Obar's plan. It makes sense."

He said, "I acknowledge all, but this is a war of retribution and vengeance. Strategy isn't at the forefront of anyone's thought, but good people will get fired if we don't get the bridge." "Get the bridge tomorrow."

I barged into a meeting in order to see Mr. Obar. I asked to speak with him alone, and he agreed. We walked outside on the deck overlooking the valley.

I said, "The attack on Mazar-e-Sharif is strategic and insightful. You gain our full cooperation, but we need the bridge." I paused, picking my words carefully, and said, "The bridge had little strategic significance to you, but it is a very big deal to my bosses." He nodded, turned his head, and looked at me. I continued, "I propose we capture it tomorrow and then attack the city as planned."

He frowned and said, "War is too important to be run by politicians. You have many politicians in America who demand action. This is a small matter, but it sets a poor precedent for our relationship."

He decided to educate me. He walked me to the map and began, "The Russians made similar mistakes. They tried to micromanage the war and failed. Control, in war, must be given to the mujahedeen leader on the ground to make the best decisions he can. The Europeans make much talk of war being an extension of politics, but this is all horse dung. War is the failure of politics, and when politics cease, war begins. The Russians lost because they confused politics with war. War is war and must be left to those who know best to prosecute it, and once a winner has been decided, politics can begin." It was an interesting perspective and one that somebody at Fort Leavenworth could discuss. All I was after was a bridge and if he didn't want to send folks, then we would do it ourselves. Finally, he turned and said, "We will capture the bridge as an appeasement to your political masters."

We took a company of General Mannel's men along with a Special Forces team. Once we captured the bridge, we would move south and begin the attack on the city. We looked like a scene from the *Beverley Hillbillies* with trucks and cars of all shapes and sizes bouncing along dirt trails. We moved to the river bank approximately ten kilometers away from the bridge and staged ourselves for the night.

The night was colder than expected and the sky was full of stars. Chad and Ray were beside me because the CIA also wanted the bridge. The Afghans built dozens of warming fires and a few of the men caught fish. It looked like we were in cookout mode. This alarmed some of the U.S. Soldiers, and the party atmosphere caused enough concern that Ray and I mentioned it to the Afghan major who was in charge. He was an older man with a thick graying beard. His name was Major Abadid and he was one of Mr. Obar's favorites. Initially, we had a hard time convincing him of our concern, but once he understood we all jumped into the Suburban and began a trek around the outside perimeter. Ray did a good job, and he said, "Guards are all around you. They are positioned high and will see the enemy coming." He pointed at a peak and said, "Look and see he has climbed the peak. All my scouts have cell phones." They didn't have any night vision equipment but given the moonlight, they didn't need it. He said, "The penalty for failing to guard the main body is death." I nodded and he continued to talk and Ray continued to interpret. "Not for one but for all." I asked Ray what he meant, and he said, "All guards on the force die if the main body is compromised, not just the single Soldier. We kill the entire guard force."

Chad said, "I get the feeling this guy means what he says."

Early the next morning we moved to our forward assembly area. We moved as close as possible without being compromised. We would attack west to east and hit the bridge on its left flank. Our guys lazed the center of the target area and before long we could hear the jets screaming across the sky. The Afghans stopped everything and watched the airshow despite our best efforts to keep them focused. Suddenly, the explosions started and the bombs landed in the center of the enemy compound. The Afghans cheered and then began a foot race toward the bridge. They were firing in all directions. It looked like a mob. We rushed forward and followed the first wave into the compound. Most of the Taliban were dead, but several returned fire and were killed. The Afghans began to loot the place. If it wasn't tied down, they loaded it in their trucks.

My phone buzzed. I answered, expecting it to be from a world way, instead it was the Task Force Commander on the other side of the river. He asked how long it would take to remove the mines from the bridge. I didn't know, but told him I would get it done. I went to Major Abadid and grabbed Ray to interpret. I said, "your men were brave and fought well."

He said, "I like the bombs, they make it easy."

I asked, "do you have anyone who can disassemble the mines on the bridge?" Ray had difficulty explaining the concept and he seemed amused.

I figured it was his arrogance talking and said, "We need to remove the mines and open the bridge. We have forces ready to cross." He nodded and began yelling. Four young Afghan's ran forward, cut the barbed wire, moved the wooden obstacles, and began to pick up the mines. I was horrified. Soviet mines have intricate anti-handling devices and once moved or tampered they explode. The Afghan's threw the mines into the river. I grabbed Ray and the Major and asked about the mines.

Ray understood and talked fast. He said, "We lost many children to Soviet mines. They like to play on the bridge. We removed the fuses years ago." I shook my head. Even Scottie didn't know.

I called the Task Force Commander. They came in a wide variety of vehicles ranging from motorcycles with sidecars to the ever fashionable Datsun/Nissan pickup truck and including several Hummers that carried communications and medical support. Chad, Ray, and I stood on the side of the road and waved. It was a long convoy with each vehicle carrying two to six Soldiers. I didn't know how many were coming, but this was more than I anticipated. A Ford Explorer passed, then circled back to our location. Two men got out of the vehicle. They were wearing a desert camouflage pattern battle dress I had not seen. One wore the rank of a Lieutenant Colonel and was the Executive Officer. The other wore the eagle of a full Colonel. I saluted the Colonel. I was wearing a red flannel shirt covered by a dark-blue sweatshirt, with a full beard and wearing a dark-blue Caterpillar hat. He smiled and returned my salute, introducing himself as the Task Force Commander of Task Force 191. I introduced him to Chad and Ray, and he asked if we could find a location to talk. His name was Colonel Stevens, and he was the Task Force Commander. His Executive Officer was Lieutenant Colonel Mark Smith.

The convoy continued down the road several kilometers, and we went to a hilltop. After we exchanged pleasantries, he asked for our assessment. Chad deferred to me, and I spent the next hour telling him all I knew about northern Afghanistan. Occasionally, Chad or Ray would add key details or facts, but overall, the briefing responsibility was mine. His mission was to link up with me and link his forces with the local Afghan leaders. His Task Force was the first wave, and he would be followed by three more large units. The US General Officer in charge planned to visit later tonight from K2, and I should brief him.

Finally, he said, "You look familiar. Where have you served?"

I said, "Basically, Fort Bragg," and I turned and moved back down the hill.

The Colonel moved his Task Force into a secure assembly area where they could join the fight. We spent several hours finding the link-up location, but once we were close, I saw it was classic Obar. He had several tents constructed in a secluded plateau at the top of a large mountain. It was difficult to find, and it was growing late in the afternoon. After dark, I doubt we would have found the site. Once we finally climbed to the top, I was amazed at the detailed view of the city. One tent was designed for operations, and he had several tables established with maps and drawings, one tent was filled with small chairs so he could brief his leaders, and the final large tent was his living and entertaining quarters.

I introduced Colonel Stevens to several members of Mr. Obar's staff. We had begun the full introductions when the Colonel's cell rang with word of inbound choppers seeking landing coordinates. This caused a mild panic among the US Soldiers, and they made their way to the other side of the plateau and hastily marked the landing zone. Soon, we heard two birds approaching. It was clear they didn't have room to land both. One of the birds went into a hover while the first landed, and in so doing, it uprooted the Operations' tent. Maps, tables, chairs, and people were scrambling in all directions. Several of the Afghans ran to hold down the remaining tents. It was embarrassing. Chad and I looked at Mr. Obar, and he said in perfect English, "Afghanistan is a difficult place to fly. Your pilots will require much instruction."

The first bird landed, and a rifle squad jumped out and acted as if they were in a hostile zone. It looked like a well-rehearsed war movie except there was no director to yell "Cut!" They spread out and established security with several attempting to run in full combat gear to the top of a small hill at the far edge of the plateau. They looked oafish and overloaded as they struggled up the hills. The pilots realized they did not have room to land, so the first bird took off and began circling the area. Anyone within twenty miles now knew something was happening on this particular hilltop in the middle of northern Afghanistan. Finally, the General landed with his large staff. He exited the craft in full combat gear and was followed by several Colonels, Lieutenant Colonels, a Command Sergeant Major, and a jittery young Captain who was attempting to carry multiple rucksacks. The second bird cut engines while the first continued to circle. The circling bird was making Mr. Obar nervous. He kept looking toward the setting sun and the helicopter.

We stayed with Mr. Obar. The general stopped several times and talked to Colonel Stevens. Colonel Stevens did the formal introductions. Mr. Obar was gracious, nodded politely, and smiled, but I didn't hear any semblance of an apology from the General or his staff for knocking down the Afghan tent. The General turned toward the three of us. He shook Chad and Ray's hand and then stood directly in front of me.

He gazed into my eyes and said, "You army?"

I nodded and said, "Yes, sir."

He stared at me and said, "You will be welcome on my team when you look like an Army officer. Shave your face. I don't need officers going native."

I nodded and didn't say a word. He moved forward as if he knew where he was going and walked into the briefing tent. This threw Mr. Obar off as he intended to entertain them in his tent.

Chad picked up on this and rerouted the group into the correct tent. He walked to me and whispered, "This man is dangerous."

I nodded but was still in shock from my introduction. I grabbed Colonel Stevens and, pointing to the circling chopper, said, "Not good for business." He agreed and sent one of his officers to work a solution.

After a few anxious minutes, the General told his staff to unload their combat gear and place it into a corner of the tent. I have few social graces, but I thought the meeting was awkward. We were joined by General Mannel and General Kamil, as well as key members of their staff. Servants brought hot tea, and Mr. Obar and the General moved off to a slightly secluded corner. The General was doing most of the talking with Mr. Obar simply nodding. One of the Colonels from the General's staff pulled me aside and said, "Who are you, and how did you get here?"

I said, "Sir, I'm JB, and I work at Fort Bragg."

He frowned and said, "You need to get cleaned up."

I said, "Sir, I don't have any uniforms."

He looked at me, gasped, and said, "The General isn't going to like that." He stared at me and said, "Don't you understand? This is not going to be a special operations war. It has already been decided. My boss is in command here. Do you understand?"

I nodded and said, "Yes sir." The General continued to talk, and Mr. Obar continued to listen and nod.

Finally, Mr. Obar moved the assembled group into the hastily reestablished Operations' tent. His mastery of English continued to surprise as he moved from table to table, pointing out key elements of the upcoming attack. He was fluent in talking tactics and, at one point, told the audience that he would use a pivot of maneuver in the final stages of capturing Mazar-e-Sharif. In reality, he was more comfortable talking tactics than any of the assembled audience. I once worked for a crusty old Colonel who told me that nothing scared a General Officer more than a tactics discussion.

When Mr. Obar concluded, the General spoke up. He spoke very loud and slow. He said, "We are allies and partners for a great and noble cause. We will fight side by side until we defeat the terrorist and together regain control of Afghanistan." The Colonel and several members of his staff began to clap and the Afghans followed suit. He continued, "We need an Afghanistan where peace is the norm and we can flourish." I was uncertain and leery of his use of the word "we," but that wasn't my problem. Finally, after much handshaking and further talks, the meeting broke up.

The Colonel who previously approached me returned and said, "Here is our cell phone. Ensure you use it and keep me informed. Don't use it to make personal calls. Do you understand?"

I was uncertain as to what he was talking about but was ready for rest before tomorrow's battle. Finally, as he departed, he said, "You need to get cleaned up and call me tomorrow. Do you understand?"

I nodded. The General and his entourage ambled back to their helicopter and headed north. Colonel Stevens and his men left soon thereafter.

I went back to the Suburban and searched my rucksack for a bar of soap. I didn't think I looked all that bad, but maybe I did. I tried to shave with some lather and my combat knife, but that was painful. My mind drifted. I thought about Jesus and how they plucked out his beard. It was painful. I finally went and got a pair of medical scissors from the kit. Eventually, I was clean-shaven.

I was up early the next morning and ready to move when one of Mr. Obar's aides came for me. I was escorted to the Operations' tent. Mr. Obar looked at me and began laughing. He could not believe I shaved. I took it in good humor.

He smiled and said, "Kamil's men were already moving and soon Mannel's. It is going to be a great day. When will we drop the bombs?"

I called Colonel Stevens but could not get an answer. The sun was coming up, and I walked back to the Suburban and asked Chad if he had any contact, thinking something was wrong with my phone. My phone buzzed, and it was Colonel Stevens. He said, "We are ready, but we still have teams that didn't make link up with their Afghan counterparts. I need your help."

I told Mr. Obar that we would begin air operations, but we still had a few units to link up with their Afghan counterparts. We worked through the details of the unit locations. This was more complex than it sounded as the Afghans didn't have any type of global positioning system, so deciphering the Afghan positions was far more art than science. Chad suggested that we drive to those locations and see if we could physically affect the link-up, and I agreed. He had two new money mule agents, and they were anxious to see the county.

The bombardment began before we left the plateau, and we could see massive explosions taking place around the town. We stopped, watched, and were soon joined by Mr. Obar and several members of his staff. It was impressive. I was uncertain if these were large bombs dropped from aircraft, or if missiles impacted, but either way, it was quite a show. Mr. Obar watched closely and then said, "It is time for the hard work to begin."

We moved south and then west in an effort to find the Afghan units. We didn't want to get in front of an attacking formation because most units will shoot first and question later. We were joined by the US Soldiers who searched in vain throughout the night. The unit consisted of ten vehicles consisting mostly of small trucks. They were tired, frustrated, and anxious to get into the fight. The explosions continued to our south and east, but the sounds were somewhat muffled due to the terrain. We continued for over an hour but to no avail. I am good with a map and finding my way. I was confident I could find this particular Afghan unit, but it was now midday. We began a slow turn almost due east and eventually picked up a small road heading directly toward the town. We entered the suburbs and passed broken down vehicles. We were on the right path. Soon, we began to see the signs of an attacking force with burned out vehicles, damaged houses, and eventually dead enemy.

We moved south into the center section of Mazar-e-Sharif. We approached the famous Blue Mosque where the cousin of Muhammad is buried. It was a beautiful structure and thankfully untouched by the chaos. We found the unit. Through Ray, we talked with the Afghan commander, and he was impressed with the bombing campaign. He had zero casualties and seemed excited to have US Soldiers with his formation. An additional Afghan Battalion made linkup on the left flank, and both units received orders to continue the attack to the far southern edge of the town.

We followed and saw nothing of significance with no real fighting, mostly driving. Once we reached the southern edge, we began to see the bombing effects. The missions, called by General Mannel's counterparts, made giant holes of former Taliban compounds. It was an awesome display of firepower, and we were joined by Colonel Stevens and several members of his staff.

He looked at me and said, "You were sold out by the martinets on the General's staff. They couldn't believe you had a beard." We stopped and ate rations. Colonel Stevens made several calls and asked, "Where did Mr. O move his headquarters? I need to talk to him about today's operations. We have another force crossing the river, and they will join us tomorrow."

Ray called and talked to Obar's staff. He had moved to the northeastern suburbs of the city. We would go to his headquarters. Altogether, we had five vehicles and over twenty US personnel.

Our plan was to head due west, get out of the city, and then turn north. We moved through several small streets, then managed to get on a decent westerly road. We passed multiple troop locations and saw every conceivable Soviet-era weapon. The Afghan Soldiers were in good spirits and established their cooking fires. We moved toward the suburbs on the far western edge of town and noticed a large formation of Soldiers in a wide variety of uniforms off to our right. We were less than two hundred meters from them, and it was odd.

Chad said, "Looks like they are having a victory parade."

Ray pointed and said, "Armies love their formations." Several were wearing long black religious garments.

I said, "Maybe a ceremony for the new recruits?"

Chad said, "There must be three or four thousand."

We slowed down. We were curious. We noticed two bulldozers working feverishly on the side of a small depression next to the formation. Ray said, "That's the first bulldozer I've seen."

Chad said, "It's odd that bulldozers are working during the ceremony."

We didn't notice the trucks mounted with machine guns until they fired. Chad hit the floor. I scanned, trying to make sense of what I was seeing. I said, "Machineguns!"

Chad screamed, "Oh my god! Oh my god!"

I jumped out and ran to the back of the vehicle. Colonel Stevens and his staff were dismounting and watching in horror. Eight or nine large caliber machine guns were mowing down the formation. It was a massacre. Colonel Stevens screamed, "Cease-fire! Cease-fire!"

My ears pained from the noise. The machine guns were grazing the formation. They were within a hundred yards. A few in the formation ran, but they positioned light machine guns on the flanks. I couldn't believe what I was seeing. They were Taliban, and our allies were killing them. I looked at Colonel Stevens. He was bent in half, vomiting. The CIA guys jumped from the vehicle, and all of us stood, gawking in amazement. In a minute, it was over. Like a routine duty, the Afghan soldiers started packing up their equipment and driving off. One of the bulldozers moved behind the formation and quickly began pushing the bodies into a large depression.

We just stood there. I glanced to the far side of the formation and noticed a small collection of vehicles on the knoll observing.

"Chad," I screamed, "who is on the hill?"

It was General Kamil. We saw him walk from his vantage point, enter his vehicle, and drive off. I heard the guttural sound of pain from several vehicles away. Chad opened the back of the vehicle, grabbed a camera, and began taking photographs.

He said, "Nobody is going to believe this." I grabbed for my phone and began taking photos. I walked forward, through a large drainage ditch and approached the mass of bodies. Chad and several US Soldiers followed. Some of the Taliban were still moving, but I didn't hear moans or cries for help. The Afghan machine gunners were ruthlessly efficient. Blood was everywhere. I was gagging. I needed to breathe and get control. I took photograph after photograph and tried to count the dead. My mind was racing and my body was shaking. Behind me, I heard the gut-wrenching cry and moan of our guys vomiting. It was ugly.

Chad screamed, "Bring me the camera connector from the bag!"

One of the new agents ran forward, stopped, bent over, and vomited.

Chad screamed at him, "Now!" and the agent tossed him the bag. I was standing beside him and watched as he inserted one end into the GPS and the other into his camera. He looked at me, his face flushed, and said, "Give me your camera." Each photograph now had a time stamp as well as the latitude and longitude embedded. The bulldozers continued to work as if we were invisible. Chad moved closer to the bodies and continued taking pictures. I walked beside him, and we moved toward the bulldozer.

I gagged, feeling the vomit rise in my throat. The carnage and blood were everywhere. I turned to Chad and said, "Why, God?"

He stared at me. He pointed toward the bodies and I pulled the camera and began taking photos. It looked like someone dumped hundreds of gallons of blood on bodies. It was gruesome and grotesque. My right hand trembled. I looked at their faces in a strange way to see if I could recognize anybody. Many were young, most were middle-aged, and each unmangled face looked as though it was still reeling from the pain of multiple large-caliber gunshot wounds. They used a combination of larger caliber 12.7-mm. and smaller 7.62-mm. weapons. They were quick and efficient in their killing. The 12.7-mm. was larger than a .50 caliber and was designed to destroy light armor, so those bullets tore easily through the mass of flesh, leaving it horribly disfigured. Arms, legs, and heads were scattered across the small hill, and the bulldozers just kept working.

In anger, one of our Soldiers raised his weapon and fired two rounds at the working bulldozer. I heard the rounds ricochet off the front blade and then saw Colonel Stevens running behind the Soldier, screaming, "Cease-fire! Cease-fire!"

LTC Smith, the Executive Officer, ran past Stevens and tackled the Soldier. Other Soldiers joined. Colonel Stevens and his men were in a fight with the young Soldier. The young soldier screamed, "Kill them!"

Chad walked the line, taking photographs as if he were a tourist. He paid no attention to the brawl taking place behind him and even went to within feet of the working bulldozers. I didn't know what to do. I closed my eyes. When I opened them, they were still there. I ran behind Chad and yelled, "I don't know what to do!"

He stared at me and said, "I don't know, JB! I don't know!" He shook his head, turned away from the carnage, and dropped to one knee.

I bent over at the waist, thought for a moment, straightened up, and said, "We record history and report."

I took the phone and was about to dial the number when Chad yelled, "Wait! We need to talk before we call."

Colonel Stevens and his men moved back to the far side of the convoy, while the bulldozer continued to push bodies into the depression and cover them. One dozer pushed, and the other dozer covered. It was mechanical and efficient. Chad and I were the last to cross the drainage ditch back to the convoy. Colonel Stevens and LTC Smith approached as well as Ray and the other CIA agents.

Chad took out a small notebook and said, "What did we see?" His face was flushed red, and sweat was dripping from under his cap. His hands shook.

Colonel Stevens said, "A massacre."

I nodded and added, "Ranging from young boys to old men." My hand was trembling, and I grabbed it and rubbed it hard.

Chad said, "Who did it?"

Ray, who was staring off into space, said, "It was Kamil. We all saw him. He is the devil who did this."

Lieutenant Colonel Smith added, "Yes, he was standing on the knoll. He gave the order."

Chad's hand was wavering as he wrote the answers. He looked up and said, "How many?"

I spoke first and said, "At least two thousand."

Colonel Stevens shook his head and said, "More, it's much more. I say at least three thousand." The young CIA agent turned away from us and vomited. Colonel Stevens looked back toward the carnage.

Ray said, "Chad, report twenty-five hundred. Let Langley sort it out. We need to get out of here."

Colonel Stevens turned back toward us and said, "What does it mean?"

Chad thought and said slowly, "It's ugly. It's politically sensitive." His body was shaking like he was freezing. He lowered his head and said, "Mr. Obar, and by extension General Kamil, were on our payroll, and they massacred prisoners of war, and we witnessed it."

I looked at the bulldozers and said, "We need to report."

Ray stared at me and said, "We need to get out of here."

I put my hand into my jeans, hoping they wouldn't notice my hand shaking.

Chad said, "I'm calling and you two"—he pointed at me and Colonel Stevens—"need to do the same." We walked in a different direction and began dialing phone numbers. The sun continued to go down, and the bulldozers continued to work.

A voice answered, and I said, "I have a report to render." I was told to standby. I waited a minute, and finally, the voice returned and said, "Give me your report."

I said, "The local time is 1711. I, along with members of the CIA and the Commander of Task Force 191, witnessed a war crime. We witnessed the massacre of between twenty-five hundred and three thousand captured Taliban Soldiers by machine gun. We are on the northeast corner of Mazar-e-Sharif. We saw General Kamil on the scene. I have photographs with embedded GPS coordinates." I listened and heard nothing.

Finally, the voice said, "You took photographs?"

"Yes," I said, "with GPS coordinates."

The voice said, "I am going to give you a complex e-mail address. If you write it down, destroy it. Send the photographs." I grabbed a pen and listened as the voice gave the address. My hand shook as I worked the letters and numbers. There was a long pause, and the voice said, "Thank you." The line went dead. It took me a few minutes to work the function on the phone, but I uploaded the photographs and hit the Send button.

I looked across the depression, and the bulldozers continued working. Colonel Stevens walked toward me and said, "Call the staff Colonel. I can't remember the turkey head's name, but you know how they are." I pulled his cell and dialed the number. The Colonel answered with only yes. I rendered the same report. The line was silent. I heard nothing and then said, "Sir, are you there?"

He was slow to respond, eventually saying, "Yes." I heard him sigh, and then he asked, "What did the CIA crowd do?"

I said, "Sir, the same as I did. We took photographs and then reported."

He said, "Standby." I stood, leaning on the front of the Suburban, rubbing my right hand. I was not going to look at the bulldozers. The temperature was dropping. I told myself the sudden drop in temperature was causing my hand to shake and my body to tremble. I walked to the back and grabbed my coat. I placed the phone down for a second, but I heard yelling coming from the other end. I placed the phone to my ear and heard the General shouting "Answer me!" at the top of his lungs.

"Sir," I said, "I am here."

He shouted, "Tell me what you saw!"

In as calm and professional manner as I could, I told him where we were and what we had seen. He said, "What is the CIA team doing?"

I said, "Sir, they are reporting."

He said, "Get me paper!" and I listened to voices in the background. He said, "Tell me the coordinates."

I asked, "Sir, do you want lat-long or military grid?"

This sent him over the edge, and he began yelling again. Finally, in my most respectful tone, I sent the coordinates first in latitude-longitude, and then in military grid reference.

He said, "What are you going to do?"

I paused and said, "We are going back to Mr. Obar's headquarters and report the incident."

He screamed, "No! You will not do that!"

Chad, Colonel Stevens, and LTC Smith gathered around and listened. His voice squeaked. He cleared his throat and said, "You will not tell anyone—repeat anyone—about what you saw. Do you understand?"

I said, "Sir, I understand." The phone went dead.

I turned and said, "Let's get moving. Get away from here." I moved to the driver's seat of the Suburban, cranked the engine, and started driving. I drove west and then veered back to the north until I found a small hilltop with good observation. I stopped the vehicle, got out, and guided the remainder of the vehicles into a circular position like wagon trains in the old West.

"Ray," I said, "start a fire."

Colonel Stevens and his guys continued to talk to the Soldier, and he appeared calmer. Chad, Colonel Stevens, and I gathered around the fire. Stevens speculated the General, who had multiple headquarters, was at K2, but nothing was certain. Chad and, later, Ray added the international perspective of what a public massacre like this meant to the war effort. I listened. I was still processing facts. I couldn't get the dead out of my mind. I asked myself, Was I any different than them?

Around midnight, Colonel Steven's phone buzzed. He said, "We meet the General at Mr. Obar's headquarters after first light." I liked the order. I didn't want to navigate throughout the night to find Obar's headquarters. We moved before dawn. We moved slowly until the sun rose, circling up the goat trails with our convoy.

We saw the helicopters coming over the horizon. This time, both landed, and nothing was blown down. The General, wearing only a black wool jacket over his fatigues, jumped from the chopper. He was followed by his entourage. His security detail didn't secure the birds but instead formed a walking perimeter for him as he made his way to the tent. He entered and went directly to Mr. Obar. They retreated to the corner. We stood and anxiously shuffled our boots. The tent flap opened. General Mannal and General Kamil entered. They shook hands with the General and Mr. Obar. Mr. Obar was stern. He spoke rapidly without an interpreter. General Kamil answered. I glanced at Ray, and he nodded.

Mr. Obar turned and spoke in soft, calm tones to the General.

He said, "General Kamil reports that one of his Commanders, whose son was killed and daughter raped by the Taliban, gave the order to fire on prisoners." The General nodded. Mr. Obar turned and made a sweeping hand motion. The tent flap flew open. Two large men escorted another. They held the man in the middle, and I noticed his hands were tied. Mr. Obar spoke to the man. The man nodded.

He faced the General and said, "This is the officer who gave the order." Suddenly, the two escorts stepped aside. Mr. Obar pulled a revolver from under his robe, aimed between the man's eyes, and pulled the trigger. The sound caused everyone to jump. I shuddered. Mr. Obar turned again and faced the General. He lowered his head and said, "I hope this concludes the matter." The General nodded. The escorts grabbed the dead body by his arms and pulled him from the tent. The meeting ended with handshakes.

My right hand trembled. The General walked from the tent and went to his chopper. The Colonel motioned for us and we walked to him.

He said, "This is an Afghan matter, and they resolved it. Do not discuss." He turned and walked toward his chopper.

MOMENTUM SHIFT

I SPENT THE morning thinking. This was an unusual place. I needed out. I needed to retire. I would soon be eligible. I thought about Lorraine, the kids, what jobs I could do, and then, the phone buzzed.

It was the boss. I wanted to tell him everything. He listened patiently to the beginning of my story and then interrupted, saying, "I know all about the massacre."

I guess he got the e-mail.

He said, "The CIA team is moving to Mazar-e-Sharif, and I owe you an interpreter. Stay with Mr. Obar and report. More forces are arriving, and it's getting complex." Finally, he said, "Hang in there, and I will join you soon." I was hoping for different orders, but it was what it was.

Around noon, I drove the CIA team to an old house on the outskirts of town. It was large by Afghan standards and was surrounded by a thick rock fence with ample room in the back to hide vehicles. This would be their northern operations center. Rolf and Curtis, from their original team, were already in place.

Chad said, "We are paying Obar electronically, so you won't see any more cash mules."

I said, "Great. Now I won't have anybody to talk with."

He laughed and said, "You don't talk anyway. It won't matter." He looked down, shuffled his feat, and said "Don't go native, man," and he handed me his secure GPS. "We will call you once in a while to check on your morale."

We shook hands. I would miss them.

When I arrived back in camp, Mr. Obar called for me. He immediately asked, "What do you know of the American media?"

I was surprised. He went on a rant about how he was called the Northern Alliance. It made him angry. He pointed at three recent *New York Times* newspapers, the oldest of which was three days old. I smiled. He realized I was not the culprit. This caused him to shake his head and eventually smile himself. He took me to the Operations' tent and showed me the plans for Kabul. We would move tonight to our new location and, within a few days, would be ready for the next assault.

Finally, he approached the issue. He said, "War is the natural state of the Afghan, and when there is no enemy, we fight among ourselves. I didn't approve the massacre. You do understand?"

I nodded. I anticipated he would discuss the tragedy of war and human loss, but he didn't.

Instead, he said, "My commanders lacked judgment. Rather than killing them"—he paused—"it would have been better to enlist them in our cause. It was another Brigade." I nodded again. He said, "Sometimes, a commander must punish personally…to get the correct…effect. Do you understand?"

I nodded again. He stared at me for several seconds and asked my view of his overall plan. I stammered for a few seconds and then managed to focus and pull together coherent thoughts. His operations crew began disassembling the tent around us, and our conversation ended.

He moved his headquarters at night. We moved along a series of dirt roads with no visible light. I was alone and the last vehicle in the convoy. The night turned colder than expected, and I had to roll the window down to stay awake. We climbed a step hill, and I was confident we were getting close, knowing his penchant for great high mountain views. We reached a nice plateau. The crews immediately began building tents and preparing for operations. I reclined the driver's seat and went to sleep.

I opened my eyes to daylight. It looked like we were on top of the world. The phone buzzed. It was the boss. He said, "Send me your grid. I have a package coming to you." Several Afghans were working off to the far right of my vehicle, and I wandered over. They emplaced a large telescope, much like those you see at scenic overlooks, except this one didn't cost a quarter. They encouraged me to look through the lens, and I could see an outline of a city. I attempted to ask the name of the city, but they tired of the language barrier and went back to work. I went to the Suburban, pulled out the map and the GPS. We were overlooking Kabul.

I heard the chopper before I saw it. My first thought was the General was coming and I needed to shave. The bird circled and landed several hundred meters away from the main camp. The pilot was skilled, and I assumed the General fired the previous group. I cranked the Suburban and made my away across several large ditches. The passengers were not in uniform.

A man dressed in blue jeans and wearing a ball cap came forward and said, "Are you JB?"

I nodded and he said, "I have a package for you."

"Wow," I said, "that was quick." A man exited the bird with a large rucksack that he couldn't get on his back without help. He grabbed an oversized duffel bag and jogged toward me. We placed his gear in the back. I shook his hand, and before we could speak, the bird was airborne and gone.

His name was Pete, and he was the interpreter. He seemed nervous and jittery. We bounced our way across the ditches back to the camp. I was tired from being up all night and nervous about the new addition.

"Pete," I said, "tell me about yourself."

He looked around the camp and said, "I'm a navy lieutenant, and I teach languages in California. I have a Doctorate and two Master's Degrees. I'm married with two kids. I don't have experience in this sort of thing, and I haven't camped out since Boy Scouts."

I nodded and said, "Welcome to Afghanistan."

Military academics wear the uniform, and many wear it well, but their focus is on academia, not on operational missions. He wore a standard issue Beretta 9-mm. pistol in a shoulder holster and was constantly adjusting himself. I pointed and said, "Cut off the straps and wear the weapon on your belt."

He stared at me and said, "I can't knowingly destroy government property."

I said, "Hand me your weapon. I will knowingly destroy government property." I cut the straps. He placed it on his belt. I said, "Get comfortable. You will sleep in the back seat. I sleep in the cargo hatch. It's a long night, so I'm going down. I will introduce you to the team here later."

He looked at me and said, "Where are you going down to?"

I shook my head and said, "I'm going to sleep."

He nodded and I crawled into the cargo hatch.

The pistol fired. I rolled to my side and grabbed my weapon. We were taking fire, but only one round. I looked up and saw several Afghan men running toward us. I looked to the side of the vehicle and saw Pete holding the pistol and totally embarrassed. I ran to him. He pointed, and I saw the damage. He put a clean hole through our right front tire. The Afghan Soldiers ran to us, trying to determine what happened. I took his pistol and walked to the back of the vehicle.

I said, "Pete, this is a mechanical safe. Unless you are an expert with the weapon, and you are not, use the mechanical safe." We spent the remainder of the afternoon changing the tire.

As the sun went down, several of the local Generals arrived and went to the Operations' tent.

"Pete," I said, "keep your mouth shut, your ears open, and act ignorant." I smiled and said, "That shouldn't be a stretch for you." He looked at me, thought for a second, and then smiled. We assembled in the tent, and I introduced Pete to Mr. Obar. I pointed out the functions of the tent and the key Afghans.

Mr. Obar opened the meeting and introduced Pete, saying, "This is the famous Tire Killer of Kabul," in English for my benefit and then in Pashtun. All had a good laugh, and he began his briefing.

This plan would be similar to Mazar-e-Sharif with General Mannel attacking from northeast to the southwest while General Kamil would attack from the northwest to the southeast. Central to the operation was the capture of the abandoned Russian Air Force Base. Mr. Obar briefed in Pashtun and only switched to English when he pointed out large enemy concentrations where he wanted air power. I nodded. Once he completed the briefing, he spent several minutes talking to the group. I noticed that Pete was hanging on every word.

As the meeting broke up, I called Colonel Stevens and briefed him on the concept. He acknowledged and said he knew where the Afghan units were and all had some US military with them.

Pete said, "Mr. Obar made fun of me for shooting the tire. He told his commanders to kill any and all resistance in the vicinity of the airfield. It was the prize. He ordered them to be lenient when entering the Capitol, but if any women or children were killed, they were to tell the people it was American bombs that killed them, not Afghans."

I nodded and said, "Pete, you have a good memory and eye for details."

He continued, "He also said to only kill prisoners whom they knew were Taliban. Any that were conscripted or pressed into service must be given the opportunity to change sides. If they refused, they were to be killed." Pete looked at me and said, "Isn't that a war crime?"

I nodded and said, "Yes, it is."

MEN FROM CHECHNYA

I AWOKE EARLY the next morning, well before sunrise, to hear voices and a different language. I checked myself to see if I was dreaming. I wasn't. They were parked ten feet from our vehicle. They were sitting in a dark blue Chevrolet Tahoe. During the night, at this headquarters, there was much coming and going, but the language was definitely different.

I punched Pete hard, and he jumped up.

I whispered, "Do you speak Serbian or any of the Baltic languages?"

He shook his head like I asked a trick question, then said, "Yes, depending upon the dialect."

I opened the door, walked casually to the back, relieved myself, and stood next to the door to assure myself it was different. After a few minutes, Pete whispered, "Yes, it's Serbian with a strong Russian influence, but its only casual conversation about some girl."

I pushed Pete to get up, and we walked into the Operations' tent. It was quiet with no activity. I was leery to enter his private tent but felt it was worth the risk. The sun was beginning to peek over the mountains, and I was curious. I entered the tent with Pete behind me. As my eyes adjusted to the light, I saw Mr. Obar sitting in his easy chair, entertaining two large males. Both men had rifles slung over their back and pistols sticking out of their belts. I stood silently until Mr. Obar called me forward.

I said, "Our air support is ready for the fight." I don't know if it worked as I usually didn't report these things to him, but at least, he didn't seem displeased I entered his tent. He nodded politely, I nodded, and we turned and walked out. I knew it would be impossible to hear the conversation taking place, but I asked Pete if he could hear anything.

When he shook his head, we moved back to the Suburban. I said, "I want to know as much about these guys as we can find. Got it?"

Pete nodded. I rummaged through the back hatch and found the small hibachi grill, pulled out some rations, and asked Pete to invite them for breakfast.

They were sitting in the front seat, smoking cigarettes with their doors open. Pete spoke in English and asked them to come over. They nodded but didn't respond. He switched to some sort of Russian, which they understood, and soon were warming themselves next to the small grill. We offered them rations, and they accepted. Pete made casual conversation. I did my best to prompt him in English, and he picked up quickly. They were Serbs, both from Belgrade, and they fought with the Islamic Brigade in Chechnya. They had my attention. The Russians fought in Chechnya since the early 1990s in two distinct wars. Like the Balkans, it was a political struggle which turned religious. It was fanatical on all sides. Chechnya was special in many ways, but once it became a religious war, it became a world war with Islamic Extremist pouring into the country. Pete talked and I gave them various pieces of MRE meals. They were hungry, but we didn't get much from them.

An hour after sunrise, I saw them exiting the tent and shaking hands with Mr. Obar. They walked toward us. I could see their faces in daylight. This was unusual, and I wished the CIA team was here. I was here to track Mr. Obar because he liked me. I wasn't a spy and didn't have spy skills. I grabbed my phone, pretending I was taking a call and managed to get one decent photograph of the two returning men. Still pretending I was talking on the phone and walking, I looked inside their vehicle. It was full of ammunition boxes. I noticed a laptop computer in the back seat and a large, long carrying case and several accessory cases. I suspected it was a Dragunov Sniper Rifle with its associated scope. The Russians were proud of this .30 caliber rifle, and I fired it in training. It was a fine piece of equipment and common in the Balkans. Whoever these guys were, they were not here for a social call. Pete offered them food, but they loaded and drove away.

Pete said, "They came from the east. I don't know if that means Pakistan or somewhere else. Our breakfast buddies were Serbs, but the two guys from the tent spoke with a distinct Russian accent."

I made the call. I asked for the boss, but he was unavailable. I said, "I witnessed an unusual activity at headquarters, and I have photographs." They again sent me a mile-long e-mail address, and I sent the photograph. I used the other phone to call the general's staff. I asked to speak to the Colonel and was told he was unavailable. I asked that he return my call.

Within the hour, Chad called. He asked for a full report. He said, "The man in the photograph was Shamil Basa." I was silent, and he was silent.

Finally, I said, "Chad, it means nothing to me." I could hear the excitement in his voice.

He said, "Shamil Basa is Russia's Osama Bin Laden. He is a killer and first-class terrorist. He is charismatic, a brilliant tactician, and, we think, an ally of Bin Laden. He gave the Russians fits during Chechnya. We think he was responsible for a school massacre as well as the theater disaster in Moscow." He laughed and said, "Based on your instincts, you might make a spy yet."

I said, "Not funny, Chad, not funny at all."

Mr. Obar summoned me later that afternoon. He knew I intruded in a business meeting, which was out of character for me. He started the conversation slowly and meandered his way through a variety of subjects including tactics for the upcoming battle. Finally, he broached the subject.

He said, "Are you a fan of the cowboy movies?" I nodded. He said, "You know the term bounty hunter?" I nodded. He smiled and said, "I placed a bounty on the sissy Bin Laden. The men you saw this morning,"—he paused, looked at me briefly, and continued—"are bounty hunters."

I nodded and asked, "Do you think they can get close enough?"

He smiled and said, "I am doing this for my American friends."

I asked him, "Do you know his location?"

He smiled and said, "Some things are best kept close," and he placed his hand over his heart.

I said, "We think he is in the mountains near the border or in Pakistan."

He said, "It does not matter."

I pressed the issue and said, "Given his status, why would a bounty hunter take the job?"

He shook his head, pointed at me, and said, "You made him. He was a lightweight, a sissy latecomer to the mujahedeen, and he does not have a special status here!"

I nodded. He composed himself and said, "The Taliban and Bin Laden are close because Bin Laden is rich. That is the only reason. Wealth goes a long way in this world, but there are people who place loyalty to Allah above loyalty to money." I nodded. He then offered, "The assassin and Bin Laden are enemies, and I will exploit that fact." He was growing tired, so we ended our conversation.

I returned to the Suburban and made two calls on separate phones. The boss was very interested in the news, but the General's staff didn't appear to do anything other than write down my report. That night, I thought of the Hiawassee River running through Clay County and how much of my life I spent walking its banks. I thought about my son and how he never had those opportunities.

The Battle for Kabul was quick. Before dawn the next morning, we heard the massive airstrikes to the south. As the sun rose, we could see the explosive white clouds rising against the brown backdrop of the desert. We spent most of the day in the Operations' tent, and Afghan Soldiers were busy talking on cell phones and updating unit locations. Bombs fell in a constant stream. At times, we could feel the concussion, and we were miles away. Before noon, he captured the Russian airfield, and by evening, the entire city was in Mr. Obar's hands. We moved off of our mountain and directly to the airfield. It was the first time we were not hidden from the world. Mr. Obar personally directed the setup of the tents and the security arrangements. It was his coming-out party.

True to his word, the boss arrived early the next morning. He arrived in a single chopper with a few guys from the plans shop. Shortly afterward, two loaded Chinooks arrived, carrying the mobile Tactical Operations enter. He thanked me for the work and told me that he was proud of what I accomplished. He was not a man to give faint praise, so I felt good. We walked to the Suburban. He kicked Pete out, and we drove off to the far edge of the airfield.

We spent the next several hours talking. We talked about what I had seen, what had happened thus far, and what should happen next. He knew every detail of the massacre and was involved in high-level discussions regarding the act. We talked about Mr. Obar, and he asked several probing questions. I told him Scottie's view of using the Afghan against the Afghan as the only winnable approach.

He said, "I argued passionately for a limited engagement and maximum use of Special Forces combined with a rented Afghan Army, but I didn't win." He looked disappointed. He said, "We will see Battalions, Brigades, and Divisions. Once they come here, it will be at least a decade before we get out. We are a very good Army now and clearly superior to what the Soviets sent, but it's all about duration. Americans don't like long and costly wars. The population is still angry about the attacks, but it will wear off, and every four years, we elect a new political order." He laughed and said, "We should never even think of engaging in a war that lasts longer than four years."

Later that day, I introduced the boss to Mr. Obar. They hit it off and began a far reaching political and strategic discussion. By nightfall, we established our operations center within walking distance of Mr. Obar's. Later that night, two more Chinooks arrived full of Soldiers, Sailors, Airmen, and Marines, and by the next morning, we were joined by Australian, British, and Canadian forces.

FIREFIGHT

My routine changed after Kabul. I spent most of my time working intelligence reports from the Afghan's and assigning our units to conduct special reconnaissance. Pete proved invaluable as an interpreter and left me to join the boss as his full-time counterpart. I was getting plenty of rest, nobody was shooting at me, and we began eating from an improvised mess hall. We knew it would take time before we could push Mr. Obar into driving farther south. The farther south, the more the culture differed. He was more than willing to gather strength in Kabul, the traditional seat of power, and let his stature grow.

The General and his entourage arrived a few days later. He walked through our Operations enter, shook hands, and slapped backs. When he came to me, he looked at me for several seconds and asked, "Have we served together somewhere before?"

I was too embarrassed to tell him who I was, so I just nodded my head and said, "No, sir."

He ordered his staff to establish a forward command post on the airfield. A few days later, they arrived. I was convinced we had more Soldiers on the airfield than fighting the war. Then it happened. Battalions and Brigades started landing.

Once the General established the forward headquarters, things got interesting. We gained a great mess hall but lost freedom of maneuver. Within days, they barricaded the airfield with external and internal patrols, guarded gates, and triple strand concertina wire. It was designed to keep people out. In reality, it kept us in. From a tactical perspective, the enemy watched our entry and exit gates and followed our patrols. In this war, we needed to be accessible to the population, not segregated from it. More and more supplies arrived, and they required more and more Soldiers to guard them. The sad thing was it made you feel safe. The enemy had us bottled up without ever firing a shot.

Mr. Obar gathered strength, listened to our strategic intelligence feeds from Herat and Kandahar and made plans for the extended drive to the south. Late one evening, I was summoned to his tent. He and the boss were having their nightly strategy discussion and somehow got on the subject of horses. They planned to go to his farm in the north, and I was invited.

We departed early the next morning in a convoy of four vehicles. The lead vehicle was a Toyota long bed pickup truck with a .50 caliber machine gun mounted on a pedestal, and the other two were dark nondescript sedans. He had the usual complement of two bodyguards in each car. When he traveled in the past, he moved only in the sedans, but since gaining nationwide exposure, he added the gun truck. I drove the Suburban with Pete, and we took up the rear. We stopped at a small Afghan village, and he drew a large crowd. He was gracious as ever and, according to Pete, thanked each of the elders by name. He was good, and the people responded.

When we arrived at the farm, we were escorted toward the stables. He wanted to impress and served a wonderful afternoon meal. It was a show with servants, food, wine, shade tents, and several of his horses grazing around us. The food was delicious, and once we finished, we were entertained by a small band that played stringed instruments and sang Afghan ballads. Pete translated for me, and Mr. Obar went into detail for the boss about the songs and their meanings.

Mr. Obar called one of his barn men to him. Pete listened to the conversation and said, "Mr. Obar wants to saddle a Galaxy. What is a Galaxy?"

I said, "It's a horse. Do you know anything about horses?" He said no. I feared he would offer me the opportunity to ride the beast. This horse was spirited; he was muscular and required an experienced rider. I was not a cowboy, but I didn't want to be embarrassed. The man brought the horse from the barn. He was impressive. Mr. Obar stood, walked to the horse, and gracefully pulled himself into the saddle. He turned the horse quickly and raced at a full sprint across the irrigated pasture. It was a beautiful sight. The boss turned and said, "The man rides like a cowboy." He brought the horse toward us at a full gallop, turned at the last minute, and jumped the four-rail fence within a few feet of where the boss was sitting. I was proud of the boss; he didn't flinch. Mr. Obar was having the time of his life. Finally, he turned the horse and pulled to a full stop in front of us. It was a magnificent sight. A mujahedeen warrior mounted on a massive horse.

I saw the bullet rip into his chest, and then, I heard the sound. It wasn't a hard shot. He was mounted high on the stallion, but it was clean. I saw the blood leap out of his back and watched him slump over. The boss was the first to react, yelling "Sniper!" and we dashed back toward the vehicles. I saw a flash of sunlight reflect off something about five hundred meters away on a small knoll. The sniper fired two more rounds, but I didn't see the impact. I guessed they were confirmation shots aimed toward Mr. Obar. We reached the vehicles, and I looked back. Two of his bodyguards dove over the fence, but I knew they couldn't help. The horse was down and kicking wildly in all directions. Blood was pouring from his neck. His guards were trying to pull him from underneath the dying animal. I ran forward to the Toyota and jumped on the back. The rounds were in the chamber, so I pulled the charging handle and began firing. The enemy dropped behind the small knoll. We had to close with them.

I yelled at Pete, "Drive!" and he moved quickly. He cranked the engine. I saw more movement behind the knoll, and I pressed the trigger. The vehicle lurched forward, and the engine died. My rounds went flying into the air and then into the ground a hundred meters in front of us.

Pete screamed, "I can't drive it!"

I didn't understand what he was saying, and I screamed, "Drive! Drive!" Pete looked at me. He didn't know how to drive a vehicle with a clutch. The boss charged around to the driver's side and screamed, "Move over!" And Pete jumped to the passenger side. He floored the vehicle and began shifting gears as we closed. I held my fire. I wouldn't be able to hit anything at this speed. He slowed as we closed on the knoll and was attempting to go to the right side. I swung the gun to the left, and we moved slowly around the corner. Off to my far right, I saw a narrow road leading northeast into the mountains, and I saw a flash. A dark-blue vehicle was making its way at high speed along the narrow and steep road. I swung the big machine gun back to the right and fired a long burst and watched as several of the tracers impacted into the right rear of the vehicle. I blinked and tried to refocus my eyes on the target. I heard the impact of the rounds before I saw the shooter. Pete slumped over the gear shift; blood splattered over the back window. The boss braked hard, and I saw him. He was fifty feet away behind a small boulder. I swung the barrel toward him and fired. Several rounds hit the rock, but I didn't kill him. I aimed carefully at the rock and squeezed the trigger. The bolt slammed forward—nothing. I pulled the charging handle to the rear and again squeezed. Again, nothing happened. I looked at the feed tray. I was out of ammunition.

The shooter fired again, aiming at the windshield. It was an old style Kalashnikov, probably an AK47. The boss dove from the driver's, side and I jumped off the side of the vehicle. The boss moved toward the back of the vehicle and began firing. He suppressed the shooter, and I ran forward pulling the hammer back on the .44 magnum revolver. His aim was good, and I could see his rounds impacting in the dirt all around the rock; then, they stopped. He yelled but I could not hear what he said. The shooter rolled to his side and was aiming directly for the truck. I was less than twenty feet away and running hard. I fired twice and both rounds struck home. The first hit at the intersection of his cheek and the weapon causing the wooden stock to shred apart and come flying from his hands. The second hit him in the nose and tore off the front of his face, exposing his skin like a Hollywood horror movie. I moved behind him and saw nothing. The boss closed quickly to the rock and was on the other side. We looked up the mountain.

The .50 caliber disabled the truck, and we could see it sitting in the middle of the mountain trail. It was some type of sport utility vehicle. We scanned the hill and saw movement.

I said, "Looks like I hit it."

The boss nodded and said, "Four hundred meters away. We can't range with pistols." The terrain was steep. Had it not been on a serious incline, I wouldn't have been able to hit the fleeing vehicle. Mr. Obar's bodyguards came screaming around the hill in two sedans. One pulled to the right and the other to the left of the truck. They stopped and jumped from the vehicle. One of the drivers ran toward the truck, opened the passenger door, and was pulling Pete from the vehicle. I yelled at the others and pointed toward the vehicle on the mountainside. I heard the bullet fly over my head. We dove for cover and were on the front side of the rock. I looked back and saw the bodyguard's body limp on the ground. The boss said it first.

"Sniper!"

He crouched beside me and said, "I saw the flash twenty meters above and to the left of the disabled vehicle."

I looked up and I saw a difference in color against the dark brown backdrop. The bodyguards were yelling and attempting to work some sort of a plan, but they didn't speak English, and we didn't speak Pashtun.

The boss said, "We're pinned, so we've got to move. We can't range them. We need to suppress and close with him."

I yelled at the Afghans. I needed them to scan above and to the left of the vehicle. They answered me, but it didn't matter. I made hand motions and finally laid my pistol on the ground and made a motion of above and to the left. One of the guards nodded and began yelling at the others. The boss crawled around the rock and grabbed the dead shooter's rifle.

He looked at me and said, "No stock, but it functions. Pull his body to you and grab his ammo." I handed him a clip. He inserted it, pointed it to the side, and squeezed the trigger. It fired. Mr. Kalashnikov built durable weapons. I took it from him and raised the rear sight as best I could. I pointed it in the general direction of the sniper and fired. The round kicked up dirt ten meters away and to the left. I brought it right ten meters and squeezed off another round. This one hit within two feet of the target. I nodded and the boss dashed behind the vehicles. I rose up again and squeezed off another round. I saw the flash coming from the far right of the vehicle.

I screamed, "Another sniper! He's on the right side of the vehicle. I don't see any other targets!"

The boss yelled, "We killed one! Do we have two or three snipers on the hillside? We can't afford to be wrong." I screamed "two...on the hillside! I rolled over, swung the rifle to the other shooter and fired off four rounds. He was well entrenched behind a rock, and I heard the ricochets from my position.

I heard the loud crack of a rifle behind me. It was much louder than any of the others.

The boss yelled, "I have a rifle. Stay put!" I glanced back and saw the boss working the bolt on one of Mr. Obar's hunting rifles. It was bolt action, probably an antique, but it had the distance.

He yelled, "Suppress!" and I fired two rounds in the general location of each shooter. One of the bodyguards crawled into the sedan and was moving forward toward me. The boss and the other bodyguard were crouched behind the sedan, while the driver hunkered down in the floorboard. The boss fired again, and I rifled through the dead shooter and found five full clips of ammunition. The boss fired again and worked the bolt on his antique rifle.

He yelled, "Out of ammo!" I threw a magazine at him, and he manually thumbed the rounds out of the clip and loaded them into the hunting rifle. It was some sort of Russian rifle, maybe a M91 or M44, but it held the rounds and the boss was firing.

He yelled, "Simple plan! Drive the sedan up the hill slowly and get close enough to kill."

If we could get close, the bodyguards could use their pistols, and we would have an advantage. We started up the hill.

The boss said, "You focus on the left side, and I focus on the right. Keep their heads down."

We made it a hundred meters when we heard the shooters yelling at one another. We continued to fire a round every few steps. It was slow. The boss had to stop, strip the clip, and manually load the bolt action rifle. As he was crouched down, loading, both snipers opened fire. They were aiming at the bodyguard driving the sedan. It was a smart move. If they could stop him, it would keep us from closing on them. They fired several rounds, and the bodyguard with the pistol kept yelling at his friend who was driving, and he kept responding. We closed to within two hundred meters, and the snipers again fired in unison at the driver. Somehow, he managed to avoid death, but we smelled the smoke and antifreeze coming from the radiator.

The boss said, "We need a kill. The vehicle isn't going to make it much farther."

I said, "Best to focus on the guy on the right. It's our best chance."

He nodded, and we both fired at the sniper on the right. As we closed to within a hundred meters, both snipers fired. We were close enough to see weapons.

I said, "He isn't going down." The boss fired, worked the bolt, and fired again. His second shot hit, and we heard the man yelling in pain. He remained a threat. The boss pulled the bodyguard toward him and made him point his pistol toward the sniper. The bodyguard nodded.

The boss said, "Now, we focus on leftie."

The snipers yelled at one another, and we could hear the agony coming from the one we hit. The car sputtered and died. We were less than sixty meters away but still outside normal pistol range. The driver tried to restart the engine, but it wouldn't crank. We heard yelling in a loud voice and saw hands come from behind the rock. The shooter on the left was surrendering. He raised his hands high into the air and slowly stood up. We began moving cautiously toward him. The boss and I focused on the sniper to the left, while the bodyguards moved toward the wounded sniper. He was wearing a scarf over most of his face. We moved closer. The boss moved wide to one side, and I moved to the other. I moved behind him, saw the sniper rifle, and said, "He's out of ammo."

He had nowhere to run; it was either surrender or die. He chose surrender. I pulled the scarf from his face.

I recognized him.

"Boss," I said, "this is the one of the guys who visited Mr. Obar. These are the bounty hunters."

The man spoke, but neither of us understood. He was motioning toward his wounded comrade. I came up behind him, conducted a pat-down search, and tied his hands with his scarf. I heard the shot and flinched. The bodyguards killed the wounded man. He screamed and kicked me in the shin. I slammed my elbow into his cheek. He fell to the ground. I manhandled him to his feet and down to the road. He was crying. The boss grabbed the sniper rifle and followed. The bodyguards were prepared to execute him. Both aimed their pistols at his head. I stepped in front of him. Both men were hurt and loyal to Mr. Obar. They wanted revenge. The boss walked between us, shook his head, and said no in a stern voice. They didn't like it, but they respected him and the decision.

I said, "He is one of the guys I saw in the tent, but I don't know if he is the mastermind."

The boss took photos and hit Send. The large caliber rounds hit the small SUV in the right rear of the vehicle, killing one of the men. His blood was all over the back seat.

I looked at the body and said, "This is one of the breakfast guys, not one of the tent guys."

The boss said, "They grabbed what they could and moved to the rocks, but they didn't grab enough ammunition. They would have been free in another two hundred meters with a clean kill, but I wonder why they left the first shooter at the bottom of the mountain."

We moved cautiously back down the hill with the bodyguards in front. The closer we got to the vehicles at the bottom, the more emotional they became. At the bottom, we saw the dead bodyguard and Pete. I shook my head and wondered why Pete and not me.

Pete took one just above his left eye. I don't think it was painful. He was a good guy, an expert at what he did, and brave. The boss pulled his phone, dialed, and said, "We have a casualty notification for Navy Lieutenant Peter J. Boone. I want a presidential letter, and I am requesting now for a SECDEF family visit."

A Chaplain and a casualty notification officer would arrive at the door and tell the family. His name would go on a wall somewhere, saying he was killed in Afghanistan. His widow would get a lot of money, and his kids received a free education. They would want to know how he died, and they would stammer without answers. My right hand trembled. I looked and saw the boss staring at me. I kept one hand on the prisoner and shoved my trembling hand in my pocket. He glared at me and said, "Two hands on the prisoner!"

We sat at the bottom of the knoll, and the boss made calls. I watched the bodyguards. They wanted vengeance. We would miss Mr. Obar. He was a skilled military commander and a shrewd politician. He was exactly what Afghanistan needed. He was their George Washington, the indispensable man. With him, we had hope. The boss walked up, pointed, and said, "This is Basa. They are coming for him." We moved back to the stable area.

His family gathered around him, and we could hear the crying and yelling before we got close. They removed his body from underneath the stallion. The stallion lie in a massive pool of blood. It was an ugly scene. I wanted Basa to see it firsthand, but we had to be careful. The boss made a motion, and I tied a loop from his hands to his feet and pushed him into the back of the suburban.

He said, "I bet he knows Bin Laden's location."

I looked at the dead horse and Mr. Obar. It was ugly and bloody.

We waited for over two hours for the choppers. The first chopper was full of musclemen. We didn't need them; the action was over. The second had Chad and Ray, as well as a half-dozen other CIA types. I introduced Chad to the boss.

Chad said, "We think Bin Laden is operating from a series of caves in an area called Tora Bora. It's rough ground, but it allows him to make strikes into the larger cities and an easy escape into Pakistan. Our operational plan is to move special reconnaissance to that area. The tactical plan is to see if he"—he pointed at Basa—"knows bin Laden's location."

Chad introduced Bruce and Les. Their mission was to interrogate. They looked intimidating, not because of the weapons slung over their bodies, but because of the way they carried themselves. They reminded me of big middle school bullies.

They asked to see him, and the boss said, "Go with, I got to make calls." They asked me to drive away from the crowd. I started for the knoll but could see our guys gathering up Pete's body, so I drove around the fence and found a ditch where they could have privacy. I stopped. They pulled him out, cut his ties, sat him on the tailgate, and began speaking in rapid fire Russian. He nodded several times. I stood on the side of the vehicle. Les pulled a laptop computer and showed him photographs and satellite imagery. He nodded and pointed. The only thing I understood was an occasional reference to Bin Laden. They took out some sort of scanning machine and ran it over Basa's face and imported it into the computer.

Bruce said, "Do you have the grid for here?"

I nodded and told him the numbers.

A few minutes later, a Datsun pickup truck driven by one of the musclemen arrived. Les and Bruce spoke to him, and he nodded. I was expecting to transfer him, but they handed him the keys to the truck. I stared forward, but Bruce stepped in front of me. Basa cranked the truck and drove away.

I yelled, "You let him go free! Obar was this place's only hope, and you morons let him go. If you don't have the guts to kill him, I will."

Les glared at me and said, "You don't understand."

I yelled, "I understand completely that you two are idiots!"

The muscleman was getting nervous. Les said, "It is in our best national interest to let him go back to Russia."

I was astounded. I stood there, not knowing what to say as they packed up their equipment and loaded it in the Suburban.

I was steaming and drove back to the boss. I said, "Team moron here just let Basa go!" The boss stared at me. Chad and Ray looked shocked. I continued, "The man killed the one viable leader in Afghanistan, and we capture him, losing one of our men, and they just let him drive off!"

Chad lowered his head and said, "This smells bad." He motioned for Les and they walked toward the barn.

The boss reached for another cigarette. I felt like vomiting. Finally, the boss looked at me and said, "We should have left him with the bodyguards."

I nodded.

It was a long ride back to Kabul. The boss finally spoke and said, "I play by the rules, but I guess I am one of the few that even has rules." He spent an hour talking on the phone and working Pete's notification. He took care of his people, even in death. When we arrived, it was like entering the White House. Security was everywhere—towers, wire, inspections, and two young Soldiers who insisted we get out of the vehicle and clear our weapons using a clearing barrel. We complied. Once I cleared the weapon, I reloaded and recharged all my weapons.

The young Soldier was respectful and said, "Sir, you will need to unload your weapons." I stared at him, and he continued, "We don't allow loaded weapons inside the compound."

We entered the main part of the airfield; we saw Soldiers and Marines everywhere. The place was crowded.

For the next several months, my mission was simple. I made briefing slides on a computer, and I walked across the compound to the daily General staff updates, and I briefed my slides. It wasn't glamorous or sexy, but it was my job. I stood in front of a group of high-ranking officers, with dozens more connected via VTC, and briefed them on our strategic reconnaissance efforts.

Two great things happened. I began receiving mail, and I called home. I slept in the back of the Suburban, occasionally turning on the heater during the coldest parts of that winter. The only drama occurred after Christmas.

I was briefing, and one of the Generals stopped the briefing and said, "Do you have a uniform?"

I replied, "No, sir, I do not."

He shook his head and said, "Find one." I spent the afternoon wandering the airfield, looking for a uniform. I wore the uniform into our cell one morning, causing heads to turn.

The boss pulled me out and said, "What are you doing?"

When I told him the story, he laughed and said, "I'll take care of it." I continued to brief in flannel shirts and jeans.

General Mannel and General Kamil, as well as a newcomer from the south named General Abdu, were locked in a power struggle. As a result, they were worthless. Despite intense prodding and massive bribery, they were more concerned about their personal status than winning the war. The so-called Northern Alliance crumbled. We confirmed Bin Laden was entrenched in Tora Bora and sent in lots of brave American Soldiers in their Battalions and Brigades. Our Soldiers acquitted themselves well and killed lots of bad guys, but we didn't destroy their leader or their will to fight. Further, the Taliban leader, who was far more dangerous *within the country*, was elusive and well hidden. We won battles, but that doesn't count.

We started public works projects and brought in dozens of civil affairs experts. In theory, if we dig wells, everything would be fine. It didn't work. If digging wells stopped wars, then they would have stopped long before I was born. We trained the Afghan Army. In some cases, it worked, and in most, it didn't. When it failed, it was generally because of the Afghan recruiting and retention policy coupled with a significant language barrier. Finally, several retired generals showed up, toured the country, and said we must eliminate the opium. Once they went public with their statements, any chance at a long-term relationship with the Afghan Military ended. They knew they produced the drug, they knew far more about its evil effects than we did, but they also knew poor. They knew poor because they lived it, and they knew they didn't like poor, so they did something about it—they grew opium. Opium was a good crop for the Afghan farmer, and due to the demand and profit margin, it was worth every hour laboring in the sun.

While the Afghan Generals squabbled, someone at the highest levels decided we would make them a George Washington. They choose a man who was a fundraiser for the mujahedeen, but he wasn't a mujahedeen. He had lots of degrees and was primarily an academic. We briefed him several times and provided a security detail to ensure he stayed alive long enough to lead. It was clear from the beginning; he was our man and not the Afghan people's man. He had ties with the Pakistan Intelligence Service and made lots of money working with large international oil companies, but these things didn't seem to enter into the strategic calculus. On the ground, our preference would have been to let the generals sort it out and continue to rent their Armies. It sounds harsh, but Civil Wars decide things. None of us thought it would come to a civil war, but it was a better option than our weak George Washington. There was plenty of money to rent an Army, but we decided to give equally to those who fought and to those who didn't. This caused even more friction. The more friction we caused, the more troops we required.

Over time, the airfield took on an international look. I continued to brief. Our senior leaders tried to determine our strategy and how to implement it. It was interesting to watch. By the early spring, we basically secured the country. Just like the Soviets, we controlled the roads and most of the major urban areas, but we didn't really control anything in the countryside. Everybody struggled with the basic question of what to do next. We didn't have a strategy other than to rid the place of bad guys, so we fought everything as a day to day action. We invaded the place, convinced ourselves we had conquered it, and now were trying to determine what to do with it. I made slides and listened. The most important thing was my hand stopped trembling.

Late one afternoon, the boss called me to the Operations' tent. He pinned a medal on my chest, shook my hand, and told me how much he appreciated my contributions.

He said, "You're going home."

That night, I walked to the small building that served as our mail center. I asked for a medium-sized box and placed the phone with all its gory photographs inside. I sent it to an address in Clay County, North Carolina.

The next morning, the boss woke me early, knocking on the back of the Suburban. He said, "Take the summer off. You have excess leave, and you need to burn it all, but draw a beeper in case I need you. Have fun."

I strapped my rucksack on my back, left the Suburban, and boarded an aircraft from Kabul. Thirty hours later, I was home.

GOOD FOLLOWED BY BAD

I HAVE TROUBLE returning from deployments. I was keyed up for several weeks, and I had a tough time calming myself. I worked to control my emotions.

Things changed. My son was taller, leaner, stronger, and smarter. My daughter was no longer a tomboy but was concerned about boys. I wanted her to be little again, but that time was past, and I missed it. I was uncomfortable with her newfound maturity. She had grown. Lorraine was so good, they actually thrived without me. They functioned better without me than with me. It hurt, but over time, I fit in. They lead full lives, had friends, participated in dozens of activities, and were happy. The alternative was to return to an unhappy and failing family, and that's worse. I was proud of Lorraine. I don't know how she did it.

Lorraine knew I needed time to process, so she and the kids gave me time and space. For hours, I sat in the backyard, chewed tobacco, and thought about life. One evening, Lorraine said, "I called Alidade, and the house is ready." I looked at her. She smiled and said, "Tomorrow is the last day of school, and we are going to Clay County for as long as you want." I was elated. We drove home, and it was peaceful.

Lorraine worked miracles, and Alidade and Israel brought food. Eventually, the kids realized we really didn't have a television and began to explore outside. We went fishing on the Hiawassee and walked the mountains and played.

Lorraine said, "I don't know why, but I actually rest here. Sweetwater is peaceful."

We took weekend trips to Atlanta and watched the Braves play, toured the zoo, and spent a night on Kennesaw Mountain. Another weekend we went to Chattanooga. We crawled all over Lookout Mountain, rode in paddleboats, and had a blast at the Tow Truck Museum and Hall of Fame. On the way back home, we stopped for ice cream and toured a working dairy farm. I was shocked to see the kids when they opened the milking parlor. This was foreign to them, but I wished it wasn't.

Lorraine was soft and tender. I loved her, but now, it was different. It was always love, but now, it was love with something added. Admiration is the best way to put it. I admired her. I looked up to her. I needed her. She possessed a sense of grace, and it was mesmerizing. We sat on the porch each evening and read stories. Once the kids were asleep, I said, "I need to get out. I need to retire. I need this life."

She laughed and said, "I know, but we need to buy a television."

One day, I went into Hayesville and bought several large tubes. We walked to the curve in the river, launched the tubes, and floated all the way down the Hiawassee into Carroll Lake. It was the most relaxing day of my life. When we finally beached ourselves, I realized it would be a long walk back, so I hoisted my daughter on my shoulders, and off we went. Amazingly, nobody griped or complained; we just walked and talked. It was the best day of my life.

I wasn't much of a father. The more time I spent with my kids, the more I realized how inadequate I really was. I tried to be home for special events, and I enjoyed playing with my kids, but when anything happened, they immediately ran to their mother. She gave them comfort, she gave them unconditional love, and she gave them affection and sympathy. They were good kids. She had raised them to be confident. It was good, but I wanted more. I wanted them to be self-reliant, but in today's world, that was a tall order.

One day, I found the mustard seed matchbox in a drawer while looking for socks. I noticed Mr. Samuels wrote Hebrews 11:6 on the side, and I found a dusty old Bible on the shelf and found the verse. I was confused. The mustard seed parable was in Matthew, not in Hebrews. I read Matthew and then went to Hebrews. Both describe faith. In Matthew, the Lord tells us if we have the faith of a mustard seed, we can move mountains. In Hebrews, it says without faith, we cannot please God. It also says 'He' rewards those who diligently seek after 'Him'. I thought about the word "diligently." I remembered Mr. Samuels telling me a man is blessed to find his purpose in this world.

Lorraine's parents came to visit. It was good to see them although it was tense with Walter. He pastored large churches in Asheboro and even in Greensboro, but for the life of me, I couldn't understand why. He floated in and out of academic life with various teaching post, boards, and commissions. He considered me a minor functionary and was constantly grooming me for the real world.

Walter was passive. He was working on a journal article, and it kept him occupied. He wasn't a bad grandfather, but he wasn't like my dad. My dad crawled everywhere with the kids, but Walter sought a high intellectual order from them and mature conversations. Occasionally, my son would cave in and thrill Walter with a mature conversation, but mostly, he wanted to play, run, and fish. Walter and I had to go to town one afternoon in order to get a toilet float.

Walter said, "These people are so lazy." I let it pass. Later, he hit me again with the question, saying, "How many of 'these people' are on welfare?"

I didn't take the bait. I just kept driving. He lived in his world, and I lived in mine, and we really didn't need to collide if I could avoid it. They were very good to Lorraine, and I was appreciative, especially when I was gone.

My mother-in-law was a sweetheart. She was kind, loving, gentle, and a joy to be around. One night, when the kids and Walter were asleep and we were sitting on the porch, she said, "I admire you. I like people who are dedicated to causes."

She was enthralled by the military. Her father served in World War II, and she was a patriot. Since 911, she was a hyperpatriot. She said, "You never tell me where you go and all these big logistic missions you do. I want you to tell me a story."

Before I could answer, Lorraine attempted to change the subject and said, "Mom, we need to talk about something different. His work is boring. All he ever sees is barren land and warehouses."

Marge shook her head and said, "No, dear, I want a story."

I said, "Well, I am going to retire soon, so I don't really do logistics. I am an operations and intelligence specialist."

Lorraine nodded at me and said, "Mom, he does very dangerous things. He has been all over the world. He does specialized missions, and I am very proud of him." I nodded. Lorraine looked at me and winked. It was sexy. She continued, "He has been to Panama, Iraq, Kuwait, Turkey, Somali, Columbia, all over Africa, Jordan, Israel, Germany, and he just returned from Afghanistan. I am sure I left several places out."

I was shocked and amazed how much Lorraine knew.

Marge said, "Oh my goodness." She paused and then asked the typical question. "Well, have you ever killed a terrorist?"

It is the toughest question to answer. You never know how people will react. I said, "Yes, Marge, I have."

She gasped.

Lorraine looked at her mother and said, "Mom, we don't talk about these things. We don't talk about them to Dad or the kids or the neighbors or at church. We keep our mouths shut."

Marge looked at me and nodded. After that conversation, she looked at me different. Finally, on the day they left, she hugged me and said, "I love you, and I am so very proud of you and what you do."

It was nice.

We took the kids to Sweetwater Baptist for services. Joel Johnson was the pastor. They didn't initially like the church because you see Dad's headstone when you drive into the parking lot. We were greeted warmly. All the services were lively, and the kids were scared. They weren't accustomed to people shouting or the preacher being excited and loud. They jumped several times. One thing was certain: they weren't bored. On the way home, we had a discussion.

I said, "God is real, and his son, Jesus, died and resurrected from the dead to give us an opportunity to go to heaven. Some believe and some don't. The people in this church believe, and they feel it. Some folks believe but don't openly feel, and that is okay, but these folks feel it."

It wasn't what they saw at Walter's services, nor was it what we normally did in Fayetteville. During the next Sunday service, Jess whispered to me, "Daddy, it's real."

I nodded, smiled, and said, "Yes, dear, it is real."

I walked them to the Samuelses' house. I told them about Mr. Samuels and how he was always talking to God. I told them about how he lived, how humble he was, how he was always willing to serve others.

I said, "I want to be like him."

They stared at me, and Jess said, "Daddy, ask God to make you that way." I nodded.

I don't know why, but being here calmed me.

Lorraine said, "JB, I don't think I have ever seen you so relaxed."

I didn't dream that summer. I slept. My hand stopped trembling, my eye stopped flinching, my legs quit itching, and I gained weight. I would go for several days without shaving until Lorraine would pull my beard. It was fun.

Lynn and Roger came and stayed a week. It was fun to have Lynn, and I realized how much I missed her. She and Roger were always trying to get pregnant, but it wasn't working. She and Jess were best friends, and it was good for both of them. Roger was a professional salesman and was constantly trying to sell anything, but mostly himself. By the end of the week, I liked him.

Lorraine and I talked daily about moving.

I said, "It's tough to find a decent job in Clay County, but we will sort it out."

Lorraine said, "The retirement check will keep us from the poor house, but I will get a job. I can teach school."

I knew enough folks in the community that I could work for wages building houses as a carpenter's apprentice, a roofer, or maybe, I could teach myself. I had a history degree. We would see, but it was fun to have the conversations and dream about the future.

I kept the beeper in my pocket and rarely thought about it. Late one night, I heard it buzzing, but when I retrieved it, it didn't show anything, so I went back to sleep. The next morning, the kids and I walked to Mr. Hill's little minigrocery store at the corner of Fires Creek Road and Highway 64. We walked and talked, skipped rocks into the river, spat off the bridge, and had a good time being silly. I noticed a large black sport utility vehicle pass as we ambled down the road, but I didn't think much of it. When we reached the store, the kids ran to the coolers in search of ice cream, and I spoke to several folks. I knew some in the community, but the county was gaining more who lived here in the summer and Florida in the winter. They were nice enough, but different. Most had money while the locals didn't. Mr. Hill's store is small with only four aisles. I worked my way back to get a

Cola and saw a man in khaki pants and blue shirt moving toward me. It unnerved me slightly, so I turned quickly.

It was Chad. He nodded, I nodded, and then, he walked to the front of the store and paid for his drink. It was him as I looked him straight in the face, but I was dumbfounded as to why he was here. I handed the kids quarters and told them to win me a hat from the grab-an-item vending game, and then, I walked out the door.

Chad was sitting in the driver's seat with the door open. He said, "Sir, could you please give me directions?"

I walked toward him. His hair was grayer, and I said, "You are an elderly man with graying hair, so I don't think you need to be driving."

He smiled. For a show, he pulled out a map and placed it on the hood of his vehicle. He said, "You are hard to find."

I said, "Yes, and I like it that way. How did you find me?"

He smiled and said, "I had the National Security Agency ping your pager for a location."

I nodded and said, "I am impressed. I guess I've made the big time."

He laughed and said, "I need to talk to you, but not here."

"Well," I said, "come to my house and have supper around six. I am certain you can find it without the help of the NSA."

He smiled, folded his map, waved, and sped off. I grabbed the kids and walked home. I was nervous.

Lorraine was gracious. I told her Chad was a friend from Afghanistan, and it was a chance meeting. She nodded and didn't ask questions. Chad brought flowers and wine. He didn't know we didn't drink, but I took the bottle and placed it in the cabinet. We had a wonderful dinner.

After dinner, Lorraine and the kids began tuning the radio for the Braves game. I suggested to Chad that we walk along the river. I asked about his team, and he gave good reports.

He said, "Ray retired. He is teaching pottery in Idaho, and I miss him. Afghanistan is settling down, but I have a new mission." We wandered to the bank of the river.

I said, "What do you mean by settling down?"

He looked around and said, "We came close to getting Bin Laden on several occasions but not yet. The Generals settled some of their disputes, and we are moving toward stability."

I nodded and said, "Are 'we' moving toward stability, or are the 'Afghans' moving toward stability?"

He laughed and said, "You are quick, JB. I will give you that. To answer your question, we are stable, and the Afghans are as unstable as ever."

I nodded. I said, "Chad, I am angry about Pete. He was a good guy. I didn't let the bodyguards kill Basa, and I should have, or better yet, killed him myself."

I grabbed a chew of tobacco, and he looked at me and said, "That is a nasty habit."

I said, "Yes, you are correct."

He turned and said, "I didn't know it, but the decision to free him was made before we got on the chopper. Les got it from the director of operations himself."

I shook my head and said, "Bad call, Chad, a very bad call."

He nodded and said, "I told you. The agency has two enemies, the US Military and the Russians."

I said, "I got it but still a bad call. You could have traded him or something. You guys make me angry, especially when I think about Pete."

He nodded and stretched. I waited for him to get to his point. This wasn't a social call.

We walked toward Mr. Samuels's shed. The sun was setting behind the mountains.

Chad said, "What's the name of this place?"

I said, "Sweetwater."

There were several old tree stumps and we sat.

He said, "It's peaceful here, really peaceful."

I said, "The old men used to sit here and talk, solve the world's problems, and pray. It's a good thinking spot."

He looked at me and said, "I have something else to tell you, and I don't want to."

I looked at him and said, "Well, then don't."

"I need to tell you. It's been on my mind for a long time, so please listen." He hesitated a moment and said, "In Belgrade, everybody—and I mean everybody—was afraid your team was compromised. They thought if you were captured and you would eventually break and tell the world it was a deliberate mission. You know where the orders came from?"

I nodded and said, "I figured."

He fidgeted for a second and said "I was the only guy inside the country. I paid Serge before your mission. It was my fault. My cover was sinking, and I needed to get out. I'm sorry and I wanted you to know. I tried telling you several times, but you were armed and"—he paused—"you have a bit of a temper." I glared at him. I started to speak, but he interrupted and said, "I found Serge three months later in Warsaw, and I killed him. He was my first."

I stared at him, and he looked down the river. I didn't know what to say. Finally, I said, "Thanks. He deserved it."

He nodded and said, "I need your help."

I said, "I figured you didn't come here to confess."

He said, "We were once a great spy agency, and I was trained as a spy. When President Clinton got his peace dividend in the early 1990s, the agency went more toward analyst. Analysts analyze things, but they do it from a distance. They do it based upon facts and assumptions but not from hands-on reconnaissance. We are an agency of analysts with few spies, and even fewer with the military skills required to conduct military type reconnaissance. In this war, we need military style strategic reconnaissance."

I nodded and said, "All good and a great history lesson, but what do you want from me?"

He smiled and said, "You don't miss, do you? You go directly to the point." I nodded. He said, "I work for the Special Activities Division. We do strategic reconnaissance, but we don't really have the skill sets."

I shook my head and said, "Are you looking for a trainer? I'm sure the boss can set up something."

He shook his head and said, "No, JB, I don't want you to train me. I want you to go with me."

"Well," I said, "it's interesting, but, Chad, I'm on my last legs. I'm tired. All I want to do is retire and live here. You see how peaceful Sweetwater is and how it makes you feel."

He nodded. We sat quietly for a minute. I looked at him and his face turned grave.

He said, "The CIA—no, not the CIA." He thought for a second, searching for the correct wording. "I have the mission to infiltrate Saddam Hussein's Iraq to determine if they have chemical weapons."

"Wow," I said, "that's a tough one."

He continued, "The agency has paid informants inside the country, and they agree Iraq has weapons of mass destruction. The good news is they are probably chemical, not biological or nuclear." I nodded again. "My mission—and yes, I have to accept the mission—is to infiltrate Iraq, conduct strategic reconnaissance on three separate sites, and determine if they have the weapons, and then report back to the Director of Central Intelligence."

"Chad," I said, "there are lots of talented guys. You could do much better than me."

He looked up the river, glanced at me, and said, "The Secretary of Defense offered to assist the CIA with people of your specific skill set." He paused, and I wondered where the conversation was going. He continued, "The military offered up three candidates. One was a Lieutenant Commander in Naval Special Warfare, one was an Army Captain from Delta, and you."

"No way," I said quickly, "they didn't offer me up. Nobody told me anything."

Chad nodded and said, "I talked to your boss. He said it was up to you." We were silent, and then, he said, "The boss said he would call you, but only after we talked."

I shook my head and said, "I don't like it, infiltrating a country to look at heavily guarded sites. That's dangerous stuff."

He said, "The United Nations Verification and Disarmament people are adamant that Saddam has disarmed, but we have informants who claim he has chemical weapons. The nation is already in a decade's long war in Afghanistan. The president and, specifically, the vice president are looking to finish off Saddam. We are going to look like idiots if we invade a country based upon the fact we think they have weapons of mass destruction, and when we get there, we find they don't." He stared at me and said, "My mission is to determine the truth."

I shook my head and stared at the river.

"Look," he said, "I need you. I have a good team. I picked the best guys possible. I'm on a timeline, and I need you. JB, you got skills and common sense, but if you tell me no, I will go up the chain to the SECDEF and ask for you by name."

I glared at him. "You wouldn't do that!"

"I'm scared. This is a big operation, and I don't…I don't like it. I need you." He reached into his pocket and said, "This is a secure phone. Answer it when it rings."

We walked back to the house in silence. He waved at me, got in his SUV, and drove away. Lorraine was standing on the porch.

I said, "An old friend needed advice."

She laughed and said, "About some top-secret mission?"

I stared briefly at her, and then John Boy yelled, "Dad! Bobby Cox just got ejected again."

I said, "Wow, he must be getting close to the record."

For the first time in a long while, I was actually a decent husband and father.

The next morning, the kids and I began our ritual walk down to Mr. Hill's store. The river was beautiful, and if you stood on the right spot on Shallow Ford Bridge, you could see the trout swimming. We took our time. The store was crowded, but we bought a few things and started back.

As we started across the bridge, the phone buzzed.

The boss said, "Are you enjoying your leave?"

I said, "Yes, sir, until last night."

He said, "JB, it's your call. I won't force you."

"Sir," I began, "do you really think they need me?"

He paused and then said, "Yes, I do."

HELEN, GEORGIA

Leaving was getting harder. My wife had a husband, and my kids, a father. I convinced myself it was my last mission. After this, I would quit and do anything but this. The trip to Fayetteville was long and tiring. It seemed longer than usual.

Lorraine wasn't feeling well, but the kids were behaved, and we arrived home. The next morning, I packed my rucksack. In the past, I spent hours planning and thinking where every item would go. This time, I just wasn't into thinking; I was more into avoiding saying good-bye. I hugged the kids, and Lorraine cried. We had done this hundreds of times, and she was always so brave, never shedding a tear. I figured it was because we had spent a wonderful summer together and didn't want it to end.

I parked the truck, walked the Mogadishu mile, and reported to the boss. We went outside underneath the lawn canopy, so he could smoke. I asked about the mission.

He said, "It's CIA business, but they don't have the expertise to get it done. They are stealing some of our talent, but it will take them time. Better they do these missions than us. It's necessary."

I spent the next several hours with the lawyers. They briefed me on different legal issues, completed paperwork, and reworked my will and Lorraine's power of attorney. If something happened to me, all the paperwork would be in a nice neat file.

The boss rejoined me after lunch and asked, "Have you ever been to Helen, Georgia?"

I said, "It's some sort of a German remake village in the mountains of north Georgia, but I've never been there."

He smiled and said, "When you're ready, I have drivers who are taking you. Be careful."

Chad met us on the edge of town. We flung my gear into the vehicle and drove to the rental cabins. The team was assembled, and I shook hands and sat down.

Chad introduced me, saying, "He started in Panama."

I scanned the room. One of the young men spoke up and said, "Dude, I was in the in the ninth grade when we invaded Panama."

The crowd laughed, and I smiled. It was good-natured ribbing. Chad let the laughter die and said, "Be careful around Papaw gentlemen."

From that day until we parted ways, I was called Papaw. He said, "Eight go on the mission and four are support. Support cell travels with us, operates from Kuwait, and assists us as required." The cabins were large with big comfortable rooms and a large billiard table in the middle of the living room.

Chad began to lay out the general concept of the operation, saying, "We spend three weeks here, followed by a move to Kuwait where we spend an additional two to three weeks in final preparation. In the recent past, three groups of foreign contractors conducted significant reconnaissance on eleven different sites of interest. A Danish group spent over a month in country, working friendly with the Iraqis and uncovered nothing. A German engineering group conducted extensive reconnaissance, almost an inspection, of five different sites in the greater Baghdad area and found nothing. Finally, we hired a group of Japanese contractors with an extensive background in chemical engineering. They scoured the northern city of Mosul for over five months and found nothing. In all three cases, the Iraqis welcomed them into the country, looking for business opportunities. Additionally,"—he paused, scanning the room, and then continued, "we conducted a major computer hacking operation on the Iraqi government. While it's been successful in providing a great deal of data relating to Iraqi military capabilities and limitations, it hasn't yet produced anything related to weapons of mass destruction. The bottom line is either the Iraqis are so secretive they aren't discussing their projects, or they just weren't that sophisticated. It's hard to hack something that isn't there."

He walked to the pool table and turned on a projector, aiming it at a makeshift screen. "Phase one is our infiltration into the county. Phase Two is reconnaissance of sites one and two. Phase three is our move across the country and reconnaissance of site three, and finally phase four, extraction."

He pulled a laser pointer from his pocket and continued, "We move using three vehicles. We use two small Toyota trucks and a Ford Explorer. Each vehicle is secure GPS equipped, allowing the support team to keep track. They also have built-in tool boxes which carry specific scientific monitoring equipment, a couple of well hidden spare weapons, and they have wenches in case we get stuck." The photographs were grainy, but we could see enough detail to understand the concept. He continued, "Each vehicle has a twenty-four-gallon gas tank with three additional external five-gallon cans. Our team in Kuwait purchased and verified several smuggler routes from Iraq to Kuwait. They are confident these routes allow us to navigate the border between Iraq and Kuwait. After the first Gulf War, the Kuwaitis built a substantial series of barriers between them and the Iraqis to preclude another cross-desert attack. While it is not as fortified as the Korean border, it is a substantial obstacle, consisting mainly of scattered point and area minefields." He used the laser and pointed at a partially covered mine and continued, "Having a cleared route is essential. Smugglers, however,…. have a way of making things happen." He pointed the laser to show our prospective route and continued, "In this case, they are running alcohol and drugs from Iraq into Kuwait and Saudi Arabia. By using their return routes, we will move through no-man's land into Iraq." He shook his head and said, "If this fails, for whatever reason, we move farther south into Saudi Arabia and then find a place to cross from Saudi Arabia into Iraq much akin to what several divisions of U.S. forces did in the first Gulf War in their famous end run." He took a deep breath and continued "The Kuwait team has driven the routes twice with no problem."

He showed a map of Iraq, pointed, and said, "Once in Iraq, we stay as far west as possible using the roads of the Syrian Desert to make our way to the north and northwest. It is sparsely populated and few would notice three vehicles moving across pothole laden and poorly maintained roads." He showed another photograph of an emblem and said, "To add an additional degree of protection, our vehicles have an Iraqi governmental emblem painted on the doors. In essence, we pose as the Iraq Department of Transportation conducting a road survey in the area. To make this appear even more complete, each vehicle has multiple clip boards of hydrology data for the region as well as several Hewitt Packard calculators." He turned toward us and said, "Given our cover, we spend the next week studying how the Iraqis build roads."

He flipped quickly to an aerial photograph. He said, "The first site is in the small town of Nami, Iraq. Nami is located just south of Hit and to the northwest of Ramadi. All this is alongside the Euphrates River." He paused and used the laser to show the river on the aerial photograph and continued, "Hit was an ancient city but not large, in its heyday it was tied to the use of boats navigating the river. Ramadi is a thriving city of over five-hundred thousand people." He flipped and showed a demographic map of Iraq and said, "Iraq is a county of division. Its most salient division is between Shia and Suni Muslims. As a broad statement, Shia Muslims are poor and are concentrated in the south and along the Iranian border. The Suni hold the majority of wealth and are

Saddam's base of power." He showed a map with an embedded triangle drawing and said, "Saddam strategically placed this site in the center of the Suni triangle. His only real ally is Syria and he is deathly afraid of Iran."

He showed several photographs of an industrial warehouse with a series of fences and a guard force. It was grainy and difficult to see. He continued, "Our informants mentioned this specific site as the place where massive amounts of chemical weapons are hidden and maintained." He showed another aerial photograph and said, "Recent satellite imagery of the place doesn't show much activity, and of the three, it appears the easiest. Our initial plan is to breach a hole in the fence late at night, cut locks, enter, and look for evidence of chemical, biological, or anything resembling weapons of mass destruction."

He showed a map followed by another aerial photo and continued, "The second site is much tougher. It is on the outskirts of the major town of Baiji. This is the tough mission. Baiji is a major player in Saddam's power structure. It's located just north of Tikrit, Saddam's home town, and it is a major industrial center." He paused and showed another photograph, but it was blurry and difficult to see anything from ground level. He continued, "The target is in the middle of a major industrial complex. I don't know how we are going to tackle this target, but we have time."

He sighed and continued, "The final target is in a most unusual place." He flipped to a map and traced a route through Baghdad to the south along the east bank of the Euphrates. "This is Al Kifl. At best, its population is ten thousand. Legend has it the prophet Ezekiel is buried here, and for years, Jews across Iraq gathered here during Passover." He flipped through a series of photographs showing the town and continued, "When Saddam took power, he killed the Jews and it became a Suni military town in a Shia neighborhood." He showed photographs of Iraqi Army locations and said, "He placed an Air Defense Brigade and a Republican Guard Infantry battalion in the city." He flipped to a map and said, "Strategically, it's south of Hillah, a major military city, and northeast of Najaf. Najaf is a Shia shrine town, so he basically built himself a small, heavily fortified outpost in the south where he can quickly project power. Multiple older intelligence sources confirmed Saddam used chemical weapons against the Shia Muslims in the south of Iraq after the first Gulf War, the weapons came from storage facilities in Al Kifl." He showed more photographs and said, "The only place sufficient to build or store weapons is an old brick factory on the northern edge of town. It is suspicious due to numerous bunkers on the property. Our plan is to focus on the brick factory and eliminate it as a potential site, and then if we fail, we move farther into the small military town." He paused and added, "the final target might be the toughest. Not because of its location, but because we travel roughly two hundred kilometers across central Iraq just to get to it. Plus, the closer we get to the Euphrates or the Tigris, the more people."

The room was silent, and he showed a map with lines and said, "Finally, we enter into phase four. This is our movement out of Iraq. We have four viable options. Ideally, we assess the target at Al Kifl, drive due west into the safety of the Syrian Desert and then back into Kuwait. Option two is drive due west into Jordan. We have numerous resources there. Option three is drive north into the Kurdish country." He paused, walked back from the map, and said, "We have an air option. Because of the 'No Fly Zone' established on the southern edge of the country, if we get far enough south, or into the western desert, we could get air recovery. All air operations carry inherent risk, so this is our least preferred option." I was glad to hear it was an option.

Chad inserted another drive into the computer and showed photos of the vehicles. He used his laser pointer and said, "We organize ourselves based upon where you ride in the convoy." He pointed at me and said, "Papaw and Mike have lead in the Toyota truck."

I looked around, trying to remember Mike. He stood and Chad motioned him forward. He was in his early thirties and in good shape. I shook his hand and said, "Tell me you speak the language."

He nodded and said yes.

Chad assembled the Ford Explorer crew, saying, "I'm shotgun on this vehicle with Jim as the primary driver." Jim moved forward and Chad looked at me and said, "Jim just finished the five-month Arabic language course." He said, "Barry and Charles come forward." For my benefit, he said, "Barry is a scientist and one of the nation's leading experts on weapons of mass destruction. As an added bonus, he is fluent in all dialects of Arabic."

I nodded.

Charles looked older than the others, and Chad said, "This guy is a good spy, mostly in Russia, but he doesn't speak Arabic."

Chad looked around and said, "The final Toyota team is Gerald and Kevin. He looked at me and said, "Gerald comes from your world, and Kevin is a chemical engineer who is fluent in Arabic." Chad turned and said, "Mitch, introduce the support team."

Mitch was a gray-haired man easily in his sixties. He stood and said, "Scott is our vehicle man. Bryan is our communications specialist." He turned and pointed "This is Lynn, Bryan's wife, and she is responsible for research and preparation."

Our days were routine. We gathered early in the morning to study the mission, view satellite photographs, used technology to look at all our planned routes, and ensured we had a complete understanding of our contingencies. Lynn taught several classes on road building. After lunch, we went outside and spend an hour dry-firing weapons and executing magazine changes. We followed this with more classes into the early afternoon, took a long midafternoon break, and started again with more classes. Each night, Chad and Mitch set up a video link in one of the bedrooms and reported our progress. Finally, Chad told us we would depart in a week.

THE LAST MISSION

Kuwait was swamped. Soldiers and military equipment were everywhere. The Army moved its entire Third Infantry Division into the country. They also had the Fourth Infantry Division's equipment floating around the Mediterranean in hopes the Turks would allow them to land and invade Iraq from the north. Security was tight as we passed either a military or Kuwaiti police checkpoint every few miles. We stayed at a large military facility on the outskirts of Kuwait City called Camp Doha. It consisted of hundreds of warehouses and was used as a headquarters and as a transit point for units moving into the desert.

We spent the first couple of days in our new headquarters behind multiple layers of security. The resident CIA crew treated us well and spent hours talking us through their preparations. They showed us the vehicles, the compartments, and we began the process of stowing and storing equipment to ensure we could get what we needed quickly. Late one evening, we loaded up our team and went on a one-hundred-kilometer drive across bad roads as a rehearsal. Once we were comfortable, we then began taking daily trips into the Udari Desert.

The Third Infantry Division is known as the Rock of the Marne. The unit's linage goes back to their actions on the Marne River in World War I. They kept units in the desert throughout the incredibly hot summer where daytime temperatures exceeded 120 degrees. These Soldiers were tough and trained.

It was impressive to see Abrams Tanks and Bradley Fighting Vehicles conducting live fire maneuvers in every direction. Throughout my career, I heard the Army's best leaders were tank men. My experience proved that to be true. As a general rule, they possessed the one quality the Army most required: common sense. They knew their men, their machines, logistics, and how to synchronize it all in order to efficiently kill the enemy. When the nation sent tanks, they weren't fooling around.

We conducted two long road marches across Kuwait to the start points of the smugglers' routes. This allowed us to work on our night protocols and how we would arrange the vehicles and guard ourselves when sleeping. Although the desert can get hot in the daytime because of the temperature drop, you freeze at night. We were into November and the temperature was decent during the day but getting colder every night. Mike and I worked well together, and he proved to be a good choice with me in the lead vehicle. The communications people were brilliant in the multiple ways we communicated not only with them but also between vehicles. Basically, if the lead vehicle stopped or engaged in any conversation with anyone, the trailing vehicles could overhear the entire conversation to ensure the stories were straight.

Our plan was to infiltrate Iraq in December and be home by early January. We knew we would miss Christmas, but if everything went well, not by much. If everything went extremely well, we would spend seven to ten days in Iraq. If it didn't go according to plan, we discussed contingencies for twenty to thirty days. Chad called the team together, and it all changed.

He said, "We won't be authorized to conduct our mission into Iraq until early February." It didn't make sense. Strategic reconnaissance was designed to provide the decision maker with facts that inform their decision. If we found chemical weapons, we would work a destruction mission which was a win for our side. If we didn't find anything, then we wouldn't fight a war. This was also a win. It seemed like the decision makers didn't want to know.

Chad said, "Whoever delayed is above the CIA Director. The vice president has a keen interest in the mission, but who knows." He brought more depressing news. "We will stay in Kuwait and continue to rehearse the mission. None of us are going home." I wanted to go home. Christmas was special, and I hadn't even called home since August. Chad knew it was tough news. I don't know if he violated protocols, but he authorized us calling home once per week using a very specific line and interface number.

Lorraine was shocked, and she screamed when she heard my voice. It wasn't unusual for me to be out of touch with her and the kids for up to six months at a time, but she wasn't feeling well and told me she had the flu. Each time I called, she was excited, and it was wonderful. I wasn't good talking on the phone. It seemed unnatural to me for some reason, but I was learning. The kids were doing great. Marge drove down to spend time with her and the kids. Lorraine was calming. I loved the sound of her voice. She sensed the calls were unusual, and something unique happened in the course of my work.

The informants in Baghdad stood by their story. Although a great deal of talk was ongoing about the Iraqi's ability to use mobile laboratories, the informants remained convinced they were stationary. The only viable targets were those assigned to us. It was possible, according to the informants, if a mobile capacity existed, it would be north of Baghdad in the vicinity of Samarra. Samarra was home of Iraq's best military units, so the assumption was they defended the capability. As a result, all technical assets turned to observe the compound. We watched anxiously for the next two months and with no indication it existed in Samarra. Either way, in the event of war, the Samarra military infrastructure was the first target.

Our days filled with routine activities. We gathered each morning to analyze the latest intelligence reports, we spent a couple of hours each day rehearsing our mission, and we went to the desert three times per week for weapons training. It became a blur. The best part of the week was my twenty minute phone call.

I remained impressed with the Soldiers training for war around us. The Third Infantry Division was at its best. They were the most prepared invasion force in the history of the world. They were training live fire operations in full chemical suits, training all night, and were determined to win. It was a risky proposition. The Secretary of Defense was determined to fight a war with the Iraqis just as he fought with the Afghans. We rented an Army in Afghanistan. Here, the strategy was to invade with the Third Infantry Division and some Marine Corps ground units. They would follow with units on an as needed basis. It was clear to me that the as-needed time was now, not later, but nobody asked me.

We watched the nightly video teleconferences. Roughly once per week, all the heavy hitters emerged and engaged in strategic discussions. While the Iraqis were fragmented, intelligence indicated they would fight hard when invaded. Yet during each of the heavy hitter conferences, someone always played the white flag card. It held that the Iraqis would simply give up and march toward us in a humble surrender. If anything, the latest intelligence suggested a strong trend in the opposite direction. This infuriated Chad who was constantly telling anyone willing to listen it would be a tough fight and to expect anything else was folly. He kept making phone calls to determine the source of the white flag theory, but the only answer was that it was a political theory.

We monitored the press and news reports. It seemed predestined we were going to war. We hadn't executed our mission, yet everyone was talking about war and their hopes and dreams for a post-war Iraq. The news cycle was full of speculation, and high-level politicians were all over the news making the case for war.

By mid-January, Chad told us we would execute the mission, and we were to make our last phone call. It was the best part of my week but bittersweet. After each call, I would wander between the buildings and imagine myself at home with my family. I needed the call more than they did. Lorraine still had the flu, but her morale was high, and she was encouraging.

I said, "You are beginning to worry me."

She shrugged it off and said, "Concentrate on your stuff and come home because we miss you."

The kids were doing great, and it was a joy to hear their voices. When I hung up the phone, I walked between the rows of warehouses and knew it was time to retire. I needed to get this mission behind me and go home.

We participated in a series of high-level video conferences where we discussed our mission, our objectives, and our projected timelines. During one of our final briefings, both the State Department guy and the Under Secretary of Defense asked again to delay the operation. Chad didn't get the opportunity to respond. Numerous senior leaders moved quickly to defend our plan. They forcefully argued the need for this mission. If the Iraqis possessed WMD capability, it had to be at these sites. They further argued these sites required human reconnaissance to confirm or deny the presence of weapons. Both the State Department guy and the Under Secretary of Defense backed down. I began to think about the benefit to me if we scrubbed the mission. I could go home and retire, that was a win. Then I thought about those Soldiers training like mad men in the desert and the tragedy of sending them to war for the wrong reasons. Chad told us not to get our hopes up as he had seen this infighting before, and it always produced some sort of backlash. We waited anxiously for several days and continued to prepare.

Chad was summoned to a high-level video conference. Mitch and I accompanied him and sat in the back row out of sight. Chad once again briefed our plan. It was an odd arrangement as we normally saw the various participants on the large screen, but this time, they were all blacked out, and all we heard were their voices. When he completed his briefing, a voice came over and said, "You need to find weapons of mass destruction."

I wondered if it was an order.

Chad said, "Our objective is to determine presence or lack thereof at three specific sites."

A long pause followed, and I looked at Mitch. He gritted his teeth and said, "This is bad."

Finally, after the long pause, the mystery man asked Chad, "How long can you stay in the country and can you execute dynamic targeting?"

Mitch jumped, and I looked at him. He looked angry and said, "'Dynamic' is an academic word. It implies we go into the country and be prepared for a call which sends us to another target."

Chad cleared his throat and said, "It's a risk decision. We are confident executing our planned mission, and it is currently rated as high risk." If you tell us to remain in country and wait for a call to look at another target, then our mission becomes extremely high risk with imminent death implications. As you are aware, that requires Presidential approval." At that point, a different voice entered and said, "It should not be difficult as the Iraqis will all surrender anyway." Chad had an emotional response. His voice was elevated and he said, "Whoever is propagating the myth of the white flag theory is not doing their homework. The daily, weekly, strategic, operational, and tactical intelligence analysis reports are pointing to a tough fight. Holding a team in country for that long is unwise." Again, all became silent. Finally, after a full minute of quiet, the original voice came over the speakers and said, "Execute the mission as planned." The screen went dead. I turned to Mitch and said, "Whose voice was that?" He lowered his eyes and said, "You don't want to know."

BUILDING ROADS

We lounged and slept for the next two days. Finally, mission day arrived. We spent thousands of hours running the mission in our minds. Now, it was reality. My father was fond of saying the hardest part of anything is getting started, and he was correct. We shook hands with the Kuwaiti team, loaded our bags, and started out from Kuwait City. Our goal was to enter the smuggler lanes in the late afternoon and exit in darkness. It was a long and hard ride across the desert. The Third Infantry Division was still maneuvering and conducting live fires in all directions, and I thought about how anxious they felt.

We entered the lanes around three in the afternoon. We knew the sun would set within the next hour and a half. It was cold, and as the night progressed, it got colder. As we had rehearsed, we rolled down our windows and began looking for anything to the side of the path that might give us trouble. Specifically, we were looking for mines. In reality, we were traversing a series of minefields. Our greatest concern was getting off the route and striking a long buried, but still active, anti-tank mine. We preloaded the route into our GPS, and we were deliberate in our movement rarely exceeding ten miles per hour. It was painfully slow. The GPS route was exacting requiring us to veer constantly to the left or right. Suddenly, two large pickup trucks appeared on the horizon. They were moving fast on a collision course with us.

"Mike," I said, "stop and get us in a position to shoot." They closed quickly. They were Ford dual rear wheel pickup trucks with large campers. Each had two men in the cab. They slowed as they came close to us. I slung the AK on my back and kept my door open. Mike moved forward and waved. They closed cautiously toward us, and the driver rolled down his window. Mike spoke to them in Arabic. He talked for a few seconds, then laughed, and walked back to our vehicle. They passed slowly on our left, picked up speed, and were gone.

Mike said, "They were carrying alcohol and drugs to a party in Kuwait City, and they were running late. They would love to stop and chat, but they had to make their delivery before midnight. It really is a smuggler's route." We relaxed slightly and drove with more confidence.

We exited the lane and found a small hill in the middle of the desert. We conducted our standard short halt drill with each person executing their assigned duties. We covered the sides of the vehicles with a combination of painted cardboard and plastic and ripped it off to unveil our replica design of the Iraqi Department of Highways and Transportation. The designs looked good and even appeared to show age. We drove another seventy miles across the desert until we reached our first blacktop oil road. Although it was pothole laden, it was easier on our trucks than the open desert. It was important for us to stay south of As Salman and Ash Shabakah while staying well north of the Saudi Arabian border.

We followed the road due west for another two hours and settled into our nighttime security routine. I slept on a small pad in the back of the truck and covered myself with a lightweight sleeping bag. It was colder than I expected. As we rehearsed, I took the last guard shift. It was still cold but the desert was beautiful. I thought of Lorraine and how one of her favorite songs was "Peaceful Easy Feeling" by the Eagles. I liked the quiet in the mornings, and it was a good time for me to focus and think about the day. Today, according to plan, would include lots of driving across bad roads. We would use our fuel reserves now, and the highlight would be our fuel stop late this evening. Yesterday had gone according to plan, and we needed today to follow suit.

We ate our rations quickly, refilled our fuel tanks using the reserve cans, and started back toward the blacktop oil roads. By early morning, we found a long stretch of road with few potholes, and we were surprised by how well maintained this route was compared to what we saw previously. Every two hours or so, we would drive into the desert, circle our trucks, relieve ourselves, and study the maps. Thus far during our tour of Iraq, we had seen a total of four men who were smugglers. By this afternoon, we would see more people. Our goal was to get to the Wild West City of An Nukhayb and find ourselves a safe fuel stop. The town was widely considered the smuggling capitol of Iraq and sat poised to deliver whatever illegal goods you desired to Jordan, Saudi Arabia, Kuwait, Syria, and anywhere within Iraq. The good news about towns like this was we didn't expect to be asked many questions. We had internal debates about whether having the Iraqi Transportation logo was a good idea entering into this town but decided it was safer in the long run.

Once we were on the road for a few hours, we began to see a few trucks and then cars. We passed a few rest stops and one or two mom-and-pop grocery stores along the road. We remained true to form and stopped every two hours to stretch and conduct map reconnaissance. Finally, we closed on An Nukhayb, and the roads got wider as we entered the small city. It may have been a smugglers town, but it was also the last stop for pilgrims exiting Iraq on their way to Mecca and Medina, so it had several gas stations. We rehearsed the plan several times, so we didn't spend a great deal of time talking. Mike and I drove slowly through the town. It consisted of a couple of mud-fenced homes, the mosque, several warehouses, a few garages, and several gas stations. We decided on the gas station on the far eastern part of the town, thinking that if something went wrong, we would be able to move north quickly. We also wanted anyone seeing us leaving the town to think we were heading east toward Karbala. It was modern, and if we hit it at the right time, we would refuel together. Iraqis, like most in the Middle East, don't venture out during the day due to the heat, but they tend to come out in droves in the early evening.

I said aloud, "The key is to blend into the surroundings." As simple as it seems, getting fuel in a foreign land while blending with the population was a critical task. The town was getting busy and lots of people were walking the streets. We moved slowly and received several curious looks.

We stopped and began the refueling drill. I started with the gas cans in the back of the truck, and as I finished the first, an older man walked directly up to me and began talking. I was clueless. I saw Mike from the corner of my eye, and I smiled, nodded, and pointed at Mike. The man moved and began talking to Mike in rapid fire Arabic as I continued to fuel the cans. Once complete with the cans, I quickly inserted the nozzle into the truck and began refueling.

Mike engaged the man in an animated conversation. Mike turned toward me, spoke in Arabic, and pulled out one of our large province maps and placed it on the hood of the truck. I noticed Chad was almost complete with his fueling, and Charles was ready to intercept anyone who spoke to him. Mike waved, and Barry moved from the Explorer to the hood of our vehicle and joined the conversation. Barry was fluent in Arabic and a natural talker. They pointed at the map, talked, pointed again, and talked more. Gerald and Kevin pulled behind me and were getting nervous. Chad finished fueling and Charles entered the store. In less than a minute, he returned. He cranked the Explorer and moved it away from the pumps. From out of nowhere, a small red car pulled behind them and filled the spot next to the pumps.

I walked back and said, " Mike, get in the conversation and move the map to the Explorer so we can refuel your truck." He walked forward and pointed toward the Ford. The whole gang then walked to the Ford with map in hand and began a new series of conversations. I moved my truck to the far side of the Ford, but I realized we left Gerald, who didn't speak Arabic, alone at the pumps. I jumped from the truck and walked casually to the Ford. I pointed at Gerald. Charles saw it and walked back to the pumps and stood guard over Gerald until he finished. He pulled the truck behind me and Charles went in and paid for the two remaining trucks. The conversation on the hood continued. I could see Chad getting anxious. We had fuel, but now three of our four language speakers were engaged in a long conversation with some man at a gas station. Finally, Barry pulled the map from the hood and began to end the conversation. The man kept talking. Mike walked back toward our truck and nodded toward me. I joined him and went to my side. He cranked the vehicle and turned toward me.

He said, "He is the mayor of An Nukhayb. We are in the Al Anbar province. It is all Sunni Muslim and very loyal to Saddam. The mayor wants us to look at a series of roads on the eastern side of town. The Army tore them up, and he is threatening to call Baghdad to the Minister's office if we don't. That might blow our cover. Conversely, if we do go and look, and we do a good job, he may call either the district supervisor or the minister and also report us."

Barry kept the man engaged.

Chad heard our conversation via the speaker system and said, "Mike, get to Barry and tell him we will take the mission. Tell the mayor we will spend the night locally and then drive the road early in the morning. It is risky, but we play the part." Mike nodded and moved back to the conversation. He pulled Barry away while Kevin and later Charles keep him engaged. Barry looked back and nodded.

Finally, we are able to extract ourselves from the mayor. Barry said, "He insisted we stay at his place, but I told him we made other arrangements. I told him we will meet him and conduct a survey of the road. I also told him he couldn't talk about this because of the political jealousies in Baghdad. I think he bought it." We drove north to get away from people. We ended up driving twenty miles before we found a small hill overlooking the surrounding area with long range views in all directions.

Chad pulled us together and said, "We are in a tough spot. If we don't return and work with the Mayor, he will call Baghdad and will arouse suspicion. The worst-case scenario is that we are picked up by the national police. If we go back and work with the Mayor, we have a higher probability of retaining our cover story."

Barry asked, "Okay, we must go back and work with the Mayor, but what's our level of commitment?"

I said, "We have stakes, flags, transient devices used in surveying, and lots of calculators."

Chad nodded and said, "The only problem is language. If any of us who don't speak the language are questioned, then things get suspicious fast."

Chad called Mitch and his team in Kuwait. Mitch looked at problems from a different viewpoint. Upon hearing the situation, he said, "When your cover is in jeopardy, go deeper into the cover rather than avoiding it. Don't just put out markers, but we will get you an Arabic concrete contract. Actually, pour the stuff. You got money, and if you build it wide enough, it might be a fine airstrip." It was a good idea. In these situations, good ideas win. We all had questions, but if we worked hard tonight, did our homework, protected those who didn't speak the language, it had the highest probability for success.

We organized and began working a list of questions. Our thoughts were far ranging. We needed workable solutions to determine where we would find a concrete producer in this region, determine the required depth and width, and a method to mark our work. We had access to three Internet computers, so we all began our research. Mitch provided us more answers than any of us could imagine, including a twelve-page bureaucratic looking contract written in Arabic. We rotated to get some sleep and then assembled early the next morning to conduct our final rehearsal. Each of us would play a role. The most critical item was to keep an Arabic speaker hovering around those who didn't speak the language.

We used the speaker system the next morning to cover the final details. True to his word, the Mayor stood with two other men at the same gas station. He was elated to see us and hugged Barry like a long lost brother. Barry was in rare form and played his part well. He jumped into the mayor's vehicle and rode with them to the site while the rest of us followed. We drove three miles to a long empty barren stretch of road. It was long and narrow. His chief complaint was that the Iraqi Army had torn up the road and he felt the national government had the responsibility to fix it. Barry agreed. We drove the length of the road, turned, and did it again. Finally, those who spoke the language, with the exception of Mike, all assembled on the hood of the Ford and began a series of discussions. The rest of us drove down the road and began to take out surveying equipment and flags. It looked real. Barry's mission was to get the Mayor to find a concrete contractor and get him to this location. We all wanted that to happen today but were willing to wait another day, if required. After an hour or more of debate and discussions, the Mayor and his partners drove off toward Karbala with a promise they would return that afternoon with a concrete man. Our mission was to make it look real. Throughout the morning, we saw traffic ranging from cars full of kids to trucks full of furniture traverse the road. We pulled out the transient and acted like we knew what we were doing. We marked off forty feet on either side of the road and began placing stakes in the ground as evenly and professionally as we could. By midafternoon, we were complete, and it looked generally square and semiprofessional.

We were eating our rations when the Mayor's vehicle followed by two trucks came into view. Chad turned on the speaker system in the Ford and Mike translated the conversation as best he could. Barry went quickly to work, saying in Arabic, "The road must be wide enough for alternate military purposes. As you know, Saddam demands everything for a military purpose so we must comply with his wishes."

The Mayor agreed. The concrete man was astonished at the magnitude of the mission, and each time Barry mentioned Saddam's name, his eyes grew large. Barry produced the large and cumbersome contract, saying, "This is our contract. We will pay half now and the remainder when you complete the job. We expect it to be done correctly."

Money changed hands. Mitch provided him with exacting specifications such as the width, depth, and density of the concrete and the current costs of labor and materials in Iraq. At times, it was so real, I thought I was an Iraqi.

Barry then went into political mode. He said, "My team must continue our mission, but I will deputize you"—he pointed at the Mayor—"to ensure this project is complete to Saddam's specifications. You will retain the money and pay the contractor. Of course, we will inspect when we return next month."

The concrete man drove the route several times and studied the problem. He had been awarded the contract of a lifetime, and he didn't want to mess up. We decided to spend the night not far from the road, each of us telling our portion of the story we just witnesses, and all of us praising Barry for his ability to play the part. As always, I pulled the last guard shift. To my amazement, the next morning, a convoy of trucks began arriving at the far end of the road. My first thought was it was a military exercise, but as the sun came up, I saw the concrete team starting their work. The Iraqis loved capitalism, and this was an opportunity they weren't going to squander. None of us expected to go into country and build a runway, but we followed Mitch's advice and went deeper into the cover.

We loaded and moved, stopping several times that morning, and by midafternoon, we turned almost due east toward Ramadi. This was a dangerous part of the mission. We were heading toward a major population center on well-maintained four-lane highways. It was an oil city, and many believe the heart of the Sunni Triangle. Our intelligence indicated it was the home of at least two divisions of the Iraqi Army. One was a conscript Division, and the other the famous Hammurabi Republican Guard Division. We moved to the outskirts of the city and then turned north toward the town of Nami. It was just south of the town of Hit. Our fuel levels were fine, and we had not yet used any of our reserve, but we did need to execute another fuel stop. We drove in a column, staying as best we could in the far left lane. We successfully executed the turn to the north and were feeling nervous but confident. Mike remained at the wheel. Suddenly, we saw a series of road blocks ahead, and the traffic began to merge. Two Iraqi cars merged between our truck and Chad's Ford Explorer. It was a police and military checkpoint, and the traffic was funneled into one lane. Armed Soldiers were manning the passenger sides while the police were manning the driver's side. We entered into the language nightmare scenario.

Each of us carried carefully crafted credentials identifying us as employees with the Ministry of Roads and Transportation as well as a basic identification card. Mike and I quickly pulled them from our pockets. We could see the Soldiers on the passenger side were carefully checking each credential. We rolled down our windows. The car in front of us seemed to be having difficulty and was drawing the attention of both the policeman and the military. They ordered it the side to undergo further inspection. Mike pulled our truck forward.

The Soldier stared curiously at the painted insignia on the side of the truck. I nodded and handed him my two identification cards. He spoke and I could tell it was a question, but I had no idea what he said. He stared coldly at me, and I lowered my eyes. He raised his voice. Mike was engaged with the police officer out his window, and I could see I was drawing attention. Several Soldiers were staring at me, and two were moving forward. I looked up at the Soldier in question as he moved directly to the side of the window, and I began making hand motions. Mike saw it and quickly stepped in and told them I was deaf. He turned to me and began making sign language, and I did my best to answer. I had no idea how to do sign language, so it probably looked far more like a bad hand of rock, paper, scissors, but the Iraq in charge bought it and slowly moved away. Mike was talking in rapid fire Arabic and was attempting to publically embarrass them. A large Iraqi Soldier who had been sitting stood and yelled orders with a violent motion, and we were waved forward and back into the highway. The window was down, and it was a very cold evening, I was sweating. We pulled forward about one hundred meters and gently moved the truck off the road. We listened intently to the speaker. We were confident the vehicles behind us listened to our conversation at the checkpoint, but we also knew that the Iraqis would not buy multiple deaf people traveling together.

We heard coughing. There were multiple conversations ongoing. Mike did his best to translate, and we could hear Barry and Charles talking. We suspected Chad was coughing. Finally, we heard Chad say, "Gerald and Kevin, be careful."

We heard our last vehicle roll up to the checkpoint and heard Kevin's booming voice in Arabic, we heard him change gears on his Toyota truck and then calmly say, "It pays to be last They waved us through." I wiped the sweat from my forehead.

If the Iraqi guard had pushed, we would enter into the fight or capture scenario. We discussed this situation during training. Each situation would be different, and each one would require the best judgment of the man who was compromised. We all agreed that if one member chose to fight, we would all fight. It was a good decision and especially for me as I didn't speak the language. If any of us were captured, any decent interrogator would break us within two hours, sooner if they used torture. The mission would be compromised, and our teammate would be dead, so we felt it a better decision to fight first and take our chances in a running gun battle than simply surrender.

We continued north and soon saw the Euphrates on our right flank. It was a powerful river and wider than I expected. It was approaching nine o'clock local, and the roads were full. People were walking alongside the river, and several of the houses overlooking the river were impressive. We passed some wealthy neighborhoods. Finally, we reached the Nami exit. Nami was a small suburb town mainly facing the river. We needed to decide our next move. We were either going to hit our target tonight or move and find a secure campsite.

Chad asked over the intercom, "Papaw, what do you think, tonight or tomorrow?"

I thought and said, "We are tired, but I really like the idea of hitting it tonight and then going to a hide site."

Gerald entered the conversation and said, "It's all about fuel, so I like the idea of getting fuel and then hitting the target."

I looked at Mike and said, "Chad, I agree. Good call, Fuel, then target, then hide."

The streets were crowded, but we found a small gas station with few patrons. It had a series of houses behind it with a small alleyway. It was as secure as we could find. Mike and I pulled to one side of the pump while Chad and his crew pulled to the opposite. Gerald and Kevin went directly to their pump. We filled our tanks, and Charles calculated the bill and went inside to pay.

We were getting ready to move, but as Charles exited the building, shots rang out. It was a long burst of automatic fire followed by yelling, screaming, and then what sounded like... laughter. I moved behind the pump and pulled my pistol. I didn't know what a bullet would do to the gas pumps I was hiding behind, but I didn't want to find out. Charles ran back to the Ford. Another burst of fire, then another. Suddenly, a crowd rounded the corner from the alley. They looked like some type of gang at first, and then we saw the AKs pointed skyward, and they began firing again.

We were all seconds away from showing our pistols when Charles said, "Is it a wedding?"

It was.

Mike smiled and waved at the crowd, and they politely waved back. I felt my body go limp, and my right hand began shaking just like Afghanistan. They were celebrating a marriage, and we saw the bride and groom walking arm in arm. They moved past us and turned away toward the center of the town, firing sporadic burst into the air. I sunk down into the Toyota seat. My hand was now shaking uncontrollably.

Mike stared at me and said, "Hey, you okay?" He was scared and serious.

I said, "Don't worry, just drive." I grabbed my right hand with my left and held it steady and did my best to massage my hand and arm. I was having some type of reaction. I felt like I was exposed to some chemical, and my brain couldn't make my hand stop shaking.

Mike turned to me again. His voice was forceful and said, "Tell me you're okay."

Chad entered the conversation and said, "Hey, what's going on up there?"

I took a deep breath and said, "I got chilled and got a case of the temporary shakes."

Mike shifted gears, cut off the speaker, and said, "Hey, man, are you having a stroke?" He was deadly serious. Somehow, I found an odd humor in his tone, and I began to laugh.

Mike cut the speaker on, and Chad was upset, saying, "Talk to me, guys. What's going on up there?"

Mike answered and said, "You guys partnered me with a crazy old man, and he's gone mad." I laughed harder. Mike started laughing, and we could hear the whole convoy chuckling. My arm stopped shaking. Maybe laughter was the best medicine.

We drove several blocks and saw the warehouse complex. It consisted of multiple warehouses with three layers of fencing. The outermost layer was a tall standard fence with concertina wire at the top, and it surrounded the entire complex. The second layer was a similar fence without the concertina, and it surrounded approximately half of the buildings. Finally, based upon the satellite imagery, we could expect a third fence surrounding two buildings in the center of the compound. As we drove past the warehouse, we could see the two outer fences as well as several guards. The outer guard house was a shack. It was guarded by two uniformed Iraqi Soldiers with Kalashnikov's slung across their back and standing next to a burn barrel. We waved as we passed but got no reaction and kept driving. The interior guard post, which was harder to see, appeared to be higher quality with electricity as evidenced by the lights and large windows. We drove down the road, past the long row of warehouses, and stopped at a small turnout beside the river. It was cold, and the wind was whipping along the river. We expected a squad of ten or eleven Iraqi Soldiers who were routinely given the guard mission. We also expected them to be Republican Guard, but that didn't necessarily mean they would be disciplined on a cold night in February. The only thing we knew for certain was that something inside the center warehouse was worth guarding.

We were in a very isolated area, tucked in behind a series of warehouses against the river. Our biggest concern was our exit route. It required us to climb a small hill and then directly into main street. As we rehearsed, we assembled and conducted a thorough equipment check. We could not afford to get inside and then determine we forgot a piece of equipment. The scout team would consist of me and Mike. Our function was to cut wire, deadbolts, and ensure the test team got in a position to conduct the test. The test team would consist of Chad, Barry, and Kevin. Gerald would infiltrate with us but would provide rear security and assist either team if we got in trouble. Jim and Charles would protect the vehicles and ensure we had safe egress. They would also be responsible for manning a well hidden machine gun in case it went really bad. Chad sent Mitch a detailed report of where we were located.

We checked our watches, and it was approaching eleven o'clock local. Each of us had earpieces, but only four would talk. This allowed all to listen but mitigated the danger of compromise. I would speak for the lead team, Chad for the test team, Gerald as our linebacker, and Jim with the vehicles and machine guns. The wind speed along the river caused my eyes to water. It was freezing, but tonight cold weather and a strong wind were friends. It should keep the most disciplined Soldier on a short patrol and hugging a stationary heat source.

I said, "Check weapons and moving." Mike I started alongside the river. It was tough, rocky terrain. We were only ten feet from the water's edge, but diving into the river to avoid detection was not an option. I was impressed by the fence. It was well constructed and pulled tight. We moved slowly alongside the river for over a hundred yards until we began to see the first target warehouse. The wind continued, making it colder and colder. My hands were freezing through my gloves.

We passed the first warehouse and found our planned entry point. The Iraqis placed three old military-style metal storage containers against the fence line. This would give us some cover as we cut the wire. Mike moved forward and began making cuts.

I could see the interior large fence, and I was fairly certain I was also seeing the third fence and the center warehouse building.

The key to cutting the fence was to make only one straight line. We used a small piece of board to hold the fence apart. Mike entered first and crawled to the front side of the old metal building, and I followed. I spoke one word into my microphone, saying, "Breached," and I crawled next to Mike. The closest warehouse was approximately fifty feet away. I tapped his shoulder and ran in a low crouch until I reached the corner of the building. From here, I could see the next fence as well as our target. The second fence was complex. It was a high fence and specifically placed to restrict access to the warehouses within its perimeter. The fence was seventy feet from the warehouses. Anyone looking in that direction would see us cutting. Our primary interest was the warehouses, but we needed to check the other two just in case.

We moved to the opposite side of the warehouse. It gave us a better view of the compound. We saw nothing moving, but to be certain, I pulled my night vision goggles and scanned. It looked deserted. I tapped Mike, and he began his sprint to the fence. I was ready to fire. He rushed forward and fell into the prone and began the slow process of cutting the fence. I saw him scoot under the fence toward the next warehouse. When he established at one corner, I began my sprint, dropped and scooted under the fence, and moved to the opposite side of the warehouse.

Mike tapped me on my shoulder, and I spoke softly into the microphone, saying, "Breached second fence, eyes on primary target." The final fence was just as large, but we would have some cover due to the arrangement of the three warehouses located in the center of the compound. They were in a two back and one up configuration. The one farthest from us was the final building and our primary target. Mike tapped my shoulder, and I nodded. He dashed forward and was soon on his back, making the cut. Suddenly, he was up and running. I ran at a low crouch, slid down, and crawled under the fence and went to the opposite corner. It was a large warehouse with several black barrels on the backside. My first thought was we found something.

As I reached the corner, I heard voices. I glanced quickly around the corner and saw two Iraqi Soldiers walking toward the back of the building. One was tall and lanky, and the other was short with broad shoulders. Both had weapons slung across their backs. I dashed back behind the barrels. Mike moved around the corner. He was in a dangerous position. He was within sight of the main guard house. The Soldiers were talking and seeking a wind break to smoke. They were standing about ten feet away, and I was in a painful crouch behind one of the barrels. I could hear their conversation, and it seemed casual.

I raised my head to see exactly where they were standing. Both were wearing pistol belts with ammunition pouches and a canteen. At least one of them was wearing a bayonet. They were Republican guard as the Iraqis would not outfit their conscript Soldiers with good equipment. I could not let Mike stay exposed. If a guard came out of the building, they would see Mike. I pulled my knife and slowly crouched back down and scanned the ground for anything I could throw to create a diversion. I found a small rock. If we fired a shot, even with a silencer, our mission would be compromised. Everyone would come running. I needed to bring them toward me. I tossed the rock hard against the side of the building toward Mike. They immediately looked and began walking slowly toward me. They didn't appear alarmed and continued to talk as they walked. The taller one passed by me focused on the opposite corner. The shorter one followed, flicking his cigarette over my head. I jumped up, grabbed the shorter man around the neck, and plunged my knife into his chest. He placed both hands on my knife, but I spun him to the ground. The taller guard turned slowly and was attempting to bring his rifle from behind his back when I brought the M4 rifle butt forward and smashed his forehead. He went down hard, and within seconds,

Mike was on top of him, putting his knife into the Soldier's chest. Both were dead, and we were alive.

I pulled my knife from his chest and looked up. Chad and his team witnessed the entire episode from the last warehouse.

Mike whispered, "We have a door on my side of the building." It was dangerous but worth a try. Our plan was to find a side door and if not to enter from the exposed front. The satellite imagery gave us an excellent top down view, but we had no clue where the doors would be located other than the front. Mike went forward in a low crouch. He used a special tool, which inserts a corrosive liquid into the key hole, causing the dead bolt to float and made it easier to pry open with a long knife or screwdriver. The problem was it took time, so he inserted the liquid and came back. We waited. We had security on both sides of the building and in our rear, so we were safe for the moment, but we hated waiting. Finally, he ran forward and used a long screwdriver to move the bolt and open the door. He went inside, and I dashed behind him. We had no idea what was inside the building, so going in alone was a mistake, but maybe worth the risk given our exposure to the guard house.

It was a long and dark building with no windows or light. We were told over and over not to enter the warehouses without masks, but it was too late. We were inside. We listened and heard nothing. Slowly, we worked our night vision devices, but the room had very little light, so all we could see were large green shapes at the far end of the building. Convinced we were alone, we went to flashlights and shined them down the length of the building. There were several covered shapes but no noise or movement. Mike turned and began tracing the wall with his flashlight looking for any signs of an electronic intrusion monitor. We saw nothing. We then moved to the other side of the building and conducted a similar drill, and again nothing. It appeared it was a warehouse without electrical power, and aside from the shapes, it was empty. I whispered into the microphone, "Enter. Building secure. We are on the far wall."

Within seconds, the door opened, and Chad came in followed by Barry and Kevin. They were carrying and half-dragging the dead Iraqi Soldiers.

Barry and Kevin pulled a series of monitors from their packs. We shined our lights down the length of the warehouse on the shapes. Kevin was the first to say, "Nothing here on my device."

Soon, Barry said, "Nothing."

We worked our way toward the shapes. They were long forms and covered with a thick cloth. Barry and Kevin walked behind us constantly looking for any sign. Mike whispered, "They look like car covers."

Chad reached down and pulled the cover up. We shined our lights. It was a car. Chad pulled out his camera and began taking photographs. It was some type of Ferrari sports car. We replaced the cover and moved to the next, and it was an older Mercedes-Benz touring car. We continued down the line pulling the covers, taking photographs, and replacing the covers. All together, there were nine vintage automobiles in the warehouse, but no chemicals nor any residue signs of weapons of mass destruction. I knew the vehicles were valuable, but the only one I recognized was a Carol Shelby Daytona Cobra. We had broken into somebody's private and well-guarded garage.

Once he finished taking photographs, Chad said, "Secure the monitoring equipment and go get the bodies. Don't leave a blood trail."

I dragged the taller Soldier, and Mike dragged the shorter one. Our kills were clean with minimal blood. Chad examined them and said, "We got to make it look like a sexual murder."

I shook my head and said, "What?"

He said, "We want the people who will find the bodies first to think it is a crime scene, not a deliberate attack."

I got the impression this wasn't his first fake crime scene. We stripped the Soldiers of their belts and shirts. Chad tied the shorter man's hand with rope and pulled down his pants. He rummaged through his small backpack, found what he was looking for, and applied a dark color of blue eye mascara to the taller man. He then poured alcohol on their shirts and arranged the bodies to look like a sex act followed by a fight and subsequent dual murder.

He nodded and said, "Can you put this guy's bayonet"—he pointed toward the shorter man—"into your original knife incision?"

It was gruesome. I took the bayonet, which was thinner and longer than my knife, and carefully worked it into the dead man's chest. Chad pointed and I took the other man's bayonet and put it in Mike's original incision. It was not perfect, but it would cause anyone finding the bodies to have a first thought and that was what we needed. If it looked like a murder instead of an attack, it should buy time.

Chad said, "Sexual perversion is not just a Western idea, and especially in Middle Eastern countries, it is brushed aside and swept under the rug."

Oddly enough, it reminded of my baseball days. I once had a pitching coach who stressed to his pitchers that it doesn't have to be a strike. It only has to look like one to the hitter. Chad added more alcohol to their shirts and said, "Anyone coming across this scene gets a strong first impression. A capable investigator will find the inconsistencies, but it will take time." Our hope was the sexual perversion was intense enough for them to take it at face value and drop the case. Much would depend on how soon they discovered the cuts in the fence.

We exited quickly and regrouped behind the building. Mike was the last man out, and he inserted another liquid into the locking device, which glued the metal. This would add to the mystery. We then ex-filtrated out and ran back to the warehouse in reverse order. I was the last man out. My mission was to tie the wire back together with a small clipping machine. I rehearsed this several times in Kuwait, but it was cold, and I was tired. I slid under the wire, used bungee cord to hold the wire together, and placed a series of clips on the wire. Anyone seeing it from a distance would not notice the cut in the wire; however, if you were close and looking, it would be obvious.

By the time I was back at the warehouse, Barry and Kevin already had their monitoring equipment operational.

Barry reported, "Nothing," which was followed by Kevin who confirmed, "Nothing."

Chad nodded, and we moved to the final warehouse. Mike floated the bolt, and we waited. This time, Mike and I went forward together and entered. It was empty, nothing. The remainder of the team entered and placed the equipment onto operation.

Kevin shook his head, and Barry said, "Nothing here."

Chad said, "Dry hole. Jim, report the dry hole. Let's get out of here."

Mike inserted the liquid and Super Glue'd the door. I saw Chad crawl under the fence, and Mike said, "Go." I was running and sweating, but my hands were freezing. Mike scooted under the fence, and I pulled the wire together with the bungee cord, but I was having a tough time getting a clip to work. I struggled.

Suddenly, Chad and Mike were beside me pulling the fence together, and I managed to get three decent clips into the wire. We ran, in reverse order, to the metal buildings and each slid underneath the wire. Mike helped me pull the wire together when we heard yelling. It was coming from the center of the compound. It wasn't an alarm; it was a Soldier yelling in hopes of finding the other two Soldiers and wondering where they were. It was worrisome. We closed and clipped the fence, then moved close to the water, leaping over the rocks and moved as quickly as possible down the river to our vehicles.

Mike cranked the truck, and I turned the heater as high as it would go. We moved up the small hill and turned into a narrow street, made a sharp right turn, and entered the main street of Nami, Iraq. We moved slowly to the north, entered the highway, accelerated, and were on the main road. I checked my watch, and it was nearing one o'clock in the morning. We stayed in the right lane and continued up the road, heading northeast toward Al Hadithah. We were exhausted, and we needed a safe place to sleep. To our right flank was the Euphrates and to our left, a few scattered homes. We would need to head west into the desert for safety.

Chad said, "Everybody okay?"

I said, "Good in the lead truck."

Gerald reported, "All good back here."

We moved another twenty miles and began to see fewer and fewer houses. We were in the sparsely populated area between Hit and Al Hadithah. We turned left, exited the road, and began driving across a series of fields. This was part of Iraq's small bread basket, and it was fertilized using water from the Euphrates. It was a bumpy ride, and I said, "Mike, don't get us stuck in here." Finally, we reached a small hill, and after driving around it in a short reconnaissance decided it was good enough. We circled the trucks and crashed. I had no idea who was on guard that night.

THE STINKING PLACE

I WAS AWAKENED by sunlight. It was easily midmorning. I jumped up quickly, and it startled Mike who also jumped up. I checked my watch. It was eight thirty local. I feared we slept unguarded, but as I looked around, I saw Charles eating a ration and looking over the hill. We were in a good spot behind a small hill with good views all around and nothing of significance other than a few distant buildings. We got up, trying to shake off the cobwebs. Kevin made coffee. We guzzled it down as soon as it was hot enough to drink. Chad called us together, and we called Mitch.

Mitch said, "The cars in the warehouse belong to Saddam himself. He purchases all around the world and uses them as presents to those he thought deserving. It is a fifty-million-dollar car collection, but I reported no chemicals or residue."

Chad said, "Thanks but keep an ear for our young lovers. We don't want it to make the news." I began to feel the slightest trembling in my right hand as I held my coffee. I shifted hands and placed my right hand in my pocket.

We had fuel, a good and safe location, and probably not more than three hours from Baiji, our next target.

Chad said, "We stay here until nightfall, move north through Al Hadithah"—he pointed at the map—"make one more fuel stop, and then head northwest to our next target." He stared briefly at me and then said, "Same method, we do a driving recon and then execute. If we don't feel comfortable with the recon, we drive north and figure it out. Today, we eat and rest."

It was a long day, and I didn't tolerate it well. I managed several quick naps, but I felt nervous. My hand continued to shake. Today, it was different and more like a tremble or tremor moving through my body. I would massage it, but it didn't appear to help. I tried to relax, I tried to control my breathing, and I tried to fantasize about being home, but nothing stopped the trembling. I closed my eyes and drifted to sleep. I saw Mr. Samuels standing near the river. He smiled and said, "The faith of a mustard seed, but it only grows with prayer."

I had not prayed in a long while. I saw the Lord perform miracles all my life, and I was a believer, but I wasn't good. I remembered how Mr. Samuels prayed. I tried to emulate. People would say he could pray down heaven, but he didn't like it when people said those things. He thought it was irreverent.

"Lord," I mumbled, "you are creator and ruler of all. I revere you, and I trust you. I beg your forgiveness of my many sins, of my killing and my anger, and my hatred. Please, God, forgive me." I was sleeping and crying. "Lord, I am selfish and evil in my core. Please deliver me from these tremors. Please, God."

Mr. Samuels was standing by the river and said, "Son, it's not about our will. It's about his will."

I said, "Lord, I need you, and we all need you. Your will be done with me, my family, and this mission. Amen."

Mr. Samuels walked toward me and poked me. I opened my eyes. It was Mike, and he said, "Who are you talking to?"

Charles and Jim were standing above me, and I wiped tears from my eyes. I shook my head, and he said, "Are you okay?"

I nodded and said, "Yes, now I am. Let's get moving."

The sun began to drop, and it was time. Moving in darkness helped. Spending the day behind the small hill was a good decision. We were rested and hydrated. Mike cut off the speaker and said, "Look, I know you have been doing this longer than I have been alive and you are the expert, but I am concerned." I looked at him. He continued, "Maybe you cut wire, and I place the clips." I was embarrassed. I wasn't pulling my own weight. I shook my head and said no, but I began to think, by my own shellfish pride, I could jeopardize our mission.

I said, "You're right. It's what we need to do." I thought for a second and said, "Only on one condition." He looked at me, and I said, "Don't enter buildings alone. It's dangerous, even for you, superman."

He nodded and turned the intercom on to hear Chad in a near panic attempting to reach us. He was upset. "Stay on intercom! Kevin and Gerald have a flat. Find a good spot."

We slowly pulled to the side of the road. Traffic was light but steady. We changed the tire as quickly as possible. We could hear rumbling in the distance, and Kevin, with his quick wit, said, "It's Iraqi buffalo."

It was a slow-moving armored convoy. Nothing makes as much noise as a tank. The first serial consisted of several-wheeled vehicles, followed by tanks and armored personnel carriers. It was a powerful display of combat power. The tanks were all Soviet designed T72s, and while they were less than the American Abrams, they were a formidable opponent. Chad, always the spy, took as many photographs as he could. The rest of us stood by the side of the road and waved. The Soldiers looked tired, but they also looked tough and professional. They were moving with a sense of discipline that I hadn't seen in Middle Eastern armies. It appeared to be a combat brigade's worth of equipment moving toward Baghdad.

Once the convoy passed, we resumed our movement and passed the convoy well before we changed roads at Al Hadithah. We decided to make a fuel stop in the town, but it was too crowded. The road became busy, and traffic did not begin to thin until we had traveled twenty or thirty miles. We noticed an isolated gas station half way between Al Hadithah and Baiji. We missed it and turned around. It was exactly the type of stop we needed. We pulled all our vehicles directly to the pumps. As we completed fueling, a black Chevrolet Suburban pulled into the station. It pulled behind Gerald and Kevin on the opposite side. Several young and fit men got out, stretched, and began fueling. Gerald nodded at them and then walked slowly over to our pumps. He leaned into the Ford and said in a quiet voice, "They are speaking Russian." Our best count was six but we couldn't see if anyone else was inside. Gerald moved his vehicle, and we followed in the other Toyota. We moved about thirty to forty feet away. The Ford stayed put as it wasn't blocking anyone from the pumps. Chad's interest was piqued, and he said, "You know the drill. Check your oil and everything else until we sort this out. Barry and Jim see what's happening."

Barry and Jim lingered and then joined the group as they entered into the small roadside store. We waited. The Russians kept two men with their vehicles, and they appeared security conscious. As they stretched, we notice side arms. Kevin took his trash to a can located beside their gas pump and spoke to them in Arabic. They were smoking, and he spoke again. They ignored him, so he switched to English and blurted out an awkward "howdy." Iraqis are curious about other cultures, and they love to talk to Westerners, so it was a good ruse. They stared at him and then offered an equally awkward "howdy" in return. He approached and began conversing in broken English. We could not hear the conversation, but it looked as though he was making progress. Barry and Jim exited the store, both engaging in casual conversation with the Russians. Jim walked toward their vehicle and tossed trash in the large outdoor can and then returned to the group. Barry stopped and talked for several minutes with two of the men. Finally, Barry and Jim shook hands and waved.

We cranked our vehicles and began moving. Barry spoke first and said, "Definitely Russian Special Purpose Forces. Their Arabic is awkward, but they were fit and followed a precise chain of command. They claim to be building contractors going to Mosel."

Jim briefed next and said, "The tall one said they were coming from Syria. I tagged them with my cell phone underneath the right front wheel well. Mitch can track until the battery runs out."

I turned to Mike and said, "I don't understand."

He said, "His cell has an embedded GPS tracker and a magnetic face, so he slapped it on the inside of the wheel well.

"Wow," I said, "that's good spy work, I never saw it."

Mike said, "When he went to the trash can." It was a slick move.

Chad said, "I have several good photographs to upload, but let's call Mitch."

We continued to drive but listened to Chad's and Mitch. Their assessment was the Russians were here for one of three reasons. First, they were here to conduct some type of direct action mission. Second, they were here to train Iraqi Special Forces, and finally, they were here to watch and report on the potential invasion of Iraq. He would track them until the cell phone went dead.

Baiji wasn't like the other cities in the region sprawled along the Tigris River. It was a mixture of industrial complexes and neighborhoods. The industrial section intermingled with the residential.

As we drew close, Chad said, "We know two things about the town and the area in general. First, it's all Sunni Muslim with the vast majority of the population being Saddam loyalist. Second, it produced chemicals. During the 1970s, Saddam worked a deal to bring in a French chemical manufacturing company. The Baghdad informants are convinced chemical weapons are produced and stored here. We know something is made here and shipped. Expect an exterior fence and a platoon-sized guard force. Remember from our rehearsal, the only way in or out of the target area is through a loyalist neighborhood. Like we talked, make max use of our cover." He didn't say it, but I thought our greatest risk was, as always, the language barrier.

We drove through the neighborhood. Although it was getting late, people were walking, and several stores and restaurants were open. I rolled down my window, and a strong stench hit me, but I could not determine what I smelled.

I said, "Anybody know where the smell is coming from?"

As we drove closer to the warehouse, it became more distinct. It was an ammonia-like smell. Finally, we turned a corner and sitting right next to the side of the road was our target. The exterior fence was adjacent to the road, which was great, but there was a row of houses facing the fence and our target. The smell of ammonia was overwhelming. Barry and Kevin were in a constant chatter as there are very few good uses for industrial strength ammonia. The area was well lit, and we saw dozens of drums lined up against the fence. We attempted to slow down in an effort to read the Arabic writing, but it was too difficult.

"Mike, stop, and I will raise the hood."

Mike said, "I can't read it. It doesn't make sense to me."

Barry tried, but due to the angle, he couldn't make out the contents.

Chad said, "Take photos and we will send them out." Our target warehouse was easily three or four football fields in length and set up as a factory. Something entered on one side, was processed in the middle, and was stored or shipped from the far end. The processing portion in the middle had several ventilation shafts coming from the roof. It smelled like a combination of ammonia, rotten eggs, and urine.

We were drawing attention. A couple of vehicles slowed to observe us, and within minutes, a police car arrived. We saw him coming, and Barry and Kevin were poised to greet him while

Gerald and I crawled underneath my Toyota. Mike interpreted the conversation and kept us abreast of the details.

Barry told the policemen, "We are from the Ministry of Transportation and have orders to survey this area for repaving. It is a priority project." He handed the policeman an e-mail and said, "This is from the Minister himself telling us we are to survey and execute contracts to repave the area within two weeks."

The policeman acted as if he was expecting it.

Barry said, "We are having some problems with our vehicle, but we are getting it fixed."

The policeman offered to help, but Barry said, "We have good mechanics, and what is the smell?"

The policeman laughed and said, "It is a present for our neighbors."

Barry didn't press the issue. The policeman drove away. It was a good con and it worked. Within minutes, Mitch and the Kuwait team identified the contents of the drums. The vast majority were industrial strength brake cleaner while a smaller portion was paint thinner. Both manufactured in Saudi Arabia.

Jim said, "Look at the batteries." I glanced and saw a small wall of automobile batteries next to the large cans. He continued, "I don't understand. Most business owners would keep them undercover." Word traveled fast in this neighborhood, and a man drove up in a dented Volkswagen Rabbit. Barry and Jim greeted him, and he offered to assist us in contracting for concrete. He wanted to be our middleman.

Barry was tough on him, saying, "Our mission comes from the Minister himself, and it needs to be complete within the next three weeks."

Jim added, "We have orders from Saddam."

I moved from under the vehicle and asked Mike, "What are they doing?"

He said, "Negotiating a price." Barry was a great actor and played the part well.

The longer we stayed, the more of a fixture we became. Barry and Gerald took the trail vehicle and brought back food from a local restaurant down the street. We used the Ford hood as our table and ate a mix of eggs, meat, hard bread, and rice. Mike said, "All we know is something is made in this factory, and the place smells really bad, but they aren't willing to discuss further with strangers, even if they are from Baghdad."

We noticed a large tractor trailer truck exiting the facility, and within an hour, another arrived, loaded, and departed. We activated the remote sensors, which were high-technology devices designed to smell the scent of weapons grade propellant, but they didn't provide us any clues.

We spent over an hour, standing next to the factory in plain view, discussing options. Satellite imagery was a great thing, but it can't smell an area, and it can't read the sides of fifty-five-gallon drums.

Chad finished his meal and said, "It looks suspicious. Thus far, we haven't seen any guards, but we must assume their inside the warehouse. It going to be difficult to get inside, but that's the mission."

He looked at me and said, "Thoughts?"

I hesitated and said, "Maybe a diversion, but getting in there without killing anyone is a tall order. If we kill anyone here, the result will be a massive manhunt, and we can't afford that."

Chad began drawing on the back of a piece of paper on his clipboard. He said, "We plant flags, use the survey equipment, and go deeper into the cover. We have enough light from the warehouse to fake a survey, and we have several mechanical drawings and mathematical calculations."

He paused, pointed at me, and said, "You, Mike, Barry, and Kevin enter the building and conduct the recon. I know it will require a significant diversion. We will set the brake cleaner on fire, and I think we can do it safely. Once you hear the action and commotion, you enter from the opposite side and conduct the recon."

Barry nodded and said, "Once the fire is out, we got to stay here and continue playing the part."

I nodded and said, "That's the tough part."

Within a few hours after our meal, we emplaced our survey equipment and all of our remaining flags. To make it appear like a large project, we even placed flags on the parallel roads entering into the warehouse. It was a good ruse. The vast majority of roads, other than highways, are pothole-laden. The idea of us repairing them was welcome news to the locals.

Mike, Barry, Kevin, and I carefully worked our way to the opposite side of the warehouse and placed flags along several of the roads within the warehouse area. We positioned ourselves on the far side of the target warehouse with our truck and surveying equipment. Although I had no idea how to read the surveying equipment, I used the long-range sights to conduct a reconnaissance of the back side of our target. If anyone saw us, we looked like we were working to carry out a rush project. It was believable. I continued to scan but saw no sign of the guard force. We checked our equipment.

We saw the smoke before we heard the yelling. Gerald used a delayed fuse device and the remainder of our team was nowhere close to the fire when it began. The fire caused a grayish black smoke which drifted across the roof of the warehouse.

I said, "I hope they didn't set the warehouse on fire." We heard someone yelling from across the compound and watched as people ran toward that side of the warehouse. Chad choreographed the remainder of our team's response. Those who could speak the language would rush to help leaving those who couldn't to drive vehicles with only one language speaker. We finally saw a door open on the far side of the warehouse and two Soldiers in various stages of dress emerged. We heard the siren from a local fire truck. It was time.

I moved forward and quickly breached the outer wire fence. It also had a small yard interior fence, but it had multiple open gates, so we ran through them. Within seconds, we all moved toward the back door of the warehouse. Mike breached quickly, and we entered. By our estimates, we entered into the shipping side. The place stank. It was bad outside, but, inside I had to work hard to control my breathing and not gag. We saw boxes and containers of all sizes and shapes.

Kevin carefully opened one of the boxes and pulled a long plastic cylinder full of some substance and placed it inside his pocket. If these were chemical weapons, then it was brilliant to ship them out in civilian industrial boxes and containers. We moved slowly down the length of the warehouse. It was a two-story structure, and we hustled up the stairs to get a holistic view of the operation. The sirens continued to blare outside. The far end of the facility was lit, and from our vantage point, we could see much of the operation. From the far end, we observed where the raw materials were stored, and we ran to the middle section and began filming. All I could see were large liquid containers, coils from one piece of equipment to another and various tables. We needed to move toward the far end to get a better view. I motioned the team forward and glanced at Kevin. His eyes were blood red and watering. It looked like he was crying. We needed goggles and a mask; the smell of ammonia was stifling. I hugged the wall and moved forward another fifty yards. I had a decent view and pulled the camera tight to my eye.

A few of the barrels had English writing on the side, but most were in Arabic. I saw large barrels of brake cleaner and what appeared to be hundreds of bottles of propane. Barry was pulling on my arm.

He said, "We need to get out."

I was finding it hard to think due to the stench. I turned to him and said, "Where are the chemicals turned into weapons?"

We should be seeing something that takes the chemical compound and puts it into a shell. None of our fancy detectors alerted. I was confused. Barry slapped me on the back of the head and said, "We got to get out!"

I began moving back toward our entry point. It seemed to take forever. I was sweating, and the sweat was pouring into my eyes, making it difficult to see anything. We moved quickly to the fence, slid under, and I banded it as quickly as possible. We moved back to our surveying location beside the truck. The sirens from the fire trucks continued, and we saw flashing lights in all directions. We managed to get in and out within thirteen minutes.

Our faces were blushing red. We all had a severe windblown look. I saw concern in Barry's eyes as he was trying to determine what we came into contact with and the best method for getting us back to normal. Kevin's face was blood red, and his eyes watered constantly. His face looked ruddy and almost blistered. Barry pulled out a flashlight and began looking into our eyes.

He said, "We've been exposed to something. Whatever it is, it is on our skin, and we don't show signs of further impairment."

Kevin said, "Water... and flush ourselves."

Barry shook his head and said, "No, no, not yet."

It was too late as Kevin grabbed a water bottle and began washing his neck. It had no immediate effect, so we all grabbed water bottles. Before long, we were all half stripped and taking a water bottle bath on the side of the truck. If it weren't for the distraction of the fire, I am confident we would have been discovered. The water helped, and since we were using my truck, I changed shirts. My hand started shaking again and I was concerned the others would see it, so I jammed it deep into my pants pocket. Within minutes we were composed and moved to the far side of the building.

We gathered around our vehicles and watched the firemen pack their gear and pull away from the factory. Barry was the first to speak and said, "I don't know what it is." He was irritable, almost angry. He shook his head and said, "It's a mass production facility for chemicals but no indications of their use as weapons. It doesn't make sense." Chad uploaded all of the videos and sent them to Kuwait. My hand continued to twitch. Chad was visibly disappointed that we didn't find anything of value. Kevin shook his head and said, "We will not know for certain until we test." Chad, Barry, and Kevin discussed how we would be able to do that and if we had the necessary equipment. It was late, well after midnight, and the excitement of the fire had died. The streets were deserted.

I said, "If we are going to test, then we need to do it here and tonight. Otherwise, we need to follow the trucks that come here and load." I pointed toward the loading dock and continued, "The chemicals are made here and trucked to another location where they stuff it into shells or missiles. I'm no scientist, but I know they are making bad stuff in there."

Chad's phone rang. He walked away, and we waited and watched to see if we could read his face. He motioned for us to gather on the hood and put the phone on speaker. Mitch was the only voice I recognized, but there were numerous other folks talking. They were all speaking with scientific overtones except for Mitch who was working hard to give us decent directions. Gerald and Mike remained on guard on both sides of the convoy.

My hand was better, and I felt like I was breathing normally again. I began talking to myself. *I am going to retire. I have had enough. I am tired. I don't have a clue about the chemicals or the long-term effects.* I tried hard to concentrate and focus on the conversation. Chad, Kevin, and Barry discussed the possibilities. The term "Mustard Gas" kept coming up; then, one of the guys on the phone began to debate that and argues the possibility of "Sarin" in a solid form. Another guy argued against that because of the delivery methodology. They continued discussing nerve agent properties, and I was back in a chemistry class. The difference is this was not theory—it was hard reality. The conversation lasted for over an hour.

Finally, Chad said, "I have to recharge the cell battery. We are going to sign off, but you better figure something out and tell us what to test. We will talk tomorrow."

We each got about an hours sleep. Gerald woke me before dawn, and I took my guard shift. The Mosque speakers clicked on with the call to prayer, and I heard Islamic chants from several different directions. The town was coming to life with people walking down the far streets. The factory changed shifts, and I watched as a truck load of soldiers entered into the factory while another departed. We had prayer rugs but didn't intend to use them unless we noticed everyone else doing the same, and at this point, the prayer calls were ignored.

Two men started walking the fence line toward me. They waved and I waved back. My hand started trembling again. This time, it took my other hand too steady it. They continued to walk toward me. I turned slowly and grabbed Mike's head as he slept in the back of the truck, and then, I walked slowly backward and kicked the side of the Explorer. Mike was up and moving just as the men approached. He spoke to them, and Barry opened the door of the Ford and walked toward them to engage. They continued talking and the conversation seemed to go on and on. I was anxious and nervous. We needed to get out of here as soon as the concrete man arrived. It was only a matter of time before the language monster grabbed us and we became spectacles on international television, or worse yet, killed without anyone knowing. They continued to talk. One of the men was of some rank, but I couldn't remember the Iraqi military structure. Barry was playing his part as subservient public servant. Finally, after more than an hour of talking, he gathered us together.

Barry was quick and went directly to the point.

He said, "We have been exposed not to a chemical weapon, but to a chemical drug."

Chad was the first to question him and said, "What?"

Barry shook his head and continued, "Look, the Iraqi officer almost expected us to show up here and repave the place due to the amount of money the place is generating."

Kevin nodded his head and said, "Yes, drugs. I got it. It's either crystal meth, or it's some derivative hallucinogenic drug." Barry nodded. This explained the lack of propellant products. Chad was on the phone to Mitch asking him to do the research and find out how we test and verify.

I was stunned. An hour ago, I was convinced that some chemical compound used in an indiscriminate weapon of mass destruction was being made here. Now, I was even more amazed that Saddam Hussein was a drug lord. It made sense—the horrible smell, the trucks for distribution, the guys in white coats and masks, the cooking process, and the guards. Before Chad could finish his call, we saw a convoy coming down the street. It consisted of several truckloads of men, framing material, and three large 1950s concrete trucks. Barry greeted the leader, gave instructions, and within the hour, we were packed and leaving the location. It was daylight, and we needed to go somewhere to test and ensure we were correct. We could backtrack and return back to our previous desert location, or we could risk a daylight move that would get us closer to our final target. We were all exhausted, working on just a few hours' sleep, and we were in transition. Transitions were always the most dangerous part.

We decided to move to the south in hopes of finding somewhere isolated where we could rest. Our plan was to drive south along the Tigris in hopes of finding an isolated rest spot. As we began moving, Chad turned on the intercom, and we heard his conversation with Mitch and the other experts. They recalculated their estimates and were now in agreement that we penetrated a meth lab. We would not know for certain until we conducted test, but we needed a secluded area to rest and conduct the test. My biggest fear was going through Baghdad. All roads south led directly to the city. Our original plan had us going through late at night or in the early morning hours. We discussed the idea of swinging either east or west to avoid it, but we knew that would also add risk.

Our vehicles were approaching half tank. We stopped and executed a fuel stop at a small station just south of Tikrit. The next major city was Samarra and then south into Baghdad. The great news was the topography. It was beginning to look more and more like South Georgia, except in Georgia, all the trees were pines. The area was grown up, and we were soon able to find a decent hiding spot roughly a mile from the main road. We established our security plan, and Barry and Kevin began testing the chemicals. It was an overcast day with occasional sprinkles, but I crawled in the back of the truck and went to sleep. When I woke, it was dark, but I felt rested. We gathered for a huddle to discuss our movement plans.

Barry and Kevin confirmed the substance as meth, and Chad turned his phone off in order to get some rest. I am certain it didn't endear him with his superiors, but we needed several hours of uninterrupted sleep. We discussed our standard movement formation and ate our rations in silence. Suddenly, Gerald's head extended as if he were a gopher, and then, the rest of us heard it. The Iraqi Army was on the move again. Tanks and Armored personnel carriers all moving south toward Baghdad. It was a huge formation.

The Iraqis knew an invasion was coming and they were preparing. Like most Armies the Iraqis had their share of good outfits and bad. The bad were the conscripts who were drafted into service, treated like dirt, given only minimal training and equipment, and most importantly they suffered under poor leadership. The Iraqi's had dominated this part of the world for a while, and they did it on the backs of their professional corps of Soldiers known as the Republican Guard. These guys were no joke. They were tough, trained, had the best Russian equipment, and generally well led. Most importantly, they were willing to fight hard to protect their homeland.

We were awake and stirring when Chad called for a huddle. He laid out the map and said, "We have one more recon target, and it was south of Baghdad in a small town on the side of the Euphrates River called Al Kifl. It has one primary target and one secondary target. The primary is the brick making complex on the northern part of town, and the other is a cola factory south of town. Remember, the place has ethnic cleansings, specifically of its Jews and later of its Shia. The Army has run off the civilian population and taken over the town. My last report says the town has a wide variety of units including armor, air defense, and at least, one Republican Guard Commando Battalion. It's a small town but central to the region. From it, you can move forces quickly in any direction—southwest toward An Najaf, northwest to Karbala, or northeast to Al Hilla. From a military perspective, it makes sense. Our mission is to determine if the brick factory or the cola factory had any indications of chemical weapons manufacturing or storage. Finally, we got to drive through Baghdad before we get anywhere so protect one another." My hand began to shake, and I shoved it hard into my pocket.

ONE LAST TARGET

WE WERE SOON mounted and moving. This part of the nation was industrialized with excellent roads. If you didn't know better, you would swear you were driving through the American Midwest. The military convoys were everywhere, but they were confined to the inside lane. At one point, we passed a convoy of tanks and armored personnel carriers over seven miles long. It must have been an entire Republican Guard Division moving south. We made excellent time and entered the outskirts of Baghdad. It was an armed city, as if it was preparing for an old fashioned siege.

Mike noticed several large cranes and said, "They are building?"

I shook my head and said, "I don't think so. It looks like they are lifting Antiaircraft weapons to the roof tops."

Iraqi Soldiers were building fortifications along every overpass and bridge, and then, it began to make sense. The enemy was placing his tanks and other major armor under each bridge and overpass for a reason. Placing weapons under some type of cover protected it from the air, and the best way into the city was using the roads. While an attacking force can maneuver its way across the open areas, they also become prime targets for well-placed, and well-entrenched, guns. Finally, if you destroy an armored vehicle underneath a bridge or overpass, it will have secondary explosions and burn for days, making it almost impassable for several hours, if not days. Although it was past midnight, we saw activity everywhere. I said, "During the first Gulf War, the Iraqi's took a beating from the Air Force, but this time, he is learning. This is an armed camp." They were ready for a fight.

Seeing Baghdad behind us was good. I was worried about checkpoints and population control, but I didn't see anything close. The roads were open, and people were traveling. The farther south from the city we traveled, the more military we saw. They ringed the city with troops, and as we moved south, we saw more and more rings. Airpower would cripple the defenses, but some poor soldier was going to have to run this gauntlet of fire to get to Baghdad. It wasn't a mission I would want.

We moved farther south and stopped at a truck stop before morning prayers. We were either good at these stops, or we were getting dangerously complacent. I didn't know which, but I knew I was tired and ready for it to end. I needed to stay focused and disciplined.

I turned to Mike and said, "The number one killer is complacency. Doing something once and being successful doesn't mean that the ninety-ninth time you do it, it won't be an adventure. Stay alert and vigilant. A person, regardless of training and discipline, cannot stay on full alert forever."

He stared at me and said, "Are you losing your mind again, old man?"

I nodded and said, "No, just charging myself up."

My mind wandered to how a fugitive could make it, always looking over his shoulder. As we entered into the outskirts of Karbala, the ground changed. We were in the Garden of Eden, the Fertile Crescent between the Euphrates and Tigris, the birthplace of mankind, and it was beginning to look like a jungle. Some sort of palm trees and tall saw grass came to the edge of the roads. I began looking for somewhere to hide during the day and found a small road that led past a few houses to a small canal. It had excellent observation of the area in all directions and provided shade against the heat of the day. We could rest here and move south into Al Kifl later that afternoon.

We took our guard shift and rested. Chad spread out the map, called for a huddle, and said, "Ideally, we cross the Euphrates and drive south on the eastern side of the river and drive right beside the brick factory, through the middle of town, and then drive right by the cola factory. If we see anything that causes suspicion, we head east and then devise a plan to get a better look."

It was a bold plan.

Barry nodded and said, "The cover has worked well thus far."

I laughed and said, "I don't know if the CIA gives awards, but you deserve an Oscar."

Chad laughed and continued, "Look and act like we belong and we won't draw attention."

Jim said, "I like it. We drive right through middle of an armed town, what could possibly go wrong?"

The team laughed, and Mike said, "The longer we are here, the sillier we get."

I nodded and said, "It's much less dangerous than getting caught snooping around the perimeter of the town late at night. Our cover works, so we shouldn't deviate. It's about being on top of our game when it comes to language. It wouldn't take long for anyone with serious questions to break us, and especially those like me who can't speak more than five words of Arabic."

Getting around in Iraq was proving easier than any of us envisioned. Thus far, we encountered one significant checkpoint, but we didn't know what would happen next. We crossed the Euphrates and began driving south. The closer to Al Kifl we drove, the more militaristic it became. We saw lots of military activity with multiple fighting positions dug for everything from tanks to individual Soldier foxholes. The Iraqi Army engineer corps was digging defensive fortifications all around this area.

Chad came on the speaker and said, "Look to the east. What is it?"

I said, "Looks like camouflage nets and lots of them. They provide no protection from anything, including rain, but if they are emplaced correctly, it's difficult to see from the air."

Gerald added, "Looks like two or three battalions worth of artillery."

Barry said, "I don't know the range, but if they have chemical weapons, the best delivery system would be from a static artillery piece or cannon. They can deliver from the air, but it's risky."

This was the first time we had seen Iraqi artillery, and it was impressive. It also made sense as it was well positioned from this location to inflict damage along multiple attack avenues. I said, "They have a problem. It's towed artillery and they can camouflage the guns, but it's hard to hide the trucks." Chad said, "If this thing starts, that will be one big hole in the ground."

We closed toward Al Kifl, thinking we should be getting close to the brick factory. We rounded a corner, and there it was, totally unguarded and looking abandoned. We slowed the convoy and turned directly into the compound. It was deserted. The last series of satellite photographs showed troops occupying this area, but they weren't here today. We pulled the vehicles into our standard protection formation and got out. Chad was convinced we were in the wrong location. We avoided using GPS and did our best to navigate by maps, but Gerald quickly pulled one out and confirmed the location. We were exactly where we were supposed to be, and we saw no sign of life, much less chemical weapons. We divided into teams, brought out the detectors, and began searching the factory room by room. Other than a flock of turkey vultures, we saw nothing. The place was deserted with no trace of chemicals. This was supposed to be our toughest site.

Chad said, "We stay here tonight. Nobody expected this. I will make calls."

Mike turned and said, "This is dangerous."

I looked at him and said, "We have a decent way out and long range views. We're okay."

He shook his head and said, "Not what I mean. Some idiot in a nice building might tell us to stay here a while." Chad had been blunt about his view of dynamic targeting, but you never knew. I established the guard shift, pulled out my blanket, and went to sleep in the back of the truck.

I dreamed about walking alongside the Hiawassee River, and our kids were throwing rocks in the river. Gerald woke me, and I took my shift. I moved toward the entrance of the factory where I could see the road. Traffic passed back and forth, and I watched as a convoy of trucks moved south toward the town. The sun rose, and we huddled. We would continue the mission through the town and onto the cola factory.

We mounted and began moving. It was still early, and it was the best time of the day in this country. Even in the late winter, it was hot by midday. We drove slowly and saw activity as we approached the town. I convinced myself we would be stopped. The place was an armed city. The storefronts were filled with sandbags, Soldiers were on every rooftop emplacing weapons systems ranging from simple machine guns to complex air defense weapons, and engineers were digging in tanks allowing them to shoot across the river. It was an impressive site. I waved at the Soldiers as they worked, and they waved back. We were driving right through the middle of their defensive position and waving at them in the process. Our cover was good, and we actually looked like we knew what we were doing. Within a few minutes, we saw the bridge over the Euphrates and continued our trek to the south. The Iraqi military had garrisoned the town mostly to the north, and while soldiers were everywhere, it was clear where they wanted to make their defensive stand.

I kept my finger on the roadmap and carefully traced our route. The road narrowed, curved, and there sat the cola factory in the middle of a large open field. It was unguarded, and we waited for a truck to pull out and then pulled directly into the parking lot. It was a cola factory, and on the loading dock, we could see case on top of case of cola stacked and ready for shipment. Two men were working to ready the day's load. Kevin got out and spoke to them, asking directions to An Najaf. They pointed us back to the road and nodded and quickly went back to work. We pulled the vehicles to the far side of the empty parking lot and watched as two more trucks came to load their daily stock. Chad shook his head, took some photographs, we all relieved ourselves, and we began driving southwest toward the open desert. Within an hour, we were all alone on a deserted road turning southeast toward the mined border with Kuwait.

HEARTBREAK

We arrived at Camp Doha, Kuwait, early in the morning. It seemed to take forever to drive past multiple layers of security and checkpoint after checkpoint. The Kuwaiti Team was waiting for us. Our orders were strict. We were to go to bed and be prepared to debrief either late this evening or early tomorrow morning. I grabbed my gear and was escorted to a small room with a very soft bed. It seemed my head barely touched the pillow when I heard the knock at the door. It was my designated assistant who asked that I get dressed quickly, allow him to escort me to the mess hall for breakfast, and Chad wanted me in a secure VTC within the hour. I had not shaved in what seemed like forever, and I was well on my way to having a scraggly beard and a full mustache. I wasn't hungry and elected instead to spend thirty minutes in a steaming hot shower. I dressed and was led through a maze of offices and warehouses toward the secure VTC facility. I asked the assistant when I was going to be debriefed, and he told me to ask Chad.

We passed through several checkpoints, and the assistant vouched my presence and used his credentials for us to gain entry.

The room was dark and he led me to the front table where I sat in a large luxury executive chair.

A few moments later, Chad entered, smiled at me, and said, "I finally got some sleep." I asked him about my debriefing, and he smiled and ignored me.

The SVTC came to life with a loud speaker squeak. We heard voices from a wide variety of locations, but all we could see on our screen was a mirror image of ourselves. A husky voice came over the speaker and announced that we would begin in two minutes and asked all stations to mute their microphones. The husky voice returned and asked Chad to begin. Chad had several pages of notes in front of him. If he slept at all, I didn't know when. He talked about our infiltration, the airfield we built, the first target as cold, movement across Iraq, enemy forces and their numbers and types of vehicles and direction of travel, the expensive automobiles, the meth factory, movement through Baghdad, and finally, the final two targets being cold. It was a comprehensive overview, and the husky voice asked for questions among the stations. All we could see was ourselves in the screen, but I heard a beeping noise as someone unmuted their microphone and cleared their voice.

He began by saying, "A good report," then a long pause and said, "Sandlapper, did you view it the same way?"

I recognized the voice, took a deep breath and said, "I agree with the report."

He said, "Anything of military significance not reported by the team leader?"

I didn't want to throw Chad under the bus, so I said, "No, sir, but I will add a couple of points. Baghdad is defended by concentric rings of forces. They are prepared for an attack. Al Kifl is militarily significant because the enemy can reinforce quickly in multiple directions. Finally, the Iraqis have learned the lesson of air power. We saw numerous instances of Iraqi forces digging in under bridges and overpasses. Any attack will be a tough mission."

The line went silent, and I stared hard into the monitor. I thought to myself, *Who was I to be giving military advice?*

I wondered if we were muted and another conversation was taking place without our knowledge. We sat quietly and stared at ourselves for another minute. A new voice entered the network, and asked Chad, "Do the Iraqis have chemical weapons?"

Chad answered quickly and said, "We saw no indications of chemical weapons during our reconnaissance, but we focused on locations listed by our Iraqi intelligence sources."

The next question was harsh, and it seemed to spew out of the speaker, asking, "Do you think the Iraqis possessed chemical weapons?" Chad was slow to respond. He seemed to know who was asking the question. He took a deep breath and said, "In my professional judgment, the Iraqis don't possess chemical weapons. It is clear they did possess them several years ago, but we had no indicators they possess chemical or biological weapons. Based upon our sources, these were the only remaining viable targets within the country. It's possible the Iraqis either divested themselves of the weapons or sold them to the Syrians."

He was in midsentence when he was interrupted. "How many sites?"

He quickly answered, "Three."

The voice asked, "Is it possible for the Iraqis, under an evil dictator, to hide chemical weapons anywhere else in the country?"

Chad remained calm and said, "It is possible, but based upon all known intelligence—"

This time, the voice gave a short rant about facts. "First, we know the Iraqis had chemical weapons, we know the Iraqis have used chemical weapons, and just because we can't find them don't mean they don't have them. This is a slam dunk."

I looked at Chad, and he remained calm. We stared at the screen for what seemed like several minutes.

The husky voice said, "All stations stand by," and we waited for several more minutes.

Finally, the husky voice came on the line again and said simply. "Kuwait drop from the network."

Within seconds, the screen was blank, and it was over. We received no accolades, no thanks, no promises, nothing. I turned to Chad and said, "I don't know how you do it."

He smiled, nodded, and said, "You got to get out of here." He stood, shook my hand, and said, "Great working with you. Thanks. We will meet again." He waved at the escort and said, "Your boss needs to see you." He picked up his papers and walked away. That was it.

The assistant walked me back to my quarters where we gathered my rucksack. My clothes stank, but I found my cleanest dirty shirt. He then walked me through the maze of buildings and warehouses. We walked for at least ten minutes before I began to see people in uniform. We finally reached a warehouse and entered. The Air Force guard stood me to one side, took my photograph, and within minutes, handed me photo badge and a lanyard. The assistant and I then worked our way through two additional warehouses where he stopped and told me this was my destination. I said thanks, and he was gone. I entered the door, wandered around the corner, and saw the boss standing at the other end of the room. He saw me and walked toward me, half-hugged me, and motioned me outside where he could smoke.

He said, "Are you okay?"

I nodded. I started to tell him about the mission, but he held up his hand and said, "I was on the VTC, I heard."

I shook my head and said, "I don't think the Iraqis have chemical or biological weapons anywhere."

He looked away and said, "I agree, but it doesn't matter. Its already started and once it starts its hard to shut down, regardless of the facts. We are in the middle of the Guns of August."

I nodded and said, "That it was a long and painful war."

The boss looked at me, frowned, and said in a low tone, "Just wait." He paused, as if thinking, and said, "Anything else from the mission you need to tell me?" I started to recount the mission in detail, and he interrupted and said, "Anything I don't already know?"

I shook my head, and he said, "I got bad news for you."

He looked down and said, "Your wife is sick. You are leaving the country tonight. I don't know the details, or how serious it is, but I need to get you back to Fort Bragg. Some of our guys will get your truck and meet you at the Charlotte airport. You will fly military to Germany and then commercial to Charlotte. Sorry, but it's as close as we could get." He motioned for his aide and his driver, and they came forward as if they had been waiting on his motion. "They will take you to the airport."

I was worried. The military is compassionate, but they don't move Soldiers out of a war zone unless it's serious. I said, "I need to get to a phone."

He nodded and said, "The Aide has one, and you can call on your way." He grabbed, hugged me and said, "Thanks, you are a great Soldier. Now, get going."

The aide handed me a cell phone, and I began calling. I got no answer at home, so I called her cell, and it went to voice mail. I jerked out my wallet and began looking for phone numbers. I found a number for my father-in-law's church. A nice lady answered, and I told her who I was and what I was seeking. She was hesitant to give me my mother-in-law's cell phone but finally conceded. I dialed the number, and Marge answered. I heard her sigh when she heard my voice. My voice was panicked as I began pounding her with questions and I heard Lorraine in the background.

Suddenly, I heard garbled sounds and then Lorraine's voice with her first words, asking, "Are you okay?"

I was emotional and noticed tears running down the side of my face. The driver and aide stared straight ahead. Before I could get a question out, she said, "The kids are fine."

I interrupted her and said, "I know, how about you?"

She was silent for a few seconds and then said, "I have cancer and am undergoing treatment."

My heart sank and I said, "I'm coming home," and I could hear her choking up. I was having trouble speaking. I shook my head and tried to sober my brain. I needed facts. I somehow managed to mumble the words "What kind of cancer?"

She said quietly, "Women's cancer."

I said, "We will beat this."

And she said, "Everything will be fine." She changed subjects and said, "I will be home to meet you."

I paused, thought, and said, "Where are you?"

She hesitated and said, "I had surgery, and I will be released later today."

I said, "I am worried."

And she repeated, "Everything will be fine. When will you be here?"

I said, "I have no idea, but I am about to get on a plane out of this place. I will call you when I when I get to Charlotte." We both tried to tell each other how much we loved one another at the same time and found ourselves talking over one another, but it didn't matter.

The driver pulled alongside the terminal, and I said, "I've got to go, but I will call when I land, and I love you."

The driver and aide dismounted and grabbed my rucksack. I sat quietly in the back of the SUV, wiped away my tears, and tried to compose myself.

I exited the vehicle and gave the aide back his phone. He and the driver handed me my rucksack and then handed me a shaving kit and a bag.

The driver looked at me and said, "Sir, you look pretty rough."

The aide chimed in and said, "There is deodorant in the shaving kit and two PX shirts in the bag. I bought them for my brother, but you need them more. Good luck, sir." They came to attention and saluted. I was unprepared for the protocol but returned the salute and shook their hands.

Flights coming into Kuwait were full of Soldiers and those going out were at best half full. I managed to get into the bathroom and clean up as best I could but kept the beard as I didn't have the scissors to trim or enough blades to cut. As I exited, a young transport NCO was calling my name, and he looked at me as if I were a crazy man when I approached.

He stared at my beard, but decided it wasn't his business. After seeing my ID card, he said, "Sir, you're the flight commander to Germany and then someone else ranks you for the flight to the states."

The last thing I needed was to be in charge of something. I asked for the highest-ranking NCO on the flight, told him he was in charge and if he had any problems, let me know. I boarded and went to sleep. In Germany, I was placed on a commercial flight to New York with a two-hour layover. I called home several times, guessed when I would be arriving in Charlotte and when I would be home. I was worried. I boarded another flight to Charlotte. It was cold and rainy when we landed, and I didn't have a jacket. I was met in the exit terminal by two guys who handed me the keys to my truck and said it was full of government gas and ready to roll. I told them how much I appreciated their assistance and was soon driving toward Fort Bragg.

It was midmorning when I pulled into the driveway. I saw Marge and Walter's car in the driveway, so I parked on the street. The door opened, and I saw Lorraine standing there. She was using the door as a prop and was weak. Marge was hovering over her, and I saw Walter in the background. She looked ghostly pale and very thin. She was sick, and I could see it in her eyes. She tugged at my beard and laughed at me as we hugged. She was frail, and I was almost afraid to hold her. She was brittle. Marge hugged my neck, and Walter was his normal acerbic self.

He said, "What kind of work allows you to dress like a vagabond?"

I shook his hand and said, "Nothing that would interest you." I wondered aloud about the kids, and they all laughed and said it was a school day. I had no idea what day it was.

Lorraine could move, but she was sore. The surgery went well, and the test results would be back in a few days. Marge pushed Walter into the kitchen. We sat on the couch. Lorraine grabbed my face and laughed about my beard.

She stared and said, "No matter what, everything is going to be fine." She was always positive. She kept staring and then said, "It's either stage III or stage IV ovarian cancer, and the prognosis is not good." I tried to look away, but she held my face. "Baby," she said, "I am dying." She never called me baby unless she wanted something.

"No," I said, "that's not going to happen. We will fix you, and I will retire, and it will be fine."

She smiled, and I saw the tears. She spoke softly and said, "I knew telling you would be the hardest part." She had come to grips with it all, but she needed me to accept it. I cried, hurting inside. I knew pain, but not like this.

She pulled me to her and said, "I am here until my purpose"—she paused, and I looked at her—"is complete." She held me, and I cried. I hadn't cried in years, and now I couldn't stop. Finally, she said, "We're done crying, and you need to shave that ugly beard. The gray makes you look like a billy goat. Besides, you will scare the kids when they get home." She tried to laugh and change the subject.

Walter and Marge got the kids from school, and it was good to hold them. Jess looked like an angel and more like her mother every day. John Boy was growing wider with the shoulders of a man. The illness was a roller coaster for them, and I was nowhere around. Jess was angry. She couldn't understand why I wasn't there. Any answer I gave didn't satisfy. It didn't make sense to her.

Her mother told them I was on an important mission, and they wanted to know what was more important than their mother. I didn't have a good answer, and it hurt. I retreated to the garage, found a chair, sat down, and cried. I needed to get control of my emotions, but I couldn't find the handle. My body was keyed up, and my mind was racing, trying to process the last twenty-four hours. I felt out of control and unstable. I needed to breathe and focus, but my chest felt tighter and tighter. I don't know how long I had been there, struggling to get control, when the kids walked in and stared. I stood and walked to the window and stared outside. They just stood. I glanced at my daughter, and she had her arms folded across her chest and her hip stuck out. It was her classic mad look, and it made me laugh inside.

I took a deep breath and said, "Get a chair."

"I have been in a foreign country with no access to phones," I began. "My mission was to conduct reconnaissance."

My son nodded.

"We will fight hard for your mother and support her and do whatever she wants or needs."

My son looked up and said, "Are we going to Clay County like Mom said?"

I was confused, and my daughter said, "If it's what Mom wants, then we will do it because it will make her happy."

We ate dinner, and Lorraine and I retreated to the bedroom. We started a ritual we kept until the end. It was the only thing that kept me sane. We sat in two old chairs in the bedroom and talked. We talked and talked. We talked about faith, the kids, their future, our history, and we talked about tomorrow. I told her every detail of every mission. I started with Panama and ended with Iraq. I confessed to every killing, from the intelligence officer in Panama to the guards in the warehouse in Iraq. I listened to every word as she talked about faith, hope, and love. I lived for those words. Finally, she would drift off to sleep, and I would move her into her bed and then move to the small couch in the corner and go to sleep.

The hospital called, and we met with a team of physicians. They were kind but clinical as if everything they said was common knowledge. There were three of them, each holding a different specialty. The news was not good, but it was exactly what Lorraine expected. They continued to use words like "invasive," "ovarian tumors," "gem cell tumors," and "fallopian tube carcinoma." I stopped them and asked for a clarification or a drawing. They were kind. Their only recommendation for treatment was aggressive chemotherapy and a follow-up in three months. We didn't discuss anything further, and I never asked about prognosis or life expectancy. I didn't have the courage to ask, and I didn't want to know the answer.

That evening, we pulled the kids from school. They knew it was coming and were very good. The teachers knew the situation and the principal, a friend of Lorraine's, supported our decision. We packed clothes, essentials, and loaded a small trailer with the two chairs from the bedroom and a few other nice items, and drove across the state to Clay County. We talked to the doctors in Murphy. They established an aggressive chemotherapy plan. We would drive to Murphy on Monday, Wednesday, and Friday, and she would undergo treatment.

Before we left, I visited the headquarters and talked to the Deputy Commander. I didn't know him, but he apparently knew me. His wife knew Lorraine, and he knew the situation. He told me I was placed on administrative leave until further notice. I told him of my intention to retire, and I was blunt in saying I wanted to retire immediately. He pulled strings, and within an hour, a retirement services civilian had me in the corner explaining my options. He insisted I file a claim with the Veterans Administration, and within the hour, a VA specialist showed up and worked me through the paperwork. I felt guilty because I was not with Lorraine, but I needed to get things complete.

By the time we crossed Balsam Mountain and were in Jackson County, it was raining. Sometimes in the mountains, it just settles in and rains. The clouds and the fog intermingle, and it makes you feel safe. Everyone was asleep when I turned onto Fires Creek Road. I turned slowly when I crossed the Shallow Ford Bridge as I didn't want to jackknife the trailer. I looked down the dirt road and put my lights on high beam. I saw a figure emerge from the riverside, walk slowly across the road, and disappear into the woods. It looked like and walked like Mr. Samuels. He walked with a wide brimmed hat and slightly swooped shoulders, just as I remembered him.

I hit the brakes and Lorraine awoke. She sat upright, looked at me, and said, "Are you okay? You look like you saw a ghost."

Maybe I had.

Lorraine did fine at first. We made our trips to Murphy, and she underwent treatments. The drugs didn't make her sick, but she was losing her hair. It embarrassed her. It began just falling out, sometimes in clumps. We would sit for hours on the front porch, listen to the river, and talk. Uncle Ray, Alidade, Israel, and Joel Johnson and his family visited, and we had some great times. She spent hours on the phone talking to people. Friends from Fort Bragg, from college, and from our neighborhood called and checked on her progress. We managed to go to church a few times when we first arrived, but by Sunday morning, she was exhausted and wanted to rest. I couldn't go without her, but we sent the kids. Lynn and Roger came every weekend and Lynn would sit and talk with her for hours. The kids insisted we get television. After some work with an antenna I placed on the side of the mountain, we managed to get the station out of Asheville. The news focused on the war in Iraq, and I didn't care. Lorraine was a great mother and very specific about what they watched. Time seemed to fly. She was getting weaker, but I convinced myself it was the chemotherapy and not the cancer. I was wrong.

One morning, I woke and went to wake her. She couldn't get out of the bed without my help. I pushed her to eat, but she didn't have an appetite. I had to carry her to the car for our trips to Murphy. She began sleeping each time I put her in the car and was growing more listless. Her mind remained strong, and we would still talk at night, but our conversations were growing shorter and shorter.

We made the return trip to Fort Bragg. We spent an agonizing day moving from clinic to clinic, scanner to scanner, and doctor to doctor. Finally, we met with the team. Her cancer had spread, the chemotherapy was not having the intended effect, and they recommended hospice.

Nothing strikes harder than the word "hospice." It is a synonym for death, and while it may mean a slow and graceful death, it still meant death. Lorraine took it in stride and actually perked up. She insisted we go to Sweetwater. It was the most peaceful place she knew and what she wanted.

As I got her from the car, she grabbed my face and said, "Take me there, and I will die peacefully. JB, everything will be fine."

I went to the chair in the garage and cried. I didn't know how much longer we had, but I knew it wasn't long. One thing was certain, she wouldn't undergo anymore chemotherapy, and that made her happy. I finally mustered the courage to check on her and found her sitting at the kitchen table writing letters. I said "who are you writing?" She smiled and said "these are for when I am gone and not one minute before. Make sure you and the kids read them." She smiled, looked at me and said "JB, don't forget".

Walter and Marge came to Fort Bragg, and John Boy and I drove a rental truck full of our furniture to Clay County. He was a good worker, and we accomplished a great deal.

On the return trip, Marge called and said, "We've taken her to the emergency room. I couldn't wake her up." She was crying. I stared crying. My son tried to comfort me, but I felt unstable. We finally made it home, and Lorraine appeared fine and was ready to go to the mountains. The next morning, we loaded up and drove.

The hospice nurse was a good guy. We talked one evening about the folks we knew. He knew my dad and had heard stories about Mr. Samuels and his faith healing.

He said, "I heard a story about him pulling a man from a burning car. The car was engulfed in flames, but Mr. Samuels walked to it, opened the door, and pulled a man to safety. The man was severely burned and sent to Gainesville, but Mr. Samuels didn't have a single scratch or burn."

I told him the stories I knew and the ones I witnessed. We talked for a long while, and finally, he said, "I need to tell you that I don't think it will be long. Be strong and I will help you and your family as best I can."

It shames me, but the kids were stronger than me. They sat daily with their mom, and somehow she always perked up, and they all smiled.

Marge was a great help, and she respected our privacy. Walter grumbled. Lorraine grew weaker and weaker. The hospice nurse tried to instruct me on pain medications, but I broke down and retreated to the side of the mountain. Lynn came and stayed for a week and helped us work through the maze of pain medications. Marge handled the pain medications when Lynn went back to Atlanta. Each night, I tried to get Lorraine up and sit her in a chair, so we could talk, but it was getting too hard on her. Her mind began to go, and she would say strange things.

One morning, she said, "Mr. Samuels is such a nice man."

I stared at her and said, "Where did that come from?"

She smiled and said, "Everything will be fine."

I figured she overheard me and the hospice nurse talking. I knew strong people, but nobody was stronger or more stable than Lorraine. I couldn't take it when her mind wandered, and I began to rely more and more on Marge to relieve me when she began talking out of her head.

She said, "JB, JB, wake up" around four o'clock in the morning. I felt my stomach tighten because I thought she was talking out of her mind again. I was afraid. I would need to wake Marge for more pain medication. She called again, "JB, please come here, baby." Her mind was clear and she said, "Let's sit on the porch."

I carried her to one of the soft lawn chairs with the big cushions. We sat there, smiled, and she said, "You have to be strong. You are the bravest man I know, but you need to be strong." I started crying.

I kept crying, sobbing harder and harder. Finally, she chuckled and said, "JB, don't be a crybaby, crybaby, crybaby." I stared hard at her, and she smiled. She said, "Please go wake the kids and ask them to come down. It's a beautiful morning."

By six-thirty, we were all sitting on the porch. Her mind was sharp and clear. She talked as if she was unveiling prophecy. She turned to John and said, "You will grow to be a great man of character and lead a successful and happy life." She turned to Jess and said, "Baby girl, you will lead a wonderful life, marry the man of your dreams, and have beautiful babies." She looked at me and said, "You are a great man. The world will never know, but I know."

It was surreal, her mind was clear, and I wondered if I was witnessing a miracle.

The sun rose slowly. She said, "Go into the kitchen and get me some breakfast."

I was the last to leave her. She winked at me like we were dating, nodded, and said, "It will be just fine."

We were in the kitchen for only a few minutes when I checked on her. Lorraine was dead. I knew it. I frantically felt for a pulse and began yelling, "Call 911. Please call 911! Please, God, don't take her. Please, God!"

No pulse, no nothing, just death. I had seen it before and inflicted it with my own hands; it was ugly. There was absolutely nothing I could do to change one part of it. I screamed again, and they all came running to the porch. I screamed as loud as I could, saying, "Call 911. She is down, and I can't get her up. I can't feel her pulse. Oh God. Oh God!"

I sounded like a wounded animal. Marge grabbed her and held her only child, and I felt sorry for her. Walter just stared, and the kids both fell to the floor crying. I hit myself hard in the chest, trying to beat the pain out of my body, but it didn't help. I was crying so hard, I couldn't see, and I walked off the porch and started up the mountain.

I walked, and I screamed, and I hit myself. I was angry. I was furious. She was dead. Who is to blame! Somebody will pay for this! She was the only good thing in my life, the only reason to live, the only decent thing remaining. She knew my secrets, and she loved me anyway. My heart was pounding. I hit myself hard, bruising my chest. I walked up the mountain. I was crying so hard I couldn't see where I was going. The anger swelled inside me again, and I screamed, "She was all, and you took her from me!"

Soon, I made it to the opening where we grazed our cattle. I screamed again, saying, "Oh, God. Oh, God, she's gone. She's gone!" It started to rain. I walked across the opening, screaming and angrier than ever before in my life. Suddenly, I saw him. He was standing by the edge of the clearing. He was wearing the old brown pants tucked into his high boots, a faded blue cotton shirt with thin black suspenders holding up his pants, and the same hat he always wore. It began raining harder. I aimed my anger at him, beat my chest like a mad man, and screamed at him like a wild animal.

I said, "You! You did this, and I will kill you!" I started forward with another guttural growl.

My legs flew underneath me, and I was lying flat on the ground. I put my hands down and rose to my knees, but my legs wouldn't move. I could not stand. He just stood there. It was raining harder.

I screamed, "You are a dead man! I will get up and kill you!"

He stepped forward, and I could see his face. He had a black spot on his nose, and I could see it clearly—it was him. He was five feet away, and I would tackle him. I tried to rise, but I was paralyzed. I was stuck and being stuck made me angrier.

"She is dead!" I yelled. "She is dead!"

He nodded and didn't move. I was crying. I shook my head and the rain fell harder and harder. He walked toward me and again the anger swelled. I tried to move and hit him, kill him. He was my objective, he was my mission, but I couldn't move. My hands fell limp to my side, and I cried again, "She is dead."

He placed his hand on my shoulder. He spoke in a soft voice, and I knew it well. He said, "It don't show smart to be angry with God, but know He will forgive you."

I cried and screamed, "She is gone! You don't understand. She is gone!" I fell forward, crying. I was soaked from the rain. I shook my head and pushed my body upright. I was free. I looked all around. There was no sign of him. I was going crazy.

I walked to the clearing looking for signs but found nothing. The rain stopped, and the sun began to break through the clouds. I ran up the mountain, trying to find evidence he was there, and I was sane, but there was no trace of him. I shook my head, and I thought of Lorraine. God knows how much I loved her. Nobody knew love like she did. My heart began beating faster. I panicked, thinking about how I would survive without her. She had been here just an hour ago, and she winked at me, and I began crying again. I was overlooking the road. I walked down the steep bank and down the road toward the bridge. I heard her voice in my head, and she was telling me I must be strong. I turned and began walking back toward the house.

As I rounded the corner, I saw two patrol cars and an ambulance. Uncle Ray pulled up behind me, got out of his car, and hugged me. He was crying and holding me. He said, "She was a beauty boy, a real beauty."

Lorraine thought Uncle Ray was a nut, and he always made her laugh. The ambulance crew moved her body to her bed and called the county Coroner.

The ambulance driver said, "He is on his way, I…We are real sorry for your loss." The kids were sitting on the couch, and I sat between them and held them. Marge moved the deputies to the kitchen and served coffee. The ambulance crew moved to the porch. Jess put her head against my shoulder, and I could smell her hair. It was like Lorraine's, and I began to cry. The deputies sat down and drank coffee. One of the deputies was a huge man standing over six-five and easily over three hundred pounds, while the other was much shorter at five-five and 150 pounds. The big deputy looked like a professional wrestler. I didn't appreciate them staring at me as I held my children and cried.

The Coroner arrived, went into the bedroom, and examined Lorraine. He never spoke to me, but as he walked out of the room, he nodded. He walked to the kitchen doorway and stood there. He glanced at me and the kids and said, "I'm sorry, it's official."

Marge and Walter were standing against the sink, and I could hear the ambulance folks talking on the porch. He looked in the kitchen and said, "Which funeral home do you prefer for her arrangements?"

I heard Marge begin to cry again, and Walter spoke up. He said, "We will transport her to Asheboro, and she will be buried there."

I bolted off the couch, moved the Coroner to the side, and stepped into the kitchen. I shook my head and said, "Ivie Funeral Home, and she will be buried at Sweetwater Baptist."

Walter stepped directly toward me and said in a loud voice, "My daughter will not be buried here with these people!"

I moved quickly and stood inches from his face and screamed, saying, "What do you mean by these people, Walter?"

He stuck out his neck and said, "You know exactly what I mean, and my daughter will not be buried here!"

I stepped forward, bumping him with my hands by my side. He turned toward the deputies and said, "Arrest this man for assault." He stepped back and pointed at me and said, "You are witnesses!"

Marge shook her head, said, "Walter," and went to the doorway and held the kids. The small deputy stood and moved slowly toward Walter, and I felt the large deputy move behind me.

Walter screamed again, saying, "I demand you arrest this man. He is crazy, and you must jail him!" He put his back against the sink, pointed his finger at me, and said, "My daughter will be buried in Asheboro."

"No!" I shouted. "She will be buried here!"

The big deputy grabbed my right shoulder. I looked down at his hand on my shoulder and said, "Get your hand off me." He did not. He moved quickly with his other hand attempting to grab my right arm and restrain me. I stepped forward, grabbed his right arm, and placed him in an arm bar, quickly stepping behind him and forcing his right shoulder downward and lifting his arm high into the air. He was slow and didn't realize what was happening. He turned his head toward the other deputy and said, "Help me, Eddie, help me."

The smaller deputy was mesmerized by the movement and his partner's increasing pain level. He didn't know what to do.

Walter seized the opportunity and began screaming at the short deputy. "Shoot him! Shoot him now! He is crazy!"

Marge grabbed the kids in an effort to move them away from the door. The ambulance crew, hearing the commotion, ran past Marge and into the kitchen. It was getting crowded.

I maintained the arm bar on the big man and also began to put pressure on his wrist by bending it upward. He shrieked in pain. The shorter deputy put his hand on his weapon, but I shook my head. He froze.

I said, "We are all going to the porch." I started walking the big deputy toward the door, and the ambulance crew flew past me.

Marge and the kids followed, and I motioned for the Coroner to move in front.

The ambulance driver keyed his radio and said, "Officer hostage." I stared at him, and he nodded and switched it off. They assembled in the yard with me and the big deputy standing on the porch.

I said, "Call the funeral home and make arrangements, now!"

The coroner jumped slightly, nodded, and began calling on his cell phone.

"Marge," I said, "get ahold of the preacher and set a date for the funeral. Also, please call Lynn and Alidade."

Walter interrupted and screamed, "My daughter is not going to be buried here!"

He turned toward the short deputy and the Coroner and said, "Aren't you fools going to do something about this?" Neither man moved. I heard sirens in the distance.

I said, "It's time to end this, so you will all get off my land." From the corner of my eye, I saw Uncle Ray. He was standing on the hill to the right of the porch. He was carrying a shotgun.

A North Carolina Highway Patrolman was the first to arrive. He casually got out of his car, assessed the situation, and giggled at the fact that Clay County's biggest deputy was in pain.

Shortly, two additional cars pulled into the driveway, one contained the Sheriff. He jumped from his car and shouted, "What is going on here?"

The smaller deputy began briefing him when Walter jumped in and said, "He assaulted me, and your worthless deputies won't arrest him!"

John shouted, "Grandpa, that isn't true."

Walter looked at him and looked at Marge. The Sheriff held up his hand toward Walter, and the smaller deputy said, "It's a dispute over where his wife"—he pointed at me—"and his daughter"—he pointed at Walter—"is going to be buried."

I kept a firm grip on the big deputy. I spread his legs and bent him at the waist with his right arm extending toward the sky. Each time he moved, I applied pressure, and he screamed.

The Sheriff looked at me, pointed, and said, "You need to release my deputy."

I saw him. He was standing behind the Sheriff's car and was staring at me. His arms were folded in front. He looked exactly the same as when I had seen him earlier.

I screamed at him, "She is dead!" He nodded. I yelled again, "I loved her so much. She was everything, and you took her away from me!"

The Sheriff was confused and shook his head, saying, "I'm sorry, but I didn't take her."

He looked calm. He was just standing, looking at me. It angered me. How could he be so calm. I screamed again, "Why did you take her from me?" He nodded but didn't move. The Sheriff turned and looked behind him, and the Highway Patrolman did the same. I began to cry and used my free hand to wipe away the tears. The big deputy saw this as a sign of weakness and moved. I put more pressure on his arm, and he screamed.

Walter pointed at me and yelled, "You took her from me. You brought her here with these people, and I need to take her home." He was crying. The Sheriff stepped in front of Walter, and the Highway Patrolman began moving to the right. Uncle Ray racked the shotgun, and everyone froze.

The Sheriff looked at him and said, "Ray, why are you here?"

Ray said, "These are my people. Nobody moves until he sorts this out."

The Sheriff nodded and said, "We can work this out. It all starts with releasing the deputy."

I wiped tears and looked over the porch, and he was gone. I scanned in all directions, and then, I screamed, "Where are you! Where are you?"

The Sheriff said, "He's having some sort of psychotic episode." He stepped forward and said, "Release the deputy."

I put pressure on his arm, causing him to scream again, and the Sheriff backed away. Suddenly, he was standing off to the far left behind the well.

I screamed at him, saying, "You owe me answers! She is dead, and you know! You owe me answers!" He nodded and just stood there.

My kids were scared. It was stressful. I remembered Lorraine's letters. I lowered my voice, pointed at John, and said, "Please go to Mom's top dresser drawer. See if she has a letter in there."

Jess ran for the door, and John followed.

The Sheriff said, "We need to resolve this. You need to release the deputy."

I stared at the Sheriff and said, "Be still."

Jess yelled, "Daddy, I found it."

Marge stepped toward them and behind me. They handed her the letter, and she opened it. Jess burst into tears as soon as she saw her Mom's handwriting, handed it to Marge and hugged her waist. Marge wiped away tears and said, "There are several letters." She counted and said, "It's five letters all addressed to us."

She rubbed Jess's head and said, "One to you," nodding at me. "One to each of the kids, and one to me and Walter." She hesitated and said, "And one says its her last wishes letter."

I looked at Jess, wiped away tears, and said, "Please read that one."

Marge opened the letter and read. Her voice cracked, and she read, "I love you all so much. I will miss you. Be kind to one another, love one another, and know I am with the Lord." Marge wiped her eyes. "On warm sunny days, walk up the road and visit me in Sweetwater, and know I am so proud of you." She paused, cleared her throat, and said, "There's more, but that's enough."

Marge bent over, crying, and Jess hugged her. They were holding each other for all they were worth. I looked up and saw him. He was standing next to Mom's old flowerbed. He nodded, turned, and walked away toward his house. Walter fell to the ground, crying.

I pushed the big deputy forward, released my grip, and pushed him gently down the steps. I grabbed my kids and held them tight. I heard the Sheriff's voice behind me.

It was a simple takedown. The Sheriff grabbed me by the shirt collar and pulled me straight back. The big deputy, seeking revenge, dropped his entire weight on me. They worked to control my hands. The smaller deputy and the Highway Patrolman joined, rolled me over on my stomach, and applied the handcuffs. I hated the feel of handcuffs. They cut my wrist and made me feel vulnerable.

The Sheriff said, "You are under arrest for assaulting a law enforcement officer."

The kids screamed. Marge said, "Let him go!"

Ray was on the porch with the shotgun, but the Highway Patrolman quickly took it from him. The big deputy dropped his knee into my lower back. It felt like he broke something, maybe my hip. I screamed. He tightened the handcuffs and jerked me to my feet. The Sheriff read me my rights and said, "You need help. You are psychotic."

The smaller deputy pulled hard upward on the cuffs causing more pain, and he pushed me down the steps. Ray yelled at the Sheriff, "Get your résumé ready. You are going to have to work for a living when we vote." They pushed my head down and shoved me inside the back seat of the car.

The smaller deputy got in the front seat and drove us toward the road. I stared out the window. He was standing under a tree just up from the riverbank. He stood there and stared at me as we passed. He had a way of slowly raising his head from underneath his hat and exposing his face.

I said, "Did you see that man?"

The deputy said, "What are you talking about?"

Maybe I was psychotic. As we started down Fires Creek Road and turned onto Highway 64, I began to panic. I trained myself to avoid even the simplest sign of panic and to keep my head and think, but all I could think about was Lorraine's funeral and my kids. I underwent numerous training situations where I was required to calm myself and think, but now, all the training failed. I began to cry. I couldn't stop.

CLAY COUNTY JAIL

THE DEPUTY DROVE to the county jail, pulled underneath the awning, and jerked me out of the back seat. I shook my head and felt my heart racing. My mind drifted to the back of the fuel truck, and I could feel my hand shaking. I shook my head to somehow get the cobwebs out and regain control. He led me into the building and up an old, decrepit flight of stairs to the second floor. He began beating on the door, and within a few seconds, it opened. He pushed me through into a small office and sat me down in a straight chair against the wall.

He turned to the jailer and said, "This is a dangerous man. He is under arrest for assaulting a police officer. Be careful"—he paused, then looked at me—"because he's crazy." The jailer stared at me and then asked, "Which officer did he assault?"

The deputy said, "Big Bill Henson."

The jailer smirked, stepped around me and sat behind his desk. He looked at me again and said, "What's your name?"

I said, "JB Smith."

He raised his eyebrows and said, "I knew JD. He was a good man. I don't recall...Is Ray your uncle or your cousin?"

I nodded and said, "Ray is my uncle." He turned, banging the keyboards of an old computer. The deputy stood nervously against the doorstop. I tried not to cry. Finally, he looked at me and said, "You went into the Army?"

I nodded again.

"Isn't your wife sick?"

I shook my head and said, "She died this morning."

He lowered his head as if he was praying and then said, "I am real sorry to hear that." I was fighting emotions and to keep from crying.

He was an older man, easily in his late fifties or early sixties. He walked around his desk toward me and said, "It will be all right. Please stand up for me." I stood but winced in pain. He looked at me and said, "Are you in pain?" and he lifted my shirt.

My side and hip were purple.

He nodded, looking at the small deputy. "Well," he said, "I need to hold your shirt up for a second." He turned and opened a file drawer and removed a camera. He held the shirt with one hand and took several photographs with the other.

This made the deputy even more nervous, and he continued to shuffle his feet standing in the doorway. When he was complete, he carefully pulled my wallet from my pocket, emptied my pockets, replaced my shirt, and gently sat me back down. He pulled out an inventory sheet and began going through my wallet and the items from my pants.

He pulled out my Military Identification Card and asked, "What is the name of your commanding officer?"

I said, "That's old. I am retired. With my wife being sick, I didn't get a retired card. My last assignment was Fort Bragg."

He shook his head and said, "I'm sorry, but you have an active card, not a retired card, and I have to notify the Fort Bragg Provost Marshall. What was your last unit of assignment?"

I said, "Intelligence Security Agency."

He began banging on the keyboards. He turned toward me and said slowly, "You understand I have to notify the Army?"

I nodded.

He slowly turned his head and looked at me. "Are you going to give me any trouble?"

It was an odd question and I said no.

He faced the deputy and said, "Eddie, take off your cuffs."

The deputy raised his voice and said, "Are you sure because he's quick. He did ninja stuff on Big Bill."

The jailer nodded and said, "He won't give me no trouble."

He took my fingerprints and my photograph and said, "You will be here for at least twenty-four hours before your arraignment. I will make some calls and see if we can do it sooner, but plan on twenty-four." He turned and said, "Eddie, go back to… whatever you are supposed to be doing." He pointed down the hallway and said, "We have four cells. You get to pick. The county is building a detention center, but this is what we have for now. It looks bad, but we have closed-circuit monitoring"—he pointed at a camera—"and it cost a pretty penny. There will always be a jailer on this floor so if you need anything, just holler, and we will come." I panicked as I walked into the cell.

I hesitated, and he said, "It will be all right." He closed the door behind me and went back down the hall. It was a small room with a toilet in the corner, a sink, and an old-style army bed with a naked mattress. I sat on the bunk and cried.

I heard him coming down the hall and wiped hard at my face. He opened the door and said, "Here," handing me a cup of coffee and a doughnut.

He walked back down the hall, grabbed two straight chairs and his coffee cup. He placed the chairs in the hall and sat down. He motioned me out of the cell and said, "Sit down."

We sat in silence for a few moments. I gulped down the coffee and ate the doughnut.

I nodded, and he sipped his coffee.

Finally, he said, "My name is Earl Hardaway and I knew your dad. I went to JD's funeral and met you there, but I guess you wouldn't remember. You lived down near Mr. Samuels, didn't you?"

I glared at him when he mentioned his name and said, "Do you remember him?"

He said, "I reckon everybody around my age remembers him." I stared at him. He smiled and said, "I was fishing in Graham County one time and got to talking to a man, and he asked me if I knew Andrew Samuels. It's a small world for us but a big world for him." I wondered why he was talking about him.

Finally, I said, "I used to work for him when he sold seed and ran his mill." He nodded.

I drank my coffee, and he said, "A boy named Mason from Fires Creek was dating my cousin. She lived on Tusquitte. She was divorced, and her ex-husband was a mean cuss named Carl. He caught them together in Hayesville and went crazy. He chased Mason down Sweetwater, and Mason ran out of gas at the Shallow Ford Bridge, right down from your place. Carl had a pump shotgun and fired two at Mason and wounded him, but he ran up the road toward the Samuelses' place. He caught Mason and tied him up and when Mr. Samuels showed up and told him to stop. Mason thought he was going to be executed. Carl turned the shotgun on Mr. Samuels and fired two blast at the old man. I reckon the Lord was all over him and not a single pellet hit him. He told Carl to go home and untied Mason and took him to get gas for his car. Now, that"—he paused—"is my best Andrew Samuels story." He paused, deep in thought, and then continued, He took another long sip from his coffee cup. "I reckon there are hundreds of stories about him and about his faith. A preacher friend told me that Andrew Samuels was on a different spiritual plane than the rest of us. It was kinda like he was God's pet. I heard he carried a mustard seed to remind him of his faith and a long nail to remind him of Christ on the Cross."

I nodded and said, "I know the mustard seed."

His wife came and served us bologna sandwiches and chips. She looked at me and said, "I am so sorry to hear about your poor wife." They walked back down the hall, and I heard her say, "Earl, it's all over the county. That poor man lost his wife and the Sheriff arresting him and all. You know Big Bill had it coming."

Earl said, "Go on now. I got work to do. Love you." Earl spent the remainder of the afternoon on the phone. He never closed the jail door again, and I was determined to uphold his trust.

Marge and the kids came about three o'clock. Jess cried all day and insisted they come. She said, "Walter sulked all day. We haven't really seen him. Lorraine's letter is specific. We will arrange everything. Don't you worry." Marge was hurting. She said, "Lynn took it hard. She is coming." I held the kids and told them I would be home tomorrow.

I heard Earl talking and then saw them coming down the hallway. Earl turned and introduced me to Henry, the night jailer. Henry shook my hand and said "I'll be at the end of the hall if you need anything. I will listen to the Braves game on the radio and you are welcome to join me if you want."

As they walked down the hall, Henry turned to Earl and said, "Big Bill was certainly in need of a whipping," and Earl nodded. I walked down and listened to the game on the radio. They won it in the eighth inning with several clutch hits and brought in a closer to finish the ninth.

I went to the bunk. I missed Lorraine. I was asleep. It was a deep sleep, and I was instantly awake. I looked up. He was standing beside me. He was wearing the same hat, shirt, suspenders, brown pants, and boots he always wore. I shook my head and bit my lip, trying to determine if I was dreaming. I felt the pain and shot out of the bed.

I said, "What are you doing?"

He didn't flinch, and I yelled, "What are you doing here?" as loud as I could, expecting Henry to come down the hall.

He said, "Henry can't hear you." It was his voice.

I said, "Are you real?" and he held out his arms. I grabbed him. I will throw him, capture him, and prove I am not psychotic. I couldn't move. I was touching his arm, but I couldn't move against him.

I screamed, saying, "What are you doing to me?"

The anger charged through my body, and I tried to scream at him, but I couldn't scream. I yelled, "What is happening?" but it came out as a whisper. I flinched and said, "You took her away and I will get you." He stood and looked at me. Finally, he said, "You are self-seeking."

It made me angrier, but I couldn't move, and I couldn't counter him.

My mind couldn't comprehend what was happening. I needed intelligence if I was going to defeat him, so I started to ask him a question, but before I could get it out, he said, "He sent me."

Before I could form words, he said, "The great I Am."

It was quicker this time. Before I could fully formulate the thought, a Bible appeared on the bed. Before I could think to tell him I knew the Bible, he said, "Not true." He was reading my mind. A thought rushed through my head. It was some sort of CIA mind trick, but before I could complete the thought, he said, "No, it's not. Do for others and expect nothing in return."

I blinked, and he was gone. It was as if he was never there. Nothing, no sign of him anywhere.

I began to shake. My body trembled. I was losing my mind. Slowly, I walked out the door and down the hall. Henry was awake, reading a Louie Lamoure novel.

He said, "Are you okay? Anything I can get for you?" He stared at me and said, "You look pale, like you seen a ghost or something." He went to the coffee pot, poured and handed me the cup, saying, "You've had some tough days, probably had a bad dream."

We sat for over an hour. Neither of us talked. Finally, he said, "Morning will be here soon so you better try to get some rest." I nodded and walked cautiously back down the hall. The Bible was on my bed. I stared at it. I cautiously picked it up. I began reading. For the next several hours, I read. After an hour, I understood the "Great I Am," but I still didn't understand why this was happening to me. I heard Henry and Earl talking at shift change.

Around nine o'clock, Earl came down the hall and said, "Your arraignment will be at four this afternoon in the courthouse, and you meet your lawyer at three."

I nodded and said, "Who is my lawyer?"

Earl said, "I'm not sure. Whoever the court appointed. Maybe the young man from Franklin." He handed me a broom. "I always ask the guest to clean up after themselves."

After lunch, he noticed the Bible and said, "I don't have your Bible on my inventory. I didn't know you brought it with you." Before I could speak, he said, "He gave us an owner's manual but most of us ignore it until the dashboard lights start blinking."

I said, "What do you mean?"

He nodded and said, "It tells us everything we need to know. He gave man smarts, but man always thinks he is smarter than the Creator. Man lost faith in God, but God didn't lose faith in us." He smiled. "Anyway, I'm glad you are reading it."

I read all afternoon.

Earl came and said, "It's time to meet the lawyer. I am supposed to cuff you, but no need."

LAWYERS

It had been years since I had walked downtown Hayesville. Lorraine and the kids came here often, but I didn't. We walked into the courtroom, and Earl pointed at a small table on the left side. A young man with glasses was talking to the Sheriff and an older man wearing a polo shirt. I watched them. Finally, the young man came toward my table. I stood prepared to shake hands, but the young man stepped back and said, "Why isn't this man handcuffed?"

Earl said, "No need."

The young man was apprehensive. I put out my hand again, and he carefully shook my hand. He walked to the side of the table, said, "Sit down," but he continued to stand. He stared at me for a few seconds and said, "I have worked a plea, so you have no worries."

I stood, causing him to jump back slightly. I said, "I need to know the details."

He looked down, then looked at me and said, "You need to understand something. You are guilty. It's in your best interest to cooperate."

I shook my head and said, "What am I cooperating with?" He stared at me, and I said, "And who determined my best interest?"

He held up a hand and said, "Best is if I do all the talking."

I shook my head and said, "No, you are confusing me."

He pushed his glasses on his nose and said, "North Carolina gives you the right to plead guilty at the arraignment."

I nodded and said, "I understand."

He continued, "This allows you to begin immediately serving your sentence, and it saves the state the expense of a trial." He cleared his throat. "More importantly, the court is much more lenient than if we proceed."

I shook my head and said, "What do you mean about serving my sentence?"

He smiled and said, "Don't worry, I do this all the time."

The courtroom door opened. An older gentleman, wearing a blue shirt and jeans, walked inside and scanned the room. He made eye contact with me, nodded, and moved to the corner and sat down.

I struggled to focus and said, "What are the charges?" He looked at me, and I continued, "And I need to know the details of the bargain."

He frowned and pulled a file folder from a briefcase. He said, "There are multiple charges, but if you agree, you should be home in forty-five days." He moved cautiously and sat beside me. I felt the anger rising, and the courtroom door opened with a loud squeak. It was Alidade, Israel, Uncle Ray, Marge, and my kids. Jess waved. She had been crying but smiled at me. I waved and managed a smile. Marge walked to me, hugged me, and said, "All the arrangements are just as she wanted. The funeral will be tomorrow at one. She will be buried next to your mom and dad."

I hugged her and felt the tears. I needed to focus on the attorney. She seemed at peace. I said, "Thanks so much. Thanks for everything."

The attorney was studying a series of documents in front of him. I touched him. He jumped and then looked at me. I said, "I need to know my options."

He nodded his head and said, "You have few options." He pointed at the man in the polo shirt and said, "He is the Assistant District Attorney. He will present the state's substantial case against you. Next to him is the Sheriff who was an eyewitness to the incident, and he will testify. Together, they will bring three felony charges and one misdemeanor charge."

I was shocked and said, "What are the felonies?"

He looked down at the paper, flipped to the second page, and said, "You need to plead guilty to assault on a law enforcement officer, holding a law enforcement officer hostage during the execution of his assigned duties, and threatening a law enforcement officer. The other charge is misdemeanor assault versus a Reverend Walter J. Bores." I gasped for air. He looked at me and said, "It would be helpful if Reverend Bores drops his charges."

He glanced toward the ADA and the sheriff, lowered his voice, and said, "You will spend forty-five days in Hazelwood, which is minimum security. The state will get you the psychological treatment you need, and you will be out before the leaves turn."

He smiled. I shook my head, not believing. My thoughts were scattered. I shook my head and said, "What happens if I reject the deal, and will I be a convicted felon?"

He frowned and said, "Yes, you are…I mean yes. You will be a convicted felon. It would be unwise to reject this deal. The judge can sentence you to medium security. That means Craggy Prison in Asheville, medium security and not good." He stared at me and shook his head. "North Carolina takes assault on a law enforcement officer very seriously."

The courtroom door squeaked again, and Joel, along with several people from the church, entered the courtroom. I glanced at the Sheriff. From his body language, he didn't like families in the courtroom.

"Not guilty," I said.

He pushed his glasses back on his nose and looked at me. His voice became squeaky and he said, "You just don't understand the process."

I said, "I fully understand the process. I am not interested in a plea bargain. I want a trial." I shook my head. "I won't do this."

His voice went higher, and he said, "Listen, this carries two to five years. Anything over two and you go to Craggy. Hazelwood is minimum security. Basically, you guard yourself. Craggy, well, that's ugly. You need to take the deal."

I glared at him and said, "You haven't asked me if I was guilty. You just proceeded without me."

He pulled back, raised his eyebrows, and then looked down at his papers. The door squeaked again and a large gray-headed man walked in, opened the gates, nodded at Earl, and went into a small office. The Assistant District Attorney smiled and waved at him and quickly followed. I could see him in the office speaking to the attorney and then grabbing a black robe. The Sheriff moved to the opposite table and took a seat.

I said, "Is that the judge?" He nodded. I said, "Are you going to go and talk to him?" He shook his head. I pointed at the Assistant District Attorney and said, "He is allowed to talk to the judge, but you can't?"

His face was red, and he glared at me and said, "You don't understand."

The judge walked to the doorway, pointed, and said, "Earl."

Earl walked toward the small office. I turned to my attorney and said, "Is this an average crowd for an arraignment?"

He started to answer, and Earl stepped forward and made a motion. The ADA moved past Earl and walked toward his table. Earl said, "This court is called to order. The Honorable Judge Wallace Inman presiding."

Everybody stood up, and he walked up the small stairs, sat down, and banged his gavel. From out of nowhere, a court reporter moved forward and took her seat. He scanned the court room, grimaced, and then said in a low voice, "The prosecution may proceed." Everybody sat down.

The Assistant District Attorney remained standing and started off, saying, "Your Honor, this is a simple case, and we discussed a plea due to the defendant's mental condition." The judge looked at me and nodded. The ADA said, "The defendant is retired military, and his wife passed away due to cancer."

I heard the courtroom door squeak again and footsteps behind me, but I didn't turn. I concentrated on the prosecutor.

He picked up a folder and said, "On the day of his wife's passing, the defendant assaulted his father-in-law, the Reverend Walter J. Bores. He also assaulted Deputies Bill Henson, Eddie Bowers, and Highway Patrolman Thomas Snyder. Present as witnesses were Coroner Mike Wallace and an ambulance team consisting of Heather Mitchell and Bobby Watson. Deputy Henson, in an attempt to deescalate the situation, attempted to restrain the defendant. The defendant then assaulted and battered the deputy, held him hostage while moving everyone from the home, threatened Deputy Bowers, and initiated a standoff, which lasted until the Sheriff arrived. The Sheriff submits that the defendant was in an altered mental state, and once he talked him into releasing his hostage, he arrested the defendant. The specific charges the state registers today are misdemeanor assault against the Reverend, felony assault, and battery against law enforcement officer Bill Henson, a felony of holding law enforcement officer Bill Henson hostage, and an additional felony charge by threatening law enforcement officer Eddie Bowers. Given the defendant's military service with no prior arrest record, the state is willing to accept a plea. Should that plea be finalized today, the state is willing to start the sentence tomorrow." He cleared his throat. "The bargain to begin after the defendant attends a funeral tomorrow."

The judge looked down at the papers in front of him, cleared his throat, and said, "Sheriff, what caused you to think the defendant was in an altered mental state?"

The ADA answered, saying "Your Honor, it was the way he looked. The defendant has undergone significant military training. He endangered multiple citizens."

The judge looked up and said, "Drugs or alcohol involved?"

The ADA answered, "No, Your Honor."

The judge said, "Big Bill Henson?" The judge held his up his hand and looked past and said, "Is there a reason for the military presence?"

I turned and saw an Army Colonel and an Air Force Lieutenant Colonel both in dress uniforms.

Both officers stood in the center aisle, and the colonel said, "You Honor, I am Colonel Mitch Smith, the Staff Judge Advocate for the Joint Special Operations Command at Fort Bragg, North Carolina."

The judge nodded.

The Colonel continued, "Your Honor, with all due respect, the defendant remains on active duty. Given that, we respectfully request time to confer with the defendant."

The judge shook his head and said, "Why?"

Colonel Smith said, "Your Honor, since the defendant is in an active-duty status, we seek time to confer with him regarding military due process options and to determine the facts in evidence."

The judge looked at the ADA and then at Colonel Smith. He said, "Who is with you?"

Colonel Smith said, "Your Honor, this is Lieutenant Colonel Mike Farris. We are both members of the North Carolina Bar."

The judge shifted in his chair and said, "Is he"—pointing at me—"active duty, or is he retired?"

Colonel Smith didn't hesitate. "Active duty, Your Honor, He is not retired but in a leave status from the military."

The judge said, "Thirty-minute recess," and he slammed his gavel.

Colonel Smith shook my hand and said, "I am very sorry about your wife. You have my condolences."

I nodded.

Lieutenant Colonel Farris shook my hand, patted me on the back, and said, "Call me Mike."

Colonel Smith looked at the young attorney and said, "Do you want to retain him as counsel?"

I said no. Colonel Smith turned to him and said, "You're fired." He looked around the courtroom, shook his head, and asked Earl, "Sir, is there anywhere we can confer with our client in private?"

Earl thought and said, "We can go outside, but I have to go with you."

I turned to Colonel Smith and said, "It's okay with me." I reached and squeezed Jess's hand as we walked out. She smiled. Earl led us out the door, and we walked across the grass to a decrepit picnic table and sat down. Earl stepped behind us, folded his arms, and stood.

Colonel Smith opened his briefcase and said, "Mike, do that trial attorney thing before this thing goes any further."

Mike nodded and said, "Did you physically touch your father-in-law, or did you just yell at him?"

I answered, "I got in his face, but didn't touch him."

Mike nodded. "Did you move toward him in an aggressive manner?"

"Yes, I but stopped short."

Mike wrote down my responses and said, "Were you fully aware that the Sheriff's deputies were in the house and what were they doing?"

"Yes," I said. "They were sitting at the kitchen table, drinking coffee."

"Did the deputy touch you?"

"Yes," I said. "He put his hand on my shoulder."

Mike said, "Interesting. Did he say anything at all. Specifically, did he ask you to calm down?"

I shook my head and said, "No, he did not. He just placed his hand on my shoulder."

"Okay. Did he tell you to calm down or tell you that you were under arrest?"

"No, I asked him to remove his hand."

"I understand. Is he physically bigger than you?"

"Yes, he is twice my size."

"Okay. Did you ever strike him?"

"No, I did not. I only put him into an arm bar."

"Good. Did you threaten the other deputy?"

I shook my head and said, "No, I don't think I did anything to threaten him other than stare at him."

"Good. How did they capture you?"

I lowered my head and said, "I asked my mother-in-law to read Lorraine's letter, and when she finished, I let the deputy loose to hug my kinds. They gang tackled me."

"I see. Did they hurt you?"

"Yes, my side and hip were bruised."

Colonel Smith said, "Can you show us?"

I stood and pulled up my shirt. The bruising was evident, but the swelling had gone down. Earl spoke from behind me and said, "I have photographs of him when he arrived at the jail."

Mike raised an eyebrow and said, "Sir, it would be very helpful if we could see those photographs."

Earl nodded, took out his cell phone, and made a call. As I turned to look at Earl, I noticed the man with the blue shirt approaching. He stopped short and asked to speak to Colonel Smith. Mike was busy scribbling notes and then asked, "Were there any bruises on the deputy?"

I shook my head and said, "None that I put on him."

Mike reviewed his sheet and said, "We will see."

I leaned back and said, "I have to go to Lorraine's funeral."

Mike smiled and said, "That's the easy part."

I noticed the Colonel and the man with the blue shirt were talking. I asked Mike, "So what do you think?"

He took a deep breath and said, "We are going to argue this was an overreach by law enforcement, and that due to your wife's death, we have exigent circumstances." He took a deep breath. "North Carolina is a law enforcement–friendly state, and you embarrassed them, so this is an uphill case. I need to tell you now that you may spend time in a hospital."

I was surprised and said, "Why a hospital?"

"Look," he said, "I know your history, and I know your wife died, but you overreacted to a situation. Anyway, we look at this." He paused. "You have anger management issues."

I shook my head and said, "No, that's stupid."

He patted my back. Colonel Smith returned and said, "This is Don from the Agency." We stood and shook hands with the gray-haired man in the blue shirt. The Colonel said, "He's from the CIA's Office of Security and Internal Investigations."

Don spoke slowly. It was irritating. He said, "Anytime someone with your clearance level is placed in a potentially compromising situation, I come and assess."

I started to speak, but Colonel Smith held up his hand and said, "Don't worry about that now. Focus on ending this before it escalates."

Mike nodded. Within minutes, Henry came loafing across the grass, carrying Earl's camera and three large pieces of paper. He handed them to Earl, waved at me, and walked slowly back toward the jail.

We walked back into the courtroom, and the ADA immediately grabbed Mike and the Colonel and walked them into a corner. The judge's office door was open, and I could see him studying papers and occasionally spitting in a coke bottle. Earl stood by the door, and the judge eventually checked his watch, stood, and put on his robe. Earl again went center stage and announced court was in session.

The judge took his seat and said, "Where we were before the commotion?"

The ADA spoke first and said, "Your Honor, the state asks five hundred thousand dollars in bail." I was shocked. He continued, saying, "The defendant assaulted law enforcement officers."

The judge interrupted and said, "Is there anything new to report?"

The ADA said, "Your Honor, we do not have a plea agreement, so we should begin looking at trial dates."

The judge turned his head and said "Gentlemen" to the Colonel and Mike.

Mike stood and cleared his throat. He said, "Your Honor, we have a case with significant mitigation and extenuation. Lieutenant Colonel Smith lost his wife after a long battle with cancer followed by an internal family disagreement concerning funeral arrangements. Law enforcement unnecessarily stepped into the situation and rather than calming it, they escalated it. This is a clear case of law enforcement overreach. It is like swatting a fly with a sledgehammer. We move to dismiss all charges."

The judge listened. The ADA said, "The people demand a bond or jail time. The defendant is a flight risk. He is mentally unstable and a danger to his family and our community."

The judge looked at the ADA and said, "Why?"

The ADA said, "Your Honor, this man has an extensive military record and was unstable at the time of his arrest."

Mike interjected and said, "Your Honor, that is a smear upon the defendant's character."

The judge shook his head and said, "Hush."

The ADA continued, "Coupled with the fact—"

The judge pointed at the ADA and said, "All of you, hush means hush." He sat quietly for a few seconds and then said, "In the past, an arraignment was designed solely to determine bail, but now, the new laws allow me discretion. I intend to hear facts before proceeding." He looked at Earl and said, "Do you have the keys to the conference room upstairs?" Earl nodded. The judge continued, "I don't have chambers here in Hayesville, so we will meet upstairs in five minutes to discuss the merits of the case. Once we determine that, we will reconvene court and will render judgment." He banged his gavel.

Mike looked at me and smiled. "Mike," I said, "I don't have that kind of money for bail."

He nodded and said, "The judge gave us the opportunity to present facts. It's a good thing." I glanced toward the other table. The ADA and the Sheriff seemed upset, and both were shaking their heads. Jess reached over the small rail and held my hand briefly as we walked outside.

THE GOOD JUDGE

WITHIN MINUTES, WE were upstairs. It was an old jury room with several straight back chairs clustered around an old oak table. It was dusty and the floors creaked. We sat on one side of the table with the ADA and the sheriff on the opposite. The judge entered, and we all stood. He was carrying legal pads and an empty coke bottle. He placed them on the table, removed his robe, and took his seat. Earl grabbed a chair and sat behind him. The judge scribbled notes on a long sheet of yellow legal paper, put his pen down, reached in his pocket and pulled out a can of snuff, inserted a small amount in his mouth, and went back to scribbling on the paper. Finally, he looked up and scanned the room.

Immediately, his eyes went to Don, and he said, "Sir, who are you and what business do you have here?" Don started to stand, but the judge motioned for him to remain seated.

Don said, "Sir, I work for the Central Intelligence Agency's Office of Security and Internal Investigations."

The judge raised his eyebrows and said, "You have my full and complete attention."

Don spoke slowly. "Lieutenant Colonel Smith has a very sensitive security clearance with access to compartmentalized information and special access programs. Whenever someone with this level of access is involved...in a legal proceeding, my mission is to observe and report."

The judge shook his head, turned slightly toward Earl, and said, "My wife has garden club tonight. My goal was to eat a Big Mac and fries without her knowledge and watch *Law and Order* on the cable, but this is getting interesting." He spit into the bottle. "Go on."

Don nodded and said, "The agency has a vested interest in ensuring the safeguarding of classified information."

The judge leaned back in his chair and said, "Army, Air Force, the CIA, and the Sheriff all here on the square in Hayesville. It's another boring day in Clay County." He pointed at me and said, "Why is the CIA shadowing you?"

I started to speak, but Colonel Smith cut me off. He reached for his briefcase and said, "This officer has a distinguished history of service to the nation."

The judge nodded, and Colonel Smith continued, "He has served in a wide variety of sensitive strategic assignments."

The judge shook his head and said, "Details?"

Don shifted in his chair, drawing the judge's attention. The judge looked at Don and said, "Do you have anything to add?"

Colonel Smith took a heavy breath and said, "Your Honor, this is sensitive. We fully understand and respect your authority to ask the question, and it is in our best interest to answer, but it is...sensitive." He continued, "Normally, we require those present to sign a standard non-disclosure agreement. It accounts for his"—he nodded toward Don—"presence here today."

The judge raised his eyebrows and nodded.

The Colonel continued, "It's in the interest of justice that you know the defendant's military history."

The judge sat back in his chair and quietly spat in his bottle. The ADA shook his head and said, "Your Honor, this has no bearing on the case and is highly irregular. We are all officers of the court."

The judge held up his hand and thought for a moment. Finally he said, "My job is to determine facts. I acknowledge this is irregular, but we are a nation at war. I will allow."

Colonel Smith reached into his briefcase and produced a stack of the documents. Slowly, he handed them out and explained them. The ADA read every word and finally signed and pushed the paper across the table.

Colonel Smith said, "The defendant is an experienced and capable Soldier. He served in numerous conflicts including the invasion of Panama, Columbia, and several South American countries, the Middle East including the first Gulf War, Somalia, and numerous actions across the horn of Africa. He has extensive service in the Balkans." He looked up from his paper and continued "He has conducted several strategic operations in Afghanistan, and most recently, he returned from a special-access mission in Iraq to care for his wife."

The judge looked at me and said, "When did he return from Iraq? We just started that war?"

Colonel Smith looked at the judge and said, "He returned to the states in February."

The judge shook his head and looked at the ceiling. Finally, he pointed at me and said, "If my memory is correct, you were in Iraq before the war started?"

I nodded and said, "Yes, sir."

He sat up, spat in his bottle, pointed at Don, and said, "I understand why you are here. You can stay."

The ADA looked puzzled, pointed at me, and said, "You were in Iraq before the war started?"

The judge looked at him and said, "We just covered that."

The ADA recovered quickly and said, "He took a law enforcement officer hostage that is the relevant fact."

Mike said, "Your Honor, we are not convinced of that, and even if it were true, it was under most unusual circumstances."

The judge held his hand to stop the conversation and said, "One at a time," and he nodded at the ADA.

The ADA looked down at his notes and said, "We cannot allow or enable any citizen to hold a law enforcement officer hostage. I appreciate his service, but he snapped, and it is in the state's best interest to ensure that doesn't happen again."

The Sheriff spoke for the first time and said, "He is a dangerous man. He could have killed my deputy, and if we don't punish him severely, my deputies will be fighting all the time."

The ADA interjected and said, "Respect for the law is a fundamental tenant. He failed to yield and is dangerous due to the background you"—he pointed at Colonel Smith—"just covered for us." The ADA let that sink in for a moment and then continued, "I feel a sense of compassion for him, but it doesn't matter. He violated the law. Your Honor, these are serious felony charges."

The judge nodded and turned toward the Colonel who nodded at Mike.

Mike slid the photograph across the table. The Sheriff glanced at it and then stared at Earl, who glared back.

Mike said, "Your Honor, this is the photograph of the defendant upon his arrival at the jail. As you can see, he is battered and shows substantial bruising all along his hip and side. Should this proceed to trial, I intend to show this photograph."

The judge looked at the photo and turned slowly toward Earl.

Earl said, "Judge, you know its standard procedure."

The judge nodded and said, "Sheriff?"

The Sheriff drew a deep breath and said, "Nobody is holding my deputy hostage and getting away with it."

The judge and the ADA stared at him. The judge leaned forward, stared at the Sheriff, and said, "I am certain you want to rephrase."

The Sheriff started to speak, but the ADA quickly interrupted and said, "Your Honor, the point is a case of this nature has significant second order effects."

The judge nodded and leaned back in his chair.

The room was silent. The judge leaned forward, spit in his bottle, and said, "I was a nineteen-year-old draftee, slugging through the jungles of Vietnam on a thirteen-month tour, carrying an M60 machine gun. I wasn't unlike Earl or your brother." He pointed at the Sheriff. "They sent the draft notice to every kid in the mountains because they knew we couldn't afford college. Most of us served in the Infantry, just like our fathers and uncles served in World War II or Korea. On the way home, I was spit on at the Los Angeles airport and called a baby killer in Chicago. I slept on the floor for over a year when I first got home because the mattress hurt my back. I hated college because I saw the world for what it was. I figured out early that idealism has its place, but there are really bad people in the world and given an opportunity they will come and kill you. It took me until '73 or '74 before I felt comfortable in crowds, and to this day"—he looked up—"I avoid fireworks shows."

We all looked at him, and then, he scanned the room and said, "The traveling wall has over fifty-five thousand names on it, and I have yet to determine why. So I know something of war and more importantly, its aftermath."

He spit into the bottle and continued. "I also know the law, and I know we cannot fight law enforcement officers or hold them hostage, or threaten them. These are serious charges. The death of your wife adds a layer of complexity." He was silent for a moment and then said, "I cannot begin to think about losing my wife. I understand."

He nodded as if talking to himself and then looked at the ADA. "In my estimation, you will lose if this goes to trial. Even if you change the venue to Murphy or Franklin, you will lose. So be thinking about your options. But,"—he looked at me—"this young man needs help, and help I cannot give. The original plea bargain was for Hazelwood which is minimum security." He turned toward the Colonel and said, "Figure out where this man can get help. Maybe in the VA hospital and consider your options. If either side disagrees with my assessment or we cannot reach a compromise, then I will rule on a reasonable bond, and we will proceed to trial. Either way, all parties will ensure this man gets to his wife's funeral tomorrow." He stood and said, "I am going to get supper. Meet me in the courtroom in an hour and tell me where we want to go with this. I remind both of you the best interest of justice is a compromise."

We stood, and he walked out of the room.

The Colonel immediately went to his phone, and Mike and the ADA argued.

The ADA said, "I respect him, and I might have to pull a jury up hill, but I can win this."

Mike nodded and said, "Maybe so, but I will make it a very steep climb."

The Colonel rejoined the conversation and said, "This is about compromise. We like the Hefner Veterans Hospital in Salisbury. They have the right staff, and it's a decent commute for any Fort Bragg physicians."

The ADA shook his head and said, "No way, if I concede to a deal, it's going to be the state mental hospital at Broughton, near Morgantown. Besides, what specialized care are you talking about?"

Mike said, "We don't know if they have the staff and specialties." He lowered his voice and said, "It's called Post-Traumatic Stress, and it requires specialized psychiatric care."

The ADA looked at Mike and said harshly, "I don't care. The VA hospital visit is off the table. It's Broughton or trial."

The Colonel, Mike, and I huddled in the corner. The Colonel said very quietly, "Any deal is acceptable. If they want Morganton, then we take it and the physicians from Fort Bragg will travel."

I stared at him and said, "I don't understand."

The Colonel looked at me and said in a very soft voice, "You need help. Please don't resist. We are seeing this more now. Going to the hospital at Morganton keeps you from being a convicted felon. We have specialized physicians who work these cases." He paused and said, "Even if we go to trial, you still need help. This is the best solution."

I shook my head and said, "I have kids and they need me."

The Colonel looked down and then at me and said, "You have been through a great deal. We will figure out the kids. Look, you want your kids to have a decent father, and the best way to do that is to deal with the issue."

I stared at him and said, "What issue?"

He exhaled and said, "Post-traumatic stress occurs after the event. Sometimes, it takes days or weeks, sometimes years, but it's a very real thing. You are a trained operator and you snapped. You had to regain control of the situation and you did, but what about next time?"

The judge returned, and the attorneys huddled in his office. I would be in an in-patient treatment program for a minimum of thirty days at the Broughton Mental Hospital in Morganton. The state would drop the charges, and I would enroll the day after tomorrow. The judge nodded, got up, and made a motion for us to leave the room.

Earl called the court into session. A large crowd gathered, and many were standing against the walls. The judge took his seat, pounded his gavel, and the attorneys repeated the agreement. I was released.

Jess hugged me and said, "Daddy, go to the hospital and get better. Please don't be like Mom." Her words hurt. I was selfish. They lost their mom, and now they would lose me. Walter was sitting in the corner by himself. He looked at me, and I looked back. He nodded. We drove to Hardees and then to the house.

It was lonely. I began having conversations with her in my mind. Thinking about what she would say about the last twenty-four hours. A car drove up and the headlights disturbed my thoughts. It was Earl. He said, "You forgot your Bible. You left it in the jail, and I didn't want you to be without it." He struggled for words and finally said, "It took me a while to stop thinking about it, but time passes. You don't need me to tell you that life ain't easy. I reckon reading my Bible kept me sane. So I'll encourage you to read and pray the peace will come. At least it did for me. Best of luck to you, and again, we are all real sorry about your wife."

I sat on the porch most of the night, thinking. I forced myself to put it all together. Mr. Samuels wasn't real. He was dead. My mind took a beating over the years, and Lorraine's cancer drained me. My imagination played tricks on me, and I saw things that weren't real. I looked down and saw the Bible. I couldn't explain what happened in the jail that night or how the Bible got there. It was there all along, and I just didn't realize it. I snapped and took my anger out on the cop. It was my fault. Mr. Samuels was dead.

I slept on the porch that night. I tried to go to the bedroom, but I kept looking for Lorraine. I grabbed a blanket and went to the lawn chair. Mornings are beautiful in Clay County, especially along the river. As the sun rose, I got up and stretched. It was a pretty morning. Lorraine loved it here and especially the mornings. I was thinking about getting my suit together and ironing my white shirt when something made me look toward the well.

There he stood. My heart skipped a beat. He was dressed in his black suit and a white shirt but was wearing the old brown hat. I took a deep breath, stepped off the porch, and walked toward him. He did not move. It's my life. I will confront him, he will go away, and I will start living again.

I stopped a few feet away and said, "Why are you here?" In a low tone, I repeated, "Why are you here?"

He said flatly, "His will." He was standing three feet away. It was him. I stared and said, "It's my mind, and I control it."

He nodded. I heard voices in the house, and Marge came out the screen door. She looked puzzled and said, "What are you doing? I ironed your shirt and made breakfast."

I turned, and he was gone. My mind raced.

We ate breakfast in silence. Walter nodded at me but didn't speak. I walked to the porch, and Walter followed. We stared at the river. Finally, he turned and said, "I'm going to the Sheriff's office and formally cancel the charges."

I looked at him and said, "Thank you."

Later, Marge told the kids about the things they would do this summer while I was in the hospital. They were sad but perked up when she said they would go to the beach. Finally, the time came. I got into my truck with John and the others followed to the Church. I was nervous and sweating, but it was a cool morning. My chest tightened. John led me inside. The church was full. Jess was on my right, and John on my left. They carefully rolled Lorraine's casket to the front and opened it. She was beautiful. She was in her blue dress and wore a gold necklace and a large cross. I started crying and the kids cried. Joel did a wonderful job, like he knew her his entire life. At the end he said, "This woman told me of her faith in Jesus Christ. Soon her body will rest beneath the sod, but her spirit is with God."

I felt some peace.

They rolled the casket from the church to the graveside. They lifted and placed it upon the rails. Walter was hurting. We moved to the graveside and a gospel group from the church sang two songs. I remembered how much Lorraine enjoyed their singing. I had been away too long. The preacher prayed, mostly for me and the kids. I felt God was listening. It was over. I stood there while the crowd drifted toward the church. Lots of folks brought food. Jess said, "Daddy, we have to go inside and talk." Lynn took her hand and Marge took Walter. They walked back toward the church. John and I stood there. The crew came and lowered her into the ground. It hurt. I started crying.

John held me and said, "Dad, it's like she said. We got to be tough." John Boy held me, but my legs wouldn't move. She was gone. I dropped to my knees and cried. I could hear Lorraine's voice telling me to get it together, that I was tougher than this, but I couldn't make my legs move.

I wiped my eyes and saw him, standing in his suit on the other end of the cemetery. I looked at him and asked John, "Do you see the man standing there?"

John looked across the cemetery and then placed his hand under my arm.

"John," I said, "do you see the man?"

John scanned the cemetery again and said, "No, Dad, I don't see anyone." We turned and walked back to the church. The small fellowship hall was full. The judge and his wife were there, followed by Earl, Henry, and their wives. Lots of folks drove from Fort Bragg, including the boss's wife who hugged me and squeezed Jess hard. She cried, composed herself, and cried more.

Jessie and his wife drove from Fayetteville, and it was good to see him. He retired and worked for the state. The school principal and several of our neighbors from Fort Bragg also made the drive. A large group drove from Asheboro, and it comforted Walter. The church prepared a nice meal, and it was special. Lorraine would have liked it.

Don was one of the last to see me. He said, "I'm sorry for your loss. Please understand I have a job to do." I nodded. "I will pick you up at seven in the morning."

I shook my head and said, "Why?"

He said, "I am a man under orders."

I slept on the porch again that night. I couldn't go to the bedroom. Marge and the kids were kind, and Walter even brought me a blanket. They planned to leave tomorrow around noon to Asheboro and then to the beach. Jess was lonely without her mother, and we sat and talked about Lorraine until midnight. The air was cool and pleasant. She finally went to bed. I stared at the darkness until sleep came.

I heard the footsteps and leapt to my feet. I turned in all directions, but I couldn't see anything. My heart was racing. I needed sleep. I spent my career telling people that sleep is the most important tool in a Soldier's toolkit. If you fail to get enough, you start into a cycle where the least things become giants. I needed to practice what I preached, so I laid down again and forced my body into calmness. I could hear the birds coming to life, and I knew it was time to get up and moving. I sat upright and scanned in all directions. I moved into the bathroom and packed a small bag, showered, and shaved. Don would be here soon, and I could hear the family gathering. I hugged them and shook hands with Walter. It was obvious, he had cried all night.

Jess held me tight and said, "Daddy, please get better."

I heard the car coming and walked to the porch. Don was driving a nice sedan. I needed to go to the hospital and tell shrinks what I was thinking, and they would help me. Lorraine was right; it was going to be fine. Mr. Samuels was long dead. This was my chance to recapture my mind.

I put my bag in the back and Don started out the long dirt road by the river. I saw him standing there. He was back in his regular clothes with his trademark hat, suspenders, and brown pants tucked inside his boots. I waved, and he nodded.

Don looked at me and said, "Do you know that old man?"

THE PEACE

"That's my story. It's the same one I have been telling you for over a month, and it doesn't change. It's a series of war stories from a man who seeks peace." I scanned the room and it was now such a routine we all had assigned seats. "You ask the same questions over and over, and I am consistent in my answers," I said.

After thirty-six days, I thought I knew where this particular Friday group session was going. We would talk about post-traumatic stress, my reactions to stress, Lorraine, and eventually, all discussions would flow back to Mr. Samuels.

Dr. Jennifer Wells sat in the corner. She was young and smart. I enjoyed the interviews with her because she was an academic, and I was one of the first real cases she worked. She was a clinical psychologist specializing in post-traumatic stress. Her working thesis for me was simple. I did fine when I had time with my family between deployments, but when I was placed into back-to-back missions, I showed classic stress signs. Her big revelation was when Lorraine died, I snapped. During these sessions, she sat to the far left and pushed away from the table. She talked with her hands and often drew out her theories for the rest of the treatment team. Today, she was quieter than usual, and I was curious. She looked at me, nodded, and smiled.

Next to her was Dr. Clyde W. Messenger. He was a psychiatrist and the top doctor from Fort Bragg. He gave me a complete physical when I arrived and sent me to Charlotte for two days of nothing but scans and MRIs. Once it was all complete, he said I was healthy. He sat with his legs crossed and was constantly writing notes. He was smart. During our individual sessions, we often discussed the Bible and our beliefs. He believed the Bible was just another book, a collection of old preacher's notes but not God inspired. He did believe strongly in a higher power and told me that he had personally witnessed several things in life he could not explain. This led him to the conclusion that there was a higher power, one that he could not understand or comprehend, but one that he didn't care to explore. His life was busy enough. He was a career Army Doc and I was not his first post-traumatic case, but I was the first patient where he was required to sign a non-disclosure agreement. When I told him the Iraq story, he became furious regarding the mission and lack of evidence of chemical or biological weapons. His theory was I had a small trust circle. When the trust was violated, I invented Mr. Samuels as a scapegoat. When I was angry at the military for the missions, I blamed him. He also said I had anger issues with Lorraine for dying.

Dr. Sherry Wilson was the CIA's representative. She flew in from Washington on Tuesday and left on Fridays. She had a rotten personality, was rude to others, and often dismissed anything they said after their first words. She and Dr. Messenger had several conversations in front of me about who the "lead" physician was, and regardless of what he said, she continued to think and act like she was in charge. Her diagnosis was Mr. Samuels represented the government, and I was angry at the government. She was convinced she knew everything. To her credit, she listened to everything I said and was able to repeat long and complex conversations from when I first arrived. She prescribed medicine and convinced herself and the others it was working. I felt sorry for her. I didn't have the heart to tell her I never took a single pill.

Dr. Felix was my favorite. He was the local physician. He wasn't in the same league with the others in terms of powerful degrees and titles, but he was the best listener. He asked lots of questions and seemed to run every rabbit down every hole. We had several conversations about life, the military, death, and coping mechanisms. He told me his job was to help me help myself. We once spent an entire morning talking about the Bible. He was well-versed and a believer. I spent hours studying the book of Job and thinking about Job's life and troubles. The next morning, he brought me a book of commentaries about Job. He told me the best commentary on the Bible is the Bible, but it was wise to seek multiple views. He was a good man, and I enjoyed his company.

Finally, there was Don. He had driven me here thirty-six days ago; listened to each conversation I had with each doctor, normally ate lunch with me because he didn't have anyone else to talk with, and never took a note. Three days a week, he worked out with me. He was the most devoted civil servant I had seen. He was married with three older daughters, and during breaks, he was on his cell phone talking to his wife or daughters. His mission, to ensure national security, was always on the forefront of his brain. He was tedious and painstakingly effective. He tabulated the doctor's notes, classified each as Top Secret and sealed them in a safe at the end of the session. He didn't compromise and even Dr. Wilson feared him coming for her notes.

I said, "Don, you are a cross between a spy and an accountant."

He smiled and said, "If I fail as an accountant, I get fired."

Over time, Don and I began having biblical conversations. I was reading and learning every day and needed an outlet. He listened but seldom spoke. I would like to think we were friends, but the closest you ever got to Don was friendliness, not friendship.

At Broughton, every day was a Tuesday. I got up early, worked out, ate breakfast, talked to doctors, read my Bible, walked the campus, read my Bible at night, and went to bed. Don gave me a cell phone to call the kids, but he always took it back when we finished. They came to see me, and we spent the day together. We were all hurting, but being together helped. John asked me to stop calling him John Boy, and Jess's mannerisms reminded me of her mother. Lynn and Roger spent one Sunday with me. Joel and several men from the church visited. The word in Clay County was Big Bill quit. Uncle Ray and Alidade came every Sunday afternoon and brought food.

On my second day at Broughton I saw him. He was walking the halls. He stopped me and said, "I am seeking a man named JB Smith. Do you know him?" He was an elderly man in his eighties of medium build.

I said, "I am JB Smith."

He smiled and said, "Pleased to meet you. I am Herbert Proctor. I have many friends in Clay County, and you look like you could use someone to talk with." He spent the day with me and came every afternoon thereafter. Don took an immediate liking to him, and we looked forward to his visits. Mr. Proctor would tell us about his latest gardening adventure. We would discuss the world. He was full of wit and wisdom. Soon, he began discussing the Bible. I began to study at night and greet him with complex questions in the morning. Don listened to every word. I was getting private Sunday school lesson, and each was more fascinating than the previous. He started each lesson with Jesus and his death, burial, and resurrection and ended each session with the instruction, saying "You must be born again."

One afternoon I asked him, "How do you know if you are born again?"

He smiled and said, "You will know." I prayed.

Finally, late one night, sitting in my room, I prayed and a great and wonderful peace came over me. I cried.

Mr. Proctor normally visited in the afternoons so the sooner this session was over, the better.

Dr. Wilson began the session. "We noticed over time, you are becoming more religious. Do you feel like God let you down during your recent struggles?"

I said, "I disagree."

She looked at me and said, "About what?"

I smiled and said, "Religion is about working your way to God. I will never be good enough to do that. Christianity is about God coming to man. It is a significant difference." I could tell she didn't like my answer, but I continued "I am a follower of Jesus the Christ. My view is your question goes back to Dr. Wells's trust theory, and you are trying to determine if I also lost trust in God?"

She nodded.

"Yes," I said, "I got mad at God for taking Lorraine, but as I read more and grow, the more I understand that it's about his will, not mine."

"Very interesting," she said, "but don't you feel a loss of control?"

I understood the question, thinking I had control issues leading to my incident. I said, "I lived my life in subordination to someone, and I guess that's how it is with all of us. I was under control of other humans, and while I will always respect that, this is different. God is in control of everything, and it's about his will. The sooner I came to that conclusion, the healthier I became."

Dr. Wilson showed a small fake smile and said, "It's a combination of things that have cleared your mind and allowed you more focus."

I nodded and smiled. She sat back and nodded.

Dr. Wells interrupted Dr. Messenger who thought he would speak next, but he smiled and gave way. "Did you have loss of control feelings before you began the back-to-back missions?"

I shook my head and said, "No, I didn't."

Looking at the others, she moved away from the table as if she had scored a goal. Dr. Messenger nodded and recounted many of the stories I told about Mr. Samuels. He said, "You admired him, he was your role model, and he shaped your beliefs. So how do you feel about him now?"

I said, "He was the most honorable man I ever knew. His life meant something. All he wanted to do was spread the Gospel."

Dr. Messenger's eyes narrowed and he asked, "What would you say if you saw him again today?"

I smiled and said, "I will answer your question directly. I haven't seen him since I arrived." I thought and said, "But if I see him again, I will thank him."

Dr. Messenger and Dr. Wilson leaned forward with Messenger asking, "Why?"

I smiled and said, "When I was adrift, he pushed me back to his Word. I was adrift and seeking truth. There is only one truth and that is the Bible. Basically, he moved me from moral relativism to the truth"

Dr. Messenger raised his eyebrows and said, "Do you think Mr. Samuels is God?"

I shook my head and said, "No, but he was carrying his"—I pointed upward—"message."

They took notes and then looked at Dr. Felix. He smiled and said, "We've been doing this for a while, and you have responded favorably. I am curious as to what you have learned since you arrived."

I nodded and said, "It's an interesting question. The first thing is I believe to my core I am a new creature. I am a new creature in Christ. I realized that regardless of my arrogance, I could not save myself. Talking to all of you has been helpful and insightful, but it doesn't compare to the sense of peace I have in God. When I arrived, I was jaundiced by the world. I knew most of its evils. I thought I could solve my own problems, and I stopped revering

God. I got to point where I thought I was smart enough to figure it out on my own. I was wrong. I learned to revere God again."

Dr. Wells said, "Why?"

I smiled and said, "For several years, I relied almost exclusively on myself. I made the missions, I did what was asked, and I produced results. I became so I focused I thought I was a god. There was a moment, when I had the big deputy on the porch, I considered using his weapon to kill, but I saw Mr. Samuels and the thought left me. I had supreme confidence, really supreme arrogance. In my mind.... I was calculating distances to targets, where the bullet would strike, if they were wearing protective vest, which deputy would react first, and my counter-reaction. I could see it all in my mind."

They leaned back and stared at me. I continued, "Mr. Samuels showing up was a sign of a far greater power. Maybe the greatest sin is human arrogance and selfishness, thinking I created myself, and I don't need divine help."

Dr. Wells pulled away from the table, Dr. Messenger began to scribble notes, and Dr. Wilson stared at me. Dr. Felix smiled.

I said, "God is jealous. He doesn't like me spending time with false gods, including myself."

Dr. Wilson leaned forward and said, "What do you mean by false god?"

I said, "Anything can be a false god. If I love the Atlanta Braves, my cell phone, my work, or whatever before Him, then I am guilty of not revering Him." Thinking for a second, I then added, "I would also add academics."

Dr. Wilson looked at me and curled her lip.

Dr. Felix nodded. He didn't get caught up in the academic Olympics but was focused on problem solving. He said, "I understand, so what's next?"

I didn't think. I just answered. "God's grace saved me. It was free. I didn't do anything to earn it. I can't earn or work my way toward God. I can do all He asks and tell others about Him, but it's not about my merit."

Dr. Wilson shifted in her chair and shook her head. She said, "What do you mean?"

I turned and said, "Jesus Christ was born of a virgin, lived a sinless life, performed miracles, was God on earth, was crucified, and arose three days later and seen by over five hundred people. He died for all my sins—past, present, and future."

Dr. Felix nodded.

"Finally," I said, "I owe him."

Dr. Messenger shook his head and said, "What do you owe Him?"

I smiled and said, "I owe Him all—my thoughts, the way I live, the way I see the world, my life. I am in his debt."

Don never spoke during the sessions. "How did the Bible get into the jail cell?" All heads turned toward him.

I said, "Don, you heard the story fifty times. Mr. Samuels showed up in my cell and gave it to me."

Don said, "We confiscated every tape. Our analyst, using the world's best technology, reviewed the evidence. We don't see anything but you sitting on the bed. You stand up and go against the wall, your arm is outstretched, and suddenly the Bible appears. We need to know how the Bible got into the cell."

I said, "I told you and every doctor here. Mr. Samuels said he wanted me to have it, and it appeared."

Don shook his head. "It's not possible, our folks examined and reexamined the tape a hundred times, and we don't know how it got there. We also examined the Bible." I looked at him and before I could speak he said, "I switched Bibles and sent the one from Hayesville to Langley."

I said, "I would like to have it back as it came from Him!" Don nodded.

Dr. Messenger said, "We can't answer the Bible question. Our job is to assess health. That's enough for today, so let's begin our note summary. He scribbled additional notes and then began. "The patient believes his being here is part of a larger global plan. He appears to be at peace without any signs of emotional or psychological distress. His coping skills appear normal. My original diagnosis stands without edit." He then turned toward Dr. Wilson, but she didn't seem ready, so he turned to Dr. Wells. She pulled up to the table and said, "The patient underwent significant emotional trauma as a result of numerous combat deployments. He continues to have trust issues but has a new found religious aspect to his life. Overall, his emotional well-being is stronger than we have previously seen, and we need to begin discussing discharge and after care treatment options."

Dr. Messenger looked at Dr. Wilson but passed to Dr. Felix. He began, "The patient shows remarkable progress, and I concur with Dr. Wells that discharge is the best treatment option."

Dr. Wilson began to speak, "The patient…" She stumbled through her words and paused to review her notes. "He had an encounter with God." She took a deep breath and said, "I concur regarding his discharge."

I smiled and said, "I like to hear the discharge talk." The doctors passed their notes to Don who began annotating. I waited until they got up and walked out the door and down the hallway. Mr. Proctor was sitting in the waiting room. He saw me coming and said "My friend, it is good to see you" as he shook my hand.

I said, "It was a good session so maybe I can get home." He smiled.

I woke early the next morning and began my routine. I felt good. Things were going well. Don came into the room. He looked at me and smiled. "Grab up your gear, Soldier. I am driving you to Clay County today. You are discharged."

I was ecstatic. "Can I have my cell phone?"

He looked at me, smiled, and tossed the phone. I called Marge. The kids weren't up, but she would tell them. Walter had a doctor's appointment today, and Jess had a long scheduled athletic physical tomorrow, so they would drive up to the mountains as soon as Jess was finished. It was great news. I said good-bye to the nurses, orderlies, and my friends on the maintenance staff, and Don and I walked to his car.

Don cranked the car and said, "I would like to stop and say good-bye to Mr. Proctor. I don't want him to think we ran out without saying good-bye."

I smiled. "Certainly, but this is Morganton, and I don't have a clue where he lives."

Don nodded and said, "I work for the CIA, and we can find anybody. We drive northwest on Highway 181 past Oak Hill and then turn left on Tucker Road. He lives on a farm about a half-mile down on the right."

We managed to find Tucker Road and then saw the house. It was a charming place with a large vegetable garden off the right side of the house.

We pulled into the driveway and saw a lady in the garden.

Don approached and said, "We are looking for Mr. Proctor."

She smiled and said, "He is working on a tractor in the shed. Go around the side and holler for him."

I said, "We should have introduced ourselves," but he kept walking.

We entered the open-sided shed, and Don said, "Mr. Proctor, we have come to pay you a visit."

"Sure!" he yelled. "I will be right with you."

A tall man rounded the corner and said, "Can I help you?"

We shook hands and I said, "We wanted to come by and thank Mr. Proctor. He has been very nice to us over the past month."

The man looked at me, shook his head, and said, "I am Herbert Proctor, and who exactly are you?"

Don nodded, smiled, and said, "I am Don, and this is JB. We were looking for an older gentleman named Herbert Proctor." He paused and said, "We must have the wrong address."

He looked at us and said, "I am the only Herbert Proctor in the county."

Don said, "Sorry to bother you. The man was shorter and probably eighty-five years old."

The man glared at Don and said, "How do you know him?"

I said, "it's a long story but I've been at the Broughton Hospital." He looked at me with suspicion. I continued, "He's been nice to come and visit us. I've been released, and we wanted to stop by and say thanks for his kindness."

The blood drained from the man's face. He stared at me and said, "How long have you been at Broughton?"

I said, "Over a month." I paused, looked at the man, and said, "Thirty-seven days to be exact."

The man stared at the ground. He looked up, took off his hat, and then bent over.

"Are you all right?" I asked.

"Herbert Proctor Sr. was my father. He died thirty-seven days ago. He was eighty-eight years old. My wife and I counted the days this morning, and he has been dead thirty-seven days."

Don's face was white, and my heart was pounding. "Mister," I said, "he came to see me daily in the hospital, and Don is my witness. We talked and we prayed, and he taught me the Bible."

"Yes," he said, "my dad loved the Lord, and he taught Sunday school for over fifty years. He was an amazing teacher." Don turned white. He turned and began walking toward the car.

Mr. Proctor was pale, and I said to him, "Your father was a great man of God." He nodded. "Thanks."

I followed Don to the car. We drove in silence. I thought about Lorraine. In isolation, I wrote her dozens of death letters, but her death letter saved me from prison. I thought about my arrogance and selfishness. My life was all about me. Everything took second place. I thought about Dad and how he tried to talk, but I didn't listen. I thought about the bad decisions. I thought about my purpose, about what Mr. Samuels, Dad, and Lorraine said about purpose. Finally, I thought about how the Lord wanted me to come to Him.

We were passing Canton when Don spoke. "Nobody, but nobody, will ever know what just happened. I won't report it, you won't discuss it, and neither of us will speak of it again. If we do, we will be locked up. They will find the doctors to commit us. Do you understand?"

I nodded. As we crossed Balsam Mountain, I asked, "Is it possible?"

He looked at me, shook his head, and said quietly, "I don't know."

He sped through Franklin inviting a trooper to pull us over, or he wanted me out of the car. We climbed through Winding Stairs Gap and entered Clay County. He turned toward me, wiped tears from his eyes, and said, "I believe." He turned toward the road.

"What do you believe?" I asked. "All of it…all of it."

We didn't speak again until we turned up Fires Creek Road into Sweetwater.

He said, "Thank you."

I looked at him and said, "What for? I should be thanking you."

He said, "You introduced me to the Lord. I don't care who knows. I am following Him."

A peace came over me.